I0672613

HEARTSTRINGS (THE WILDER BOOKS #2)

SAVANNAH KADE

GRIFFYN INK

This book is a work of fiction. Names, characters, businesses, organizations, places, events and incidents are either a product of the author's imagination or are used fictitiously. Any resemblance to actual persons, living or dead, or locales is entirely coincidental.

Published by Griffyn Ink

www.griffynink.com

Copyright © 2016 Griffyn Ink

All rights reserved.

No part of this book may be reproduced, stored in a retrieval system, or transmitted by any means, electronic, mechanical, photocopying, recording, or otherwise, without written permission from the publisher.

For ordering information or special discounts for bulk purchases, please contact Griffyn Ink at Mail@GriffynInk.com.

For Victoria and Andrea, who opened arms and hearts and red pen caps for me.

CHAPTER 1

E very wedding had that point. The pictures were taken, the reception was over, even the bride and groom were gone. A bridesmaid's job was done. She'd had just enough fun and just enough champagne to find herself standing in the low surf and having big thoughts as the tide rolled in.

Shay was drunk enough to make the effort to hold up the hem on the gown she'd spent painstaking hours on, and sober enough to understand it wasn't working.

"You're going to ruin that dress." The voice came from behind her. From back on dry sand, it rolled over her, deep, masculine, and maybe a little concerned.

"I'll just hem it. That's what you're supposed to do with a bridesmaid's dress anyway, right?" In fact, she'd designed it to be hemmed and worn again. Not that she believed any of the other four bridesmaids would do that. Even if she hemmed it, even if it were shorter, flirtier, less formal, she still wouldn't have anywhere to wear it. So she let go of the wad of taffeta in her clenched fist, allowing the beautiful gauzy fabric to swish with the waves at her feet.

She was officially on vacation now.

Ten minutes down. Two more days to go.

"Are you okay to be standing in the waves? I'm afraid one might knock you over." Definitely concerned.

She smiled and still didn't turn around. It was good this way. A man talking to her, worried about her well-being. It was probably only a clerk who didn't want her to get swept out to sea and create negative publicity for a hot Miami Beach hotel that had just hosted the wedding of country star Hailey Watkins. "Oh yes, I'm really good."

The slightly off answer probably only proved that she wasn't all there. *Oh well.*

"You want some company?" The voice was closer behind her now. He was already standing in the waves.

Shay hoped for his sake he'd taken off his shoes. She knew what salt water did to clothes, shoes, more. "Sure. If you want."

Then he was beside her, though she still didn't look. She just got a glimpse of a sleek suit, worn well, but she wasn't ready to give up the fantasy just yet. His hands went in his pockets. "That dress is amazing, but it doesn't do you justice."

She laughed. "I'm not *that* drunk."

She hadn't been that drunk in a long time, and she wouldn't ever be again. Truth be told, there had been a time when a man hadn't even needed to get her drunk. Just a compliment would do it. Anything she could latch onto and pretend.

Not anymore.

"Good." He chuckled. "But the dress is amazing."

"Thank you. Are you saying that because you know I made it?" She turned and caught his surprise at that.

Hailey had always been really good about talking up Shay and her skills, but never about making her seem like the help. Maybe because Hailey had been the help, too, once upon a time.

They'd grown up next door, fed each other when pantries went empty, waited tables together, partied together, and then Hailey left, taking her guitar and heading to Nashville. When she made it, she'd done as much as she could for Shay. Having Shay as her maid of honor was a touching gesture. Shay's heart had warmed, knowing that Hailey really did still consider her a friend and equal.

She couldn't say the same of the man beside her.

Craig Hibbets. Bass and backup vocals for Wilder. Despite a few rocket-hot, smash singles off their first album, they hadn't faded away. Their new stuff was climbing the charts even faster.

She gave a small smile, glad the fantasy held up. Craig Hibbets was a pleasure to look at.

She knew him intimately. The breadth of his shoulders. The length of his leg. The taper of his waist. The distance from elbow to fingertip. Where his tattoos were. He didn't know her at all.

Shay blinked. She'd made the tie he was wearing. Hailey had requested them as presents for the guys for Christmas. When she'd first been signed, her friend had shared a tour with Wilder, alternating tour dates and allowing each music group occasional breaks. They'd become friends, working under the same label.

Hailey had given her handler at the label Shay's name for costuming. The handler had given it to other groups. It kept Shay employed. For that she was grateful. But the tie was also a reminder of the distance between them.

"Did you make all the bridesmaids' dresses?" He asked, still not realizing who she was. That some of the things he'd worn on stage were things she'd sewed for him.

"Yes."

Shay didn't offer more. It was nice having a stunningly good-looking man standing next to her, while warm water licked at her feet and the hem of the nicest dress she'd ever owned. But she didn't want him to talk, didn't want him to ruin it with reality.

He waited a moment, looking at the last of the light on the

water as the sun set behind them. Then he spoke again. "You were pretty busy back there. Did you get anything to eat?"

"Sure. About an hour ago." She smiled as she turned and felt the world tip a little. "What time is it?"

"Almost eight."

"Shit." She regretted the word as soon as it flew out of her mouth. "I had probably one of the appetizers?"

"That was not an hour ago." He grinned, his eyes lighting up. "Let's get you some food."

She shook her head to protest right as a wave hit her shins. The water had gotten higher while she'd watched the ocean. That wasn't as much of a problem as the fact that the whole lower third of her gown was soaked and wafting with the tide, pushing her to land then pulling her out to sea.

She stumbled, grabbing onto his arm as he caught her. So when she righted herself and stood on her own, Shay agreed. "Okay. I do need food."

He took her hand firmly, probably just to keep her upright and they began the slow trudge of getting her gown out of the water. Finally on dry sand, he leaned over and picked up both their pairs of shoes, not handing her the sandals that were so gorgeous she'd never have a place to wear them again either.

"I'm good."

He didn't let go. "Let's get something to eat." He gestured to the restaurant tables on the patio looking out over the ocean.

Shay could not afford to eat there or anywhere near the posh hotel. But Hailey had booked the room for her as long as she wanted. Covered all the bills, including anything she charged to the room. Even encouraged her to get her sister to babysit so she could stay a few extra days and have a real vacation while Hailey and Adam went off on their honeymoon. Still, Shay refused.

"I have to change. I have sand on my feet. My dress is wet."

He shook his head. "It's a beach-front hotel. You're supposed have sand on your feet when you eat on the terrace. You look stunning. Join me."

He didn't let go of her hand.

"Okay." It was a small concession. One she hadn't made in a very long time.

Shay didn't know if the hostess recognized him, but they were seated quickly at the railing, putting each of them parallel to the beach. The light had disappeared, and though the night was warm, her dress made her chilly.

At the first sign of a shiver, Craig peeled his suit jacket and draped it around her shoulders. She was pulling it up when the server came by, offering wine.

"Maybe just water for us." Craig said, then had her choose appetizers.

"I'm not a lush." She commented. *Who was he to order for her?*

"You didn't eat." He shrugged. "You can order what you want. You want a glass of wine, a margarita, get it." He grinned at her, redeeming an action that had seemed heavy-handed. "But I want to ask you something later, and I'll only ask if you're sober."

"What is that?" She frowned at him.

"Not until later." He became evasive, hiding behind the water glass as it was filled.

He asked her how she knew Hailey, and she explained that the two had grown up together. She didn't tell that their 'houses' had been trailers. Or that Hailey had finally saved enough to get out of town. She answered as evasively as he did, then turned the tables and asked him about Wilder, about touring, about playing on stage.

"You recognized me?" He tipped his head.

Of course she did. She had a file on each of the four guys. Measurements, favorite color, fabric preferences. She didn't say it, just let him talk about what it was like to become a star. Shay compared it to Hailey's story, finding some similarities, some differences.

They ate appetizers while he talked. Then they dug into beautifully plated entrees that couldn't have been enough food for him.

Shay commented.

"I ate at the wedding. You didn't. I'm good." He cleaned the plate with gusto, a second dinner not beyond him.

When she finally sat back, sated, she sighed. On the tail end of her breath came his question.

"Do you want to come up to my room with me?"

Startled, she looked at him.

Craig held the glass of water casually, his big hand drawing her attention. He looked at her through surfer-blond hair that kept creeping over his eyes.

"Was that your 'later' question?"

He nodded, but didn't ask again.

She was completely sober now. She'd heard him.

He waited for nearly a full minute, then asked a follow-up. "Is it that hard to answer?"

She laughed. He wasn't mean or pushy about it. He seemed sincerely interested in having her up to his room. Instead of yes or no she tested the waters.

"You just looking to snag a bridesmaid?"

Despite the catch in her voice, he managed to keep the mood light with a charming grin. "Nope. There were other bridesmaids and single guests that would have been easier to catch."

That was true. The champagne had flowed, the bar had been open, and after the bouquet had been thrown more than one single lady had tried hard to not be single for the night. Shay had not been one of them.

She really hadn't considered this. "And tomorrow?"

"We each fly home. You go your way, I go mine." He was open about it at least. Not leading her on.

They'd only had a few hours together. Could she trust him?

He seemed to catch on and held his arms out to his side openly. "Ask me anything."

She didn't. "Yes. Let's."

CHAPTER 2

Shay's heart hammered even as he signed for the bill, a sweet grin settling on those lips. Now she looked at his mouth again, wondering how it would feel on her. Now it looked sinful.

He stood, picking up shoes again, holding out his hand to her. His fingers were rough, the fingertips calloused. Something in her shivered. She had never done this before. She was an adult, she was single, and she needed this.

Sure she'd had one night stands before, but she'd never intended them to be. Before, she always believed she'd found the *one*, the right guy, the man she needed. They usually walked out the next morning leaving her wondering how she could have been so wrong again. The ones who stayed were worse.

This was the first time she'd gone in with eyes wide open.

She hadn't been with anyone in so long she almost couldn't remember. Her sister had even commented about it last week, encouraging Shay to have a fling at the beach despite protests that she'd given all that up a long time ago.

Here was Craig Hibbets, offering his hand and reaching for his hotel room key. Even as she wondered if she was just doing a boy from the band, she followed him down the lushly carpeted hallway, her bare feet leaving faint sand prints right next to his.

She thought there was something poetic about that. About the fact that they moved just fast enough for the now dried dress to billow behind her a bit. Exactly as she'd designed it: airy, slightly sinful, romantic.

As the elevator doors closed, she could feel herself leaning toward him in anticipation, but he stood still and held her hand. The doors dinged and his fingers squeezed hers.

Though the car stopped once, no one got on. Still, he didn't make a move.

Finally, he offered one word. "Cameras."

It hit her like a ton of bricks. She was about to go into the hotel room and spend the night with a bona fide star. She wouldn't wind up on any tabloids, would she? Surely not. Surely Craig Hibbets had his share of trysts and no one cared.

Her heart hammered a little harder at the thought, her breath catching again, making her wonder how many times it could do that. When he turned and smiled at her, she realized there probably wasn't a limit to his capabilities to make her breath catch.

Craig's mouth opened to speak, then closed, then opened again as he decided what to do. "I've been dying to do this since I saw you."

He didn't kiss her—cameras—but he reached up into her hair and began pulling the pins on the beautiful updo. Piece by piece, the soft, sweet curls the stylist had given her fell around her shoulders. Shay closed her eyes as his talented fingers found her scalp, gently searching for more pins.

At the ding of the door she looked up at him, surprised when he reached down and picked up the shoes he'd dropped. He left a scattering of bobby pins on the elevator floor—as telling as the footprints in the lobby.

He slid the key into the lock and led her into a suite identical to hers. As he closed the door behind them, she looked out the window. "I think I'm in this same room two floors up."

A slow smile crept across his face as he let the shoes slide from his fingertips and took her hand in his again. "Do you want to look at the city lights?"

She was pulled around to see a much better view, so Shay shook her head 'no' as something magnetic drew them together. She heard his soft inhale as his arms pulled her close enough to feel the heat coming off him.

That same heat flared in his eyes as he pushed the suit jacket off her shoulders and let his hands trace their way up her arms, leaving a trail of feverish goose bumps in their wake. His long artist's fingers found her shoulders, her neck, her face, and only then did he lower his head and press a slow, nearly reverent kiss to her lips.

She'd been tense, waiting for a change. Sometimes it came, sometimes it didn't. But it didn't come with Craig. In fact, the moment his lips met hers, she sighed out a surrender. It might be a bad idea, but there was something liberating in knowing that they'd each walk away tomorrow morning. She wasn't clinging, hoping, wishing for something that wouldn't be. For the very first time in her life, she was happily playing the cards she was dealt.

As his lips opened against hers and his tongue moved slowly across hers with a sigh that turned out to be his, Shay decided it was a very good decision indeed.

His hands caressed her shoulder blades, her back, her sides while his mouth gained entry. Her hair tumbled when her head tipped back, loopy curls brushing the exposed skin at her shoulder blades, tickling her, making her feel heady and wanton. His mouth moved down her neck, up around the shell of her ear, over her shoulder, and it was her turn to sigh.

All the while his hands roved. So did hers. She pulled the tie from his collar—the tie she had folded, pressed, and stitched— then tossed it onto the floor.

"Don't stop touching me." The words were his, whispered as his hands left her to undo cuff links.

Shay obliged and helped, starting with the front of his shirt. She popped button after button, then pushed the cotton slowly down arms that could bench press her, but never seemed to push. She tugged at the tank he had underneath, reaching up high to get it over his head, only achieving that with help.

Naked now from the waist up, he dove for her, effortlessly lifting her onto the counter in the middle of the suite, one hand finding its way to her calf and slowly climbing, taking the gauzy skirt higher and higher until he hit her hip. He pulled back, leaving his hand there on her hot skin, and watching her as he slowly inched it higher, higher, questioning until he hit the thin lace side of her thong.

He only growled.

His hands pressed against her sides, then slid around her back, pulling her in for his mouth once more. She kissed him with everything she had, clutching at bare, strong shoulders, grabbing biceps, feeling the taper of the waist she already knew the perfect measurements of. When his mouth found her ear again, she tipped her head, sucking in air for the heady sensation of his tongue, only to find she got ground-out words instead.

"How in hell do I get you out of this dress? I can't find . . . I'm two seconds from ripping it and it's a damned piece of art. Tell me."

Shay laughed. "I hid the zipper."

"Why the hell would you do that?" He looked completely at a loss, as though she'd made the dress for his consumption and not for her best friend's wedding.

So she helped him out with a hand and a whisper. "It's a good thing you're here. I don't know how I would get out of it myself." Then she talked him through finding the tiny tab under the row of buttons that he hadn't been able to open.

His eyes lit up as the back of the dress opened with the soft synthetic hiss of the zipper. In a moment, he'd shimmied the dress down and under her, leaving her in the sunshine yellow strapless bra and matching thong. Hailey had provided the very high-end lingerie she said every girl needed at a wedding.

By the look on his face, she'd been very right.

"I am way too dressed for this situation." He was looking her up and down and she would have wondered what he saw, except that he seemed so in awe. The one good bit of advice she'd gotten from her mother had been, "If he doesn't see your flaws, don't you go telling him what they are."

Shay kept her mouth shut and let a grin do the talking. If Craig Hibbets wanted to show her his tattoos, she was all in.

His breathing was heavier now, his words gruffer. "Wrap your legs around me?"

It was truly a question, so she reached out one foot, snagged him and pulled him in until she had her legs locked around his hips and her arms tight around his shoulders. His hands molded her ass as he lifted her and walked them down the hallway.

The light was off in the room, but the curtains were cracked and he didn't remove a hand from her to close the door. So she could easily see him as he shucked the finely tailored pants. He shouldn't have looked better naked, but he did. He shouldn't have felt more amazing under her fingertips than the superfine cotton of the fabric, but he did.

He left for a moment, rustling in his luggage. Probably looking for a condom. Shay stared at the ceiling and hoped he grabbed a handful. She was still on vacation tomorrow. So while he flew off home, she could make up on sleep—sleep she fully intended to miss tonight.

She studied the ceiling for a moment, her hands slowly

moving, one at her hip where she was deciding if she should peel the thong or let him. The other hand touched her shoulder, as though she could evoke the feelings he did, but she couldn't.

"Jesus." He was standing again. In his fist was a clutch of foil packets and he seemed almost unable to move. So she got very brave and climbed to her knees near the edge of the bed. What else was there to do when a hot musician was standing naked in front of you and not seeing your flaws?

Reaching behind her, Shay flicked the hooks on the bra, then reached to the side and dropped it. Next she hooked her thumbs into the sides of her thong and slowly lowered it. A bare-legged, airy summery wedding dress had been a good impetus to shave like she meant it, and she was glad now.

The look on his face begged her to continue, but warned her he might break if she did. *Heady power that*, she thought, but happily played with him.

When she was naked on her knees on the bed, he reached out blindly setting the fistful of condoms on the bedside table. His hand came back with one still in his fingers and without looking at what he was doing, he ripped it open and sheathed himself. Then he crawled onto the bed, stalking her as she giggled and scooted backward.

Grabbing her ankle, Craig held her in place until he was far enough up that he could slide his hand all the way to her hip, this time encountering nothing but skin.

His mouth lowered to her belly, and two sets of lungs gave a sharp intake at the contact. He kissed her everywhere, making her gasp and sometimes giggle. He whispered words she couldn't quite understand and some she couldn't repeat. Magic hands played her like a finely tuned instrument, bringing her alive for the first time in a long time.

Maybe she'd never been alive like this at all before, because she'd never been able to let it all go. But she let go now and let Craig touch her. She touched him the way she wanted, unconcerned for once if she was doing it right. When he stroked her, then entered her, she let her head fall back with the pure sensation of it. Something between a sigh and a moan escaped her lips, then he caught it with his own just before he devoured her.

CHAPTER 3

Boneless, Shay rolled from the bed, away from the man who managed to seem even just a little larger asleep than he did when he was awake. For a moment, she stared. He'd earned that deep, deep sleep, that was certain.

Her underwear was on the floor and she stepped into it, bare feet padding out the bedroom door in the barely-there pieces. The dress had fallen across the chair next to the island, and she picked it up. The stain of the saltwater was much more visible in the daylight. Likely it could no longer be hemmed and saved, but she couldn't say she regretted it.

Feeling the dress, she found the lump of the cell phone in the pocket she'd tucked it into. It had been set to silent during the wedding. Stashed in the hidden spot she'd stitched just for that purpose; she would have felt it vibrate. But she'd never turned it back on, and she hadn't been anywhere near it for hours.

Shit. She was a horrible mother.

Closing her eyes for a moment, she opened them again to see that nothing new had come in. She almost smiled. That was Zoe. She'd tell the boys not to call, and she'd hope Shay had been doing . . . well, exactly what she'd been doing.

Quickly, Shay checked in. "Morning. How are O and A?"

"All good. Why are you texting?"

"You?" She ignored her sister's hint. If only she knew. But she wouldn't; Shay wouldn't tell.

"Fine. Why are you up so early?"

"Habit." Maybe a lie, maybe not.

"We are awesome. Aunt Zoe is the bestest. Go away. Go back to sleep. Love you, Z."

Shay shimmied into the dress, contorting her ribs and arms to get the zipper even partway up. It had never occurred to her that she'd be sliding back into it in a stranger's room the next morning. She managed to get it closed enough so the dress wouldn't fall off on the way to the elevator, then she picked up the sandals she hadn't even worn up here and slid her feet in. She was going to make the walk with the least fanfare possible.

She grabbed the leather bound notebook with the embossed hotel stationery. It had taken a minute to find it because she'd been looking for a small tear-off pad like the ones she found in the places she'd stayed before. This one had a fountain pen in a leather loop in the middle.

At least her script was pretty.

Thank you so much. Hope you have a good flight today. — Shay

As she propped the note upright and open on the counter, she had a brief flash of what she'd done there last night. Just the memory left her hot, and she hoped it would for what might be several years to come. Then she slipped out, letting the door quietly click behind her before she walked down the hall with her head high.

The elevators were tucked around a corner and there were enough that no one had to walk too far. She wound up in the same one as last night, but no bobby pins littered the floor as a reminder. Her hand went to her hair where the curls still lingered, though now they were a bit mussed.

Two floors up, she reached into the little pocket with her phone, and found no room key.

Crap.

Pulling her phone out of the way, she reached in again—empty. Had it stuck to the phone? Nope. No room key.

Shay stared at the door as though she could will it to open. Then she took stock. She was locked out of her room and the room where the key probably was. Craig was likely still asleep. She could knock, but she didn't know if he would wake up. And was that any more or less embarrassing than showing up at the front desk with no ID and a partially-zipped bridesmaid's gown?

She felt her shoulders sag.

"Need this?" The voice was velvet and closer than she'd expected. She gasped a little at his nearness, at the jeans and t-shirt and bare feet that made her look incredibly overdressed for the hallway.

Craig offered her the room key and a half grin.

"Thank you." She reached out. While he let her grasp it, he didn't let go quite yet.

"Don't fly out. Stay another day with me."

She thought her heart stopped right then. "Tonight?"

"Yes." He still held onto the card key, and so did she—like a dolt.

"You know that kind of violates the idea of a one-night stand." It was a question really.

He nodded and grinned a little. "So let's go for a fling. I can stay until Tuesday morning."

She was already booked until Tuesday at noon, when the shuttle would pick her up. Shay had been looking forward to blessed alone time. She never got any at home. Well, not much that was worry-free. She scrunched up her lips. "I was going to spend the day on the beach, reading."

A dream in her world.

He let go of the key, and he looked . . . disappointed.

As he turned to go, she asked a question. "How did you find me?" She imagined him calling the front desk and pulling strings. Or stalking her up the stairs. Some men didn't like to be left, they liked to do the leaving.

"You said you were two floors up." He nodded softly. "Have a good day reading." And he walked away.

She called after him. "I'm looking forward to it. So . . . you could pick me up, here, around six?"

The way his face lit up told her she'd made the right decision.

~

Tuesday morning came way too fast. Shay was at war with herself.

She missed her babies. And she wanted to stay here, with the soft beds and the hard man.

She promised herself she'd get out quick if she felt uneasy or threatened at any time, but she never had. She'd felt desired, interesting, even though she hadn't talked much about any details. Not her boys, not her home, not anything that was personal. He knew she had a sister that she checked in with, but he didn't even know Zoe's name.

She learned a little about the band, and never divulged that she'd compiled info sheets on all of them long before the wedding. She wore clothes Hailey had bought her for the wedding, things she could never afford for herself. She went to the spa the second afternoon and emerged feeling like a noodle —and like a princess.

Craig fed her. Danced with her. Swam with her in the warm

waves and found a hidden cove they were pretty certain everyone knew about. Then they made love there anyway because it was Monday and the hotel was nearly empty.

Tuesday morning found her in her own room, alone. She packed her old suitcase full of new clothes. She had a hanging bag with the probably ruined gown inside. And she put on her own cheap t-shirt and jeans that she'd bought secondhand for the flight home. She wore her hair in a ponytail along with the wonderful sunglasses Hailey had decided they both needed.

Then Craig showed up at her door one last time as she was doing an idiot check. She couldn't afford to leave anything behind.

"Just wanted to say goodbye. And thank you. I had a wonderful time."

"Me too." She grinned and bounced on her toes.

One last kiss turned long and sweet. Then he turned and pulled his own suitcase behind him as he headed to the elevator.

He had a tour to go perform. She knew that now. And she had life to return to. It was time to head home.

CHAPTER 4

T he bus rolled into Nashville, a sight Craig had seen many times before. For some reason, this time it felt different.

He looked out the window into the dark night as they approached the city. I-40 came in on the west side of town, passing more and more exits with businesses, houses, and even schools. The city didn't really start anywhere, it just slowly picked up steam as you drove in. He couldn't see much by the street lights, but then he never could.

It was an unintended Wilder tradition to arrive home in the early morning hours. When they'd started, JD had a five-year-old who needed him, so they came straight back after the last show whenever they could. No one complained, though part of what JD was coming home to was his neighbor, Kelsey. Though Craig didn't like people interfering in general, Kelsey had redeemed herself early on by helping the band get their start. So no one begrudged her much of anything.

That had been two years ago. Since then, JD married Kelsey, and their combined brood plus the new one equaled four. Craig wondered if JD's announcement about a new baby had anything to do with his own odd mood.

JD and Kelsey were expecting kid number five. Just the thought of five kids made Craig shudder, but it made JD glow. The lead guitarist was the most stable of them, while TJ and Craig were known for partying and occasional bouts of musician's depression, JD only merely got grumpy sometimes. He was normally upbeat. Add in the positive pregnancy test and the man glowed like he was the one carrying the baby.

Alex and Bridget now had little Olivia. She was cute as a button, just a naturally sweet child, though her mother doted a bit too much. If Craig had to hear one more time just how perfect the toddler was, he might toss his lunch. But lately, there was something about the other two that drew him.

He didn't want what they had, he was not cut out for babies and wives and "Hi honey! I'm home!" but he wanted to be as happy as they were.

TJ was maybe a little too happy. The two of them had run the tour going out late each night, drinking and partying. A good car rental, a local bar, maybe a local girl . . . that was the way they usually did it. But lately, Craig had been letting TJ leave before he did. Then he'd catch a cab or a ride back to the bus and sleep in his own bed alone.

He thought it was just a standard mood swing. Craig was known for the occasional bout of paranoia. He'd grown up in southern California, then hit L.A. for a while before getting his shit together and leaving for Nashville. To say he'd done things he wasn't proud of was to undercut it severely. Each time a Wilder song climbed higher on the charts, each time the venue got bigger or they traveled farther west, he got more afraid that someone would recognize him.

There were a thousand Craigs out there. He didn't think anyone in L.A. had ever known his last name. He only hoped the bleached hair, the broader shoulders, and the change in his personal style were enough to keep anyone from recognizing him and linking him back to the boy he'd once been. Then

Wilder would play the westernmost venue, or they'd do a few big shows, and no one would call him out. And he'd feel fine again.

Sometimes everything was just wrong. Sometimes he wondered why he was on a tour bus doing what he loved. Sometimes he was alone in the crowd, in the band, or at the bar, despite all the people around him. In those cases—not the paranoia, but the bona fide depression—he'd write a song or two and then feel better. Did he feel better because he got it out of his system that way? Or because when he wrote something like that he invariably got told what an amazing songwriter he truly was? Or was it just the way his moods swung? He had no idea.

This time he'd written his melancholy song. He'd been told how awesome it was. The band had added it to their set list. TJ had sold it and the crowds had gone wild. The fans had screamed.

Sand was going to be one of the singles off the new album. Everyone loved it. Still he didn't feel any happier.

The world still looked a bit off. The city looked different, darker despite the fact that he always saw it in the same lack of light. He always rolled in between two and five a.m. These days, when he let himself into the nice house he'd bought with the money they made, the air inside pushed back at him. It felt like even his house didn't want him.

They'd been on the road for three months off and on. Craig had figured it was the tour, but he was home for a stretch now. The guys had a break from each other, he wasn't going to hear from TJ or see JD's glow or Alex showing picture after picture of the perfect Olivia on his phone for at least a week.

He hadn't slept well, which was why he'd been up and watching the town roll by. His house was a three bedroom, something he could easily afford. TJ had himself a small mansion he was making payments on. JD and Kelsey had added on to her house. Alex and Bridget lived where the homes were brick and the schools were good, and Craig was pretty sure they were in hock up to their eyeballs.

The band was doing well. The others were spending their money.

Craig was socking it away. No kids to spend it on. Small house, a few neighborhoods over from JD and Kelsey. Far enough to not be asked to babysit, close enough to call them family. Or as close as he got to it.

He almost owned the house. That was a win. Each month was a struggle to decide—pay the mortgage off faster or have cash on hand, just in case something went wrong? He agonized over it. But he was here and content now with the decisions.

Tired as hell, he finally walked in his own door and first took care of the guitar and the bass he carried with him. When he was in high school, he'd read something about the pioneers, and how they always took care of the horses before they took care of themselves. Because the horses made their lives possible. When he'd gotten his first acoustic guitar that had been the real deal, he'd cared for it before himself. He still did.

He'd sold that guitar what seemed like a long time ago, and he regretted it to this day. With that last thought, he crawled under the covers and fell into a sleep that was as melancholy as his waking hours had been.

He woke up the same way.

With nothing left to occupy his time, he admitted to himself that he'd been happy. That all these shows and tours had happened and no one had recognized him. He was as safe from his past as he could be. This time he wasn't going to come out of the funk he was in just because he'd written a great song about a girl on a beach and how she'd slipped through his fingers like sand.

That was just musical stylings. She hadn't slipped through his fingers at all. He'd kissed her goodbye. She'd walked away.

She wasn't the one who'd gotten away, not like the song suggested. She couldn't be, because he hadn't tried to keep her. He'd simply let her go.

Maybe she could become the one who got away. Or maybe she wouldn't. But he had to find out. Craig stood on his back patio in the middle of the afternoon, jeans slung low on his hips the only thing he was wearing. He hadn't done anything other than roll out of bed and think he needed fresh air and to at least try to get back the girl he had known.

The one that he'd written into *Sand*.

CHAPTER 5

"What do you mean, you're going to be late, Jason?" Shay gritted her teeth.

She never learned. Jason never learned. He said he was 'going to be late' but he was already late. The fact that he was calling to say so was a step up, but he was so far down that a single step didn't mean much to her these days.

"I'm stuck in traffic. I'll be there. Don't be a bitch."

It rolled off her. He was always stuck in something: work, traffic, maybe some girl. Shay didn't care about it for herself, she cared for Owen, who sat reading a book—something he could drop at a moment's notice—and waited for his dad to show. Her heart twisted that her little boy already understood at six that his dad didn't think he was important enough to show up on time.

"We'll see you when you get here!" She chirped into her phone and hung up.

The way Shay considered it, she owed him nothing emotionally or effort-wise. She would owe him literally nothing except that the court had disagreed with her. The court said she'd hit him too, and she had.

He'd smacked her around after Owen was born. Then he'd escalated to pushing or slamming her into the wall. The last time he'd punched her, she'd pulled the dirty frying pan he'd left on the stove and whacked him upside the head with it. If it hadn't been such cheap aluminum, it might have knocked him out for longer.

She'd leapt over her husband, run into the tiny closet they called the baby's room and grabbed the sleeping child. Owen had screamed, his face turning red, but she'd cradled him close, once again jumped over Jason where he lay directly in the way of the door and made it out the apartment door. She was in the central hallway of the apartment building, when Jason grabbed her hair.

If the neighbor hadn't been coming out the door right then, Shay might have a very different story. But the couple across the way had ushered her inside. She'd filed for divorce the next day.

The downside of hitting him back was that they both had injuries to show the judge. His head, her face. The judge ordered parenting classes and anger management classes for both of them. Shay attended every one. Jason attended none. But it was too late. The judge had set visitation that same first day, and Shay didn't have the money to fix it. She was saving to fight back, though that was a long road. How much would it take? She couldn't run out halfway through.

Then there was Aaron. Her toddler was out with *his* dad right now. While she was certain Jason would never hit Owen, and she inspected him every time he came back, Aaron's dad was a different breed.

Brian Wilson imagined himself as talented as the lead singer for the Beach Boys. Shay knew now what her ex had most in common with the legend was his mental instability. He'd never hit her. She didn't make that same mistake twice. No, she'd chosen a new one.

He'd called her ugly and stupid. He tried to ignore Owen out of existence, and sometimes her, too. She'd been useful as a way for him to get a son. Though why he couldn't have done that with any of the other women he was screwing on the side, she didn't know.

When—at eight months pregnant—she'd come home from running errands to find her second husband in their bed with another woman, she'd known it was over even before he asked her to shut the door so he could finish. He'd be out to talk about it in a while.

She hadn't been there when he was done, despite the fact that he was done pretty quickly. She hadn't talked about it to him except through a judge. And she'd thought if she left before there was a baby, maybe this time she could get out. Big mistake.

It was a boy. A man laid claim to a boy, Brian said. That might be true, but Shay had pointed out that since he wasn't a real man, she didn't know what that had to do with their situation.

Brian was not amused, and she and Aaron had paid for that true, but snotty, remark ever since. Aaron was out with his dad since yesterday afternoon. She'd loaded him up with things to do, but that was hard because he was three. Brian did not know what to do with a three-year-old, and he didn't bother to try to figure it out. Shay was afraid her toddler was second-hand-smoking weed, and probably watching porn or at least adult shows. The only good news was that Brian had a girlfriend who seemed a little more together than he was. Shay wanted to warn the girl off, but she didn't dare take away her son's best care provider when he visited. So she kept her mouth shut.

It seemed she spent too much time working around her ex-husbands. Even now, she was in loose workout pants and a sweatshirt with all the cuffs cut out. With UCLA emblazoned across the chest, it was the closest thing to trendy that she had on. Zoe sent it when she got into grad school there. Shay loved to wear it, both because it was from Zee and because it was a reminder that there was a way out.

Her hair was finger-combed up into a loose knot held in place by a ponytail holder and a fabric pencil. She was supposed to be working, but she'd known that wasn't going to happen. The few times she'd been actively doing something with Owen, Jason had showed up, miraculously on time, and demanded to know why his son wasn't ready.

So she puttered around, dealing with a schedule not her own. She fed Owen what he was willing to eat between chapters of the book he clutched. She pulled out her machines and set up the kitchen table for work. She purposefully hadn't put makeup on. The last thing she wanted to do was make Jason think he might want her again.

He'd done that a few times when he'd been lonely. After she'd divorced Brian. He'd talk her up, tell her she was pretty, and how much he wanted her. It was all bullshit, and Shay had wised up.

Though she would never trade either of her sons, she'd sure managed to tie herself to two royal bastards for the next fourteen years, nine months, and twenty-seven days. That was how long it was until Aaron turned eighteen.

She could handle it. But while Owen wouldn't be Owen if Jason wasn't his father, and Aaron wouldn't be Aaron without Brian, she wished she'd done a hell of a lot better job picking out their fathers. Instead, she lived a life of trying to be the best parent she could be. On top of that, she worked to make up for what their fathers lacked. Then, when the day was done, she just let a lot of it go. She wasn't making her kids eat extra vegetables or watch less TV because their fathers had no control or concern about their children's well-being. She could only do so much, and in the past year she'd worked on the fine art of saying "fuck it."

She kissed Owen on the forehead, then turned to check her work. "Whatcha reading?"

He held up the book. "It's about a boy who gets a car that he fixes up."

"Oh?" She didn't look at the book; she was looking at the bolts of fabric she had stacked on her shelves. The boys had books, she had bolts. They had hot wheels, she had embroidery machines and sergers. Hailey needed something flirty, knee length, and one-piece for on stage. Must go with teal blue cowboy boots.

"Then, the car starts fixing itself." She could tell by the sound of his voice that Owen was eating one of the peanut butter crackers she'd set out. He continued, "But now, it seems like the car is killing people! Which is kinda cool."

She turned and oh, shit. There was Stephen King, in paperback, face down on the table while her angel ate crackers with peanut butter and a blob of jelly he'd apparently added to each when she'd turned around.

Fisting her hands, Shay reminded herself that his independence and his advanced reading skills would serve him well in the future. And she would survive the now. "Is it a good book?"

"It's really good, Mom." He popped another cracker in his mouth, almost letting the jelly slide onto the upholstered chairs she'd found for a song.

She took on the other problem. "Don't you think that's a little old?"

"Mrs. Vreeland says we need to read as high a level book as we can, so we become better readers. I'm trying to do that." He sounded so adult.

Shay forced a grin. She couldn't take the book away. Well, she *could*, but he'd found a way around her the last time she'd tried. If she was going to do it, now was not the time. Which meant he'd have the book finished by the time he got back from his dad's tomorrow night. She also tried to remind herself that Mrs. Vreeland probably hadn't meant for her son to read adult horror novels.

The knock at the door jolted her. She was both relieved that Jason had finally showed and a little heartsick that she'd be sending her baby out with that asshole. In a reminder of why she did all this, she looked to Owen as she opened the door.

"Jason." She said it without turning to him, with as little feeling as she could, and stepped out of the way before he could push his way in.

"Shay?"

Her head snapped around. That was not Jason's voice. "Craig?"

Her heart thudded against her ribs, her hands started a fine tremor, and her voice quit working.

He stood in the doorway of her tiny house in a neighborhood made up of people who couldn't afford anywhere better. Neither of them spoke. She stared. He stared.

No wonder. The woman he met at the beach had flowing curls, not hair that had dried in a towel and couldn't decide if it was wavy or straight. It now couldn't decide if it would stay in the knot or break loose and hang haphazardly around her face. The beach girl wore high end clothes, not sweats.

Shay had only worn a bra because she didn't want Jason staring at her breasts. Now she was supremely grateful. She wanted to invite Craig in, but she couldn't. There was a tiny entryway, so Owen couldn't see the doorway and Craig wouldn't see Owen.

She heard her son's feet hit the ground and his voice asking without excitement, "Dad?"

Craig jolted at the sound of a kid.

So did Shay, but for an entirely different reason. "No, Owen. It's not your father. Go back to reading." Then she turned to the man who managed to look incredibly out of place on her doorstep, and she hissed. "What are you doing here?"

"I . . . I just wanted to see you." He stammered. Thrown off by circumstances, or maybe by the sight of the real Shay Lynn Leland, he was no longer the assured man she'd had her one-night-stand-turned-fling with.

"How did you even find me?" She stepped forward into the doorway, hoping to keep Owen from seeing him. She didn't date, and she didn't want her sons to be exposed to boyfriends. Since this was the closest she'd come in the last three years, her instinct was to keep the two separate.

"I called Hailey." He looked lost.

Well, he *was* lost. He shouldn't be here. Didn't he know that showing up in reality ruined the fantasy? Did he not understand that he was a snow globe to her? Something she took out and shook occasionally to spark a memory. Damn Hailey for giving out her address. She hadn't even given the man her last name! The whole three days, she'd never said she had two sons, or lived in Virginia, or that she was usually a mess.

And good God, Jason could show up any moment. What would he do if he found a man on her doorstep? Would he haul her back to court? Get jealous or violent? He'd done okay with Brian, but Brian had been a mellow musician-wannabe. He'd been no threat to Jason's perceived masculinity. One look at Craig and Jason would know he'd been bested. That was a bad combination.

Putting her hand square in the middle of Craig's chest, she pushed him back even as she fought the zing that raced up her arm. The feel of him beneath her fingers was wilder than any imagined memory she had of how good the two of them had been together.

But that was fantasy. Three days out of reality.

Right now, reality was that her ex-husband might be pulled over down the street, watching her. Right now, she was what she usually was: a mom fighting to put food on the table for her kids, to get them a decent education, and help them grow beyond the crap roots they had. So she pushed against his chest and told him, "You have to go."

Then she closed the door in his face.

CHAPTER 6

Craig had booked one of the better hotels in Bristol. He normally would have saved the money, but he'd gotten used to nicer places when other people put the band up somewhere. More than that, he'd decided that—should he fail miserably—he'd want to come back somewhere pleasant. Somewhere he could order room service and wallow in what went wrong, rather than having to eat from a vending machine or suffer the wall bangers in the next room.

It seemed like a good idea at the time.

But after getting the door slammed in his face and dragging his ass back to the nice hotel, he flopped onto the bed and didn't do anything else. Numb to his bones, he asked why the hell he'd ever thought this was a good idea.

Until he'd seen his file, just after his tenth birthday, he'd harbored the ridiculous hope of getting adopted. Some kids did. Before that day, he'd checked out the house, the parents, and made a decision. If he liked the family, he would flat out ask them to adopt him.

There was always a different reason not to. They were just a foster family. They would help him find an adoptive family, but it wasn't them. They already had enough children. Looking back as an adult, he could read the refusals for the excuses they were.

At one point, he'd been plucked from a relatively cushy family and dumped into a group home. He ran away. Ran back to the family he thought had loved him. He told them what was happening at the group home.

They sent him back.

No report. No help. Just, "Your time with us is over and we all should move on."

Then, once he'd seen his file, he knew that asking was useless anyway. Eventually, he got out. Made mistakes. Hit bottom. Worked hard and clawed his way to where he was. He didn't ask anymore.

So why the hell had he gone to her and asked?

Of course this was the outcome. This was always the outcome. Every time he asked, he was kicked like a puppy. He'd learned that a long time ago. He thought he'd also learned not to ask. Not to get kicked. But it seemed the lessons wore off after time and he had to learn them again.

So he lay face down on the very nice, fluffy white comforter and reminded himself of what he already knew. This time he would make sure it stuck. This time he wouldn't need to re-learn it in another ten years.

He ignored the ringing of his phone. Probably Hailey calling to check up and see how it had gone. He almost barked out a harsh laugh. He wasn't going to tell her. Let Shay gossip about how her three-day fling had showed up at the door wanting more.

He wondered if she believed he'd just driven here almost on a whim. Or if she wondered if he thought, because she agreed to an extra few days originally, that she'd just agree to more now.

Rolling over, he looked at the ceiling and considered Shay's house. The woman he'd met had been refined and elegant. The house was anything but. The siding was faded and sagging. The front steps were concrete with pieces missing and cracks that made you wonder when the next step would just break off. The door hung slightly askew in the frame.

He'd lived in a house just like that once. He'd been five or six, the family packed in. The father—Mr. Green—complained that the house leaked like a sieve and he was glad there were so many kids to keep it warm. They ate white bread and cheese squares that came in plastic. Craig understood the dynamics now. When he'd been moved from the Greens, he thought they'd come get him.

It had taken six months in the new house to realize that wasn't going to happen. He remembered clearly the day he'd given up hope on them. But he'd gone and gotten attached again, three homes later.

When he looked back, he told himself he was only a kid then. He could have had it easier, had he kept his head down, and not tried to become part of the family. But he didn't know. What was his excuse now?

The phone rang again.

He didn't even look. He couldn't talk to Hailey with her bubbly, just-got-married enthusiasm. She'd been excited to hear that Craig and Shay had "met" at the wedding—at least that's all he'd told her. That he talked to the beautiful bridesmaid not long enough to get her last name. That was kind of a lie. It had been plenty long, but she hadn't volunteered it. He probably wouldn't have volunteered his if it hadn't been public knowledge.

After only a little cajoling, Hailey had happily given up Shay's phone number and even address when he said he'd like to just show up and surprise her.

Hailey told him that Shay had been her best friend growing up. It wasn't a casual mention. It was a warning; they all knew Hailey had it hard before hitting success with the label they were all on. But what Hailey didn't know was that he could make her 'poor' look positively stable and elegant.

He assumed Hailey was warning him that Shay-at-home was not the same elegantly dressed bridesmaid he'd seen at the wedding. So Shay's house had not been a surprise to him. Now he realized that what she meant was that Shay was not normally as open and welcoming as she'd been at the wedding.

He'd almost expected the yard that needed to be mowed. Maybe even the sweats and haphazard hair. He knew from the start that she probably didn't usually spend her days reading on the beach and getting massages and blowouts at the spa. But he had not expected the kid. Nor the door in his face.

She'd looked harried and tired and worried, and it made him worry about her. Craig pushed those thoughts aside. No point in worrying about a woman he'd known for three days three months ago.

He told himself it was better to get kicked now. Not later when he was invested. And why risk an investment now anyway? The only ones he'd ever made that worked were the guys in the band and himself.

He told himself he'd paid for a nice hotel, and it was worth heading down to the bar to get a cocktail. It didn't matter that the day had turned gray and was threatening rain. It had been sunny on his way out to Shay's—almost as if his mood was controlling the weather. But not anymore. Now he could get a nice drink in a nice bar. Maybe find a nice woman, or at least a warm one, and break his three months of apathetic celibacy.

Grabbing his phone, he headed for the door and saw the text.

Not from Hailey.

A string of numbers showed across the top. He frowned, but he hit the button.

—This is Shay. Can you come back? I'll explain.

Shay turned up the volume on her phone and ran to the bathroom. She wet her hair down and tried to give her hair some direction. Any direction. It was the fastest track she knew to something decent. There wasn't time for a shower.

She didn't know how far away he was.

She didn't know if he'd come back. If he'd text first, or just show up at the door. If he did, at least this time she'd be ready.

Her hair wasn't really styled, but it was better. She'd never get it straight in this kind of time frame, but at least it was relatively smooth. She changed into a pair of jeans that fit and added a draped cottony top.

"Too much." She muttered. He'd already seen the house. Seen the yard that hadn't been mowed because the neighbor who'd been mowing it had lost his job. He no longer needed her to watch his kid, and so her lawn wasn't getting mowed. If she had an extra twenty, she should have hired him to do it. Maybe he'd work for a casserole? But too little, too late. Craig was in town now.

Why? She had no idea.

Shay peeled the nice top and traded it out for her best fitting long sleeved tee. She was pretty sure it had come from the discount store. Then again, Shay herself pretty much came from the discount store. If Craig was going to show up at her house, he was going to get the real deal. He'd probably run screaming, but at least she'd know the score.

She started to grab for her makeup, then stalled her hand on purpose. She could only do so much. She didn't want to answer the door in any way that suggested she was going to roll right back into bed with him.

Laughing at herself, she applied a small amount of concealer and about two more minutes' worth of work. She declared herself done and figured he probably just realized something was missing—his key, a favorite bookmark?—and wondered if it had gotten mixed in with her things. She'd say "no." He'd say "thanks anyway." And it would all be over.

The phone hadn't dinged. No return text.

Though she told herself it was nothing—that she'd already ruined anything that might have happened from Craig showing up on her doorstep—she was still incredibly disappointed. What did she think was going to happen?

"Shay, I've finally found you! I'll take you away to live in my McMansion in Nashville and treat you like a queen!"

She snorted at the thought. Surely she was nuts, because one —she was talking to herself. And two—she wouldn't take that offer in a million years. Men who offered to take you away could do that because they had everything and you had nothing. In three years, you'd live in a bigger house, but you'd still have nothing. You'd have a man who told you how to dress and act. A man who provided like that constantly remembered that he was the provider, and wanted you to remember it, too.

No thank you. Shay had shit to do.

And she was late. She was supposed to be working on that dress for Hailey. Also, there was a set of gowns to be made for the local theater. That was some of her most favorite and most hated work. The gowns were interesting, bright and showy. They had to be for the stage. But the unfinished seams—who would see them? The theater didn't want to pay for it—drove her bonkers.

After five minutes of staring at her fabric, picking out complementary textures and colors for Hailey, then scrapping them and starting over, she decided to work on the theater gowns. She couldn't afford to sit around and wait for a man who wasn't likely to show. He hadn't even responded.

She cranked her cheap dress form to match the measurements of the lead actress and pulled out a bolt of a shimmery burgundy fabric. It was relatively cheap and scratchy.

Perfect for theater. The woman would wear petticoats the theater already had. She could wear a low cut t-shirt under the top.

Pulling out a white gauzy fabric, Shay held it up, eyeballing if she had enough. Then she stepped back and thought about the dresses. Ten of them. She had enough of the white for three. Good.

She'd been ten when Hailey had seen a skirt she told Shay would be awesome. Neither girl could afford it. So for Christmas, Shay had saved up, bought fabric and a pattern, and made a similar one for Hailey using her mother's old sewing machine. She made a second one for herself, and she'd tweaked the design a little, making the lines better, the waist smoother. Both girls like the second skirt better.

It had taken two years for the old sewing machine to give out and take her heart right along with it. Shay had been making clothing for both of them by that time and Hailey felt the loss, too. For Christmas that year, it was Hailey who saved, hunted, and bartered. She found a used professional machine. And she kept it at her house. It wasn't safe at Shay's. Nothing worth any money was. But they were back in business, with Shay and Hailey both handing clothes down to Zoe as they were outgrown.

By the time she graduated high school, Shay was earning some of her own money as a seamstress. The small local theater —two towns over—paid her for costuming. She had three machines, all used, all at Hailey's. Some classmates bought prom dresses and such from her.

She'd graduated. Waited tables. Met Jason and fallen so hard in love. Had Owen. When Jason needed money, he sold off her machines one by one. Saying she didn't need to work. On the contrary, she needed to work more, he could stay home with the baby. That had been the first threat of violence. The first hint of lockdown. She hadn't liked it, but she hadn't recognized it for what it was. By then, Hailey had blown town. So no one was there to tell her she was making a horrible mistake thinking —as Jason said—that things would be better once he found work.

Jason had once swept her off her feet.

No one would ever do that to her again.

She had just given up and gotten down to real work, when the knock came at the door.

CHAPTER 7

He didn't know why he was back. Standing on the broken steps again. He'd raised his hands to knock twice before without actually doing it. A good sign he was more broken than he'd thought.

That was why the third time, he actually struck his knuckles against the door. Then he braced himself. She'd told him to come back, so she shouldn't slam the door on him. Then again, she shouldn't have done it the first time either.

Shay opened the door, looking definitely more together and, it seemed, a little relieved. "I'd decided you weren't coming back."

"So had I." He shrugged, then stepped into the small entry as she moved back and offered a sweeping gesture much grander than the house warranted.

"Welcome to reality." She offered half a grin as he moved through the small entryway and directly into a well-used living room. Toys were piled in a laundry basket in the corner, small shoes in a smaller fabric basket next to it. The carpet was worn, the couch was worn, the TV was deeper than it was wide. Yet there was something about it that called to him.

"This is my house." She seemed to feel the need to speak to fill the space.

He must have been staring, but he couldn't not stare. The small dining room held a large table hidden under a plastic tablecloth. Fabric draped the backs of chairs, two machines sat perpendicular to each other at one end, and a bookshelf that didn't match anything else was shoved into the corner. A clear box with a million little cubbies inside held every color of thread imaginable. "You're sewing?"

"Yes." The way she said it held an undertone of "duh," and he couldn't say she wasn't right.

But he was putting the pieces together. "You made the bridesmaids dresses. Hobby?"

Even as he asked it, he realized that was stupid. People who lived in houses with the siding sliding off didn't have hobbies that required several machines and dedicated bookshelves.

"Job."

"Did you make the wedding gown? It was amazing." He looked at her, hands in her pockets, shy. Not the gregarious woman he'd met at the resort.

"No, I didn't. Not enough time." She looked around as if deciding what to tell him. "I made Hailey's pieces for the tour and TV and such."

He was putting it together. "And you make ours, too."

She smiled at that. She was proud of it, not ashamed. "I made the tie you wore to the wedding. I recognized it. Hailey wanted them for presents for Christmas. She keeps food on my table. She's a good friend."

He laughed out loud, some of the tension finally breaking. Some of the Shay from the frothy dress and lush hotel room was breaking through. "No she's not. I mean she's not just being 'a good friend.' She's paying for talent."

Suddenly startled, he looked down at himself. He'd kept

some pieces from tour and didn't know if he was wearing one of them now.

She caught him. "No, you're not currently wearing anything I made."

"My suit at the wedding?"

She shook her head. "I can tailor suits just fine, but I don't generally make them. Usually the place you get them takes care of that. Not much business for me there." She paused a moment, then tipped her head.

He wasn't really sure what he was waiting for. Maybe he'd hoped she would just start telling him about her life, but she wasn't doing that. She hadn't addressed that there had been a kid here earlier. And that it looked like a smaller kid lived here as well. She had two? Three? He didn't ask.

She beat him to it. "Why are you here?"

He shrugged. They'd agreed to go their separate ways. They'd said goodbye. It had all been very clear. And then it wasn't. He sighed. He didn't know where to start or if there even was a start. He made the decision to come here on the spur of the moment—a long moment once he factored in travel—and then he'd even come back. If he didn't answer with something, it was all a waste. So he tried.

"I don't know." He watched as she raised her eyebrows, probably thinking that was all she was going to get. Instead he motioned to the couch. "Can we sit?"

She didn't answer, just walked over and curled her mismatched socks up under her in the corner of the cushions. He took a seat at the other end and started again. "After Miami, Wilder went out on tour. I get depressed on tour sometimes, but I've done it enough that I know how to fix it. Only this time, the fix didn't work."

That wasn't enough. He tried again. "I went home, and still didn't feel at home. When I thought about the last time I was happy, it was in Miami . . . with you."

He felt like he'd laid an ugly puppy at her feet and was asking her to love it. She looked at him. Tried looking into him. None of it seemed to satisfy her.

"You can't get Miami back. It was vacation. I can't live on vacation."

"I know. I—"

She interrupted him. "It wasn't about *me*. Why didn't you just go back to Miami and find another beach and another bridesmaid?"

"That's not it." He didn't look at her. Couldn't stand the thought that she'd reject the ugly puppy.

For a full minute, no one said anything. He just sat on the old couch, sinking further into the bad springs with each passing moment. When she finally spoke, she didn't reject the puppy, but she didn't accept it either.

"I'm going to tell you three facts about my life and you're going to run screaming."

I dare you, he thought, but he just looked at her. Her blond hair tumbled, not in ringlets but saner waves now. She was scrubbed and fresh, much like she'd been after they went swimming. Though she'd been pampered and done up in Miami, she'd never had an issue with him seeing her bare-faced or rumpled. The unadorned outfit from earlier that afternoon had not been off-putting. It was just that he had no idea what to expect, and a woman obviously mid-crisis had not been it.

She started her list. "I have two sons. A six-year-old and a three-year-old."

He flinched. He knew it. He wasn't one for kids. Aside from his bandmates' children, he hadn't been around them since he'd been one. And his current child-exposure-level was still as low as he could keep it.

She nodded. "You don't even need the other two."

"I do." He stayed put. *Kids, huh?*

"I'm twice divorced. My boys have two different fathers."

He nodded this time, now wondering what number three could possibly be. She was trying to make him run.

"I'm flat broke."

"Why?" He spoke it before he thought about it. What a horrible question. But if he was going to leave and never come back, he wanted to be sure she had this straight. "Is the label not paying you enough? Wilder is making enough—and so is Hailey —so that you're well-paid for your services."

That he could do. Maybe he walked out of here with nothing else accomplished but making sure she didn't have to live "flat broke."

"It's not that." She looked away.

"Then what is it?" He scooted just a little closer. Something about her drew him, whether she was in a gown, or just the hotel sheets, or in her old jeans, sitting on a lumpy couch.

"Look, you and I aren't in the same spheres. Miami was great, but it's over."

His face must have showed the hit his heart was taking, and he didn't even know it had been exposed. That was stupid, of course. He was here. So somewhere along the way, he'd gotten his heart involved. Only it seemed he'd done that entirely in his own imagination.

Shay backpedaled as fast as she could. "It's not you. You're great, but I can't keep that up. I have too much here. My kids need me. And you don't even like kids."

"I don't dislike them."

She clutched a throw pillow to her stomach and raised one eyebrow at him.

Exasperated, he threw out one last attempt. "Let me take you out to dinner. Give me one date. One real date, then dump me."

He didn't know why he was begging.

Apparently neither did she. She was rejecting the ugly puppy. "I can't. I'm supposed to be working. I have to earn as much money as I can. I have kids. I don't have time to date."

He sat back. "So you're earning enough money but you're broke. Kids aren't that expensive."

He knew from experience you could raise kids on the cheap. From the looks of things, her toddler wasn't running around in Air Jordans or anything. She was probably lying about making enough, but she wouldn't admit it to him. Didn't he know a thing or two about pride like that?

It only made him want to push harder. There was no good reason to do it, but he did it anyway. She didn't want him, but it didn't stop him. Craig stared her down.

"Fine. I make enough, but I'm saving everything I can. I shop at Goodwill and use things until they are beyond dead. I don't have cable or a nice car. I can't even afford the clothes I make!" She threw her hands up.

"What are you saving for?"

"Why are you making this worse?" She seemed really upset. Affronted, even, that he would ask such a thing, but she answered. "I'm saving for a lawyer. Both my ex-husbands have partial custody of my kids. Both of them are abusive in different ways. But I have to fight two separate court battles. I can't free one kid and leave the other one in there, can I? And I have to be sure I don't run out of funds halfway through and lose." Her voice was rising. "I'd waste all that money and I'd just make them mad. I have to have enough in case one of my kids comes back from his visit with bruises! If that happens I have to save that one first. But . . ."

She reached up and wiped away a tear that had fallen. But even though she got it, the next one replaced it and the next and the next.

Jesus. His heart clenched, surprising him. Somewhere along the line he stopped believing he really had one.

He'd been that kid—shuffled back and forth. He developed a tough shell of 'well, I turned out okay.' When he heard sob stories, he remembered he'd lived through it. He never talked about it to anyone. Even the guys in Wilder didn't really know. So no one talked about it to him.

Something about her vehemence cracked him. Something about the way she fought for her boys. The way she was fighting for them every moment. It wormed its way under the shell he'd built.

It pissed him off, too. He'd wanted a damn date. He'd wanted some of Miami Beach back. Not only was she not going to give him even a glimpse of that, she was determined to run him off.

Shay started talking again before he even got himself a little bit together.

"Every guy starts off as this knight in shining armor. But they turn into assholes." She stared at him. "I'd finally gotten it all figured out. I stayed with you in Miami because I wanted the fun beginning. I got out before you became an asshole. And it worked." Tears fell as she talked. She clutched the pillow closer as though it could protect her. But the tears were evidence that it didn't, couldn't. "Why did you have to show up again? I had the good part. Don't come back and ruin it!"

CHAPTER 8

Though Shay finally got Craig to leave, she couldn't get back to work. Her hands wouldn't quit shaking. Her heart wouldn't quit pounding.

He didn't kiss her—the first time they met he'd kissed her within a few hours of saying hello, and it had sent an electric jolt through her. The good kind. Now though, when he touched her hand, her arm, she felt that same thing.

In the past, love and lust had turned to revulsion. Clearly she wasn't at that stage with Craig. She really hoped to keep it that way.

No, she told herself, it was just because he showed up, demanding answers he had no right to, making her dig up her past and show her underbelly. Despite the fact that she tried to keep as much of it to herself as possible, she still felt exposed.

Not shamed. That wasn't right, but she was definitely jittery. He'd made her put into words what she usually just put into action. She had more in savings than a lot of her friends made in a year. But she never touched it; it was for her boys.

They were in a bad spot and might need that money one day.

No, they *would* need that money one day. They might need it on a moment's notice.

Shay breathed in and out. Mad.

She'd had that wonderful memory of Miami Beach—of surf and sand and three days with a hot musician who seemed to think she was something special. Now she couldn't cut a straight line or sew without threatening to run her finger under the needle, so she scrubbed her crappy kitchen. The cracked tile countertops could always use another round of bleach. Maybe the smell would get her brain going.

Her whole day had been for shit. Jason had finally showed up around four. He'd been due at two. Owen read another five chapters of a book he shouldn't have had in the first place during that time. Craig had come back at seven. And by ten—after scrubbing the entire kitchen—she was finally able to get herself together enough to sew three bodices for the costume dresses for the theater. By two a.m. she fell asleep in the house that was always eerily silent without her boys.

By six a.m. she was awake again. Habit? Nervous energy? Couldn't sleep without someone trying to wake her up? She didn't know. What she did know was that every penny saved was a better lawyer, a quicker resolution to getting those men out of her sons' lives, a safety net in case Owen ever came home with a bruise, or Aaron told her something his dad said that wasn't safe.

Her heart squeezed.

She lived a life of work and worry. Shay was not the kind for wishful thinking. She didn't date—and why would she? She sucked at it. Royally. She'd also learned some pitiful lessons from her mother. One—if you love a man, or even just think you might, marry him. If he doesn't ask, get him to. Shay knew now just how terrible that was. But she hadn't figured it out until recently.

Two—if you love a man, have a kid for him. What her

mother had neglected to teach her was that she'd be tied to that man until her kid turned eighteen.

Three—that man should take care of you, and it was your job to do whatever you had to in order to keep him taking care of you. Like the other two things her mother had taught her, that last one was also complete bullshit.

Her mother hadn't just told her daughters these things, she'd led by example. Case in point, Shay and Zoe had different fathers. But there were two things Shay's mother had done better than she did. Things she hadn't managed to pass along. First, she had daughters. Men didn't care about daughters, it seemed. And second, her mother somehow got the men to completely disappear. Shay didn't seem to be able to shake either of them.

What she did need to shake was this melancholy that Craig brought with him. She'd started in a hole, and she'd dug it deeper, but she was finally climbing out. That was something she was proud of. She'd also taken care of Zoe. Maybe it was just Zoe, or maybe Shay had helped, but none of their mother's messages had stuck with her brainy little sister. Zoe was doing well. Zoe was single and had never been surprised to find she was pregnant. Shay decided she deserved to be proud of that too.

So she ate a bowl of cereal and started back in on the dresses. More work, more money, more savings. She rough hemmed what seemed like miles of fabric. It would become swooping, regal skirts on stage. Shay imagined kid leather shoes and curtsies. She always liked to work with an image of what the clothing would do, what it would go with. It helped her tweak the design along the way. She'd given up on patterns after that first skirt. It was all pretty clear in her head anyway.

When the phone rang, she popped up to see that it was going on ten a.m. She jumped the way that mothers do and ran for the phone. It might be the only exercise she got all day. The caller ID said "Jason Masters." *Shit.*

"Hi Jason." She picked up and tried to be positive.

"Mom?"

"Owen!" She was both happy and fearful at the same time hearing his voice. He was her big kid—always older than Aaron —and she tried to remind herself all the time that he was still little. "What's going on, honey?"

"I just wanted to say hello." There was a smile in his voice.

Should she be happy that her son missed her, thought of calling her, or should she be worried? A six-year-old might say that if he didn't know how to say something more concerning. Forcing a calming breath, she remembered the code they'd developed.

"Are you worried about me getting sick?"

"No, mom. I just wanted to say hi. And ask if you can get me another book for when I get home? This one's almost done."

Of course it was. He'd brushed off her code question. "What are you up to?"

"Will you get me another book? The author's name is Stephen King. Get one by him." The voice was way too small to be saying that. Shay almost slapped her hand to her face. That was just like Owen. She could try to evade, but he never let her.

"Can we talk about it when you get here?" Two more days. Two more days with Jason. Her son sighed at her and she asked the other question again. "What are you doing with your dad?"

"We're watching football."

Owen didn't really care for it. That meant he was reading. His book would be gone in no time and who knew what he'd find at his dad's house. She hoped he'd packed a backup book. Then again, even at six, he'd probably packed three. Shay frowned. "It's Monday afternoon. What football is on?"

"It's a recording from yesterday."

"Oh."

Right then she hated Jason with all her heart. It was hard being so full of hate, but she was. Jason had their son for the last days of summer. School started on Thursday. He'd taken her child and set him in front of a football game. Jason didn't seem to know or even care that Owen didn't like it.

She chatted a bit more, trying to keep her fury at her ex out of her voice. Eventually, Owen had enough of her and hung up. Jason didn't get on the phone. She'd read about other dads who were good dads. She'd seen things about being a good divorced parent online. And she'd experienced nothing like any of it. Then again, she could pick the real losers.

After a second bowl of cereal, and a firm decision to get dressed, she went back to sewing. By the time the doorbell rang she had two dresses done to spec if not her own satisfaction. The damned rough seams bothered her, but she wasn't doing work she wasn't getting paid for.

Once again, she hopped up. Thank god she'd thrown on the summer t-shirt dress and put her hair up in a pony-tail. She'd added some sunscreen and mascara and one of the two shades of lipstick she owned. When she threw the door open, there stood a delivery man behind a disturbingly large vase of flowers.

"Hello ma'am." She still couldn't see him, but he held a clipboard.

It seemed he'd done this before, and in a smooth motion, he set the bouquet down on the small cement step beside him and held out the clipboard asking for her signature. She wasn't getting her delivery until he got his confirmation.

Sure enough, though she signed and thanked him even as she frowned at it, he thrust the overflowing vase into her hands and was down the steps before she even finished her words.

Cradling the flowers, she stepped inside and kicked the door closed. The flowers fought for space, in bright, almost teal blues and a peachy salmon mix. It was beautiful if not a standard color combination. Then it hit her.

The colors called back to Miami, and she sighed. Sure enough, in the middle, almost buried, was a stick holding a disturbingly thick envelope. The single word on the front said "Shay" but she knew.

Setting the vase on a nearby end table, she plucked out the heavy card.

Inside was a greeting card with simple watercolor lines on the front. It was bent around a jewel case holding a CD or DVD. She couldn't tell. On the front of the disc, in what she was disturbed to say she recognized as Craig's handwriting, was one word. "Sand."

She had no clue what that meant, but she sighed. He'd sent her old tech. Not a USB, not a download code, but a disc. Because he'd seen how she lived. Knew she didn't have cable, and knew she probably wouldn't be downloading things. She hated that he was right.

Turning back to the card she saw his clean script.

--**What if I don't turn into an asshole?**

Dinner, tonight.

Please.

Dammit. Why was that sweet? That shouldn't make her heart twist. But it did. She wasn't agreeing, she told herself, she was just finding out what he'd seen fit to send her.

Her old laptop whirred and even chugged when she popped the disc into the player, but the window came up and she hit the arrow to play before she could think about it more.

The song was about a girl on a beach, how she'd slipped through his fingers like sand. It was a story of how she'd been something more than just a one-night stand, but he hadn't understood until she was gone.

It was Craig's voice on the disc. Not TJ's. So this was his demo, or he'd sung it just for her.

"That bastard." She said it out loud, her face wet though she hadn't felt the tears fall. She wiped at the tears and did what she always did when there was a crisis she didn't know how to handle.

This had moved well beyond her zone and she needed reinforcements.

She called Zoe.

CHAPTER 9

Craig could not remember the last time he'd been this nervous. He also couldn't remember the last time he'd taken anyone out on an actual date. He'd slept around plenty, not anything he was proud of, but it was what it was.

But this—this was something else.

Somehow Shay said yes, then when he suggested a nice steak place—he wanted to take her somewhere she didn't normally go —she said she only had one suitable dress.

"So wear jeans." He failed to see the problem. He wasn't much for places that demanded a jacket and tie himself.

"I can't wear jeans." She'd thrown her hands up and he hadn't been sure if he was supposed to wait on her or come back later.

Since coming back later would give her a chance to change her mind, he'd sat on the couch and scoped the place again. The toys remained eerily untouched, still piled in the basket. The kids were nowhere to be seen. Could both her exes have the boys now? It was the only thing that made sense. He'd never known a six- or a three-year-old who could stay quiet long enough to not give themselves away. Not a normal one anyway.

And for all her fierce parenting, he'd bet Shay's kids were as normal as could be.

Still, Craig wasn't ready to ask about the boys. So he'd waited until she emerged in a blue skirt and white blouse. Her hair was curled and pulled around to one side. She wasn't the fairy-siren from the beach. She was something sweeter and far more wholesome, but he only said, "You look perfect."

Shay did not respond, but she followed him out the door.

He'd rented a Mercedes the day before. More money than he would have spent, but he'd wanted to have some class. At least that was the way he thought of it then. Now it just seemed showy. Hailey had warned him about Shay's background. So what had made him think 'showy' was a good way to go? Had he thought he'd impress her with money?

The drive into town was awkward. He'd asked how her day went and she said only that she'd gotten a lot of work done and that she'd talked to her sister.

There was no tone in the words to tell him if this was a good thing or if the sister had said to take him for the highest priced dinner she could get out of him then tell him goodnight. Shay didn't seem like the type for that though.

He hadn't asked another question. When they arrived, he went around to her side of the car and took her hand, led her inside, and sat quietly across from her at the white-clothed table.

He watched as she listened intently to the server and ordered ice water. Her hands grabbed both sides of the menu and she held it up nearly in front of her face.

Why had she come? He'd asked himself that about five times, then realized he'd pushed her . . . a bit. That was a mistake.

"I'm sorry."

The menu dropped to the table top. "What?" She asked again. "About what?"

"I pushed you." He couldn't quite look at her. "The first night

56

in Miami, I waited until you were sober, because I didn't want to push you. I don't push." He took a breath. "I've always been a take-it-or-leave-it kind of guy. I don't like to push. I don't ever want you to be with me because I badgered you into it. I shouldn't have done that, and I'm sorry."

Her eyes went round and she looked at him like he was a lizard at her table or something equally odd.

One more try. It wasn't something he wanted to do, but he wouldn't be able to live with himself if he didn't. "Serious offer: if I was too pushy, we'll just order and get it to go, and I'll send you home with your food and I'll take mine back to the hotel. I won't bother you again."

She was still looking at him like he was a lizard. Finally, she spoke though the words were soft and he strained to hear them. "I wanted to come. I have a lot of reasons not to, but I *wanted* to come. I just—" she took a breath and tried again. "When we go out, Taco Bell is a treat for us." Shay looked around the restaurant. "I don't come here."

That was when he saw it. She was nervous, and that was something he understood. "I'm buying. I asked you out, so I'm buying. You don't worry about what it costs. I promise I'll only take you places where I can easily afford whatever you order."

It was just a steakhouse. But he'd been there. In the past few years, he'd been thrust into new places, new things to consider. He remembered the first time someone had offered him a steak that cost enough to eat for a week. And he remembered wishing he could have just had the money.

She raised an eyebrow, as if to say 'duh.'

So he went for broke. "When you ask me out, you pay. You set the menu."

"When I ask you out?"

"Wishful thinking." He shrugged again. He'd been doing too much of that, and decided that all the times he'd been uncomfortable in places just like this were finally going to be worth something.

She almost laughed and he tried a little harder. He was normally a take-it-or-leave-it guy. So why wasn't he being one now? He couldn't figure it out. Though he told himself he was on break and had nothing better to do, that didn't really explain any of this. So he didn't even try. "Scoot over here."

Even as he said it he slid his chair toward one corner, inviting her to come closer. Grabbing his menu, he reached for her hand and helped her slide over next to him. He told himself to let her go if she protested.

Slowly, Shay slid his way. He didn't let go. Just laced their fingers together and looked at her. "Would you like a drink?"

When her brows pulled together, he dove back in. "Just one. I'm not trying to get you drunk, I just want you to be comfortable with me and you're sprung tighter than a bad toaster."

She smiled at that at least.

"Shay, you know I grew up in Los Angeles? Well, I grew up all over the area. Mostly the bad parts. I ran away at sixteen. Before that I lived in nineteen different places."

She gasped a little. Tried to hide it, and offered some quick math. "That's less than a year each."

"Some were longer. Some were very short." It wasn't the whole truth. He wasn't sure he could even speak the whole truth. But it was true. "Some were so bad . . . and most would make your house look like a castle. I know a well-cared for *home* when I see it."

She'd broken. Whatever the wall was that she'd had up in between them, this had dissolved it. It had hurt to say it, even as much as it was just a scratch on the surface. But it had been worth it. She flipped the menu over to check out the drinks, then finally confessed, "I don't know what to order."

"I've got you." He called the server over, hoping to take

advantage of someone's knowledge for the evening, because it wasn't his own. "I need a rum and coke. And she needs a drink, but we don't know what." Turning back to Shay, he asked, "Sweet, sour, strong?"

"Sweet." She looked to the server who talked her through flavors and textures and helped her arrive at fruity, peachy, and fizzy. Craig was not going to touch that, but she seemed happy. And he wasn't going to tell her he'd learned that you could ask for recommendations by picking up women in bars. Not everything needed to be told.

"I don't know what I'm getting." She seemed puzzled, but glad.

Before the server came back with the drinks, Craig got Shay's attention. "Only one. I'm not trying to get you drunk."

"And you?"

"Only one. Unless you're trying to get *me* drunk?"

She laughed at him. "I'm sure I'm not insured on your nice Mercedes."

"It's a rental. I didn't want to show up in my old truck." It had been a bad call; he could see that now. "Okay, dinner. Steak? Fish?"

"Is the salmon good?" She shook her head.

"Do you like salmon?"

"Not really, I've mostly had it from a can. So I can't say what a good fillet will be like."

"Then don't get it. I made that mistake once. Had to drive through Hardees at midnight to get a burger after that. Most expensive food I ever had that I didn't eat."

She laughed at him again. "Is it wrong to just want a really good burger?"

"Not at all. This will ruin you for all other burgers though."

"Bring it on."

They ate fat burgers on parmesan buns, with sliced roasted mushrooms and three kinds of cheese.

"Oh my god. Why is it so good?" She moaned and made it halfway through a burger that was almost as big as she was.

"Quit. Save room for dessert. Take the rest home."

She looked at him funny. As if she knew he was pushing extra food on her. She would have enough to eat for the rest of the week. Craig didn't let her dwell on it. "Why are you so timid now? You weren't in Miami."

The way she looked at him, he was pretty sure the peach fizzy thing had made her tongue a little looser. "Because in Miami, you didn't pick me up at my house. I was in a princess dress, had no kids. And it was beachfront. Barefoot. It was pasta and things I could pronounce."

"True. But tell me that wasn't the best burger you ever ate."

"It was." She conceded. "I can't eat dessert. I'm too full."

Forcing a smile, Craig conceded the evening. The check would come soon. He'd take her home. There was nothing else holding him here. Certainly not her.

Then she was. "Order a dessert to go? I'll clear off my table if you can handle a plastic tablecloth after all this."

He ordered three.

CHAPTER 10

S hay was sugar drunk. They'd driven the winding road to her neighborhood on the outskirts of Bristol, the bag of take home food heavy between her feet.

After that burger, she'd thought she couldn't eat again, but after sitting on the couch and chatting for a little while, they'd dug in.

"You were right." A grin tugged at her lips. "That drink helped relax me."

"That was several hours ago. You're not drunk."

She shook her head no, and he leaned back in the cushy chair. They'd pulled two of them up to one end of the table, pushing her work safely out of the way of peach cobbler and chocolate mousse and raspberry cream cake.

They talked of nothing, something that seemed more comfortable than the rest of it.

"Where do you keep your patterns?" He was looking over the bookshelf crammed with all her supplies. Games loaded the lower shelves where Aaron could reach. "I had a . . . someone once told me you can keep them in a big book, or a file."

The hesitation seemed odd, but she didn't want to ruin the

ease they'd finally achieved. She didn't ask. Besides, it didn't seem odd to be telling him these little things, but she wasn't sure about digging into the big ones. "I don't have any."

"So you just do all that from your head? And you think your sister is the brainy one?"

"She's getting a masters in chemical engineering at UCLA." Shay shrugged. She'd finished high school just fine, but with no college plans had wound up waiting tables and falling right into Jason's arms. Zoe was definitely smarter.

"So?" He shook his head and looked up into the corner. "I have a GED. I ran off at sixteen. It's not for everyone."

The laugh bubbled out of her. That was one of the things she'd so loved about their long weekend. He made her laugh, smile, relax. And here he was, doing it again. "But you're a big star now. Rich, renting Mercedes. Sometimes I've even seen you in the tabloids."

He flinched. "Renting the Mercedes was because I didn't want my old beater truck here. I wasn't even sure it would make the trip."

She gave him a look that said she didn't quite buy that. He'd probably been trying to impress her, and she was flattered. "Are you even allowed to park your old beater truck in your rock star neighborhood?"

"I'm not as rich as you think I am. Wilder is flush for the first time, but not rich. I had nothing when we started. My house has three bedrooms and it's in a decent neighborhood, where the home values are going up." He sounded like he was reciting a real estate agent. Then he turned serious. "I sock away a lot of my money, too. I'm saving up."

"For what?"

"My house. I want to own it. No more bank." He took a small sip of the water she'd served them in plain glasses that looked out of place on the plastic tablecloth. "It's a very good house. It has two bathrooms."

Shay put her hands over her heart and pattered them. "Oh, I'm so jealous. And you don't have to share them with anyone? *Two* bathrooms?"

"Sometimes I share them."

The comfort fled. She really didn't want to hear this. Why would he come all this way and then tell her about other women in this house he was proud of?

Seeming to catch on, he leaned in. "Olivia is a bathroom hog."

Who was Olivia? Shay's face went blank.

"Olivia is three and just got potty trained."

That made her head snap back. "You have a daughter?"

"Oh god, no. No." His hands flew up like he was warding off a bad presence. *No kids*, she was reminded. Probably a good reminder. She had kids. It was already a given. He explained. "Olivia is Alex and Bridget's little girl. Her mom is overbearing and . . . One of those moms whose kid is the best at everything. Olivia learned three new words. Olivia potty trained in a weekend. Olivia can recite the entire Declaration of Independence."

"At three?" Shay leaned in.

"Okay I made the last one up. But maybe by the time I get home. Bridget's all over her. But when you get the kid alone, she's really funny." He grinned, and Shay just didn't know what to make of it. How was she supposed to contribute? It turned out, she didn't really have to.

Craig lit up. "I remember when Allie was that age—Allie is Kelsey's. Kelsey is married to JD. When we first met Kelsey, Allie was three, and she was like this little whirlwind. A ton of energy, always wanted to play and interact. It was like she didn't have an 'off' button. If I hadn't actually seen her sleep a few times, I wouldn't have believed she did. But Olivia isn't like that. She's more reserved, more cerebral. The kid's three, and she made a joke the other day. Not a joke she memorized or anything, just off the cuff."

"Oh. I know those kinds." She almost said Owen was like that. Almost confessed to him that it was the worst possible combination, that Jason had a son who was brainy and introverted. And, of course, Brian had a son who was active and couldn't give two shits about sitting still or listening to music. But she didn't say it.

Though she was sitting in her house and Craig had intruded into her real world, it still wasn't real. She'd sworn early on that she wouldn't parade a string of boyfriends through her home, not in front of her boys. It seemed she wasn't quite ready to parade the boys in front of anyone either—even if it was just in stories. And Craig wasn't her boyfriend.

He was just another stitch out of time.

She wasn't still drunk. The one drink they'd each had was long gone. The sugar was wonderful, but she'd never done anything she regretted because of sugar—well, except the sugar itself.

"Why are you looking at me that way?" He asked softly, no longer leaning back. Now he was forward, his elbows on the table, something leonine about the sway of his shoulders.

"You could stay." Her words were soft, even to her own ears, and she wondered if he'd heard them.

He heard them. "That's not why I came out here."

"Then why did you?"

The ease climbed out of him almost visibly. His back stiffened. He didn't look at her. "I really don't know."

"You got in the car and drove—what?—five, almost six, hours, and you don't know why?" This time she was skeptical. The distance sure didn't make it a reasonable booty call. She believed him about that, but she wasn't so sure he didn't know. And she sure would like to.

This time it was his voice that was soft. "I missed you."

To ease his nerves, she responded in kind. "I missed you, too." It was the truth. "You were a great memory that I would think of when I was alone. But now you're here and we only have until tomorrow afternoon at three."

She took his hands even as he asked, "What happens then?"

"Reality." She tugged. "I turn back into a pumpkin."

Though he laughed at her, he let her lead him into her tiny bedroom. The bed was a full, not the huge, lush, plush thing in Miami. But he wasn't looking at the bed.

Craig didn't have to be asked twice. The soft tickle of his fingers slid around her waist as he pulled her closer, his mouth making hot contact with hers even before she made it fully flush against him. On tiptoes, Shay tried to even the playing field, but he was simply bigger and stronger than she was. She was on the bed before she knew it, gentle hands and rough fingertips pulling off her high heels and tossing them.

The bed creaked and gave a little as he climbed over her, not bothering with pulling back the covers. Grabbing her hands, he laced their fingers together and pinned her arms to the bed by her head.

The first zing was heady, and she sucked in air heated with the scent of him.

The second zing was in her brain. *Don't let him pin you down.*

But in her experience, men turned into assholes by degrees. Never all at once. All at once and you would leave. You wouldn't stay and hope for better; you wouldn't believe things would change. Zoe had been right: Shay should enjoy Craig until he changed. Besides, if Shay's a-hole meter wasn't top notch these days, then whose was? The moment things were less than wonderful; she'd cut him loose.

"Where did you go?" He was looking at her, clearly wondering what she'd been thinking. His eyes were soft, curious. He probably blamed himself.

"Nowhere." That was a lie. "I'm back." Arching up, she fused her mouth to his and took the ride.

He kissed her exposed skin until he became frustrated with her clothing, and only then did he let go of her hands. Shay reached for his shirt, their arms tangling as each worked on the other's buttons. She figured she had reason for her hands to shake. Craig was good. She hadn't gotten any in three months, and this time she'd missed it.

But why were his hands shaking? Surely, he'd taken advantage of the women who threw themselves at him. Though she put her hands everywhere on him, she couldn't put her finger on what it was that told her he hadn't. For some reason, Craig Hibbets wasn't sleeping around.

Maybe it was because he touched her reverently, as though she was something amazing. Maybe it was because he was the only man who'd ever suggested that she had a purpose beyond his pleasure. He called her smart and together. He used his mouth until she moaned his name.

Helping him, she peeled the last of her own clothing while he searched his wallet for a condom. There was something comforting about the fact that he wasn't slick with it. He hadn't been ready for this.

But now she was.

When he entered her, she felt it from her head to her toes. Her fingertips curled into the sheets, her legs wrapped around him as her head fell back. She heard her name through the fog that enveloped them. She heard a plea to God, and she heard a 'please' or two. Then she didn't hear much beyond the sound of her own voice screaming his name as she came undone.

Together they collapsed into a tangle. Heavy breath mingling. The scent of sex in the air.

For a long time neither spoke.

Shay was screwed, in the metaphorical sense, she knew. Even as she cooled down, the thought lingered that this was the best sex she'd ever had. That wasn't a heat of the moment assessment. It was really the best.

His showing up like this, her being bold enough and maybe stupid enough to bring him into her bedroom, broke the fantasy. He was no longer *there*. He was *here*. He was no longer a memory, he was better. He was flesh.

How was she going to hold him at bay now?

Rolling slightly to his side, Craig relieved her of his weight, but she missed it. Reaching out, he curled her into him. Her eyes squeezed shut. What was she going to do?

"Tell me I can stay."

CHAPTER 11

The pounding on her door transported Shay from a comfortable slumber to a cold sweat.

Up on one arm, she looked down at the naked man in her bed. Somehow he was sleeping through what might be her worst nightmare. Then again, maybe he'd just sent more flowers.

Either way, more people had knocked on her door in the past two days than in the past two months. Standing rapidly, and leaving the warm cocoon of the bed, she hauled on a sweatshirt and some handy yoga pants.

As Craig was still out cold, she waited until she was out in the main room to yell. "Coming."

No makeup, hair not even brushed, and her yoga pants were red beneath a candy pink sweatshirt. She hoped it wasn't anyone important. Shay threw the door open.

"Brian."

Her second ex stood on the doorstep, holding their son's hand. Aaron looked a bit sleepy and confused and Shay worked to fix that. "Hey, sweetie! You're early."

Why were they early? But she didn't get to ask that.

"Why is there a Mercedes in the driveway?"

She stared at him. Shay owed him nothing but a weekend of her son's time once in a while. In fact, he owed her five more hours of care for her son. Brian repeated himself, getting angrier. "Who owns the Mercedes?"

"A friend." She kept her expression as flat as she could, despite the fact that she was getting angrier herself by the second. Shay was opening her mouth to redirect him when Brian looked her up and down.

"An overnight friend?"

It was pretty obvious to her mind, but she stayed as calm as she could. "I don't legally owe you any explanation."

"You do when my son is in the house with you." He was getting more and more upset.

The problem wasn't that he was concerned, it was that Shay hadn't asked his approval. And it was because the mystery man owned a car Brian couldn't afford. Brian still seemed to think she deserved no happiness, even though he firmly believed he deserved a girlfriend for every day of the week. Brian had been the opposite of Jason—Brian encouraged her to work. So he could pursue his music.

God, if she wasn't falling for one load of crap, it was another.

She ignored Brian and turned to Aaron. "Why don't you run inside and grab whatever you need?" As he meandered past, she reached down and grabbed her baby boy for a big hug. His small arms slowly hugging her back the best feeling in the world.

When she let his small shoes hit the floor, she saw movement out of the corner of her eye. The bedroom door opened softly. Craig stood silently in the doorway, pants on over bare feet, his hands pulling his t-shirt over his head. He looked at her, quietly asking if she needed him. For a flash of a moment, she wondered if he knew he could make things worse for her if he barged out, or maybe worse if he didn't. He knew to ask. Where had he learned that?

SAVANNAH KADE

Then again, maybe he was just protecting his famous face from becoming tabloid fodder. Maybe he was protecting her from the tabloids that might follow his famous face around. Whatever it was, she waved her hand at him behind Aaron's back to go back into the bedroom. Craig didn't, but he crossed his arms and stayed in the doorway. There was no line of sight from the front door to the bedroom door. It was something she'd liked about the house when she rented it. A disturbing thing to like, but she didn't want her exes to see into her room.

Turning again to Brian, who'd decided to let himself into the entryway and was coming farther inside, Shay stepped forward, blocking him. "You were not invited in."

"I need to see who's in the house with my son."

"Since your son wasn't supposed to be here now—he's supposed to be with *you*—you have no such right. Please step back outside." She hated this. Hated that she had to fight so hard for her own personal space. She shouldn't have to. But she'd picked Brian and inadvertently picked this for herself somewhere along the way. It was worse that Craig was watching.

Brian didn't leave, but at least she stopped him from coming farther forward. Was it worth the battle to make him do what he should have done in the first place? Shay stood her ground, and it took all of zero seconds for Brian to bitch about something else.

"If you answered your damn phone you'd know that I was dropping him off early."

"Actually, I'm not obligated to answer, and you are required to ask me before you return him early." Her chest squeezed, and her heart beat against her ribcage. She hoped with all her heart Aaron didn't hear her say that. As though she didn't want him back.

"I have a gig in North Carolina. Debbie and I have to leave now or we won't make it."

"Okay." Shay said. "You leave now and I'll take Aaron and not report you to CPS."

"You can't report me." He tipped his head at her, as though he knew her.

He hadn't known her for a long time. "Watch me."

Desperately, she longed to throw the exact amount of back child support he owed. But she couldn't. If she threatened him with it, then he'd know that she knew and that she was keeping track. He could get prepared.

"I don't like that you have someone staying over." He glared at her.

"I don't like you. Don't be late to your gig." She walked forward, all but putting a hand on his chest and shoving him onto the step.

Brian went reluctantly, and she shut the door. Then she bolted it.

Turning, she passed Craig and headed back to the boys' room to find Aaron. He'd grabbed some of the generic click blocks she'd bought for him, but it seemed he'd then crawled into bed and was almost back asleep. How early had Brian woken him this morning? She kept her voice calm and soft as she tried to bring her boil down to a simmer. "How was your trip, sweetie?"

"Okay." He didn't look up at her and she figured that was okay. He was safe here.

"Can I have a hug?" She crouched down next to his toddler bed and held her arms out. Her baby went willingly and even gave her a big kiss on the cheek.

Then she had to deal with Craig. Aaron seemed to not care that a strange man was standing in the doorway to his mother's room. Did that mean he trusted her? Was it because *she* obviously wasn't upset by this, then *he* wasn't. Or did it mean that he was used to strange people coming and going—which could only have happened at his dad's house.

Shay turned back to her son. "Are there a lot of people at your dad's house?"

"Mmmm-hmmm." He looked up, answering like the innocent he was, then focused back on the blocks clutched in his hands, his eyes drifting shut. She rotated cleanly away from him before clenching her fists and giving a silent yell of every swear word she knew.

Craig saw. Reaching out, he grabbed at her clenched hands and opened them, rubbing his fingers down her palms, soothing her hands and her. She let him, until he put their foreheads together, and whispered. "It's going to be okay."

She smiled at him.

That's what you were supposed to do—smile and agree—but it was not going to be okay. She needed another fifteen thousand dollars to match what the lawyer had suggested she have on hand. It was enough for a slightly protracted court battle. It would be enough, she hoped, to outlast both of her exes. Winning one was not enough.

When he leaned in to kiss her, she twisted away. Everything was wrong. Even having Craig here, even stealing what was supposed to be her own time didn't work. "You have to go."

He sucked in a breath, but he understood. With a quick nod, he ducked back into the bedroom and gathered his things, shoved his feet into his socks then his shoes. He moved past where she stood in the hall, watching her son sleep and being grateful she had him home. Owen would be home the next afternoon. Then she would have both her boys for one evening, until school started. Until next time.

"Shay!"

She startled. He must have called her several times, and she looked up to see him motioning her into the living room.

"I'm so sorry." She shrugged at him. She'd told him she had kids. Told him her life wasn't a fairy tale or a fling. Not shockingly, it had played out exactly that way.

He shook his head at her, seemed to understand she didn't want to introduce him or parade him in front of her son either. He did pull her close and offer a sweet kiss that made her long for a home she'd never known. Something like she'd seen on TV as a kid, but with a deeper bedrock than even that.

He kissed her once more, then nodded at her and left.

He didn't say goodbye, and she wondered if that was on purpose.

It was all she could do to stand and watch out the small front window as the Mercedes backed out the driveway, turned in the street, and drove away. She hadn't meant to let it happen, and he probably hadn't meant to do it, but he'd taken a piece of her with him.

She wanted to think it would bring him back, but it didn't matter if it did or not. She'd had a fling in Miami, and she'd mistakenly tried to bring it home. Even without the boys here, it didn't work. So she worked on cutting loose the part he took with him.

He hadn't turned into an asshole. Yet. So it was still a good memory. Something to take out and turn over and replay in her mind when she was lonely. Something she could think would happen, maybe one day when everything was sorted out.

Forcing herself to turn away from the empty street she'd stared at long after he was gone, Shay enjoyed an evening with her youngest. Once he woke up, they threw the ball on the lawn, played blocks, and ate the best left over hamburger she'd ever had. Aaron invited her in for a slumber party, so she slept in Owen's bed that night.

The next night, she'd have her boys back. In the past, she always thought of that as being whole again. But even with Owen's return, she didn't quite feel whole.

Three days later, another bouquet arrived. No note this time, no card, nothing but the feeling she got inside to identify the sender.

The day after she got two texts.
—How did you like the flowers?
—I loved them
Then
—When?
—I can't.

CHAPTER 12

C raig sat in rehearsal like a lump. He hit notes, sure. Played all the right chords at all the right times and managed to do so with exactly zero enthusiasm.

It disturbed him at a cerebral level. He'd fought hard for the right to play music for money. Getting to this level, there had been many nights he'd eaten ramen noodles or nothing at all. Times he spent the only money he had on guitar strings instead of shelter or needed clothing.

But now his lack of energy affected more than just him; he wasn't a solo artist. As much as it pained him to be relied on, he'd set himself up as an integral part of the band. This was the only true family he'd ever known.

They didn't seem to notice that he wasn't even really there.

Or maybe they did and they didn't care? Craig didn't really see that as a possibility. It was more likely that they noticed and they simply figured that's the way he was; he'd snap out of it soon.

No one asked about him disappearing for five days. Then again, it was possible they had no real idea what he'd done. After all, he'd answered texts and returned phone calls. They might have no clue he'd even been out of town, or that he'd thrown his heart at the feet of a woman.

It hadn't been stomped on. Just turned away.

Stomping might have been better. It would have been a reaction. Had she been a bitch, he could have hated her.

Instead, she wouldn't carve out a space for him in her already overcrowded life. It was hard to be mad at that. Having been on the receiving end of both good mothering and bad, and despite all that never having had a real mother, Craig couldn't fault her.

How could he ask her to take time from her children?

How could he ask her to stand up to not one, but two, ex-husbands who wouldn't take kindly to his presence? It would create shock waves in her life and create battles she shouldn't have to fight.

Despite his knowledge of the situation, and his belief that she'd probably made the right choice, his heart caved in, and he hit his notes with perfunctory attention that his skill and talent managed to hide a bit. By the end of the rehearsal, JD had only said that they all sounded a bit rusty.

JD probably thought Craig sounded like he was rusting, more like. But they all slapped each other on the back. JD headed home to be with his wife and kids. They were tight-knit, JD's little family. The six of them—soon to be seven—were like magnets always pulling back to the others. Alex and Bridget didn't seem quite that way.

Craig hadn't examined it before, and he didn't know why he was doing it now, but he couldn't help it. Alex and Bridget seemed to like their life more than each other. Like they each had found a spot they fit into perfectly, and each was content in that role. It was an interesting concept to Craig. He hadn't really considered that he needed a spot. He'd always thought he needed a someone.

He tried to shake it off. So when TJ asked if he wanted to

head downtown for drinks, it felt like a terrible idea. "We can find an open bar, maybe an open stage, and maybe some open chicks."

"Sounds great." Craig slipped his bass strap over his head and locked the instrument away with practiced ease.

Nash-Vegas—as the downtown strip was often referred to— lit up like fireworks. Every door was open, and every bar had live music playing. Craig knew. Wilder played some of these places before they got signed. Before their songs hit the radio. Before he realized that fame was a web he could easily get tangled in.

He was in the passenger seat of TJ's hot new ride before he realized he'd actually agreed. The bar they chose was another door among many embedded along the buildings standing shoulder to shoulder for blocks. Restaurants flanked bars, and even sat atop them, open to the air and the generally good weather of the beginning of fall.

TJ didn't choose one of those.

He rode the crowded street with the top down. The smile on Craig's face was more something he was in the habit of doing, rather than something he felt.

"Here we go, man." TJ swung a quick right and let himself out of the low-slung car even as he made a smooth movement to hand over the keys to the street-side valet.

Mimicking the slick motions, Craig unfolded himself from the passenger side and turned to his friend. "Where to tonight?"

"Wherever the women are hot and the drinks are flowing." TJ's wide grin showed off straight teeth and the confidence needed in a lead singer and front man. For the first time Craig looked at him through jaded eyes.

He loved TJ. The man was as close to a brother as he had. But TJ was built for fame. Wide smile, genuine laugh—or it sounded that way even when it wasn't. A quick answer, a ready comeback, or a smooth line. And he never missed a beat. The velvet voice didn't hurt him any either.

Craig had been happy to be along for the ride.

TJ had three beers to his one when it happened.

"Don't I know you from somewhere?" The blond was looking at them, her eyes narrowed but her mouth wide. It was a look that was coming more and more often lately.

"Maybe." TJ drew out the word, leaned on the bar and waited her out.

This was the moment they'd started counting about two years ago—how long before someone recognized them?

When they stayed out all night and it didn't happen, TJ would bar crawl hoping for someone to say they loved him. Craig had done it, too. He'd enjoyed the sly smiles, the moves, the conquests. He was reaching for that feeling tonight, to find that it slipped through his fingers each time he thought he grasped it.

"Are you in a band? Did I see you on stage?"

"Maybe at the Ryman." TJ casually threw out the name of one of the most famous local theaters.

Craig leaned on the counter, knowing the blond's brunette friend was sauntering over in her short skirt and cowboy boots. She was eying what her friend was reeling in. Craig felt his eyebrows lift in an invitation he hadn't meant to invoke.

"What's your name, drummer boy?" The brunette asked him, a quirk to her lips as she checked him out head to toe.

"Craig." He responded, easily, cockily maybe despite the fact that he was not the drummer. Did she think he was Alex? The smile though was just his natural response to her question. Coming as much from habit as rehearsal earlier had. "This is TJ." He tipped his head toward his friend and watched as TJ winced just a little.

Craig had just thrown the game.

TJ liked to make them figure it out. He toyed with them until they recognized him themselves. But the two first names together were often enough of a clue, and Craig wasn't up for a drawn-out game tonight. Focusing on the woman who was looking at her friend as though they'd discovered a secret, he at least enjoyed when they figured out who they'd netted.

"Oh my God. Y'all are from Wilder, right?" The blond gushed, her body leaning closer to TJ. He didn't lean back towards her. He liked to let her do the work.

"Yes, ma'am." He took another swig of his beer and left it at that.

The brunette eyed Craig again, until he felt like he was a car she was having trouble deciding if she would buy. He wouldn't have been surprised had she run her hand along his leg to check the upholstery or asked if he had a Dolby sound system. Then she seemed to make her choice and stepped boldly between his legs.

He leaned back. It was no longer about making her do the work. Suddenly she was in his personal space, and suddenly he cared.

He didn't usually and found himself confused by his own reaction. The woman's makeup was too heavy. Up close, he could see that she was painted like a canvas, three shades lined her eyes and he wondered at the amount of effort required for a temporary effect.

"Buy me a drink?" Her grin turned an odd combination of sweet and feral, but he signaled the bartender and put her pink mojito on his tab. Thanking him and grinning slyly, she licked the straw. The blatantly sexual move just didn't grab him and he was getting pissed about it.

Next the two started into asking them to play something. As though, by virtue of being musicians, they always had their instruments and always played music. Though TJ was prone to let himself get talked up on stage if there was a gap in the music, there wasn't one tonight. Despite the women's efforts, the two guys wouldn't interrupt another musician on stage.

There had been an incident early on, where TJ and Craig had been drinking and had let the crowd get out of hand. Another band had ended their set early due to the uproar in the bar about having half the hot new band Wilder in their midst. The way they had hurt that musician still left a sour twist in Craig's stomach when he thought about it. But it joined a handful of other sour twists. There was plenty of easy company among his regrets.

Suddenly, TJ was signaling him that he was out the door.

Craig knew the drill; he'd find his own way home. TJ was getting lucky. Then again, TJ was born lucky.

"I have my own keys." The brunette dangled them in front of him, even the sway of the metal tag was seductive. The cold note it hit in him wasn't.

He wanted to think he wasn't drunk enough, but that wasn't the problem. "I'm going to catch a cab."

He turned away, catching instead an indignant huff from the woman he'd just bought an overpriced drink for. She blended back into the crowd a little too seamlessly Craig thought. It was easy; she looked like every other woman in here. When he checked back with the bartender, he saw the question. "Are you paying your friend's tab, too?"

Of course he was. Craig nodded.

It wasn't the first time and it wouldn't be the last. TJ often forgot things like money when a hot piece of ass was involved. Craig never forgot about it. But all things equal, he had an old truck and TJ let them arrive in style. TJ made all of it possible, because despite Craig's moves, he didn't have TJ's magnetic power. And Wilder wouldn't be Wilder without TJ up front. So if he picked up the tab once in a while, it wasn't a problem. What he needed now was a ride home.

Leaving the change on the counter for the bartender, Craig

pushed himself away and then wound his way out the door. Though it was only twenty feet away, it took a while to make it past the throngs pushing their way inside and despite swimming in a sea of people, he felt horribly alone.

Maybe it was because they were all moving into the club and he was the lone person headed out. Maybe because something seemed to have broken recently and he didn't know how to fix it. For a kid who started broken and stayed that way, it was definitively disturbing to think there might not be a way around it.

On the street, more people moved in masses, leaving gaps that echoed the noise of the people off the brick siding. They laughed, they chatted, they took pictures of themselves and each other. They all looked happier than he felt. Were they hiding it better?

Or did they simply have something he lacked?

Craig was pretty sure it was the second. There was something magical about a mom and a dad and a house and a dog. He'd had these things sometimes, but they'd only ever been lent to him. Each time, the lender had taken his things back and sent Craig on his way without them, on his own, his own meager belongings in a black trash bag as he headed to the next stop.

Even when he'd run out on his own, he hadn't had more things than fit into the cloth grocery bag he'd stolen. It had been a huge step up from the disposable plastic bags he was used to carrying around. And no one had gone with him.

Hands shoved down into his pockets, Craig found himself at the sidewalk, in one of the gaps between people. He shouldn't be standing there alone. As he hailed a cab, he thought of the first way to fix it.

CHAPTER 13

Had he been able to, Craig would have gone the night before straight from the bar, but it wasn't open. Nashville, despite having a party section, wasn't a party town. Unlike New York or L.A. and a ton of other big cities, most of the town rolled up their sidewalks after ten or eleven.

So when the cab dropped him home at nearly two a.m., he was the only one up and about in the neighborhood, and there were no businesses willing to speak to him.

But he was able to hop online and look up what he needed and found that seven a.m. was the time. After a shower and some food, he realized he still wasn't going to be able to sleep. Two infomercials later he went to Walmart and spent an hour checking out his options.

At four a.m. as he was staring at the beds, a woman recognized him. "Aren't you the bassist from the new band 'Wilder'?"

Craig shook his head, "I just look like him." He offered a sad grin and an expression that he hoped suggested the woman had made an honest mistake.

"You sure sound like him, too." She smiled.

"I'll take that as a complement." He turned away, hands in pockets, a good place to keep them.

For some reason, two things struck him then. One, that the woman might have been hitting on him. You'd think he'd have a better handle on that. He had plenty of experience getting hit on, he should recognize it. Where had that skill gone? Why was he even questioning her motives rather than confidently assessing them?

The second thing that struck him was that sticking his hands in his pockets was a remnant of one of his foster moms. She'd told him to do that to keep from touching things that didn't belong to him. So why had that lesson stuck so well? Why was it that nothing belonged to him?

He was out to change that today. He couldn't have Shay. He wasn't going to get what JD had. But he could have his own little slice of things. And he could touch the things in front of him on the shelves and he could buy them if he broke them.

He loaded his cart, paid, and returned home, then started setting things up. It was the only thing in weeks that made him feel better. Partying, drinking, moping, even the thinking he'd done, didn't make things easier. He'd realized too many things about his life over the last few days. Too many things he'd never thought about, he'd just lived with.

He'd seen the foster system's file on him when he was ten. He'd learned the circumstances of his birth, and though none of it was about him, he couldn't change it. Though none of it was about him, it had dictated his life. Maybe it always would.

But maybe it wouldn't.

He was still awake at six forty-five when he threw on a jacket and headed out to his truck. When the animal shelter opened its doors, he was standing in the brisk wind, waiting, hands not in his pockets despite the morning chill. Because fuck them.

"Can I help you?"

"I'd like to adopt a dog." He frowned. Was that not the usual response here? He wasn't at the main metro center, he lived a bit out of town.

"Oh good." The man perked up and Craig had to ask.

"Is it unusual that people come here to adopt dogs?" *Wasn't that what an animal shelter was for?*

"It's not unusual, but sadly it's not the bulk of our business." The man looked over his shoulder as he led Craig down a freshly painted cinderblock hallway. "We get way too many of drop-offs and doorstep creatures. A lot of the people who want to adopt go to private rescues. But we're here to help. What are you looking for?"

"The right dog who needs a home."

There was some back and forth as Craig explained his situation and the man from the shelter—the only one Craig saw on the job that morning—tried to assess what would make the best pet for a man who was sometimes on the road.

"Is there someone available to watch the dog when you're gone? Or will the dog go with you? Would you prefer a cat?"

The questions were far more than he'd expected and Craig took a moment to sort them out. He'd thought he would simply look at the dogs and then go home with one. This was far more than he'd bargained for.

"No cats." He paused. "Can a nine-year-old look after a dog?" Maybe Daniel would like a job. Craig sure would have loved one at that age—and one with a dog. He surely could talk JD and Kelsey into letting the boy walk the eight blocks and watching the dog, couldn't he?

"What's the boy like?" the man was tipping his head as though he'd asked the question before and Craig hadn't responded.

"Oh, really good kid. Good parents. Mom would help, make certain he's on time. He'd play with the dog a lot, I'm sure. That's good, right?"

"Have you ever had your own dog before?" The man looked again, checking Craig's face or his expression, assessing him more deeply than he was willing to be assessed.

"No." He'd never had a dog at all. All those foster homes and the closest he'd gotten to a pet was the mouse he'd fed occasionally after finding it behind the washer and the stray cat he'd sometimes petted and given part of his baloney sandwich to on the way home from middle school. This was all new to him and the man was reading all that pretty clearly by the look on his face. The old anger rose again. He couldn't do things because he hadn't done them before. He couldn't have things because of the way he was born. He couldn't . . . "Is that a problem?"

"No." This time the smile was genuine. "Honestly, we just attended a class on the fact that we aren't adopting out dogs fast enough. That we've maybe missed out on good families for our animals because they haven't had one before, or because they already have a dog."

Craig looked at the paper he was filling out. At the bottom were a handful of questions just like the man was saying.

"We just use those to help determine what *kind* of dog you should get, that's all."

"I don't get to pick?" Craig frowned again. Really, he'd thought he'd walk in, look around and say "that one." He'd been here thirty minutes already and he barely had the preliminary paperwork filled out.

"Yes, you get to pick. I'm just going to try to be helpful, that's all." Then his expression turned dark. "And I have to assess whether you're training fighting dogs or picking out bait dogs."

"What!?" Craig felt his whole body pull back.

"It's a problem around here. People come pick out puppies, then sell them to the fighting rings." Clearly, from the expression on his face, the man wasn't here for the paycheck and he wasn't even here to give Craig the run-around. For the first time it was obvious that the worker had one priority: the animals.

Something pushed inside his chest.

These abandoned dogs and cats had something more than the kids in the L.A. system had. They had someone fighting for them. Craig pushed back, ignoring the pressure inside him. He was getting ready to open his mouth when the man asked, "Do you want to see the dogs?"

"Yes." Now he was getting somewhere.

The kennels were noisy, the cinderblock walls echoing the sounds, making it louder and sadder. Craig's entrance set off a cacophony of barking that threatened to shatter his ears. Looking at the shelter worker, who didn't even flinch, he decided this must be pretty normal.

He was looking at the slightly older dogs, the ones who hadn't been adopted yet. Craig didn't have to look very far to find his motives there, so he didn't. A bell sounded loud enough to be clear over the barking and it set off another round.

"I have to go check that. Don't put your fingers through the cages. I'll be back." The man disappeared around a corner in a different direction from where they came in and Craig was left with more dogs than should ever be in one place barking at him from behind chain link. He walked the aisle and tried to make a decision.

Five minutes later the man came back. "I'm sorry. That was a drop-off. Or an abandonment, however you want to call it. Twelve puppies. At least he drove them here."

The man looked both irritated and relieved. Craig frowned. "I don't understand."

"They're pit mixes. The man was from Metro Nashville, and like a lot of other big cities, Metro puts down pit bulls as soon as they come in."

"Even the puppies!?" Craig was appalled.

There was a grim nod. "Even the puppies. They don't get adopted out, nothing. Just euthanized."

"Why?"

"The breed has an undeserved bad rep. And there is a lot of dog fighting. But I think it just perpetuates the problem to put the dogs down. They're actually really sweet."

"Pit bulls?" Craig frowned again. The only one he'd ever known was down the street from foster home number ten, and it had barked and yanked his chain and generally scared the crap out of a small Craig as he walked to school each morning.

"Exactly!" Said the man as he led Craig down the hall and turned the corner to another full set of kennels Craig hadn't realized were there. So many dogs.

"See these two?" The man pointed to two brown and black fuzzballs who looked at his pointing finger and sauntered over. "Seven weeks old, ready to go home. Pit/Rottweiler mixes. There were three of them and one got adopted."

"Only three?" Sounded like a small litter to him, but what did he know? He was thinking he should have kept his mouth shut when the man responded.

"Yeah, there were more but they didn't make it. They were dumped on the side of the freeway, most of the puppies and the mother were killed."

And that was it. Craig only looked down to see the two now-round puppies toddling toward him. Their black and brown coats gleaming despite some of the dust they'd rolled in at the back of their cage. On his knees with his fingers between the chain links before he even realized what he was doing, Craig found himself getting his fingers licked and even gnawed on just a little. One of the puppies made a plasticky noise in the back of his throat as he tried to get through the fencing and out to Craig.

He sat like that, leaning on his heels, his hands pressed through the links to try to scratch behind ears or feel soft fur.

"Hold on. I have to go settle the dogs I just checked in."

But instead of leaving Craig alone, the man opened the gate, expertly scooped a puppy under the belly in each hand then walked down the hall as they hung squirming from his grip.

"Open the door for me?"

Craig obediently turned the knob on the unmarked door revealing a small square room with several large square cushions on the floor.

"Sit." The man said, gesturing with a small dog now hanging limp in his grip.

Craig wondered if he was going to get told to "stay." But he lowered himself to one of the cushions and waited to see what would happen. It went like he expected, with the man setting the two puppies into Craig's lap and grinning. Next he turned and went out the door. Right before he closed it he said, "I'll be back."

Then Craig was alone in the tiny box of a room with two squirming puppies who were trying to lick his chin and crawl on him like a jungle gym.

It must have been ten minutes or so later that the man came back and opened the door unexpectedly to find Craig laid out on the floor. Puppies scampered over him like an obstacle course, his own laughter barely contained.

"So you'll take one of them?" The man asked, his grin a bit knowing but Craig didn't care. He'd been suckered, but he wasn't upset about it.

"Both."

CHAPTER 14

C raig woke to the sound of small, pitiful whines.
　　Despite the very early morning trip to the store, he hadn't been ready.

It had taken another hour to get out of the shelter, to sign the paperwork and finish his background check. He then waited while a vet in the back did a preliminary checkup for the two little fuzzballs without names but with energy to spare. In a fit of good feeling, Craig asked about making a donation and drastically over-paid the double adoption fee.

He'd been sent to a pet store nearby, which was open now because things took so long at the shelter. The two small dogs sauntered in the door he opened for them, tugging at the leashes looped around startlingly tiny necks. He'd been told they'd likely each top sixty pounds before they were done growing.

Though he'd gotten food and a bed at four a.m., the bed was too big and the food was made for an older dog. A pair of very nice teenagers in smocks and pet store name tags swarmed the puppies as they entered. The young workers' expressions changing from put-out at having to be up early on a

Saturday morning to being completely enamored with his two tiny dogs.

Despite being young, the kids knew far more than he did. They bombarded him with questions, then with sales, probably racking up a huge commission as they went. They even helped him load the car, the tiny no-name dogs thanking the kids with yips and licks.

He'd intended to get a dog. He'd gotten food and a dog bed the night before, holding off on a collar because he didn't know the size. Now he had two puppies—unwanted because of their breed. He had food bowls and a mat for the food bowls. He had toys and a bin for the toys. Toys that squeaked, toys that crackled, toys that held hidden treats. He had a dog crate and book about training the dogs for the crate. He had collars and harnesses and an understanding that he'd probably have to install a dog door soon.

He'd been saving to pay off his house. While the other band members had spent some of their future money, he hadn't. JD bought his wife a classic Ford Mustang, and TJ bought himself a flashy new car. They'd all gotten houses, but Craig's was the least expensive, the least showy, the smallest, and the least mortgaged.

Wilder was growing in fame, and they'd hit the big time, but the fame came faster than the money, and Craig lived with the knowledge that shooting stars sometimes burned out. He didn't want to be working mall security as he got older. He'd scraped his savings. He was close to paying off the relatively small, cheap house.

But that morning he'd blown a small stash of his savings. On a whim. He knew was going to continue to spend as he took the dogs to the vet, repeatedly, as he shored up the fence so they didn't get out as they got older. He was going to go nearly broke feeding them, he'd surmised after watching them scarf down the first bowls of puppy food he'd placed in front of them. They had terrible table manners, too.

Eventually, they'd eaten, made messes in the backyard while he waited in the warming air, and he'd put them in their crate, as the book told him to do. They whined for a moment then settled into a tiny puppy ball together. Pulling a pillow from the secondhand couch he called his own, he'd curled up on the floor to watch them, only to find out he'd fallen asleep himself.

Metallic noises indicated tiny paws were raking at the crate and he blinked himself awake, remembering what he'd done.

The clock on the wall suggested they'd all managed four hours of sleep. Though the puppies may have slept through the night before, Craig hadn't. He'd been awake, full of his crazy get-a-dog scheme, and now it was staring him in the face. Four deep brown eyes watched him with curiosity.

He'd done it; he was stuck with his decision. But he wouldn't go back. He didn't believe in returning animals to the shelter because things didn't work out. While he might not sleep until the dogs were older, it was nothing worse than what he'd been through before. This time for a much better cause. Lifting the latch, he watched as the two tumbled out, unconcerned with any etiquette or hurting themselves or each other.

He stretched himself up, barely managing to catch the scampering critters and click huge leash clips onto tiny collars. Then he led the puppies out the back door before they could start sniffing around inside the house. Four hours with no accidents was making him happy. After two tiny puddles were made, he led the now quarreling pair back inside and looked again at the clock.

"Oh shit."

He must have said it out loud, because two small sets of eyes looked up at them, and one planted his—her?—butt on the ground as though on command. He was about to be late for practice.

The garage yielded a cardboard box that he thought was big enough to hold puppies. The bathroom gave up an old towel, not that he had any new ones. Making them comfortable and throwing in a few toys, he stashed the box in the passenger seat and made it halfway to practice before he nearly died.

When the trio walked in the door of the studio he was greeted with a variety of welcomes.

"Oh wow. Who are they?" from TJ, who immediately leaned down and started rubbing bellies.

"Don't let Olivia see them. She'll squeal and Bridget will get her one." From Alex.

"Man, you look white as a sheet." It made sense that JD was the only one actually paying attention to him despite the adorable distractions he'd brought in.

Craig gathered his breath, seeing that the puppies were safe for the moment. "I didn't know they could get out of the box, and I didn't know they could fit under the brake pedal." He was still breathing heavy. "I couldn't get him out of there, and I couldn't stop the car without squishing him! Her? I don't know which one."

JD only nodded as though Craig's brush with near-certain death was nothing of real importance.

His next words made it more clear. "You're a parent now. Your kids are fuzzy and will grow a lot faster than mine and Alex's, but welcome to the club."

Craig proceeded to look at his guitarist and sometime co-writer as though JD was batshit crazy. Then he tried to get to work.

The puppies interrupted everything. Craig worried that he'd ruined practice. Then he worried that the dogs would chew a cord and electrocute themselves. He didn't even know where the nearest vet was. Alex and JD exchanged knowing smirks while Craig scrambled.

He took TJ and the guys through a few chord changes he'd

decided to add to *Sand*. They listened to a new one JD had that was only an outline. Then one of the producers came in and asked them to both sell a song to an upcoming band who wanted to cover one of their non-singles from the first album and to do a quick run of a song the company had purchased and wanted to know if they wanted to record it. By the time they finished the four-hour set, Craig was exhausted again. And he wasn't done.

His first stop was another pet store, this one on the way to the vet he'd looked up. Three times on the drive there, he pulled over and picked up one puppy or another—jeez he was going to have to learn to tell them apart!—and scooped them into the small backseat of the truck. Each time he told them "No!" using his best harsh voice, but it was difficult. They were adorable and weren't trying to be mean. They just wanted to get into the front seat with him. He wasn't sure his heart could take the beating.

He purchased car harnesses and strapped them into the backseat, increasing the volume on their little wails and howls. A carrier crate went into the truck bed and it only took ten minutes to get them both inside at the same time to go into the vet's office and wait for about thirty minutes because he didn't have an appointment.

He paid for two initial check-ups to find out that the shelter had indeed taken very good care of them and no one appeared to have any congenital problems. Then Craig realized it wasn't a girl who was slipping through his fingers like sand, it was his money. But he couldn't—wouldn't—change it.

Back in the car, with everyone harnessed in, Craig climbed into the driver's seat, realizing he was keeping up a constant chatter to the dogs, who couldn't really respond. No one climbed into his lap and he sat with the key in the ignition and his heart in his throat.

Why had he done this?

It had been a whim. But the kid who'd been shuffled from house to house and had never belonged to anyone really wasn't able to turn a puppy away when it wanted his lap, his attention, his time. He didn't want to tell them no, and he was suddenly petrified that something would happen to these little dogs he'd had for less than twenty-four hours. What would he do? How would he handle it?

He wouldn't. That's what.

So he had to keep them safe. That was the only option. Though the vet had chided him for being too soft—which Craig wondered how that was possible since they were puppies—he fought the urge to let them out of the harnesses. Other people got dogs and left them in the yard. They didn't get vet check-ups or worry like this. But some switch had been flipped and he'd become both fierce and weak.

Driving home, he talked to them, told them they'd been good at the vet. At least the vet had said so, despite the fact that they gnawed on her hand, licked her face and tried to bite her chin. She was gentle but firm when one pawed at her and left scratches.

He had her card and was told he could see any of the vets at the clinic, but if he wanted to, he could make an appointment for them with her. He wanted that, wanted them to see the same doctor over and over, to lessen the chance that anything might get missed.

Dr. Naman was young, beautiful and intelligent. She might even have been hitting on him, but he hadn't cared. He'd pocketed her card then put it on the fridge with tape since he couldn't find a magnet.

He walked his puppies. Played with them. Fed them measured bowls of food. Walked them again, then put them in their crate and tried to leave them in the corner of the living room.

They let up tiny attempts at howls, mad at being left despite the fact that they had each other. He lasted fifteen minutes.

They lasted longer.

Craig let them out, toggled the crate through the bedroom door and set them up in the corner of his bedroom. He was proud that he had his time down to five minutes to get them both into the crate at the same time.

He crawled into bed again.

They howled again.

With a weak laugh, he pulled his pillow from the bed, grabbed his soft, fuzzy comforter and curled up on the carpet next to them.

Finally, they were quiet. Coming over to the side of the crate close to him, one stuck a paw through the metal wire and rested it on his arm, as though touching him reassured the puppy that Craig wasn't going anywhere.

He reminded himself the dogs had been abandoned on the side of the road, watched their siblings and mother die, spent several weeks in the shelter and went unadopted. Despite their cuteness, they had bad blood. Pit and Rottweiler was unwanted.

Craig sighed wearily to himself. He hadn't meant to understand Shay.

He'd been trying to forget her—thinking a dog would take up his time, need his attention, and pull him out of his funk. It was supposed to help him get over her. She'd made a sound decision about what she could and couldn't do. He understood that he didn't fit into her life.

She'd chosen her kids over him. Shay had to.

Despite the fact that he'd intended the dogs to help distance himself from her memory, it brought her back to the forefront. The switch had flipped. The harnesses, the right food, the constant vigilance, it was all part of his 'parenthood.' Somehow, in no time at all, he loved them.

He wasn't sure he'd ever loved anyone or anything before.

Maybe the comforter—he'd wished for one as a kid. As an adult, it was one of the first things he'd bought when he had a place of his own. He didn't think he'd ever really loved a human being.

But this was so easy, it had snuck past him.

He broke. There on the floor, his comforter under and around him, he started crying. First tears fell that he couldn't get under control, then the silent defeat turned to great sobs. Unable to stop himself, he tried not to look at the puppies, but felt another paw reach out as though to comfort him. Though he fought to stay silent, Craig couldn't tamp down the pain that wracked his chest and clamped his lungs.

He'd never cried as an adult. He hadn't cried since he was sixteen. He'd cried his first night on the street, just a little. He'd cried his first night off the street, a lot. It had been scarier and worse than his first night on his own. But he'd never cried again.

Not until now.

Not until he understood how easy it was to love something small that needed him. And not until he saw that—despite how easy it was—no one had ever done that for him.

CHAPTER 15

"What are you reading, Honey?" Shay looked down at Owen. To say he was 'sitting' in the chair was a misnomer. He was sprawled sideways across the one recliner they had. It didn't recline anymore, but that didn't stop him from reclining in it.

"It's about a dog."

Thank God, better than what he was reading last time! Shay sighed to herself and looked at the clock.

Saturdays and Sundays were rough. Often one boy or the other had something with his father. Weekends like this one— with no father visits—were both easier and harder. The boys were far enough different in age that finding a single activity for both was a difficult task.

Though the sky was bright and the sun out, the weather forecast wasn't good, and she decided to take a chance.

"Aaron?" She called toward the back of the small house. She was pretty sure the youngest was playing with his click-blocks in the bedroom. She'd seen him back there just five minutes ago. But to a three-year-old, five minutes was more than enough time to get into serious trouble. Luckily, he came out when called and Shay managed to get Owen's attention away from his book.

"Look what I got!" She held up a printed ticket to the local indoor bounce house and grinned.

Both boys lit up like little firecrackers and yelled. Her heart warmed at seeing even Owen have more than just a mellow reaction, and for something physical. He was so subdued normally that she wondered if she should become concerned.

As excited as they were, they were easy to herd through the many steps to get ready. The money she'd spent on the ticket was a discount, but she hated spending when there was a park for free down the street, a community pool for cheap in the summer, and so on. But the kids needed variety, both in where they went and who they saw. She'd hoarded the ticket for the right day, and was glad that today seemed like a good one.

Both boys had slept well the night before, the day wasn't gloomy enough to drive everyone inside and overcrowd the place, and she hoped it would be a good visit. They went to the bathroom in order, Aaron insisting he didn't need help and Shay watching and monitoring as she 'not helped.' They put on shoes with little fuss, ate a quick snack as she packed more for the car —she wouldn't spend on the expensive pizza slices and sugar water drinks they sold at the place.

Then they were in the car and off.

Other parents plugged in laptops and hooked into the Wi-Fi. Shay was too afraid to unplug hers from her home system. One day a reboot was going to crash her dinosaur, she knew. Besides, though Owen could go off on his own in the enclosed space, Aaron still needed someone watching him pretty much the whole time.

Once through the door and past the ticket counter, her boys shoved their shoes in cubbies, not noticing that their shoes were older and more beat up than the others they were next to. They didn't notice that only a few of the parents had presented discount tickets at check-in. Shay wondered how long it would be before Owen started seeing the differences.

Luckily, it wasn't today. He was off like a shot, lost in the crowd of kids and inflatables. Shay told herself not to worry; he was a smart kid and well street-trained. Aaron grabbed her hand and pulled her to watch him climb a bubble climbing wall.

Though she grinned and responded to his every question and his every "watch me," her mind wandered.

Brian was an idiot. Her ex had told her with great joy that he'd given Aaron Benadryl and he'd slept like a charm. When asked—with great alarm on Shay's part—why Aaron needed medication, Brian had proudly said, "So he'd go to sleep!"

"That's great, sweetie!" She smiled up at her son. He seemed to have no lingering effects from being doped. She told Brian he couldn't do that, then she'd looked up all possible side effects and lasting damage online and found there wasn't much. It was nearly impossible to even have an allergic reaction to the stuff. But while Brian agreed not to do it again, she didn't trust him to remember or even to keep his word if he did. She knew Brian and current girlfriend Debbie smoked a lot of weed, too.

Aaron grabbed her hand and pulled her to the other side of the large room, still bouncing despite the fact that he was no longer on an air cushion. Her son tugged her past several large slides and she looked up to see Owen, helping a little girl climb the rope rigging to the top.

"You can do it, honey." A voice told her, and Shay's attention was unexpectedly jerked to the man at the bottom of the steep slope. Her breath caught.

Craig.

She knew the blond hair, the broad shoulders, narrow waist. The twist in her heart. But then he turned as their two kids reached the top and she got a glimpse of his profile.

Not Craig. Of course not. Craig didn't have kids, didn't want kids, didn't even particularly like them. He didn't even live in the area.

The problem was that it wasn't the first time she'd seen him. Once, she'd almost approached a man in the grocery store, thinking Craig had come back and simply hadn't called her yet. The boys hadn't been with her; it had seemed so easy and so obvious.

She'd come up behind him and even said his name. When the man turned, confused, he so obviously wasn't Craig that she'd become embarrassed and turned beet red. She'd even stammered, "I'm so sorry, I thought you were someone I know."

But she didn't know him. And why was she so flustered? She'd given up being embarrassed about anything long ago. She owned her mistakes and stupidity. She'd had to tell the women's shelter, then her lawyer, then everyone in the mediator's office exactly what Jason had done to her. She'd used up her shame a long, long time ago.

But it didn't seem to matter, she'd been so embarrassed that she thought she'd seen him, and now she did it again. He wasn't here. He wasn't coming back. Maybe that was why she was embarrassed—because she somehow truly believed it would all be different. She was upset that she mistakenly hoped he would come back and sweep her off her feet.

It was upsetting to know that in her heart she'd wanted it. Even just a little. Even knowing what that kind of thing brought. It was shameful wanting something that wasn't right for her kids.

Turning her thoughts back to the boys, back to her real life, Shay helped Aaron climb yet another house-sized blow-up toy. He came down the slide ass over teakettle, but seemed to think it was fun enough to do it again. Shay wasn't going to tell him he wasn't doing it right.

Wanting to milk the day-pass for all they could, she stayed until the boys said they were ready to leave. Exhausted, they could barely get their shoes on. She was as tired as they were, and she hadn't even jumped on anything.

Hauling them inside once they were home involved waking them up from the backseat. It made her think again about Brian giving Aaron Benadryl, and made her wonder if it wasn't time to dig into that account.

The boys ate their dinners and headed off to bed, ready for school the next day. Shay sprawled on the couch. Her body was sluggish, but her mind ran disturbingly fast. So much for getting extra work finished this evening.

Each time she finished a project early, she could ask for the next one. She could sock away more money. But tonight she was afraid she'd mess up her stitches, match fronts and backs of fabric badly, and cost herself time. Those kinds of errors made her slower rather than faster and made it not worth even trying to work when she saw she wasn't in the right frame of mind.

Instead, she lay there, her brain thinking about Brian, about Owen, and the book she'd managed to put away before sprawling there.

Cujo.

It's about a dog, Mom.

She should have known. He was still reading Stephen King.

Staring at his bookshelf, she thought about his rejection of all the books she'd tried to get him interested in. Goosebumps. Treehouse of Horrors. There were so many that were for his age, and Owen wanted nothing to do with them. She'd found *The Amityville Horror* tucked under his pillow a few weeks ago.

Maybe it was time to meet him halfway. Maybe he could read adult books, but she could steer him toward dragons and elves and such. She'd try to hit the library tomorrow morning when she could talk to the librarian and explain her problem.

Her eyelids drifted closed and she thought of several sets of parents she'd seen at the bounce house. It would be nice to have someone to bounce ideas off. Someone who helped instead of hurt. Shay knew it existed. Somewhere.

Craig's words flitted through her head. *What if I don't turn into an asshole?*

That shouldn't be romantic, but to her, it was. Other people had long, good, solid marriages. Why couldn't she? Why couldn't she *learn* to pick the right kind of guy? She wasn't doomed!

Then again, maybe she was. Brian had gotten horribly upset just from seeing Craig's car. Had he seen the man, he'd have known he could never measure up.

She'd neatly sewn herself into a pocket.

If she found anything for herself, her very happiness would trigger both Brian and Jason to take it out on her. To take it out on her boys. Until Aaron turned eighteen, or until she got the men to relinquish their parental rights, it would not be an option. Her own doing, she knew it.

Shay took a moment to be grateful that Zoe hadn't followed in their mother's footsteps anywhere near as well as she herself had. Zoe was twenty-four and still had never been pregnant. That was such a big family victory that Shay almost cried at the futility of it all.

She'd considered bribing the men to sign away their rights. Brian would do it for cheap. He had no concept of money. And she had the money saved up to buy his agreement. More than once she'd thought about just trading cash for rights. But if a decent lawyer ever got a hold of Brian, the fight would be on, and her money would be gone.

Jason would squeeze her for everything before he signed anything. Then he'd find a lawyer right away and sue her for trying it. Shay didn't doubt any of this.

She struggled with the decision to start suing Brian for custody. The Benadryl concerned her. But as always, if she started with Brian she would have to finish. Would there be enough money left to take on Jason?

Could she sacrifice one boy to save the other? If she didn't, would she lose them both?

Then she did cry. She lay there on the couch, with silent tears rolling down her face. She cried because there were no good answers. No safe paths. And she cried because she wanted something that wasn't good for her boys. She dreamed of Craig at night. She thought she saw him when she was out and about. No matter how much she told herself it was fine and she'd get over it, it was only getting worse.

Shay woke up on the couch the next morning, and barely got the boys to school on time. She headed straight to the public library where the librarian set her up with some guaranteed attention-holding books that didn't involve rabid dogs tearing their families limb from limb or—God Forbid—fathers burying their dead sons in a pet cemetery.

She headed home, armed with a full bag of books for each boy. She sewed like a madwoman and turned in two projects ahead of time.

When the weekend came again, she had each kid ready on time, and entertained until his father showed up late. Both men. She sighed. But once again threw herself into her work.

Sunday morning, a knock startled her from the lace she was hemming onto the bottom of another stage outfit for another country star.

"Open the door, Shay!" The pounding came again.

She recognized that voice. Brian. Was he returning Aaron early again? And if not, then where was her son?

As she peeked out the window, she saw her toddler over his father's shoulder, unflinching despite the shouts. "I'm coming!" She hollered back as she headed to the door.

Brian thought she jumped for him. Never. Always for her son. But never again for him.

She barely had the door open before he was pushing Aaron into her arms, only Aaron didn't come. Didn't hold out his arms. He just draped like a sack of lead and she nearly dropped him.

"What's wrong with him?" She almost yelled it. Still the boy didn't react at all.

"He's asleep." Brian brushed it off. "I got another gig. I gotta go." He was already down the steps.

"Aaron?" She tried to wake him, but nothing happened. He wasn't this deep a sleeper. "Aaron!"

In her panic, Shay slapped at his face but got no response.

Brian looked back at her. "He's fine. Just asleep." His voice was mocking as if to say *How could she be so stupid as to worry?*

Normally, if something was wrong, Brian would say so. He'd make up some song and dance about how he knew she'd want to be there for the boy, blah blah blah. This was nothing like that.

Suddenly Shay realized that in her panic, she'd been slow.

Brian was at his car door when she yelled out to him, "You gave him Benadryl again, didn't you?"

The ass had the nerve to shrug.

"You said you wouldn't!" She was furious. He lied and didn't even care.

"You weren't supposed to know." Brian shrugged again. "He would have been awake before he got here if I hadn't caught this gig. Don't worry about it. It's fine. You're being hysterical."

Then he opened his car door and climbed inside. Shay could see Debbie, filing her nails or some crap, in the passenger seat, while Shay stood in her doorway, holding her limp son, his overnight bag left carelessly at her feet.

The two sons of bitches drove away while she stood in her open doorway staring. As she turned to take her son inside, she held him close. That's when she smelled it.

They'd been smoking again.

CHAPTER 16

S hay drove Aaron to the doctor despite the cost. Sure, she'd
scrimped and saved, but this was what it was for. She
honestly wasn't as concerned as she might be about her son not
waking up. She'd given him the same medication before—for
legitimate reasons—and he'd been out cold then, too.

No, this was for documentation. She wanted the doctor to
say that her son had been returned un-rousable. Shay needed a
medical record stating that a professional smelled weed on her
son. Luckily, she'd told this doctor all about her issues with the
fathers and the doctor was ready. She was opening the clinic on
a Sunday, to get Aaron in fast, before the meds wore off, before
the smell faded from his clothes.

When she met Shay at the door, the doctor led her and her
sack-of-cement son into the back room to wait a moment. Shay
was surprised to see the physician return with a uniformed
police officer.

"This is Officer Patel." Doctor Devanii introduced the
surprise guest. "He's here to assist with the documentation."

Shay tried not to seem upset; she wasn't the parent in the

wrong, but she was struck with the sudden and gripping fear that they would take her son from her. He was medicated to the point of comatose and smelled like pot. Shay looked back and forth between them, trying not to look guilty of things she hadn't done.

"Don't worry. Please." Officer Patel tried to assure her. "Dr. Devanii called me in to help with documentation. She mentioned that you had talked to her previously about prior issues with the boy's father. Do you wish to open a case?"

Shay took a deep breath. *Go time.* "Yes."

She'd never been more scared in her life.

"Lay him down here." Dr. Devanii told her. Though the doctor was young, Shay trusted her. She'd been bringing the boys here for several years, since they'd moved into the tiny house. Each time, Dr. Devanii had checked the boys for any bruises, asked about any interactions with either parent, and more. All documented for Shay's records.

Fortunately—or unfortunately?—there hadn't been any marks on either of the boys before. Shay was ultimately grateful.

The doctor moved her hand, waving the officer over. "What do you smell?"

"Weed. That's pretty strong." He shook his head, then turned to Shay. "When did you take possession of him?"

She checked her phone. "About half an hour ago." She shrugged. "I think they were smoking in the car, but I can't prove it." Then she looked at her son, still peacefully sleeping. "And he slept through it, so he can't give you anything either."

The officer nodded. "While the court will talk with him, he's not old enough to testify to facts."

Shay considered also what the ramifications might be if her boys wanted to keep seeing their fathers. Why would they? Neither boy ever had anything nice to say about his dad. She took a deep breath and calmed herself, she didn't need to keep the boys from their dads. Not really. She simply needed sole custody. She needed to not have to hand them over every other weekend and holidays, held hostage by men who were known to be abusive.

"Do we blood test him for the Benadryl?" She asked the doctor.

"We can." The doctor nodded. "But it's expensive and it's not an illegal drug."

"Still, it would prove that his father was medicating him for no reason." Shay protested, pushing down the thought of the money.

"No. It would only prove that he *was* medicated. Maybe by the girlfriend. And it doesn't prove there was no reason."

As Shay started to protest, the doctor held up her hand. "But as the father is responsible, it's definitely a concern. It might also show if he was over-medicated." She sighed. "Which I suspect, given his lack of response."

Dr. Devanii picked up one of Aaron's hands and it hung limply in her grip. She let go, letting his hand thump onto the bed, not a soft landing by any stretch. Aaron didn't react at all. "Don't worry, his breathing and heart rate are fine, but I would expect some reaction to that test on a normal dose. I also lifted his lids and checked for pupillary reactions. They're fine, but again, he should have reacted. He didn't."

"Do the lab test." Shay was solid. If Brian had over-medicated him, she was going to sue him for the money to replace her damn savings. Then she turned to the officer, unable to watch as the doctor used a small butterfly needle to draw a vial of blood.

"Officer Patel, Brian—his father—told me he gave my son Benadryl to make him sleep. This would have been in the morning on Sunday two weeks ago. He then promised not to do it again. He did it again this morning. He admitted to doing it. He admitted to doing it just to 'get the kid to sleep.' Does that help?" Her heart was pounding and she wondered if it would ever stop.

"Honestly. I don't know." The officer looked rueful. His hands were tied by a system that believed in biological parentage. Shay no longer did. She loved her sons because they were hers. Their fathers didn't seem to have the genetics for it.

"Will your ex-husband admit to that tactic? It's not an illegal drug. We don't arrest over marijuana either. But exposing a toddler to it can be problematic when trying to get or maintain even partial custody. Do you want me to test for it?"

"Yes!" She turned back to the doctor. "Can you do that on the blood panel?"

She nodded and made more notes into the computer.

"I can also do a residue test. Do you want that?" The officer added.

Shay nodded frantically. What she wouldn't give to have someone here. Strong arms to support her while she supported her small child. No, not someone. *Craig.*

But he wasn't really the type, was he?

And she didn't need anyone. She straightened her spine and watched as the officer pulled out a stick with a detector on the end and inserted a small cloth he pulled out of a single pack foil. He rubbed it across her unresponsive son's clothing and skin, then put the cloth into some kind of evidence baggie which he labeled. When all the tests had been done, and her statement taken both for the medical record and for an official police record, it was starting to get dark.

"Do you want to stay until he wakes up?" The doctor put her hand on Shay's shoulder.

"You're so kind, opening the office on a Sunday, and bringing in an officer. I need to be home to meet my other son.

Will Aaron wake up on his own?" *What if he didn't?* Worry was starting to set in about something new.

"He should." She rattled off times to expect certain changes. If and when Shay should call the doctor's cell number again. Shay thanked them both and hauled her son back out the door, the toddler blissfully unaware of the war that had just ignited over him.

She had Aaron back in his own bed, the timer set to check on him, right as Jason showed up with Owen. Owen looked sour, but Jason hardly spoke at the exchange. Crouching down, Shay ignored her ex and hugged her son, managing to bring him inside with no words spoken to a man she'd once believe she loved with all her heart. After she closed the door, she turned to her son. "What's wrong, sweetie?"

Owen was close to tears, and so was Shay. She couldn't take another trauma today.

In a very tiny voice, he told her, "He broke my book."

"Broke it?"

A nod. A loose tear running down a cheek. A whisper. "He tore out the pages and told me it was for pussies."

The last word was almost inaudible, but Shay recognized it. One of Jason's favorites. Right up there with "fag" and "queer" and "bitch" and a few others, none of them favorable. Her only consolation was that he'd been nice to her when they were dating. What she hadn't known then, was that if a man was nice to her, but not anyone else, that he wasn't a nice man. Jason was not a nice man. He wasn't even neutral. He was a cold-hearted, bigoted son of a bitch. Shay could not tell her son that.

"Which book?" she asked.

"The library book." He whispered back.

"No worries. I'll take care of it." She smiled at him, hugged him and wished she could make it all okay. But she couldn't. That book was going to cost her an arm and a leg in replacement fees. Another trip to talk to the librarian. Shay had considered getting her son an e-reader, but once again opted not to. He couldn't have nice things because his dad ruined them.

"I was in the middle of it. What will I read tonight?" Owen was angry. Pissed as hell. Not at being called a pussy. He simply didn't buy into his dad's bullshit. But he was mad about destroyed property, kicked puppies, and general meanness. Whatever gene his father lacked had the opposite mutation in Owen. Much to Jason's irritation, his son was sensitive. "The library is already closed."

"I'll tell you what. I'll buy an online copy of it and you can read it on my computer until you finish or until we get another book from the library, maybe tomorrow." *Ouch.* Ouch to the money of now needing to buy something she had gotten for free in the first place. Ouch to Owen reading on her computer. Ouch to all of it.

She set him up on her screen while she sewed at the kitchen table. Around nine p.m. he declared himself ready to go to sleep and by nine-thirty he was out cold. Unlike Aaron who'd woken up just a little while before and was finally coming out of the room and saying he was hungry.

Shay was never going to get to sleep. Her exes weren't even here and they still managed to steal from her—her sleep, her peace of mind, even the man she loved.

Scratch that. She didn't love Craig. She loved the idea of Craig.

And even the idea of him didn't work in reality. So Shay set Aaron in front of the TV with some cereal and managed to catch a few winks on the couch. She'd managed by herself when he was a baby and never slept, and Owen had been just a toddler. She'd do fine now.

The next morning, she shuffled her grumpy bunch off to school and to Head Start. Then she hit the library where she tried to explain that yes, his father had ripped the book and could there please be some reduction on the sixty-dollar replacement fee?

She managed a pity rate of fifty percent. Next she marched into the office of the lawyer she'd chosen three years ago when she first thought she'd had enough money. An hour later, when the woman was finally ready to see her, she said, "I'm ready."

CHAPTER 17

C raig sat in the comfy chair across the big mahogany desk from the woman who took his case. "This is all confidential, right?"

The lawyer worked for HeartBeats, Inc.—the label that owned all of Wilder's music and produced all their albums and such. Brenda, their personal manager and co-owner had recommended the woman, but he couldn't have this getting back to anyone at work.

The woman on the other side of the desk had her hair scraped back into a severe bun. Her clothing was boxy, and she intimidated just by sitting there. Not really the soothing presence he was hoping for as he swallowed his tongue.

The last weeks had been eye-opening. It turned out he was a good father—if the puppies were anything to measure by. He thought they were, since they kept trying to be little terrors and he handled it with some level of grace.

The night he'd cried by their crate in the room, he'd woken to late daylight, painful whines, a puffy face, and half a comforter. The other half looked like it had been cherry-bombed. The fluff that made it into the crate had been peed on and then played with.

He'd gotten angry but held himself in check. Despite the destruction, they'd just been doing puppy things. He could buy another comforter. Not another first one, but he told himself it had been getting old anyway.

After cleaning the mess and purchasing a new bed set, he sat down and found the chapters in the dog book on 'chewing' and 'destruction.' At which point he learned not to have fluffy things near puppies. *No shit, Sherlock,* he'd thought. Lesson learned. He'd slept in his own bed the next night—poorly because of the whining. Then the third night, things finally calmed down.

He followed the book religiously and was generous with playtime and exercise. And Scarlett and Gunnar—names plucked from a TV show—had both learned how to sit and how to come when called. For his part, Craig had learned how to tell their faces apart.

He even trained Daniel to feed them appropriately and walk the pair without letting them tug the leashes too much. Together he and the nine-year-old worked with the small dogs on hand signals and vocal commands. Daniel was a disturbingly competent kid. He was full of good ideas, and even finished reading the training book before Craig did.

It shouldn't have surprised Craig. After all, Daniel's mother Kelsey was uber-competent. Despite her claims that her old life was anything but, she lived and managed a drama-free home. Quite the opposite of Shay, he thought more than once.

But Kelsey didn't intrigue him. Didn't tug at the back corners of his memory when she was gone. Good thing, too. JD would kill him.

It was uber-competent Kelsey who got the only earful of what he was about to do. And she didn't get much. Instead, he'd sat her down and told her how good Daniel was with the dogs. Then he asked her a crazy question.

"If something happens to me, I want Daniel to have the puppies. Is that okay?" He didn't know what he expected. Really just a yes or no answer, but that had been really stupid, he realized.

"What's going to happen to you, Craig? Is something wrong?" She'd stared him in the eyes, tried to pop up and grab his shoulders only to be thwarted by the extra weight at her waistline.

"Nothing is going to happen to me." He lied. "But I have these dogs and I couldn't stand it if they went back to the shelter. I'll leave a trust fund for them—"

"You're going to leave a trust fund for your dogs? I'm their god-parent? *Dog*-parent?" She looked at him sideways.

"Daniel would be. But obviously a lot of that would fall to you. Can you do it?" He stared her down hoping to prevent further questions.

"Why?"

Well crap. "Just yes or no, Kelsey. Please?"

She sighed. "Yes. Of course. Now tell me what you're about to do!"

"I'm not about to—"

"Are you suicidal!?" This time she did jump up despite the prominent baby bump. They all knew she'd lost her brother that way and Craig immediately dispelled what was clearly a bone deep fear in her.

"No. I'm not. I just have some business to take care of out of town and the flying is . . . I just want to be sure."

So he'd told the lawyer to draw that up legally. She'd pulled up a standard document and let him talk her through any changes for his heirs to not be human. To name a minor— Daniel—in charge of the dogs and Kelsey as the legal adult. Craig wasn't even certain if "Kelsey" was her legal name or a nickname, but he wasn't going to get into that now. He'd signed the printed document and left it in the lawyer's hands to file before getting down to the real meat of his business. "I need to confess to a murder."

That at least got her attention. "A murder? There's no statute of limitations on murder. You know that?"

Craig nodded. He'd looked that up online. It would never expire on him. So he thought he might do better getting out in front of it rather than letting it catch up to him later. It would destroy the band either way, but at this stage of the game, they might be able to replace him if he spent the rest of his life in jail. He would just be that guy that was on the first two albums.

His heart was beating heavily; he had no idea how this was going to turn out. Despite the fact that he was literally beginning to sweat, the lawyer stayed cool. Craig wondered if people confessed odd shit to her all day long. Maybe she dressed that way to discourage it. *Too late.*

His throat was closing. Why had he done this? He'd never told anyone—*anyone*—what he'd done. Why now? Why this sudden need to unburden himself? It wasn't like the dogs cared what he'd done. They loved him anyway.

It occurred to him maybe that was the key, as stupid as it was.

The only creatures that had ever loved him unconditionally weren't even human. But he'd walked taller these past couple weeks. He was more certain of himself. And more convinced he needed to become the man he could be rather than the grown up remnants of the kid he'd been.

"When was this murder?"

Looking up into the corner of the room, he realized he should have thought this through a little better. He back calculated out loud, using the year he'd run away for good to figure out when it would have happened.

"Can I get you a drink? And what month of that year?" She asked as though ten-plus-year-old murders were taken with tea most afternoons at three.

"A Dr. Pepper if you have it." He answered in what might be the most bizarre conversation he'd ever had. "June."

He'd run away two springs before. Right before finals in his high school classes. He'd thought he was hot shit, but he was out of money and on the street, just like every other kid, before he knew what he was doing. He'd sung on street corners to supplement the crappy savings he'd started with. But being mugged and beaten up for even those meager amounts had driven him to worse things.

A knock at the door signaled a disturbingly classy service of an iced tea and his Dr. Pepper. Then the kid disappeared and the questions continued. "Where?"

"Santa Monica Boulevard."

She frowned. "Where?"

"Hollywood. California."

"So, not even in this state?" She looked at him over the rims of frameless glasses. Given her calculating stare, Craig figured she didn't even need them. He shook his head.

"Whom did you murder?"

"I don't know his name." His guts rolled and he thought he might puke despite the fizz settling in his stomach. He'd been horribly ill prepared for his own confession.

"So tell me how this happened. Where, time of day, circumstances." She waved her hand at him to go on.

"It was about three a.m. when I met him. We were in the old Dixie hotel. I'm not even sure if it's still there. I didn't give him my real name." Craig paused. He couldn't tell all of it. "Everything was normal until he was supposed to pay me. He pulled a gun and pistol whipped me with it."

She still didn't flinch and Craig respected that. It wasn't an easy story to tell and probably not easy to hear either. Not without judging him. But she didn't. "Do you have any scars from that?"

The question surprised him, his hand automatically flying

to his hairline. He nodded but didn't speak. Only once in every few blue moons did he even touch the remnants of one of the worst moments of his life. But he now turned his head to the side and pulled back the hair he always wore shaggy as though that would hide the whole year and a half and not just the scar.

She looked at it clinically and made a few notes before nodding for him to keep going.

"When he turned, I jumped him. I grabbed the gun away." He shrugged awkwardly, struggled for the words. Maybe he should have practiced the story. "I thought I was going to die and I just got mad. I didn't care that he was going to shoot me. I just wasn't going to die like that . . ." He stopped as though waiting for her approval.

She nodded, her expression finally turning softer, finally understanding. Craig thought maybe it was easier for people to talk to the stiff old broad than the comforting mother type.

His voice was quiet, as though the softness lessened what he'd done. "I hit him with it. Over and over."

"Where?"

"In the hotel room."

"Where on his body did you hit him?" Though she asked it gently as if it were a follow up question, Craig felt stupid. It was what she'd meant the first time she'd asked. But he answered.

"His face. His head."

"Until he died?" Now her voice was soft, too.

He only nodded.

"Then what?"

"I took all his money. Dropped the gun and ran." What he didn't say was that the man had been up and down Santa Monica before. They knew him, all the kids on the boulevard after dark. They all hated him. It was rumored he often carried a lot of cash. And that was right; Craig had taken all of it. Including three gift cards to stupid chain restaurants and a shoe place. Only after he'd spent them did he realize the police might have traced him through those cards.

Bloody and beaten beyond recognition, he'd taken the money, gathered the stash he'd managed to keep hidden from everyone on the street—the money he'd been saving to make his escape—and he'd left the area in a cab, his head ducked low, his heart racing with leftover adrenaline and new fear that his street bosses would come after him. They'd be worse to him than the fat man was.

"Did you fire the gun?"

It sounded like she'd maybe asked the question before. "No."

"Can you describe him?"

Oh, yes. Craig could describe that man. His round face still haunted bad dreams. He'd deserved what he'd gotten and more. For the first time Craig wasn't sure *he* deserved to live with it any more. He told everything. He'd survived the streets off Hollywood for over a year. He'd come cross country and survived in a mean business. He'd survive the rest of this, too. He could wish for a different life from jail just as easily as he could do it from a tour bus.

Maybe easier, if he could do it without the guilt.

Despite becoming a comforting mother figure, the lawyer had taken down an extended series of notes. By hand. Craig appreciated that. No computer document to hack. He wasn't ready for her answer.

"Let me see what I can do. I can probably call you by early next week with some idea of how to proceed."

118

He wasn't prepared for the jolt to his system as the plane touched down. It wasn't the jerk to the seat caused by the wheels grabbing tarmac for the first moment, it was the fracture of recognition of a city and a life he'd left behind.

Despite Wilder's traveling, despite coming close to Southern California—they'd made it to San Francisco and to Nevada— he'd not been back to Los Angeles since fleeing over a decade ago. Not since the night he'd murdered the man who'd threatened him.

A week passed since he talked to the lawyer. A week of rehearsals without puppies. Daniel babysat while he was out, something that seemed to work out well for all parties—except maybe Kelsey who had to oversee things.

A week of his heart beating just a little stronger than normal. A week of jumping every time the house phone rang. A week of playing harder with the small, fuzzy family members he'd just gotten and hoping he didn't have to leave them soon. But for the first time in his life, Craig had a strong need to put things right. He'd lived with things being wrong for so long.

Also, while the bank might repossess his house, and the band could go toes up and take all the money with it at any point, he now had family. No one was going to repossess his dog crate, or the leashes, or the toys. He had family that would be with him if they were kicked out, or even on the streets again.

But his desire to set things to rest had led him here, and here he was afraid there was no rest. Just breathing the air twisted him inside. Luckily, he was a master at fighting to look normal. He could pass as calm when he was anything but.

So he pulled his carryon bag from the overhead spot and slung it over his shoulder, wondering if he would make his return flight in three days or if he'd be in jail. He hadn't commented on his trip to the rest of the band, only informed them that he was taking it.

"Back to L.A.?" Alex had asked. "What for?"

"Trip home for a few days, just some old business to put right." He'd shrugged into his guitar thinking he'd start playing and they'd shut up.

"You have 'old business'?" TJ teased him. "Do you have a surprise kid!?"

A decent question, given JD's odd circumstances a few years before, but not at all like Craig's issue. "No." At least he could grin at that.

He'd set Kelsey and Daniel up as relief sitters for the actual babysitter he'd hired to stay with his puppies for the three days. So Kelsey was worried about the trip, probably because of what he'd said before, but she didn't seem to have opened her mouth to JD. Or if she had, he was keeping the story quiet. "Let's get started. I'm missing the next couple of days."

Or decades. He thought, but didn't say.

So he'd hopped the flight, everything in place, and then stood at the edge of LAX, flagging a cab in a strange reversal of his flight out of here. He was staying in Santa Monica on the instructions of his lawyer, something about jurisdictions. It was intended to buy him time if everything went south, despite the fact that the lawyer didn't think it would, given what she'd already dug up.

When he got to the hotel, he stood in the lobby and called the number he'd been given.

"Mr. Hibbets. Good to hear from you." His local lawyer said kindly. The man—Kip Darrow—had been referred from the Nashville office and had all Craig's notes from his previous sessions.

No, it's not good. It was simply necessary. "Thank you." Was all he responded.

"Do you need a rest or do you want to meet right away?"

It was only ten a.m. here, the early flight and the time zone changes working in his favor. "I'd rather just jump in than wait around."

Darrow promised a call back and Craig took the time to do an early check in and find a sandwich, not that easy at ten in the morning. He was just polishing it off, sitting in his seventh floor room looking out over the sprawl of Santa Monica, when his phone buzzed. Despite expecting the call, Craig jumped.

"Yes?"

"Can you be ready in twenty minutes? I'll pick you up and we'll head into Hollywood where we'll meet a Detective Valverde."

Craig agreed, his heart jumping erratically. The twenty minutes in the lobby, staring at the walls, was one of the longest stretches of time he could remember. And there had been some bad moments he'd waited on. That this was the worst was telling.

The town car pulled up and Craig remembered the fascination Angelenos had with their cars. It must still be going strong ten years later. Status was a big deal out here, and it came by way of corporate titles, neighborhoods, and wheels. This navy blue car, buffed to an almost disturbing shine, was no exception.

The lawyer shook his hand, then looked over Craig's pressed slacks and button down shirt. "Good."

The value judgment didn't mean much. It was pretty much exactly what he'd told Craig to wear. There was nothing he could do about a few tattoos that snuck out beneath the sleeves he desperately wanted to roll up. He hadn't even tried for a tie— tugging at it would be worse than not wearing it.

On the drive in, he was given instructions. "This is just a fact-finding mission. Right now, despite your confession, they can't tie you to a crime."

Craig had heard that before, from his lawyer back in Nashville, but it was good to hear that things hadn't changed for the worse since planning this trip.

Kip Darrow continued. "I should be sitting right beside you. You can answer any questions honestly, but don't elaborate. If you want to say more about something, ask me first—we should be able to step out for a minute if you really need to chat."

"Won't that look bad?" Craig asked, already starting to sweat.

"Not really. These guys deal with lawyers all the time. A sidebar, or me shutting you down mid-answer . . . well, it happens a lot. It won't make you look guilty."

Craig nodded. He'd been told that the fact he'd initiated the investigation, that he'd confessed, played in his favor, too. But he'd never done this before. His only interactions with the police had been to run when he saw the cars coming down the streets when he was a kid. Then, his fear had been going back to foster care, or worse, to juvie. Where he'd wound up was far worse. Maybe he should have thrown himself at one of those cars. But past mistakes were past. Nothing he could do now, not that he wasn't already doing.

They parked in the side lot at the Hollywood Police Station, the car gliding into the spot as though it knew it belonged there. Craig got more and more nervous as he was checked in. Though he waited for someone to fingerprint him, call him out, basically blow his cover of normalcy, no one did.

His lawyer even pulled out the heavy, padded swivel chair for him as they sat at a table in a conference room. It was a far cry from the metal chairs and cinderblock interrogation room he expected. There wasn't even a two-way mirror. For the first time his heart started to slow. Then it kicked up again, when he thought maybe they were playing with him. He'd killed a man, after all.

Kip Darrow reached out tentatively, putting his hand gently over Craig's. "You're going to be fine." He nodded, sensing Craig's distress. "You're helping them. No one has any plans to charge you. Have you told me everything?"

Craig nodded, unable to speak past the lump in his throat.

"Then there's nothing that can happen today except a conversation." The hand lifted, but Craig had been grateful for the touch.

Just then a very young-looking officer came through the door. Though she wore a plain black pantsuit, she had a badge clipped to the waistband of her pants. She smiled, just a bit, "I'm Detective Jessica Valverde."

Darrow shook her hand and did quick introductions while Craig sized her up. For some reason, he'd expected an old, grizzled man, like on a cop show. Jessica Valverde was not bubbly, but she was strikingly beautiful. High cheekbones and a wide smile were offset by tanned skin and brown hair shot through with highlights. The blond streaks seemed to be her only concession to girliness, but Craig suspected they might be all California sun rather than salon.

She sat down across from them, setting down a fat folder that Craig only just then noticed she'd carried in with her. "I'm going to level with you both. I only just made detective, and that's why I was given this case."

She folded her hands and looked at each of them. "Mr.

Darrow, you and I have spoken and I've pulled everything I can find. After a decade, this was all getting dusty in storage and I cannot tell you how much fun it was to dig it all out." She almost grinned before turning to Craig. "Mr. Hibbets, we really appreciate you coming forward. Honestly, I don't even know how we would prosecute you."

Craig felt his heart start to flutter. *Was he going to be okay?* But he only blinked.

Valverde continued. "You said it was at the old Dixie hotel. Right?"

He nodded blankly.

"The building is gone. There's zero way to collect evidence." She sighed heavily. "And we aren't going to. I've read the case notes from Mr. Darrow. I can only guess at what you were doing in that room."

He couldn't even respond.

They *knew*. They understood. That strip was well known. And his presence there was a shame he'd carried for a very long time.

But Valverde didn't give him time to sink deep. "I understand that you're with a band now. Wilder?"

He nodded.

"I've heard you guys on the radio. You're very good." She grinned.

"Thank you." Just a whisper. He had just felt the final click of his old life linking to his new one, and he didn't like it.

She must have seen it. Darrow must have seen it, he was leaning across the table, but Valverde had her hands up. "We don't prosecute those crimes. I'm not here to put kids in jail for surviving." She stared at Craig, "Nor am I here to ruin a decade of amazing work. What you've done with your life is nothing short of miraculous, Mr. Hibbets."

The words hit him like a shockwave.

He'd done nothing. He'd only clawed and dug his way out of a hellhole. Nothing more.

But Jessica Valverde disagreed. She looked him in the eyes, her words earnest. "I come from a bad section of L.A. myself, and I had it very good compared to you. Kids often don't survive what you went through. The numbers show most become addicts. They commit suicide or disappear. They sure as hell don't very often buy houses and become famous on what is very clearly an amazing talent. I'm impressed. I'm not here to put you in jail. But I'm hoping you can help me. Maybe we can close an old file or two."

"But I killed him." Craig whispered.

"I read the file. I'm calling it self-defense. Nothing more. And no one can call it anything else." She nodded, looking down at the papers now.

Darrow patted Craig's hand and he found himself fighting the urge to grab it and squeeze for dear life. His words came out in a cathartic tumble, "But I kept hitting him after he was down."

She nodded. "Feel free to unburden yourself. I get that. But no one's going to prosecute you. You lived through it. I get the feeling you've carried it with you for years. Isn't that enough?"

He started to breathe; maybe it was enough.

Detective Jessica Valverde wasn't done with him yet, though. "We don't have a body. So I'm not even confident that you actually killed him. If he got up and walked away, then you're only looking at assault. And I'll book that man for what he did to kids up and down that strip, because you said he wasn't a first-timer, right?"

Craig shook his head. They all knew him. They were all afraid. He'd left knowing the others would be glad the man was dead.

Suddenly, it washed away. The guilt lifted, and though it wasn't entirely gone, it was so much lighter it might as well have been. She was right. He'd been petrified at the time. Maybe the man had gotten up eventually; Craig hadn't stuck around to find out. The asshole sure wouldn't have reported the crime—not from where he was and what he'd been doing. Craig almost had to hold onto the arms of the chair to keep himself from floating away.

Kip Darrow and Detective Jessica Valverde had cut the strings. Even if he killed the man, he'd paid his debt. He wasn't wanted. He wasn't going to have his life pulled out from under him. The weight had been heavier than he realized.

"Do you need a drink?" the detective asked him.

He nodded and she left him to look through photos.

Darrow seemed to know what was going on and he turned the pictures toward Craig. "These are unresolved missing persons in the right age bracket, from the right time period. Let us know if any of these are your guy."

Craig was still thumbing through them when Detective Valverde came back with a glass of ice water.

"What are these? Possibilities?" She frowned at the three photos he'd pulled out. There were a disturbingly high number and Craig wasn't finished looking through them yet. "No. None of those were him."

There were a variety of shots. Many were mugshots and Craig didn't ask what they'd been brought in for. He figured he already knew. "Those two were frequent flyers." He pointed, then shifted to the third. "That's 'Jim.' He was a street boss and ran coke through some of the girls."

Valverde only nodded, not shocked by any of this. Had she been testing him? Probably, but he knew the players. He'd never forget some of the faces. He didn't think he'd ever forget any of it, but maybe he should think like she did. He was still standing. He was earning money and making a name for himself. He'd come out the other side.

It took another hour sorting through stuff. "He's not here."

"Is it possible that you didn't kill him?"

He'd considered it the first time she said it, but it only now sunk in. No one in the greater L.A. area had been reported missing and never been recovered from that time. They had no bodies reported at the Dixie that night or even that week. None were dumped anywhere nearby that matched his description. "It must be. All this time I thought I killed him."

She shrugged. "I guess it's possible. But that would mean the body was moved and never identified. Or not found in time to even make my list here." She folded her hands and looked at him, her sharp gaze coming from sympathetic chocolate brown eyes. "If he did get up, or if someone dragged him out alive, he'd wind up in a hospital probably. He wouldn't have pressed charges against you or he'd face his own. There's nothing anyone can do."

She held her hands out. "I suggest you go live your life free of this. Know that you did the right thing coming forward, but we *can't* prosecute you for a crime there's no evidence of. And you were a minor. We'd more likely prosecute him." Valverde smiled, seeming to call it a day. "Thank you for all your help. I will call you if anything happens in the case, but I don't think it will. I think you should get back to your regularly scheduled life. Is there anything else I can do for you?"

She looked to both men, but Craig was done. She was right, they'd done everything they could. If the man was dead, good riddance. If he wasn't, then Craig would take the stand and defend himself. It was the first time he'd ever thought of his position in that whole mess as defensible.

He thanked Darrow and headed back to the hotel where he moved his flight to the first available seat back to Nashville. He wanted to wash the residue of his life in L.A. completely off.

There was nothing with any reasonable layovers open until the next morning. So he called the lawyer back in Nashville. After thanking her and explaining how it went, he asked her for another favor. "I need a custody lawyer in the Bristol area. Can you recommend the best one?"

Then he tossed and turned the whole night, popped up with the sun and hopped on the plane with far more energy than the day before. He wanted to go home.

CHAPTER 19

S hay sat in the lawyer's office, her knees knocking as the woman looked through her stack of papers. Shay had saved everything.

"You have information regarding the birth, beyond the birth certificate?"

"What do you want?"

"Any hospital records regarding the father's genetic relationship to the child?" The lawyer looked at her over her glasses, sheaf of papers still clutched tightly.

"Did I have a DNA test? No." Shay shook her head. How was she going to get one now? "I don't have any doubt that Brian is the father. Brian may have been cheating on me, but I never cheated on him."

"He was unfaithful? Do you have proof?" The woman flipped through the pages.

"I saw him with his . . . well, in the act. That's when I left him." Shay wrung her hands. She'd hoped to come in and have the lawyer tell her she had everything she needed and everything would be okay. It wasn't going down that way and Shay was getting even more nervous than when she'd come in.

"So the infidelity precipitated the divorce?"

Shay paused a moment, "Yes. It did. I walked."

Then she waited, watching as the woman looked at paper after paper, occasionally making a small noise of thought. When Shay couldn't take it anymore, she blurted out, "Is this even possible?"

"Should be." But the woman didn't even look up. "The back child support is the biggie."

Shay wasn't sure "biggie" was a plausible legal term. She wasn't ready for the follow up question.

"Will he be able to back pay it? He'll be given the chance to make amends first." She'd stopped looking over the pages and was staring at Shay again, as though this was going to be the roadblock.

"No." Of that, Shay was certain. "He does not have the money."

"Will be able to set up a payment plan to cover it?" She still hadn't looked back down to the papers, just kept staring at Shay.

"Well. That depends." Shay looked down at her hands as she was wringing them and willed herself to stop. "He can set up a plan. As in, he can tell you about it. But about a week or two in he'll be dead in the water. Does that help?"

"Not now. But a week or two after he fails it will boost your case. Depending on the judge he may be given several attempts to pay it." The woman sighed. It wasn't a good sound, and Shay was growing only more frustrated.

"What about the weed? The Benadryl?" *Wasn't that the whole point?*

"Neither is illegal."

"But endangering my child is!" Shay burst out.

"How is that?"

Why couldn't the woman see that for herself? "Because he's doing something that could precipitate a house fire! Not only would he not be able to save my child, he's drugged my son to the point that he can no longer save himself!"

"That's a good point." She made notes.

Shay blinked. Wasn't that the lawyer's job to think of those things? Why was she building her own case? The woman had seemed solid the first time Shay met her. She'd even handed her a list, which Shay had followed to the letter. So why wasn't everything all set? That's what she'd waited so long for.

"What about your other son? You have another son, right? Younger?"

"Older." It was the easiest thing to answer. "Why?"

"Different father, right?" But she didn't wait for an answer. "If you do this with one father, will it tip off the other? Will he have the money to back pay *his* child support and ruin your case against him?" The woman was staring at her again. All the papers had been set back down.

But Shay was stopped cold. "I only meant to start the one case now. Do I have to start both?"

"It may be in your best interests." This time the woman folded her hands and looked at Shay.

Of all the things to remember. Why didn't she remember that she'd told Shay to gather what evidence she could? To let the men get as far behind on child support as possible.

"But I did everything you said." She was close to tears. Then she bucked up. "Okay. Let's do both."

Now or never. She'd been prepping for this. "I have a certain amount of savings . . ."

By the time she got home she felt like old laundry, wrung out and hung on the line in a high wind. She hugged her boys despite their surprise at the ferocity of her moves. Then she paid the sitter, thanking her and trying not to look longingly at the cash as it left her hands. It was hard not to round down for the sitter when every penny counted. But she couldn't make enemies.

SAVANNAH KADE

Instead she fought her fears by microwaving popcorn and watching Lilo and Stitch for the umpteenth time with the boys.

She told Owen to put down the book—the next book in the series from the dragon book he'd been reading at his dad's. He was trying to finish it before he had to go back his father, in the hopes that the bastard wouldn't make fun of him.

Though the movie was playing on the TV and the book was open over the arm of the couch, Shay found herself wondering if her son had been reading Stephen King books to impress his father. It was a sobering thought.

She couldn't wish her sons away. She also knew that Owen wouldn't be Owen if Jason hadn't fathered him. But she did wish different circumstances on him. She wished he had a different father.

Craig's face popped into her mind. Though she tried to shake it and concentrate on the movie, the fact was she'd seen this one too many times to pay it any real attention. She could probably run scenes from it alongside the boys. She couldn't keep her brain off Craig and the beach and being free.

After she put her boys to bed, Shay sat herself down for a good hard think. She'd never questioned that Owen was Jason's son. But the lawyer had brought up the possibility, and when Shay was honest, there was a possibility. Jason had been a terrible husband. He'd been a terrible man, and she had scant evidence that he was any better now.

The lawyer didn't seem to think that Jason's abusive tendencies toward her were enough to get a judge to terminate his parental rights regarding Owen. Especially since he'd been seeing the boy for a number of years, and those visits hadn't produced any evidence of abuse. Never mind that he claimed he didn't owe her as much child support because he was watching the kid at least part-time. Jason had the most beautiful blue eyes, but they should have been brown, he was so full of shit.

Shay didn't like to think about what he'd done to her, about

132

how little he'd valued her, and how little she'd valued herself in return. Mostly, she ignored it. It was done.

Early on, she'd needed the child support money. So she hadn't looked for ways to unhook Owen from Jason. She didn't need the money anymore. Thank God, too, it wasn't like she was getting it. Even when she had been, it had been sporadic at best.

She was going to have to dig up some long buried past to get Owen out from under Jason. She was going to have to admit, out loud, in court, that Jason had passed her around to his friends. She'd complied because he'd talked her into it. He'd bought her flowers afterward; told her she was good.

Looking back, it was all stupid, and reckless, and dangerous. But it hadn't happened all at once. It came in small steps, each a little darker than the last. Each step was nothing she hadn't done before, but always in a new way. Each time, she'd earned some small praise or affection from the man she desperately wanted something real from. None of it had been real except the damage to her soul.

Maybe the physical abuse had rattled her brain and that was why she agreed. Maybe she was simply horribly stupid when it came to men. Both were a very real possibility.

She never wanted to revisit that part of her life. She was going to have to do it. Even though it just might prove that Jason actually was Owen's biological father. Shay tossed and turned all night, barely sleeping. She sent the boys off to school with lunches and kisses, and she felt like a robot doing it.

Her sewing table called to her. There were deadlines to make, and tonight she was going to have to buck up and sew, even if her brain wasn't in it. But she had to go back to the lawyer.

She'd shown up at the office only to find out the woman was in court that morning. Saving someone else's children, Shay hoped. It turned out she was handling a defense of an arsonist.

"I can have her call you this afternoon." The receptionist offered. He was a nice young man today, looked enough like the lawyer to be her son.

Shay smiled. "Is a call okay? Does it still have the same confidentiality laws?"

She didn't know, and she didn't like sounding stupid. Though she'd tried getting online and educating herself, she hadn't been able to untangle what she found. Instead she'd wound up down a rabbit hole of blog entries and websites on her "Constitutional Rights!" She wished she'd gotten an education like Zoe. Instead, she asked stupid questions.

"Have you paid a retainer fee yet?"

Shay nodded.

"Then yes." The boy knew. He looked about fifteen, but must be older because it was a school day. At least he knew the law. "Once you hire the lawyer, everything you discuss is confidential, unless you are actively threatening to harm someone."

He said the last almost like it was a warning to her to keep her foul plans to herself.

Shay shook her head. "None of that." Then she left a message with her number and went home to work on her pieces.

The boys were home and settled into their dinner before she got the return call. At first she was irritated at having the meal interrupted, but then she was glad. She was able to take the phone around the corner and out of earshot of her kids. So far, she'd managed to do all of this away from them. Eventually she'd have to explain, but the last thing she needed was her boys worrying over eventualities and bad possibilities the way she was.

"What happens if we get a DNA test and Owen isn't Jason's?" It felt odd in her mouth to speak it.

"Well, it's never simple."

When was it? Shay wondered.

The lawyer continued. "You may be able to get his rights terminated very quickly. If he agrees. Many men do when it turns out the child isn't theirs. He may at that point sue you to return child support he paid."

Shay snorted. "If the case goes that fast, I'll have plenty left over to pay him. It's not like he paid that much!"

"Well, we'll barter the amount down, too." The lawyer assured her. "There's another possibility. He may sue to get parental rights."

"What? If Owen isn't his? Why . . ." Shay couldn't fathom that.

"He can argue that he loves the child, and that he raised him as his own for six years, believing Owen was his. This can give him rights in some instances."

Shay put her hand to her forehead, certain she had suddenly developed a massive fever. "He's abusive."

The lawyer paused a moment. "Have you decided? Are you ready to file these cases?"

They should be filed as close together as possible, Shay understood. So that neither man caught wind of what she was doing and could become the plaintiff in his own case. She took a deep breath. It was time. "Yes."

"We'll argue every angle." The lawyer reassured her. "But be ready. You're in for a fight."

Didn't Shay know that? When was she not ever in for a fight? It was a fight to get her boys picked up, a fight to get them back, a fight for the child support and the boundaries of her own home. So many fights that the fight for Shay and what Shay wanted or needed had been abandoned a long time ago.

She hung up the phone both lighter and heavier.

She'd done it—put a plan into action that she'd been working toward for years. But she'd also come up on a game that would change things. She only hoped she could win.

She tucked her boys in with extra stories and hugs and kisses that night. She packed treats in their lunches the next day figuring they were smart kids and understood that mommy was worrying about something she couldn't share with kids. The next evening her dinner was interrupted by the doorbell.

A strange man stood at the door in a t-shirt and jeans, his hands in his pockets as he tilted his head just shy of peeking into the window at them.

Wiping her hands on her old yoga pants, she pulled open the door, leaving the screen between them. "Can I help you?"

"I'm looking for Shay Leland?" He said the name as though it didn't roll off his tongue easily. His words were a little stilted as he spoke before she could answer. "I have a delivery."

He didn't hold a box or flowers or anything. Unless he had something in his pocket? She frowned at him wondering what this was about. "I'm Shay."

As he opened the screen she saw him pull an envelope from his pocket. Full manila sized, it had been folded over several times to fit. "Shay Leland, you have been served."

CHAPTER 20

S hay was stunned. For two days she floated in a sea of disbelief. She'd barely filed her lawsuit and Jason had slapped her with a countersuit that same evening. And "slapped" was the right word. He was somehow both suggesting that her request for a DNA test was harassment and also suggesting that if Owen wasn't his it was because of her promiscuous ways.

She wasn't sure if she was more offended that Jason handed her around to his friends or that he was suggesting it was all on her. What was on her was being stupid, believing that she could get him to love her and be good to her and their baby. At least she was now mad enough to readily admit that in court.

The lawyer had assured her that Jason wouldn't be able to get the DNA test stopped—or at least not for long. Everyone involved in the case would want to know whether Owen was genetically his or not. Everyone except Jason who would know that it might not come out in his favor. Then again, Owen did look like Jason.

Shay found herself praying that was coincidence. She also found she was kicking herself repeatedly. She'd gotten out from under Jason. She'd quit whoring around for him when she became pregnant, she'd grown a backbone, she'd thought. And she put those dark times behind her.

Jason had never used protection with her, though he'd insisted his friends did. He didn't realize that his friends were just as awful as he was, and they didn't like to follow his orders.

Leaning over to catch her breath, Shay realized she'd taken this position far too often the past days. She had her hands on her knees and she looked like a runner after a marathon. Only hers wasn't over. She was just glad she could openly hyperventilate now. When the boys were home, she just silently gasped for air and hoped they didn't notice.

She was inhaling deeply when the phone rang. Her heart fluttered as she looked at the strange number on the caller ID. The home phone was too puny to display the entire name of the caller, and said only "Office of W. . ." Probably a lawyer. Probably Jason's lawyer. Or God forbid Brian's. She hadn't heard from them yet and honestly couldn't decide which situation was worse.

So she didn't answer. She was under strict orders not to talk to any other lawyers without her own lawyer present. Who knew what she might get twisted into saying?

Hands still on her knees she watched the phone sitting in its dock as it answered for her. She heard her boys' sweet voices say "Hello? Hello? You should leave a message."

It had been cute until now. Now it sounded like she was putting her kids out to the world rather than protecting them. Every step she made now, and every step she'd made before would be questioned.

The voice came on, tinny through the crappy recording system. "This is Parker Wilcox of Wilcox, O'Malley, and Bordeen. I'm calling to extend my services to you. I'm a specialist in child custody cases . . ."

She quit listening.

Shay already had a lawyer. Her heart rate slowed. Just

someone who wanted her money. He wouldn't have wasted his time had he known just how tight her money was. It was still her biggest fear to run out before the cases were done. At least her lawyer would let her set up a payment plan.

By the time Owen climbed off the bus, her heart had slowed. She'd realized something very important, too. This time was precious. Even more than she'd already known it was.

Jason was playing a vicious game. Brian a silent one. Who knew how it might all go down? It was more important than ever now that her boys both know and feel that their mother loved them more than anything.

"Who wants pizza?!" She asked excitedly as Owen climbed into the backseat, clicking himself into his booster.

"I have homework." Owen's serious voice overlapped his brother's squeal of approval.

But Shay knew both her boys. Owen would worry if he got behind, or even might not have time to finish everything to his satisfaction. "So let's go to the store and buy our stuff, and then you can do your homework first thing when we get home. Does that sound good?"

He nodded then, tapping into the joy that was pizza.

"I'm hungry now!" As soon as she told him, Aaron whined, already passing from pleasure to despair at imagined pizza detention.

It didn't bother her today. Her boy was three. Three-year-olds did this. "Well, if Owen's homework takes too long, then you and I will start the pizzas. That way Owen can have his as soon as he is done! Is that good with everyone?"

Owen thought for a moment before nodding. Aaron threw his hands up in the air and yelled "Pizzaaaah!" by way of response.

She drove them to the store, held hands, even bought bacon to put on the pizza, because Owen had heard another kid in his class liked it. Then when the pizza was cooked, she ate all the slices with bacon on them because Owen scrunched his mouth, saying he could "taste the pig."

She'd fought hard to keep a straight face.

A text from Zoe popped in after that.

—Hey S. I'm on my way.

Shay frantically responded. Tried to keep the boys from seeing. Owen could read.

—No. Stay in school.

—Already booked flight. Not missing anything. Too late.

"Shit." Shay whispered it. But she'd be glad to see her sister. Apparently, she'd see her around eleven thirty that night.

She made it through baths and stories with enough happiness to counter the dread of her situation. Zoe rolled up right on time, and Shay spent the night with her sister in the bed next to her—a throwback to a time when they had each other's backs. They still did. It was just nice to not have it be from across the country.

"I love you, Zee. Thank you." Shay whispered before she fell deeply asleep.

The next day she got a phone call from the other lawyer again, trying to solicit her business. This time she picked up the phone as Zoe looked up from the fat textbook she was taking notes from.

"Hello, this is Shay Leland." They had used her name already; it wasn't like she was giving them any info.

"Oh, good. Mrs. Leland—"

Her brain rolled. As though she was claiming a "Mrs." title. She'd had enough of that shit. But she didn't correct him because she was going to hang up on him.

"—I saw that you filed a lawsuit against each of your ex-husbands."

Though it made her heart clench, she knew the suit was of public record. Not all the details, but that she'd filed it. "Thank you, but no thank you, I already have a lawyer."

She was setting the phone back in the dock—a little harder and less satisfying than the easy slam she could do with her grandmother's old corded model—and if she hadn't missed the dock, she wouldn't have heard him.

"Mrs. Leland! Wait! I've already been retained for you."

Picking up the phone she'd fumbled, Shay pressed it back to her ear, "I'm sorry?"

"I'm covered already. Free of charge to you." The voice was soothing, educated, ready to respond. "Allow me to explain."

She didn't. "Craig?" It was the only thing that made sense.

"Yes. Mr. Hibbets is covering the charges." There was a smile in the voice now. "When can we meet? Since the two suits are already filed, and there's already a countersuit in process, I'd like to get going as soon as possible."

"I have a lawyer." She gritted it through her teeth, Zoe watching with narrowed eyes now. Shay sighed. She'd also had a lifetime of owing people. Either for things she needed, or for them just stepping in, doing something for her, then telling her she owed them. "Thank you, but no."

"Mrs. Leland!" The voice was sharp enough to make her jerk.

Shay's eyes darted to Zoe's as she thought to hit the speaker button. Her sister was now at her side, quiet as she listened in.

"I'm sorry. I shouldn't have burst out like that." The apology sounded sincere, but there was something in the tone that told her he'd caught on to the change in the phone. He knew he was on speaker. "Is either of your ex-husbands present?"

"No."

"Are the children in earshot?"

"No." She was giving as little as possible.

"Then, assuming I'm on speaker, there's a reason. Who is there?"

"A friend." She ground it out. It wasn't his fault Craig hired him without asking her.

"A bit of legal advice: it's not wise to have friends in on your legal discussions or correspondence. Especially if they have ever been associated with your defendants."

"It's my sister." She sighed then explained. "I'm sorry that Mr. Hibbets hired you and that you won't be able to collect, but I have a lawyer."

"May I speak, please?"

She rolled her eyes at her sister. He was so damn polite she didn't have it in her to say no. But she wanted to. "Fine."

"If you truly refuse my services it will be the easiest money that I have ever made. Mr. Hibbets paid a large retainer that's non-refundable. I've already made the money."

Turning to Zoe, she mouthed, *He probably did it so I wouldn't say no!*

Zoe nodded her head in agreement, understanding all of it in the way of sisters.

Before Shay could comment, the lawyer began again. "I've met your lawyer. She's solid, but takes a variety of cases. I take only child custody cases and only after I've vetted the parents in the case. I have, on more than one occasion, offered my services to the parent the person who originally contacted me was trying to sue.

"I. Won't. Lose. Mrs. Leland, children's lives are at stake. Mr. Hibbets told me your story, and I agreed to take your case."

"What if he's lying?" Zoe blurted out.

Shay's eyebrows rose in shock.

"Hello, you must be the sister. I told you, I check the background for all my cases. I know the records—one Shay Leland Masters gave birth to a singleton son, 'Owen,' in Knoxville, Tennessee, listing Jason Gregson Masters as the father of record."

He went on listing both the boys' dates and places of birth, as well as their fathers'. He listed Shay's information, then paused. "Need I go on? I know this case already."

"That's disturbing." Shay admitted, feeling a little cold at the recitation.

"It's all in the public record. Including the dates of your divorces. We can win this one." His voice was soothing now and his words hit her hard.

"I need to make a decision. I'll need some time." Shay said, taking charge in a conversation that had run off the rails a while ago.

"Take some time. But honestly, I've seen lawyers mess things up in cases like these. For example, what has your current lawyer done to research the men's past interactions with the law? Please decide sooner rather than later." He left her with his private number and said he was leaving the office for the evening. Then he added that the number would go to his cell, and she should call any time.

Shay hung up, shaky now. She looked to Zoe. "What do I do?"

"We research the hell out of him, that's what." Zoe tromped over to her bag and pulled out her laptop—much newer and shinier than Shay's. "If he knows that much about you, then you should know that much about him."

"You're right. We need fuel for this." Shay headed into the kitchen while Zoe began tapping around. "Hey Shay, get this, he's in Elizabethon, works all three of the tri-cities."

"That's a drive." Shay commented as she emerged from the kitchen with bowls of chocolate ice cream, then squished into the corner of the old couch next to her sister.

"So far, so good." Zoe commented before taking a bite. She tapped some more, balancing the bowl and her laptop. Then she was silent for a moment before turning the screen toward her big sis. "Shit Shay, read this."

While Zoe ate, Shay read an interview her sister had pulled up. In the article, a child had been murdered by his biological mother. Parker Wilcox had lost the case for the father and the step-mother just four months earlier. The quote from him was "Every time I lose a case, I fear it will go this way. I pray for the best, and I fear this. When I lose, I know there's a child in the wrong place, and I don't sleep until they're home."

Shay looked at Zoe. "That's pretty heavy handed isn't it?"

"Shay, it's from seven years ago. He didn't set us up. He's been doing this a long time and according to this—" she hit a few more buttons "—his win-to-loss rate is excellent. Better than your lawyer. Did your lawyer check out Jason or Brian's criminal pasts?"

"No." Shay admitted, but stayed mad. "I don't want to owe Craig! I don't want to owe anyone!" She stood up abruptly, nearly spilling the dregs of her ice cream.

Zoe became quiet. "I understand that. I do. But I don't have enough money to fix this. I have *some*. Give your money to this guy, then. I'll help with the rest."

"Zoe." She sighed her sister's name. "I can't take your money any more than I can take Craig's."

Zoe nodded, speaking quietly. "You have your standards, and that's good. But your case—*cases*—are complex. You've already got a countersuit filed against you. Are your standards more important than your kids?"

CHAPTER 21

I t was the tiny, high pitched attempts at barking that woke him. Craig scratched his head and stared at the small dogs, frowning. They were going off like there was a siren outside or something. But there wasn't.

He checked his clock—3 a.m.—and rolled his eyes. "What do y'all want?"

But they just kept going. As tired as he was, it was still disturbingly cute. They were trying to bark like little badasses, but they couldn't bark yet. Their voices hadn't dropped. "Do you need to go outside?"

They seemed to say yes to this, hopping back and forth on their front feet, almost like they were dancing. He opened the door to the crate, comfortable now with them running through the house if he was watching. They still needed leashes in the back yard until the fence was installed. *Back yard*, he thought with a dejected sigh. He'd need shoes, the grass would be wet. But they were sitting at his bedroom door, looking to him and he grinned.

Once he opened the door, Gunnar and Scarlett beelined down the short hallway, but instead of going to the sliding glass door that led out to the backyard and their play space, they went straight to the front door and sat, looking at the knob as though it might do something interesting.

"Is someone—" He didn't even finish. The knock interrupted him.

Who was at his door at 3 a.m.?

Then he didn't finish the thought. Either he was getting robbed, or someone was in trouble. He threw open the door expecting to see one of the guys or Kelsey or—

"Shay?"

She looked up at him, surprised, as though she hadn't expected him to be at his own house. Or that maybe he just wouldn't answer his door for her. Then, quick as a lightning strike, her expression changed. "Can I come in?"

She asked before he could decipher her look. A tiny paw on his foot reminded him that there were two adorable terrors running loose. "Um. Sure."

He turned away from her, scooping up the closest puppy, who was hiding behind his legs, and looking around for the other. "Gunnar?" He called out, then turned the little dog in his arms and looked it in the face. "Yup, you're Scarlett."

"Gunnar and Scarlett?" Shay raised her eyebrows as though she could mock his choice of names in the middle of the night unannounced.

He didn't answer, but he did find Gunnar hiding behind the couch. "You two are going to be watchdogs one day, right?" He spoke to them as though they would answer. They looked away, ashamed. "No worries. You're little." He kissed them each on the head then sat down on his couch, one dog tucked under each arm. They didn't squirm, just watched Shay as she looked around for a moment then decided on the armchair. It was just as old and worn as the stuff at her house. If she'd been surprised that his furniture wasn't better, she was hiding it.

She perched on the edge, hands clasped. "I didn't know you had puppies."

"I didn't either." He just looked at her while she frowned back at him. Her silence forced him to explain. "I mean, I just went to the shelter on a whim, and *boom*, suddenly I have two puppies. Why are you here?"

Then, suddenly it struck him. "Is everyone okay?"

He'd been reading her nervousness, but maybe she wasn't nervous about something she was going to say or do, but about asking him for something. She nodded, looking around the room at everything but him.

He wasn't sure what to do. She'd told him no. She was clear. And he was the last man to pressure anyone into anything. So he just sat, stared at her for a moment, waiting.

Finally, she looked him in the eye. "You can't give me a lawyer, Craig."

He opened his mouth to ask why not, to explain, but she railroaded him.

"I have spent my whole life owing people for what they did for me. Things I thought I wanted. Things I truly needed but no one would give to me. Everything." She was standing now, almost but not quite pacing around the room. "I've had a long drive to think about this and I can't take the money."

"I—"

She held her hand up. Apparently she was here to speak her mind, not to have a conversation.

Long way to drive to yell at me, he thought, but sat still. He'd been here before. Sometimes it was better to be quiet and just let the other person ride it out themselves. Things hurt less that way.

"I appreciate that you found the best lawyer in the tri-cities." She looked at him and nodded, then looked away, her hands still wringing. "I will take the recommendation, but I can't take your money. I have my own savings and I can't owe you."

"Okay." He stayed on the couch, watching her.

She broke his heart sometimes. So strong because she had to be, but also sometimes she had to be because she pushed people away. Here he was trying to help, with no strings attached, but she insisted that she hold up the entire sky herself.

He'd never done that. Never held up the sky for anyone. Just helped hold things together with the band when times had been lean. But never had that been all him. Even the puppies—he kissed their little, fuzzy heads—didn't pose the kind of struggle Shay was going through.

She turned to face him. "That's it? You'll take your money back?"

"No." He looked at her like she was nuts. "Those aren't the same thing."

"What do you mean? You can't do this!" She opened her mouth as though she had more to say, then closed it.

Just as he was getting ready to speak, she started again. Craig shut his mouth.

"Thank you." She took a deep breath, just long enough for him to think *That was easy.* But it wasn't. She spoke again. "It was a generous offer. No, it was well beyond generous. But I can't take it. I'll pay for the lawyer myself."

She said the last line with far more conviction than anyone should have if they'd driven almost six hours in the middle of the night.

Craig waited. The puppies squirmed and he set them down, telling himself he'd keep an eye on them.

Before he could speak, Scarlett closed the distance between herself and Shay and pawed at Shay's pant leg. She leaned over. "Aren't you just the cutest thing?"

Though both puppies had shied away from Shay at first, they seemed to be warming up. They also seemed to not have ever been petted before. They acted as though Craig had ignored them for weeks on end.

Stunned, he looked at the dogs while he spoke. "I swear, I feed them and pay plenty of attention to them."

She grinned up at him, as beautiful as the moment he'd seen her standing on the beach in that yellow dress. "This is normal. At least it is with kids. No matter what you do, they want attention from everyone else. They act like you never give them ice cream or popsicles or love."

"Well," He conceded. "I don't ever give them ice cream or popsicles."

"They're clearly very well taken care of." She smiled again, picking up Gunnar who'd weaseled his way in between his sister and Shay. "You got them on a whim?"

He nodded. Best whim ever. Right up there with saying hello on the beach.

She rubbed a little head and set the puppy down. "So you'll call your lawyer and get him to send your money back?"

"No."

Stunned, she only stared at him for a moment, then found her voice. "Why not? I told you, I'll take care of it."

"Did you ask what he charges?" Craig looked at her. She'd told him how much she'd saved. She could get started, and if everything went perfectly, she might be able to cover it. Might.

"I'll figure it out." She said.

"Don't. It's taken care of. Get yourself a new car or start college funds for the boys with it." He sighed. He should have known it was going to be a battle. But he thought, if anything, she'd call. Then he could tell her no, it was done, and hang up on her. Hard to hang up on the person standing in your living room.

"I can't owe you." Her hands were clenched at his sides.

"You don't. It's a gift. You don't owe me anything." He was about ready to assume the same stance himself.

"It doesn't matter! What happens when you want a favor from me? That's how it starts. You'll think I'm not grateful enough or I'll spend every moment being so grateful you can't possibly fault me. I can't do that again." Tears were forming in the corners of her eyes and he tried to forgive her the harsh judgment of him. One he didn't deserve.

"Then don't. Don't owe me. Don't be grateful. I don't want it anyway!" He was yelling by the time he'd finished, the puppies running behind the couch from the vehemence of the words, and his heart fell that he'd scared them. Instantly on his hands and knees, he forgot about the woman behind him as he spoke soft words, stroked little heads, and apologized until they came out.

A few licks to his face un-seized a heart he hadn't realized had stopped when he saw what he'd done. Sitting on the floor now, puppies sequestered in his lap, he looked up at Shay. "I'm not an asshole. I'm not going to turn into one. You know how I know?"

She shook her head.

"Because I haven't become one yet. Because you keep pushing me away, and I'm still not being one. Even in my thoughts, I'm not. I try to understand and most of the time I do." He took a breath. "I've been with the guys in the band going on five years now. I have never once not had their backs. I'm good to these little guys. Didn't think I had it in me, but I'm a good dad to my dogs. So you can stop looking at me like you're waiting for a monster to crawl out of my skin."

She opened her mouth to say something, but this time he railroaded her. "I get it. That's all you've seen happen, but judging me by what other people did to you is a shitty way to treat me."

She didn't move. Just stood, towering over him, not speaking, not visibly reacting.

So Craig kept going. "There's a lot you don't know about me." He almost started to say what he'd been doing these past weeks without her, but he held his tongue on that. Instead he gave her something else.

"I told you I moved nineteen times in sixteen years, but what I didn't tell you was that I was in foster care. Those moves weren't just to new houses or new apartments, they were to new families. Some good, some bad, some not even families, just facilities. I ran away when I turned sixteen and I can't even count how many places I lived after that. So I don't need your shit about not understanding."

He took a breath, anger radiating off of him, but he tried to keep his voice calm for the little creatures in his lap who trusted him and looked to him as their beacon.

"I see how much you protect them. I see how you take care of those boys, even though you won't let me meet them. Even though you don't even want me around. In sixteen years, no one adopted me. I ran away when I gave up. No one looked out for me like you do for those boys."

He was grinding his teeth. The fact that she'd finally reacted with a hand to her mouth and tears starting to roll down her cheeks only pissed him off more. "No one. The truth is, I'm jealous that someone is there for them. Because my case worker was the greatest constant in my life and, honestly, I had about nine of those. So you don't owe me a damn thing because I didn't give *you* the money. It's not yours to give back. It's *theirs*. You can help your boys by giving their lawyer all the information you have. Your call."

CHAPTER 22

S hay drove home with tears in her eyes. She didn't want to cry, but it seemed the best she could do was leak tears down her face and sniffle silently. Sometimes, when she thought about what he'd been through, she sobbed. For Craig. For her boys. For the shit way she'd treated a good man.

She was still mad that he'd taken away her chance to save her boys herself, but she was also grateful that he was doing it in a way far better than she could. Even if she worked her ass off, it would be three more years of visits and bad weekends before she could get that lawyer. Three more years at the least of waiting for fathers who didn't show up and didn't know how to show love, if they were even capable of feeling it.

She had her pride. And it meant nothing when it came to her boys.

She made a decision then. Her money was there for all the extras. She no longer needed to worry about the cost of this DNA test or that investigator. She could afford those things now. It meant she could do this right. Parker Wilcox didn't doubt that he could get Jason and Brian's part of the joint custody taken away. He thought he might even get visitations reduced or removed all together.

As soon as she got home she was going to ask Wilcox how to go about getting a DNA test between her son and Jason that would stand up in court.

Shay started to take a deep breath in.

Then she cried again. There were so many things she hated about her old life. One constant had been that she chose men who expected her to fail. They told her what she couldn't do, what she couldn't accomplish. When she did fail, they said it was inevitable. When she tried, they told her not to, that she didn't have it in her to do great things, or even normal things. She was stupid, or wrong, or . . . always something.

Getting into that over and over was her own fault. Sure her mother had drilled it into both her daughters that nothing much was expected of them. Mom still waved her hand—the free one, the one not holding some beer or other—and dismissed Zoe's degree. Why she didn't marry was beyond mom. Mom even held Shay up as the good one. *Look at Shay, getting married, having kids!* As though Shay was an example of anything other than what not to do.

Putting herself into that same situation over and over was her own fault. Living with men who told her she wasn't good enough and that she was going to fail was a shadow she'd finally crawled out from under. But treating Craig that way? That was actually failing.

He was right to call her on it.

She felt like shit about it and she wasn't sure how she was going to make it up to him. She needed to, though. And not the way she'd tried. Or like it had looked like she'd tried.

He was probably right about the other thing, too.

She was over halfway home, driving through the familiar territory of Knoxville, when she finally let herself think about it.

When he'd told her she didn't owe him anything, that he was giving the money to the boys, she'd thanked him.

He'd calmed down pretty quick, which impressed her. He'd been very angry. Her past experience with angry men wasn't good. But he didn't say anything more about it. He'd only sat there on the floor, stroking a happy little puppy's head and alternating when the other got jealous. Then he asked her a question. "Did you come to Nashville just for this?"

She nodded.

"In the middle of the night?"

Shay had nodded again, then tried to explain. "Zoe, my sister, is home with the boys. And I was so confused by the whole thing. So mad." She shrugged at him as though not being able to really explain was an explanation in itself. When he waited, she tried to find words. "In the past, when men have given me something, it's always called in later. You know how people always say that women hold onto things and bring up old problems in a fight?" She waited until he nodded. "Well, men always did that to me. Something they gave me—some help, some favor, some service—would get called in. Even if I didn't ask for or didn't need what was given. I was expected to pay for it. Just whenever they wanted something from me."

Tipping her head to one side as though to minimize it, as though to spill away all the old hurts, she stared at him, hoping he'd understand.

"I won't do that."

Suddenly, she'd believed him. Even that first night, he'd made sure she was sober before he asked her to his room. When she said she had to go the next morning, he told her he wished she would stay but took her at her word.

Somehow, it had escaped her notice that Craig had never once thought she didn't know what she wanted or needed. He never doubted what she said. He never cataloged what he'd done for her or suggested that she owed him anything for any of it. Even the thousands of dollars in legal fees he'd ponied up for her boys. He wasn't keeping score.

The only other people in her life who didn't keep score were her boys—which Shay admitted didn't really count—and Zoe. Even her mother had often thrown it in her daughters' faces what she'd given up to have them, how she'd done X or Y and how the girls owed her. Shay had been fighting that all along.

She'd been sitting there, on his chair when she recognized that, watching him hold those dogs. His hands had scratched them under their chins, rubbed their heads until the tiny creatures practically purred. And it hit her, she knew what it felt like to have those hands on her.

When the small dogs whined in concert and ran for the back door, he calmly stood and clipped leashes onto their collars. The leashes were big, thick ropes and looked ridiculous holding back a tiny dog that probably needed yarn at the most as a leash. He clearly expected them to get larger.

Without looking back at her, Craig had disappeared out his back door, leaving her to sit there with her realizations. For Shay, what she'd just figured out was stunning.

She'd found a decent man.

She looked around the house without him in it, seeing the old couches that looked like they'd been picked up at a yard sale. The kitchen had pots and pans, but not a nice set—these were mismatched pieces that he clearly used. Only the TV and sound system reflected the money he was making.

It occurred to her that this was a man who was not only decent, but one who understood her. He'd come from a place that didn't buy for show, but for need. He didn't throw things away because they weren't pretty anymore. Despite his on stage persona, he didn't need the flash and excess of fame.

He'd grown up in foster care. He didn't want a house. He wanted a home.

Shay didn't have a house, but she finally had a home.

Only her home was six hours away. Until the court cases with the boys were resolved, she couldn't move. She was legally bound to stay within a certain distance of the boys' fathers and couldn't leave that area for more than seven days without permission from men who couldn't even show up on time for what little time they had with their sons. Sometimes they didn't show up at all—and she was left holding the bag, trying to explain to her sons why the man who was supposed to love them didn't do a decent job of it.

Since she'd started the court case, she'd started reading up on it. No more library romance novels before bed. Now she was learning about what to do, how to dress for court, what was normal for divorced parents. Not that there was anything normal about her case, but she needed to know what she could push for and what she couldn't. What she'd found was a treasure trove of "me, too." It seemed most divorced mothers with bad or barely passable fathers went through a lot of the same troubles she had. In fact, her case seemed better because her boys didn't spend their time crying over their dads. Shay simply created back-up plans, and if dad didn't show, she was ready with something else. Her boys seemed just as happy if their fathers didn't come.

The lawyer told her that would play well in court.

For a moment, a spark of hope took hold deep inside her chest. Parker Wilcox told her she could expect to be free of the men in her life. Hopefully soon. And there stood a man, just beyond the glass of the sliding doors, carefully helping two small puppies navigate the grass wet from the day's rain. He didn't get frustrated when they tangled their leashes. He was patient when they played, even though they'd seemed to need the services of the grass, and he gently tugged them back in the right direction, never yelling, never angry, when they didn't pay attention.

Her heart turned over.

She watched as he scooped them up and fumbled with the door handle, a squirming puppy under each arm. Jumping up, Shay slid the door back, and he passed by, not speaking. But he moved the air around him and stirred her, too. She smelled him as he came so close. Then he was down the hall, but the memory of him lingered, mixing with older memories she had of him. She'd tucked them all away, savoring every last one each time she pulled it out. Now they all washed over her, moving her toward the hall and the sounds of tiny puppies protesting being put down for bed.

She understood that. So she waited at the entrance to the hall, not wanting to interfere with whatever routine he had, and wondering why his competence at it turned her on so much. When he came out from his room, pulling the door shut on the whimpering behind him, he looked at her. His eyes met hers straight on and he looked tired. Sad. Maybe a little beaten down by the night.

That was her fault, she thought.

So when he said, "It's almost four in the morning," she whispered back, "It is almost four in the morning," and closed the distance between them. On tiptoes, her lips met his with the slow lightning that permeated her whole body each time she kissed him.

He almost responded, and she tried again, reaching her hands up to his shoulders, pulling him a little closer, pressing her mouth to his a little more firmly.

This time he began to kiss her back. His mouth moved softly over hers, his tongue darting out against her lips, hers answering back.

Shay sighed as her fingers threaded into his hair, holding him there for her to explore as she wished. Her feet stretched, trying to reach his height, to make the most of it, and she found herself pressed full-length against him. When she bounced up further on her toes, her whole body moved against his, eliciting a soft moan as he moved them just a few inches to the right to press her back to the wall.

Craig leaned into her, his hands at her ribs, clenching as though his fingers twitched on their own, as though he was holding her there lest she get away. He kissed her while his hands then skimmed the sides of her breasts, crept over her shoulders and planted on the wall on either side of her head.

He pushed back from the wall so smoothly, it took her a moment to realize it wasn't a move.

Craig closed his mouth and looked at hers. The deep breath he took turned her insides cold. His words turned her colder.

"I can't do this."

"What?"

"With you, Shay. I can't be with you anymore." This time his hands left the walls, tucking themselves into his back pockets as he turned away.

"What?" She asked again as though she couldn't remember any other words.

When he turned back, his eyes were sadder than they'd been before she kissed him. "You're going to leave again. I can't do this just so you can walk out the door."

When she opened her mouth, it was his voice that sounded.

"You'll go back to your boys. You'll say you can't bring men around them. They're your first priority." He closed his eyes. "And you're right. But I can't be your backup player anymore."

"I—" it was all she got out.

"You should go." He walked toward his front door, opening it to the pre-dawn blackness outside. Then he said the worst thing. "You don't owe me anything."

Turning, she stared at him. He thought she was *paying* him? But she was too slow, too numb, and when he gestured her out the door, her feet moved. She wandered into the dark of his front yard, fumbling for her keys as she heard him click the lock behind her, the bolt sliding heavily into place as though she might try to break back in and break his heart.

Instead hers cracked.

She'd been awake for over twenty-four hours. She was exhausted, but she had to get home to her boys. To Zoe, who didn't keep score. To her bed. So when the sky opened up and rained on her, it only seemed appropriate that it was crying with her.

CHAPTER 23

Craig watched as three sets of small feet scampered past the dining room table. Each of the kids had put their dishes in the sink—with great noise and little care, but it seemed enough for Kelsey and JD—then ran past on their way to play in the back room where he'd parked the puppies in their crate.

He watched them go, thinking for the first time how little they'd been when he first met them. Allie only three. She still popped like popcorn, and Kelsey said it had never been about her age, she was just always energetic. They had all grown. Daniel was nine now, able to talk to adults, and clearly in charge of the small trio.

Beside Craig, Ari squirmed to get down from her high chair.

The only one still at the table—Kelsey and JD having disappeared into the kitchen for a moment to clean up—Craig reached out and undid the tray from Ari's seat. There was a buckle, too, and he unclipped it, sliding his hands under her chubby little arms.

"Wait." He told her, and set her bare feet on the floor before he wiped at her smeared face. Then he told her, "Go!" and she scampered off to join her brother and sisters. She still had the bow-legged run of a kid in diapers and he watched her padded butt disappear around the corner into the hallway before he yelled out to Kelsey, "I just set Ari free. Do I need to follow her?"

Kelsey reappeared from the kitchen, her rounded belly preceding her. Craig knew she was barely halfway there, but the whole process didn't seem to bother her. "Did she head in with the other kids?"

Craig nodded.

"Then she'll be fine." Kelsey hollered back over her shoulder, "You okay in there, honey?"

JD yelled back. "I've got it. You sit!" and she smiled softly, her expression a clear indicator of the simple but strong love the two seemed to have for each other.

Craig fought a flash of jealousy. He'd lived in houses like this, but he'd never been part of that circle. Sometimes it hurt more to watch. "Thank you for dinner, but—"

She put her hand out, covering his and effectively stopping him from getting up from the table, unless he wanted to be flat-out rude—which he could never be to Kelsey.

"How was your trip?" She asked, her voice not loud but not low. She seemed to sense his need to talk and also his need to not be overheard.

He nodded, thinking. "Better than I thought it would be. Things worked out well."

"The plane didn't go down." She grinned at him, and it took a moment for him to remember that was the excuse he'd given her for getting all his affairs in order before he left. So he nodded.

"It was actually a pretty easy flight."

She wasn't done with him. "You seemed lighter when you came back. You got your business taken care of?"

He nodded again, thinking that if TJ had made it to the weekly 'family' dinner, this wouldn't be happening. In fact,

Kelsey hadn't asked about it last week. She'd probably been waiting for this, knowing sooner or later, TJ would call in and say he couldn't make it. There was usually a hangover or a woman involved. Sometimes both.

Kelsey's voice was too soothing for the knock of her words. "So why do you look upset again? You were so much . . . I don't know the word, *happier*, I guess, last week. And now you're down again."

"Lost some sleep last night." He offered. He'd actually lost a lot of it, never having gotten back to sleep after he showed Shay out the door. He second guessed that decision enough times to stay awake for hours. Then the sun was up and he was certain Shay was already back in Bristol.

Kelsey raised her eyebrow at him. Even though what he'd said was true, she had a phenomenal bullshit meter and never hesitated to call people on it.

Without his permission the words fell out of his mouth. "Shay came by around three a.m."

Her eyebrows rose even higher now, surprise across all her features. "All the way from Bristol?"

Kelsey was the only one who knew the real story of Shay, and even she didn't know all of it. She just had a way of cornering him and getting him to talk. For the first handful of months he'd known her, he'd managed to keep a distance, but then she'd helped them get their first record contract and she'd hugged him. He'd hugged her back.

She didn't know it, but that had been the first time anyone had hugged him without an agenda. She'd done it again. Casually reaching a hand to his shoulder sometimes. A smile of understanding here. A cupcake there. And he couldn't keep anything from her.

Kelsey may have seemed like the all-American wife, but she had a background almost as fucked-up as his. Her old family history included alcoholism, sometimes violent mental illness, suicide, raising a kid that wasn't hers and more. Maybe that was why she was easy to talk to. He didn't—couldn't—truly surprise her.

"Shay was mad. I paid for something for her kids and she wanted to tell me not to." He shrugged. Shay's story wasn't his to tell, so he didn't give any details.

Kelsey didn't ask for them. "Did her kids need it? Was it something she could handle?"

"Yes definitely, and no, not entirely. Not as well as I can."

"Did you talk her into it?"

He nodded.

"But you're still sad." It was just a statement.

He nodded, feeling it deep in his chest. Kelsey was the perfect person to unload on. She asked him to do it, so for once, he obliged. He looked into the kitchen, wondering if his bandmate was still in there or if he'd pop out at any time. He didn't really want JD to overhear. Kelsey's smile told him it was taken care of. Maybe somehow she'd known he needed to let something off.

So Craig talked the long way around, something he never did. "You know I grew up in LA—all over LA, really—but what I don't tell people is that it was entirely in foster care."

She only nodded once. "I figured. Did you go to LA to visit?"

"No, just to clear up some old documents, that kind of thing." He turned the conversation back to Shay, "So I understand that Shay's boys come first. I know legally she can't move them away from their fathers. But I can't move there either. She doesn't want me there. It creates too much of a problem because her exes are complete dickheads who got upset that I had a nice car in her driveway." He shook his head at the memory. "It's not worth it to her to fight them off."

I'm not worth it.

The phrase rang through his head and he would have thought it wouldn't hurt so much anymore, but somehow it did.

It hurt more from Shay who found her sons to be worth anything, and Craig not much.

"I'm sorry." The simple words from Kelsey meant a lot. "I liked her."

"You know her?" Craig was surprised.

"I met her at the wedding. Us girls hung around a bit." She shrugged.

He hadn't expected that. He'd thought Kelsey might vaguely remember the blond bridesmaid, not that she had met Shay enough to form an opinion.

"I wish there was more I could say." Kelsey seemed upset that she couldn't offer more to him. "But I can't change her decision. I hope she didn't upset you too much last night."

"I sent her home."

"Ah." That one word told him Kelsey had figured out some semblance of the situation. She might not know all the details, but she had the basics. "I'm really sorry. That's hard to do." She reached out and grabbed both his hands in hers. "But it's right. You're amazing and you deserve someone who will give you everything."

Craig could only nod.

This was maybe why he loved her. He could admit that now. He wasn't trying to steal JD's wife. He didn't feel the tug and need for her at all. That was all for Shay, but he loved Kelsey. Just like he loved the guys. She truly believed he was worth someone's everything.

Just then, Daniel came running out. "The puppies have to go outside. Can we take them?"

Craig tugged his hands from Kelsey's, or he tried. She held on to him as she spoke. "You kids can do it. Take the scooper and clean up after. I'll be mad if I step in dog poo in my own back yard when I don't even have a dog!" But she tempered the instructions with a smile for her son and Daniel dashed off.

JD appeared then in passing, never questioning that his wife was holding another man's hands. "I've got this. I'll just supervise, but I'll make sure it's all done."

Something about the simple interaction cracked something in Craig. He'd seen them like this a thousand times before. From when they were first together, to when they were fighting and it almost broke JD, then for the last handful of years when they'd hit some harmonic balance between comfortable and unable to get enough of each other.

Craig didn't want their life. He didn't need four kids with a fifth on the way. Two puppies were more than enough. But he wanted the shared chores, needs, support.

It wasn't JD and Kelsey, he knew. It was *him*. Things inside him were breaking off and floating away. Anchors were being cut and he was being set adrift, free from his old ties and scars. It suddenly occurred to him that he wanted to keep them as his friends, forever. TJ was probably his closest friend. But JD and Kelsey were the best at being his friends. He saw that now. It was the first time he'd ever let himself think of forever. If he wanted to keep that friendship as solid as it was, she needed to know more.

The room was theirs again. So he opened his mouth.

"I was in a lot of different homes in foster care. Some were good, but not that many. And I just happened to miss having a birthday at any of the good places." He didn't know why he was telling this now, other than it seemed important. "The birthday party you threw me three years ago was the first time anyone threw me a party. Just for me. Not all the June birthdays or anything like that. It was my first birthday party."

Her mouth opened.

Well, he'd shocked Kelsey after all. "I didn't know."

"I figured. So I wanted to say thank you."

"You thanked me at the time." She pushed a still-shocked grin at him, but offered no pity. He loved her for it.

"I know, but I thought you should understand it was a bigger thanks than it maybe sounded like." He sighed. "I wish I'd had someone like you for a mother."

Her mouth opened and her face crumbled as fat tears rolled down her cheeks. Kelsey sniffed in, a great gulp of air as though she was surfacing from a deep dive.

"Don't cry!" He commanded, panicking. "It was just a thank-you. Why are you crying like that?"

"Because." She gulped again. "I'm pregnant! You can't say things like that to pregnant women and expect us not to cry." She started to get it under control. "You can't bring us pizza and expect us not to cry. I cry at commercials. I cry at country music."

She was grinning by the time she finished and so was he.

"You are married to the wrong man then." He commented and she cracked up, the tense moment gone as she tried to laugh and wipe her face at the same time.

She took his hands again. This time her eyes were rimmed in pink, the remnants of her bout of tears. "I hate to say this, but if Shay can't be with you, then I'm glad you sent her off. You deserve everything. It's your turn. And I hope you find it."

Yes, he thought. He should thank Shay for starting the cracks that opened him up, but he needed everything. He needed more than she could, or would, give. This time nothing cracked. Something fused together, and with it, the drive came. He was going to find it.

CHAPTER 24

S hay sat at the conference table, nervously twisting the water glass in front of her. If she paid attention, it would ride around the glossy surface in the ring it had sweated there.

Reaching out, Wilcox stilled her hand. "We've got this. If he refuses, we'll crush him in court. No worries."

But she worried.

She needed to be here. Needed to show her face, maybe answer some questions. Mostly, she needed to—wanted to—put on a good front and show Jason that he didn't have any hold over her any more.

Wilcox was young, but very competent. Each day Shay sent up a prayer of thanks to Craig for finding him, let alone paying for him. The lawyer was an animal when it came to kids' rights. He made no bones about the fact that he'd grown up in foster care, that he'd been beaten and molested. He'd graduated high school and been dumped unceremoniously out of the system on his eighteenth birthday.

Apparently, Parker Wilcox had it worse than she had, and he'd had his shit together better than she had, too. Because he'd made sure he had a summer job and a friend's couch to crash on. Then he'd enrolled at the community college, gotten an A.A. degree, earned a scholarship to finish his bachelors at a prestigious university and went on to law school from there.

Given his past, he trusted his gut when it came to parents. He charged an arm and a leg, and told Shay that he would have taken her case for what she could pay. The more he learned about her exes, the more he'd been willing to take her on for anything. Not that it mattered. He had Craig's money.

Wilcox had sat her down and told her he needed a few things from her. He requested paperwork, DNA testing, and more. But he'd also said she owed him. She was never to marry another man like either of her exes again. Then he said if she found herself in a bad situation she was to come to him so he could get her out. He made her agree to those terms and swear it on her children's lives—because that's what was at stake, he said. She believed him. He was a pit bull.

So she sat here in her best pantsuit. Actually a nice one from fine fabric, even though she'd found it at a cheap resale shop. She was trying not to look nervous.

Tapping her hand again, Wilcox said, "If you can't find your backbone, find your anger. Think about what he did. Each time you go to open your mouth, think about every time he left your kid high and dry. Think about the awful things he said to you. And let it bleed through a little."

Shay nodded at him just as she heard the shuffling of voices in the hall. She glanced at the watch she'd strapped on this morning, only now noticing that the gold was rubbing off in spots. Cheap. But no worries, Jason was late.

Her ex-husband sauntered in, followed by his lawyer who looked as slimy as he did. Though Jason wore a pinstriped navy blue suit, he still looked like a low-rent player. With a smooth style he'd clearly practiced, he shrugged out of the jacket and rolled his sleeves up.

Wilcox stood up and shook their hands, "Welcome, gentlemen."

Shay almost snorted at the term, but kept her head ducked and stayed seated. Briefly, she looked up to see Jason smiling as though he had this in the bag.

Fear shot through her heart. What if he won? What if he refused the deal Wilcox was laying out for him? That would be stupid, but Jason was only above average in charm and smarm. So it was reasonable for her to believe he might refuse it, putting her and Owen through the nastiness of a now unnecessary trial.

Wilcox put a gentle hand on her shoulder and she looked up to see a feral smile cross his lips. Then she remembered: every time Jason had ignored Owen, ripped his book up because he didn't approve, called and told her to tell his son that he wasn't coming. She turned and stared him in the eyes, her expression flat.

Jason pulled back a little from her glare, and she realized that she had some power over him after all. She should have pushed him out of her house and backward down the steps each time he'd shoved his way in through her front door. He would have threatened her, but she should have looked him in the eye and said, "Bring it, asshole."

So now she let her steady stare do the talking for her. Wilcox had told her not to initiate conversation with Jason, or even respond if her ex tried to start anything.

"I'm glad you made it today. I was beginning to think you weren't going to show." Wilcox threw out the first barb, and Shay watched the other lawyer come to life.

The man sighed, offhandedly introduced himself to her as "Miller" as though he was doing her a favor. "It's just an initial offer. We're only here as a courtesy."

What a dick. She wished she had an Erin Brockovich move

up her sleeve, so she could say, "We had that water brought in just for you." But she didn't have one. Wilcox did though.

"It *is* just an initial offer." He unbuttoned his suit, making a show of getting comfortable. "But it's one I hope you'll thoroughly consider." He smiled as though offering them tea.

Jason looked at Shay, his eyebrow raised, "You can't win this, babe."

Feeling some new steel in her spine, and even though she knew she wasn't supposed to speak to him, she did anyway. "Watch me."

Wilcox gave her an approving look then started in. "Let's open with the results of the DNA test." He flipped a sealed envelope to the other side of the table. "That's your copy."

Jason shrugged. "Kid's mine. Have you looked at him?"

Wilcox nodded. "Do you remember what you did to your wife? Would you like to pony up the money you collected passing her to your friends? She didn't see a dime of it."

Jason's lips pursed, but he returned volley without acknowledging the charges. Typical Jason. "The kid's mine."

Wilcox only tipped his chin at the envelope. "Open it."

Jason did, his hands shaking as he read that he wasn't the father of the child in question. "This is a lie. It's a mistake. What shoddy company did you send this to?"

Wilcox flipped a second sealed envelope at him. "Yeah, we thought you might suggest that. Remember that second swab we made you pony up? It went to the same facility that the FBI uses. Shockingly, they got the exact same result."

Jason's lawyer put his hand on Jason's arm, holding him back before he exploded. "How do we know you used the right swab?"

"Here you go." Wilcox opened the file and pulled two pages from the top. "For the first swab, his teacher at school as well as the school psychologist, principal, and two police officers verified Owen's identity, along with a notary. Want to ask who was present for the second swab?" He plucked a page and waved it in the air until the other man refused to look.

The DNA was a done deal. Wilcox had told her that's where he was headed first. The other lawyer then went on the offensive. Though Shay stiffened at first, she forced herself to relax. Wilcox hadn't batted an eye yet. So neither would she.

"So while your client has lied about the paternity of this child for six plus years, she's been conning my client into paying child support and investing his time and other money into the child." The smarmy lawyer shot back.

"Stuff it, Miller." Wilcox shot out the first bit of anger from their side of the table. "She only DNA tested the child because I told her to. She believed Owen was this asshole's son all along, or she would never had turned her kid over to him."

"She was in it for the money." Miller countered.

"Yes, why don't we read the court transcript from the initial custody case when the judge awarded joint custody to Mr. Masters." Wilcox threw out a thick print copy bound with brads down the side. "Enjoy reading the fifteen minutes of Shay Masters—at the time—begging the judge not to let her child go with her abusive ex-husband. Read where she offers to forgo child support in exchange for custody. Read where she tells the judge what this man did to her."

Miller made a show of flipping through the pages, but he didn't seem to care. "Her allegations of poor treatment are entirely hearsay."

Jason started to grin.

"True." Wilcox conceded with a smile. "But there's not a jury in the land who will buy the bullshit you're pedaling that she was lying about the child to get your money." He then turned to Jason and looked at him with narrowed eyes, as though trying to remember something. "How much money was that anyway?"

Jason mumbled the disturbingly low number.

"And how was that calculated?" Wilcox looked at the other two men as though he didn't know.

When they didn't answer, he threw another blow. "And that hasn't been adjusted in six years? Even though your income has changed, you haven't claimed the increase. That's positively illegal."

"You—" Jason's epithet was cut off by his lawyer grabbing his arm and pushing him back into the seat he was rising out of. Again.

Wilcox flipped another page their way. This time he didn't even wait for the counter from the other side. "You can try to sue her for the money back, but since you haven't been paying it regularly, you'll be hard pressed to find a judge who thinks you deserve it. And, oh, you still owe her over ten grand in back payments."

This time Jason looked at her. *"Bitch."*

It wasn't loud; it was low and feral.

Old Shay would have flinched. New Shay was on the winning side. Finally. "Yes. And proud of it."

Wilcox played his end card, sliding yet another page across the table. "This is a termination of parental rights. I'd like you to sign it."

"Not until I get my money back from that whore!" Jason nearly yelled it.

"We'll take you for emotional damages, too, honey." Miller was talking to Shay, taking her for the weak link, but she didn't budge a bit.

Wilcox actually had the balls to laugh out loud. "Look, you don't need to sign it." He looked at Jason. "Mr. Masters, this is just a formality. Your rights terminated the moment the DNA test returned negative. Your signature is just your agreement that you were here today, that you understand the results, and that you'll make no future claim on Shay or the child."

"I don't have to sign it." He was on his feet now, shrugging back into the jacket to go.

"No, you don't." Wilcox didn't get to his feet yet, so Shay stayed seated, too. She tried to keep her expression some cross of neutral and satisfied.

Jason stared at her again, his venom even worse now. "I'll find the fucking sperm donor, and get him to sue your ass off." He seemed satisfied with his last gambit and he was almost at the door when Wilcox spoke again.

"If anyone threatens Shay Leland for money or for custody or, honestly, anything related to the boy, I'll head to court with your records Mr. Masters." His voice was low, almost singsongy.

Shay turned to look at him. Records? She didn't know.

As Jason froze and the lawyer, Miller, tapped him on the arm as if to say "What is he talking about?" Wilcox went on.

"I dug into your past. None of it's good. I have five women willing to testify in court that you pimped them out, just as you did to Ms. Leland. Want to go up against that?"

"You have no proof." He ground his teeth and Shay enjoyed watching him squirm, even if she wasn't out of the woods yet.

"Nope. But five witnesses with almost identical stories—six with Ms. Leland—is pretty damning. And I do have proof of your arrests for dealing meth from three years ago." He tapped his finger on new papers he'd produced.

Shay looked over at the arrest warrants and documents.

"It's done. I did probation for those."

Wilcox nodded. "Yeah, but I have a PI on you, too. And you're still dealing. That's a violation of your parole."

"You're violating parole!?" This time Shay jumped up, hands on the table, body leaning forward with fury. "You can't see him if you're on parole! You *know* that."

Wilcox looked at her now. "Oh, you didn't know he was on parole? He also recently robbed someone at gunpoint. It's a violent crime." Then he turned to look at Jason pointedly.

Though no one knew how he'd gotten that information, no one doubted him. Not with the expression on Jason's face, admitting the truth of all of it. Next, Wilcox stared at the lawyer. By his expression it was clearly dawning that he had no case.

Shay was shaking with her own fury now. Jason had done all that while he had her kid on weekends? She couldn't breathe. Through the roaring in her head, she barely heard the next words.

"I have a warrant for a blood test for you, right now." Wilcox pulled out another page. This one with a scrawled signature of some judge at the bottom. "Take the test or sign the paper."

"This is making me sign it under duress!" Jason protested.

But by then, even his lawyer was looking at him and shaking his head. "No, it's not. You're lucky they don't have an officer waiting to arrest you outside the door."

With that, Jason tried to look out the slim glass windows bracketing the wood door. Shay sucked in air through her nose and tried not to look like she was gulping it. She was still furious, but a sense of satisfaction was starting to creep in.

His lawyer looked at him and in a low voice said, "My legal advice is that you sign the papers. Or you'll be spending the next ten to twenty in prison."

Angry, maybe as angry as she had ever seen him, Jason stomped back to the table and signed the page hard enough that the paper ripped. When he shot a smartass look at Wilcox like *what are you going to do with that?* Wilcox simply produced another copy and said, "Try again."

Once it was signed, Jason turned to Shay and said, "I'll get you for this, bitch."

Then Wilcox changed from lawyer to man who had grown up on the wrong side of everything. "No you won't. If anything happens to her, if any word gets out on the street, anything happens to the kid, this packet goes right to the police. You'll be arraigned faster than you can spell 'bitch,' if you can even spell it."

"I signed your god-damned paper!" Jason bellowed the words, his face red, spit flying.

Wilcox didn't flinch. He apparently wasn't afraid of assholes. Shay was only afraid for whoever Jason took his anger out on later. She'd seen that rage before, and someone always paid for it.

"Yes, you signed the paper. And you and your lawyer didn't even ask for a deal where I destroyed the evidence or anything like that. So I hold both now."

This time, it was Miller who looked chagrinned at the error.

Shay didn't fault him the shoddy work. Jason had blindsided him, too, by not telling him the whole story. He'd let Miller be surprised by all the evidence against him.

Wilcox leaned into Jason's face. "Remember that. Now get the fuck out of my office."

One Mississippi. Two Mississippi . . . Shay started counting in her head, looking straight in front of her while she waited for the door to close behind the two men. Even when it clicked shut, she still didn't find her space and it took another minute before she was able to look up at Wilcox, who was gathering the mess of papers Miller and Jason had left behind.

"Thank you." The words came out as more of a whisper than anything.

"You are very welcome." He offered a small smile. "One down, one to go."

CHAPTER 25

I t took two more months for Shay to fight Brian. Wilcox had warned her it would be a battle, and it was.

Jason—probably the worse of the two fathers—had actually been the easy case. A lot of prep on Wilcox's part, but then one big strike and he was gone.

Jason hated her. *Hated* her. Shay knew it. She didn't like the idea that someone out there had that kind of rage toward her, but she'd chosen him. She made that bed; at least she didn't have to lie in it anymore. She only had to deal with the fact that it existed.

Three weeks later, Wilcox had called her. "Do you want the good news?"

Shay perked up, "Brian is consenting to sign the paperwork?"

For a moment, she'd thought it was all over. But that wasn't it.

"No, this is about Masters."

Jason.

Wilcox continued. "Police picked him up for brawling the night of our meeting where he signed over rights."

"Oh?" That was news, though it wasn't surprising to her at

all. "We didn't know about that arrest before now?" She knew Wilcox was following the man. He told her he did monthly checks on a handful of clients' exes. The checks would extend to annually after a few years if the ex stayed out of trouble.

Wilcox told her the story. "Apparently they gave him a warning and let him go. He spent the night in the drunk tank but that was it. That's happened again since then, but if they just give a warning, we won't hear about it unless I set my guy to specifically dig into it. What happened is that this time Masters broke someone's jaw, and got arrested. So we know about it. Do you want to release his papers to the arresting officer?"

Shay took a deep breath. "Can I think about it?"

It had been a week and she finally had an idea. She tried to call in while the boys were at school. But as the weather loomed closer to the holidays, she started worrying about them being at home more. Snow days, bad weather, colds, things like that. Aaron was at home with her that day and she'd had to wait until he was asleep to contact Wilcox about the problem.

Taking a deep breath, and hoping there was more information about Brian that would end that case earlier rather than later, she dialed the number. After being on hold for several minutes she got through to the man.

"What's happening to Jason because of the current charges against him?" She already decided that she would use this information to make her decision.

"He'll being going away for five to ten. He'll probably be out early though if he can swing good behavior."

Shay barked out a laugh. That was the most absurd thing she'd heard in a long time. "I don't think Jason could even recognize good behavior let alone exhibit it." She took in a breath. "The deal was that we'd release our information—*your* information—if he came after me or Owen. I'd like to keep that in our back pocket."

There was a silence as he seemed to think it over. "That's

fair. Hold your cards. I don't think you have to worry about him anyway for at least the next handful of years."

She asked about Brian and found out that nothing had changed. He wasn't willing to negotiate. He was holding out for a court case. But Wilcox had checked out Brian's lawyer and told her they didn't stand a chance. "He just doesn't have the resources we do. And to be honest, you have the uterus."

That had jolted Shay. "Is that really still a factor?"

"In the South, outside of the big cities, yes. We haven't quite made it to the modern age of men as actual parents rather than 'father' being an honorary term for 'sperm donor.' I'm always happy when the parent I'm defending is a female. Makes it easier, that's for sure." He mentioned a few more things which Shay tucked into her memory before she thanked him and hung up.

Another brick rolled off the weight she'd been hauling for years. It wasn't gone yet, not by any stretch. In some ways it was worse. There was always the mild possibility that Brian would present a really great case, and the judge would give him more rights as a parent. But as Parker Wilcox, amazing lawyer and savior, had told her, it was a really low possibility, and you had to risk it to get your kids out from under.

He'd also assured her that the idea was absurd enough that if that happened, they'd file an appeal before they even left the courtroom. So there was a backup plan in case it all went to hell.

Shay needed those backup plans. She'd learned to have one when she lived with Jason. And when Brian hadn't turned out to be the one who took care of her, she'd learned to take care of herself and to be ready for any eventuality.

Still, the specter of Jason was gone. Owen was at home every weekend now. He seemed happier with that. Shay had been so pleased at the outcome, at not having to spend her whole savings to make it happen, she'd taken him out after school the day before. It had been one of Aaron's days to stay at Head Start until five. Apparently it was also a good day to catch something contagious from one of the other kids. But she hadn't known that.

So she picked up Owen at the bus and took him to the local used book and electronics store and bought him a used e-reader. He didn't have to worry about his dad breaking it anymore. Neither did she.

"Mom!" He'd glowed and clutched it to his chest. "I can have it! I can have books on it?"

She'd smiled. Inside, she acknowledged that it was a crap thing he hadn't had one before now. The very idea that his father might have broken it was unreal. She was glad Owen didn't have any of that man's DNA. Unfortunately, he had the DNA of one of Jason's friends, so that didn't make it any better. But Owen was wonderful. "You deserve it, sweetie. You're such a good reader."

They'd gone home without picking up Aaron yet and sat on the couch side by side while she set up an account with an online bookstore. He could look up new books but couldn't buy them without her passcode. He didn't care.

Once they had three books lined up for him, she told him, "We want to turn it to a black background and white letters. Help me figure out how to do that . . ."

He had no fear of breaking it like she did. So he pressed buttons and opened menus and changed options until he found the right one. "Mom, that looks weird."

"It's better for your eyes." She looked at it and handed it back to him. "When you are almost finished with these books, let me know and we can borrow a new one from the library."

He frowned at her. "Maybe I can do chores to buy e-books?"

"Maybe." She looked at him a moment before she realized

what his concern was. "Oh. You can get e-books at the library, too."

"You *can?*" His awe lit her up inside, too, and she ruffled his hair as he opened the first book and ran his finger over the color version of the cover that popped up on the screen.

She let him read that way for a little while, doing dishes in the other room and peeking in to watch him flip the pages back and forth with a button, wondering at the e-reader as much as reading the book. Surely some of his friends at school had one? He seemed so enamored with it. She'd thought it was simply a good idea and such a neat gadget for a kid who reads all the time, but it was as though she'd given a regular kid a flat screen TV and a gaming system.

Maybe none of the kids at his school had them? None of the other first graders were avid readers like him probably. But they had tablets, right?

After she finished the dishes, she packed him in the car and they headed out to pick up Aaron, Owen with e-reader in hand. He showed it to Aaron's pre-school teacher when she asked him about it, and the woman grinned up at Shay.

"Mommy!" Aaron tugged at her pants as Shay watched her older son interact. "I want one."

She picked him up, savoring the heaviness of him. It wouldn't be much longer that she'd still be able to carry him around like this. She touched the tip of his nose. "You have to learn to read. But if you become a really good reader—" she stopped herself before saying 'like your brother' "—then I'll get you one, too. How does that sound?"

He nodded then ran to grab a book off the shelf. Shay hated having to shut him down but promised him reading time after dinner. He made her teach him letters that night and impressed her by learning seven easily. She'd wait to see if the lesson held the next morning. But then he'd woken up sick, and she'd called the lawyer, and she rescheduled with the psychologist.

At Wilcox's request, she was getting Aaron interviewed by two different psychologists. She was getting the interview transcribed by a court reporter. No small expense, but nothing like what she'd planned to pay out.

Wilcox had also told her that the court would most likely order another interview and report from a therapist they appointed. But by having these done independently, they would have counter records should the court-ordered psychologist come up with anything different. And Aaron would be comfortable talking to the person. The lawyer had warned her that it was possible that no one would care at all what Aaron had to say, and they may just be presenting the ones they'd done on their own as additional evidence.

One was already done.

The information had gone to Wilcox, and Shay hadn't seen it. He didn't want her to. Wanted her to be able to say to the judge that she had no idea what her son had said to the therapist, good or bad. So she didn't look.

When she finally got the boys into bed—Aaron holding a book to his chest, Owen asleep curled up with his new e-reader —Shay looked around the house and out the window at the neighborhood in the last of the light. There was a glass bottle in the gutter; she could see the glint of streetlight on the round surface. Looked like a beer bottle.

The porches down the street sagged like hers did. One home had fresh paint, but the others only needed it and didn't receive any. Some of the grass was fresh cut, but others had let it grow out as it was wont to do even as they headed into the cold season. It didn't get dry enough to stop the grass until late November. One house, not the one with the fresh paint, had a small garden. Several had a bicycle out front; hers had a big wheel and a small bike.

When she thought beyond the neighborhood, the local elementary was the worst one in the city. The gate behind the school was falling down. The parking lot went right up to the front door, no yard there, cars and buses everywhere.

Once Brian was out of the picture she could move without his permission. She could take the boys somewhere better. Better schools, better neighbors, somewhere to ride their bikes without worry.

Brian wasn't gone yet and she didn't want to get her hopes up. But Shay began to dream. She made a few plans that weren't plans; she didn't want to be too disappointed if it didn't work out.

Then, several weeks later, she woke up bright and early and put her good suit back on. She dropped the boys at school and Head Start and she tucked her fears into her purse with the lipstick she'd been nervously applying.

Wilcox met her in the parking lot. "Ready?" He asked. When she nodded, he only smiled. "Let's go set your little one free."

The smile was infectious. The previous victory over Jason bolstered her confidence, and she was able to "approach the bench" even though the judge had come down to the front table, keeping the hearing formal, but not ridiculous with only five of them in the room. She stated her name and occupation, address and all manner of stupid facts calmly for all of them. She was grateful the hearing was closed.

Brian basked in the silly comments the judge made about his name being the same as a Beach Boy and asking if he was into music. He leaned back in his seat as calm and relaxed as he could be, the judge nodding politely at him as he answered questions. When the judge asked, Brian openly admitted to giving Aaron Benadryl, said he didn't realize it was wrong. He admitted to smoking pot. He admitted to doing it with his son in the house.

With each answer, Shay saw tiny twitches in the judge's expression. Each twitch was a candle lighting her hope. Then at last, the judge looked directly at Brian to ask another question.

When his lawyer tried to stop the judge, the judge overruled. It wasn't a formal courtroom after all, he could ask what he needed to ascertain the well-being of the child in question.

Then the older man looked directly at Brian Wilson and asked, "Mr. Wilson, are you stoned right now?"

CHAPTER 26

The tour bus had rolled into town around ten a.m.—late for a Wilder tour to get home. Three or four in the morning was more the norm. This time, Craig had come fully awake on his own with the wheels still rolling underneath him.

Usually JD was the one who went room to room and woke everyone up. Craig always understood that was because JD had something to come home to. Alex did, too, but he seemed less anxious to get back to his wife and kids than JD did. JD seemed to truly miss what was quickly becoming an entire herd of kids.

Craig had only compared the two married men to each other. Certainly he and TJ didn't have any such compunctions. They were the rolling stones of the group, happy to land wherever, whenever, as long as there was beer and company.

This time, however, Craig found himself a bit irked by the late arrival. He knew the puppy sitter would have taken them out this morning before she left, but they'd been in their crate since she'd taken off for work at seven. She usually came back during her lunch time and Daniel came after school and played with them, so they were being cared for just fine. But Craig found that he missed them.

He missed getting his face licked. He missed having them curl up on his lap when he watched TV. He missed having something small to scamper after him and someone to work with and be proud of. He was beginning to see why some people loved their dogs—and maybe even their kids—so much.

When the wheels finally ground to a stop, the guys all nearly fell out the door, laden with overnight bags, instruments and more. Each man lugged his stuff to his parked car in a well-rehearsed routine that was practically a ballet by this time.

JD was not surprisingly the first one to holler out "Great trip! Bye y'all" as he pulled his car door shut and rolled out of the lot. But this time it was Craig who hustled and hollered out second. He was hot on JD's heels even as TJ shot him a look of confusion. His friend had probably been about two seconds from asking him to hit a bar for a little day drinking and maybe a pizza. Craig was happy to have avoided saying no.

He pulled into his driveway imagining he could hear Scarlett and Gunnar whining. Surely they could recognize the sound of his engine. Hauling his bags in the back door, he found he could actually hear them rattling the dog crate. He wished they could run free, but the vet assured him they were not old enough to be on their own. Given the number of times he'd had to pull them back from chewing the couch, or worse the TV and computer plugs, he had to agree.

"Hi, guys!" he hollered out as he made it in the door, barely dumping his stuff. The only thing he paid attention to was the acoustic guitar he traveled with this time. His stage bass stayed with the set-up, but this one was a replica of a model he'd had on the street in LA. The one he'd sold. Both guitars had been taken everywhere, used for his own comfort, for writing songs, and whatever musical opportunities came along.

After setting the newer version into the waiting cradle in the living room, he headed down the hall into his room where the puppies had spent the last seven nights without him.

"Oh, God. You're huge!" He was speaking even as his fingers struggled to open the crate door. It wasn't hard to open normally, only that changed with two puppies trying to break out by pushing against the door. They were now about twice the size they'd been when he first got them.

"Here you go." He murmured as they finally tumbled out and over each other in an attempt to reach him. For a moment, he sat there on the floor basking in the overwhelming joy they had just at seeing him. He figured that went both ways and acknowledged that he'd thought a dog would be a good friend. A housemate maybe. A creature to be there when no one could come watch a football game. But these guys were so much more.

They were a massive responsibility. If he'd been asked to take it on, he would have said no. But he now happily headed down the hallway, watching them romp along behind him, still not in graceful control of their limbs. Their ears flopped with their exuberance, and they skidded and slid into each other as they attempted a neat stop at his feet. He tried not to laugh as he held the leashes in one hand and gave a command for 'sit.' They looked at him with their feet still dancing.

Craig waited. It took three tries and him pushing their butts down and showing them 'sit' again, before they were ready to go. The sitter hadn't trained them much, he could tell. Maybe he needed a pro, not just one of Kelsey's sitters for her kids.

Scarlett and Gunnar scampered down the steps, hitting the ends of the leashes and he tugged back a bit, letting them know he wouldn't be dragged. The vet and the dog book had both warned him. They couldn't do much damage now as far as tugging him around, but if he didn't train them he could have eighty-pound terrors on his hands in about six months. So, with one pocket full of small dog biscuits and the other full of plastic baggies, he let them head down the sidewalk.

The air was definitely getting colder, but the sun was out and he even said hello to a mom with her two toddlers in a stroller. He looked at the kids differently now, after thinking about all that Shay was going through. He didn't even ask for updates from the lawyer. Shay would tell him what she wanted him to know, when she wanted him to know it. *If* she ever did.

He had to be okay with that. A gift was a gift.

His little duo made training stops where Craig worked them on some basics and handed out treats liberally. About an hour later, when he was on his own block and the dogs were starting to drag, their energy happily used up, he turned the corner to see his front door step was occupied. He couldn't see clearly who it was, but the clench in his heart told him with no uncertainty that it was Shay.

She hadn't seen him yet. In fact, she looked like she'd been waiting there a while. Her purse was set beside her on the stoop, and she was looking down at her phone, maybe texting or playing a game.

For a moment, he stopped and stared.

It had been nine weeks since he'd seen her or heard from her. He'd gone out with TJ, but hadn't been impressed by any of the women at the bars they were frequenting. He'd then let Kelsey set him up with an acquaintance. Kelsey had tried to be casual, inviting the woman to family dinner. But at the end, she'd found a moment when only Craig could see her face, and Kelsey shook her head 'no,' her face scrunched up like she'd been offered a distasteful food. It wouldn't work out. Craig had agreed.

But now, sitting on his porch steps, he could see the reason why nothing appealed to him. He wasn't over her.

Given what they'd been through, he hadn't quite understood how deeply he was under her spell. She kept leaving him, pushing him away, and he let her. He had to. Somehow, she kept turning back up.

When he slowed his pace, the puppies picked up theirs,

tugging at their leashes. Craig wondered if they remembered her, or if they were just drawn to her like he was.

He was a little closer before her head popped up and she spotted him, immediately reacting. Shoving her phone down into her purse, she jumped up to standing, then wiped her hands on her jeans in a clear show of nervousness.

She stood like that, unmoving, as he approached his own front door, Scarlett and Gunnar tugging harder on their leashes, trying to get to her. A few times she pushed a smile onto her lips as she watched him come closer, but it didn't look natural or overly happy.

When the puppies made it to the hem of her jeans, Shay wiped her hands on her thighs one last time and offered a tentative, "Hi."

"Hi." He looked at her, wondering what it was this time. Though he waited for a moment she didn't say anything else and he had to prod her. "To what do I owe the pleasure of your company?"

He hadn't been able to make the overly polite words come out with a casual cadence, and she clearly picked up on that. While just the sight of her—just the knowledge that she was here—grabbed him in the gut and twisted, he walked around her on his way up the steps and slid his key in the lock as though she were the mailman and not the one he couldn't forget.

He heard her take in a breath. "I was hoping we could talk."

He nodded and motioned her to follow him inside. The door led almost directly into the living room, so he waited until she picked up her purse and closed the door behind her before he unclipped the dogs and went about setting up the baby gates he'd purchased. Craig did it to avoid talking to her for another minute, and as he looked at the puppies he realized they'd be over the gates in another week. Maybe sooner if they put their minds to it.

By the time he'd set everything perfectly, she still hadn't said another word. She looked nervous, and he wondered what made her drive all this way again after how it had gone down last time. "I do have a phone."

She nodded. "I really wanted to talk to you in person." Then she licked her lips as he waited her out.

Craig had no reason to make this easier for her. But as he watched her nervously try to start, he realized that response was petty and jealous. He wanted her for his own and he couldn't have her. End of story. No need to make her upset about it too.

Though she was the one who'd chosen this path, he didn't think it would have been her first choice either had things been different. So he opted to crack the door a bit.

Making the first move toward peace was another thing that was new to him. As hard as it was, he made a mental note to tell TJ thank you for each time he'd reached out to Craig when he'd been acting like a dog backed into a corner. He found himself taking his own deep breath of awkward air. "Would you like a drink?"

She nodded and he found ease in working out the details— soda or tea or water? Ice? Would she like to sit at the table?

Shay did, hanging her purse over the back of the chair, and holding the glass as though it were a talisman. "It's over."

He looked at her, wondering why she'd driven so far to tell him that.

Then she clarified. "With the courts. With the boys."

"Oh." He nodded and took a sip of the tea he'd poured himself from the jug. "I know. I got the last bill."

"So you know what happened?" She asked, her head tipped.

"No. It was a gift. I paid the bill. I didn't follow up or ask how you were spending it." He shrugged, growing uncomfortable again.

"Well, it turns out Owen isn't even Jason's son."

189

That shocked him. It would mean Shay was cheating on Jason.

"No, I didn't." She looked at him sharply, reading the path of his thoughts. "Long awful story for another day, but that terminated Jason's parental rights pretty quickly. Wilcox, the lawyer, shook him down with some criminal records and then Jason got himself locked up for assault. All in all, he's gone from our lives for at least five to ten years and hopefully for good."

She took a breath and smiled.

"If it's over, then you got Aaron's dad's rights terminated, too?" Craig asked it as though it was a casual question and not a key to his soul.

"No." She shook her head. "But I got sole custody. And Brian can't claim any visitation without me present, and he can't claim any at all until he passes six biweekly drug tests in a row, all clean. He has to initiate the testing then request visitation through the court."

"Wow." Though it would require a lot from Brian, Craig thought that was a reasonable solution. A man should be able to see his child if he was clean and sober and the mother was present.

"Yeah. I agreed to it. Honestly, I don't think he'll ever do it." She took another sip. Then she dropped the bomb. "Since I'm not tied there anymore. I'm moving away from Bristol."

CHAPTER 27

Craig felt his heart slip up and lodge in the back of his throat.

Though he'd told himself he was done with Shay—even as he acknowledged that he wasn't over her—her words sparked the knowledge that he'd harbored some real hope that things would come back around. That at the very least, he could hop in his car and drive to see her if the urge hit.

What if she took off for L.A.? Her sister was there.

Colorado? South Florida? Montana? They were so far away.

He inhaled a deep breath through his nose and tried to look unaffected. He wasn't sure whether he pulled it off. So he offered her what he thought was an encouraging nod. "That sounds like a plan."

She looked nervous, and for a moment it occurred to him to wonder why. She wasn't tied to him anymore. Even the bill had been paid. But as he watched, she swallowed.

"You said to put my savings into a college fund for them, but I think I have something better." She wrung her hands together, and he watched as she took another fortifying breath. "I'm going to try to get us a decent house in a good neighborhood. The boys can get a better education, grow up where there aren't beer bottles in the street. If other kids have parents that encourage them to be educated . . . maybe they can get scholarships like Zoe did. It won't wait until they're eighteen. The benefits can start now. And if I buy, I can take the equity to fund their college."

"That sounds like a great plan." He still had no clue why she'd come here to tell him that. He was attempting to force his words to sound normal around the thought of her being even farther away.

"So I went online and I did some research. You know, schools, real estate value, neighborhoods." She reached into her purse. "I have about five different places that fit."

Somehow, her hands managed even more fine tremors as she retrieved what looked like a map of the entire United States. Shay spread it out across the table with her hands flat. "Here's what Zoe and I found. There's a place in Irvine, California. It's good, and we'd be close to Zoe, but I don't know that she wants to stay in L.A. forever. And with traffic, we wouldn't be that close. Here's another one in central Florida. There would be a beach we could drive to and that would be cool. But I don't know anyone in Florida."

She worked through one in upstate NY that apparently made the most economic sense in a 'house-to-school' ratio she'd worked out. "But I don't know if I could find the right kind of work there."

He wasn't paying attention.

There was a red circle just northeast of Nashville.

When she finally looked up at him, the words dripped out of her mouth and faded away. Her finger drifted to that circle. "That's why I'm here."

He nodded.

"Craig, I know people here. I should be able to get some intros to other musicians who need stage costuming hand-made. There's a lot of that business here. Plus, the theater scene is pretty big in some parts of town—I have a referral from Bristol. It's a small theater, but my portfolio should speak for itself."

He nodded.

She looked him in the eyes. "It's my favorite location out of all of them. It's where I want to be."

"Why are you asking me?" He could hardly breathe. Having her here? Maybe running into her? "Nashville is big enough for the two of us."

"This area of town. This county has the best schools for the home values. But I wanted to ask you first—"

He interrupted, barely able to keep from jumping up from the table and asking why she couldn't just leave him alone and let him get over her. "It's a free country. Move wherever you want!"

"I can't live here if you don't want me here." The words were breathy, light, far too worried for the woman who held all the cards. "I can't live here if . . ."

She trailed off, as though unable to speak the words.

Craig almost bit his tongue trying to hold back and not yell something at her. But what, he didn't know.

"I can't live here and see you sometimes, I mean, we have some of the same friends. So if I was here and ran into you, if you were seeing someone, I mean."

She wasn't even speaking English, her words were so jumbled. He was about to say something to make her shut up and leave, when she finally pushed it out.

"I couldn't live here and not be with you. It would break my heart." She looked straight at him, tears shimmering in her eyes.

Craig stared back. His own heart stopped beating, surely. He thought he understood what she meant, but was horribly afraid that he was inventing the interpretation he wanted. "What?"

"I want to move here." A tear broke free and ran down her

cheek. "And I want to be with you. I want to give *us* a try. I need you to tell me if there's any hope—"

Later he would wonder if he'd jerked her to him too hard. He was never sure if he went around the table between them or over it. He only knew that the last words didn't get out of her mouth because his lips were on hers.

He had her out of the chair and pressed up along him before he even realized he did it. But the taste of her hit his veins like sugar. The feel of her tingled and buzzed where he touched her and radiated outward from there. Hardly able to breathe, but unwilling to pull back, he held her to him. His mouth fused hers, tongue seeking before he even consciously understood that, yes, she was kissing him back.

It took a minute of holding her, tasting her, savoring the feel of her, to know that she was holding onto him, too. Only then did his hands move up into her hair, keeping her where he needed her. Through the fabric of his shirt, he felt her small, capable hands cling to him.

It was relief washing through him. The need for her that he'd been holding at bay for months was finally loosed. After the first tidal wave passed, it changed. To hunger.

For just a moment, he broke the kiss, pulled back to look into her eyes, to see if she was with him. Craig didn't bother hiding the need he was certain shone there. Shay might not know all the details, but she understood. It was more than he had ever hoped for. So when he saw the want returned in her own gaze, it was all he needed.

This time when he kissed her, he bent down and scooped her knees, as though if he picked her up, held onto her, nothing could take her away from him again. The weight of her felt right in his arms. Though he waited for it, she didn't protest as he carried her down the short hallway and into his room. He barely registered the small noises as he carefully laid her on the bed and waited a beat to give her time to comment.

Her only reply was to sit up and wrap her arms around him, move him until his mouth came to hers, and she sank into him, into a kiss driven by her needs and wants as much as his. Desire shot through him, crackling like lightning. Knowing she wanted him as much as he wanted her set his hands free to touch and test. It had been far too long since he'd felt her skin beneath his fingertips, since he'd been naked against her.

Toeing off his shoes, he climbed onto the bed. Overwhelmed, Craig reached up and pushed her hair back from her face, framing her features for him to see clearly in the dim light of the room.

The sun was outside in full force, but inside a cocoon held only the two of them. He always gave her time to back out, to turn away from him. Some small part, deep inside, even after all the times she'd come to him, was afraid she would turn away, that she would reject him. But she didn't. Shay reached up for him, her eyes closing as she neared. She inhaled as though she were breathing him in, and Craig reveled in her choice. She chose him.

He leaned toward her, fusing his mouth to hers again, full with the knowledge that she was choosing more than just this once, more than just today. The knowledge that she could finally be his swamped him, leaving him drowning in desire for her. His hands sliding under the hem of her sweater, touching skin that felt like the silk of her neck tasted under his tongue. The sound that breathed out of her lungs was a siren call, some undeniable cross between a whimper and a moan. He answered it by pushing the knit up and over her head, tangling her arms above her while he looked his fill.

Her round breasts strained toward him, her back arching up to meet him as she writhed on the bed. Her legs, still in their jeans, wrapped tight around his hips, triggering adrenaline and need. Blood rushed from his head, leaving him light but never more sure of himself than he was right now.

Pushing his hips against the juncture of her legs, he heard the same whimper/moan from her. His fingers trailed down the inside of her arms, still tangled in her sweater over her head, until he found her breasts. His touch there, over and around her bra, changed her movements from writhing to jerking in an attempt to get her hands free. He unsnapped her bra and pushed it, too, up and over her head, taking one hard nipple in his mouth.

He needed to be inside her. Needed it a long time ago. And though he wanted to take it slow, he didn't have it in him. It didn't look like she needed that either. Pulling back and almost crying himself at the loss of contact, he reached behind him to find her shoes. Her feet had hooked behind him, using that force to pull him close, and grind her hips against his erection.

The sounds he heard now were her shoes hitting the floor and the moan that escaped his own lungs from the feel of her against him. He reached for the snap of her jeans, lust taking his control as he worked under the sole knowledge that he needed her naked. Now.

Even as he moved her legs deftly to one side, stripping her jeans and panties in one motion, her fingers found the skin at his waist, moving and twisting him until he realized she only wanted his shirt off.

Taking over the task as though he were drowning and that would get him air, he peeled the shirt up. As it passed by his face, he realized that she was no longer helping with his shirt, but had nimble fingers working the snaps on his jeans.

Craig tried to concentrate on the task of getting the shirt off, but the feel of her fingers stroking him as she pushed his jeans down just far enough to set him free made him fumble more than he could get past. When he finally tossed the shirt blindly behind him, it was to the feel of her warm hands stroking him until his hips jutted forward, pressing into her touch.

Groans, deep and guttural, escaped him as he moved against

her talented fingers. He knew there was more, but was unable to think beyond the feel of her on him. It was only when she reached up to pull his mouth down for a soul searching kiss, only when she released him did he realize he had seconds to save himself.

Reaching out, he fumbled in the bedside drawer purely by feel. Shay trailed her fingers down his chest, came up to her knees on the bed, placing her just a little above him, so she leaned down to kiss him. He tilted his face up to meet her, a drowning man surfacing for the only touch he'd ever known that would save him.

Hastily, he shoved down his jeans and underwear, awkwardly kicking the knot of fabric away. He was clumsy pushing the condom on, rolling it haphazardly down, until he was ready and his hands were free.

The fingers of one hand threaded through her hair, holding her face to his, so he could kiss her, breathe her in. The other hand reached behind her thigh, lifting and pulling her up against him, naked skin to naked skin. Thinking it was a sensation he hadn't felt in far too long, he tipped her backward onto the sheets of the unmade bed, her body naturally lining up to his.

And he pushed into her. The heat of her closed around him, gloving him in a sensation that spread to every cell of his body. His hips moved of their own accord, the pull and slide of her, the feel of the heat of her breasts flush against his chest stealing all other thoughts from him.

His eyes came open as he pushed into her again, the sounds from her throat pulling return cries from him. She was looking at him. Into him. As no one ever had.

His hips flexed again and again, pounding into her, feeling her push against him, straining for the same thing. His lower back clenched, his core following, the rush of his orgasm taking him over as his body moved in uncontrolled waves with hers.

He registered the cries of her own orgasm, her legs tightening on his hips, her fingernails digging into his shoulders.

As the last breath was wrung from him, he looked at her again, taking in the dreamy look on her face. And he wrapped his arms around her, both of them still breathing heavily, but unable to give her space.

Shay was here. Here. With him. He tumbled over the edge into a deep sleep.

Later, Craig woke to the sound of puppies whining. He'd forgotten they were there, that they'd likely watched him with Shay.

Shay.

She was warm in the crook of his arm and he didn't want to move. Didn't want to wake her, didn't want to leave her side to clean up little piles of dog poop. But Scarlett whined again and Gunnar put a paw to the lock, rattling it.

"Shhhhh." Craig whispered as he rolled away from the soft heat of the woman he loved.

He stood for a moment, naked, stunned, and wondering why he didn't know it before. It didn't hurt. It didn't scare him. It simply was, and that was wonderful. He loved her.

Quickly and quietly, he pulled on sweats and undid the clasp on the crate, noticing for the first time how noisy it was. He made a mental note to put WD-40 on it, then a second mental note to find out if WD-40 was harmful if a dog licked it.

He slipped out his own bedroom door, looking back at Shay, rumpled, naked above the sheet gathered at her waist, and sleeping like an angel. Want shot through him again, but he ushered the small dogs down the hall and out into the newly fenced backyard.

In bare feet, he stood on the back patio surveying them as they sniffed around. Then, he turned and looked back through the glass door at the table with the map still spread out. Two glasses made rings on the surface of the already-scarred table and he didn't care. It spoke of home to him.

A movement beyond the dining area came to him and he watched as Shay walked into the living room, dressed and ready to go. She picked up her purse before she spotted him.

CHAPTER 28

S hay reached down into her bag, looking for her phone. She'd checked in with Zoe when she arrived, but that was yesterday. Her phone volume was set loud enough for her to hear it over the boys yelling, or the dishwasher running, but now she questioned whether she would have heard it over the sounds she and Craig made last night.

Aside from seeing that she had no messages when she and Craig came out to find food late in the evening, she hadn't done anything. So she hadn't texted Zoe to say she was here with Craig, or that she even had a safe place to stay. If things had gone badly and she'd hit the road right away, yesterday afternoon, she might have been home by now.

Shay looked up to see Craig watching her through the glass of the sliding door, an odd look on his face. But she turned back to the phone and sent a quick message to her sister. She knew the power of getting involved with Craig—he could easily make her forget to check in. He'd already done it once.

His attention away from his small, scampering dogs, he slowly opened the sliding door, but didn't come in. "Leaving already?"

The flat tone of his voice worried her. "No. I mean, I have to go relatively soon, but not without saying goodbye, and I had hoped not without breakfast."

He nodded, then turned back to the dogs, clapping his hands and calling them in. Once he got them both over the threshold, he slid the door shut behind him and stood facing her.

He looked good, standing there in only his old sweatpants, his feet bare despite the chill. His chest looked good enough to lick, but it was rising and falling in measured beats. Not good.

He said he wanted her here. And, after last night, it was clear he still wanted her. Better to just ask. "What's wrong?"

"You're leaving?" His eyes were as flat as his tone.

"I have to go home to my boys. And if I'm moving to Nashville, I should see if I can find an apartment today. Put down a down payment." Her own heart stuttered as she wondered what could be so wrong after last night.

He nodded. "When will you move here?"

"Over Christmas break." She swallowed, the stilted feelings stuck between them, clogging her throat. "In three weeks."

He nodded.

That was it, it seemed. Maybe that was enough. But Shay broached another topic. Before she laid down money and made her plans, she needed to be sure. "Have you been seeing anyone else?"

He shook his head. "Not really. You?"

"No. I don't date." She shrugged and fought the fear in her chest. Old Shay didn't ask the hard questions, and Old Shay got shit in return. "What do you mean 'not really'?"

"I went out bar hopping with TJ a few times, but I always went home alone. Kelsey set me up with someone, but it was just at family dinner and it was pretty clear there was no chemistry." No, he was looking at her with a little more of the old heat. "So no. I haven't slept with anyone else or even kissed anyone else since Miami. I couldn't shake you."

She smiled, surprised at how shy she felt given what they'd been up to last night. "I couldn't shake you either."

"You sure tried." At least he didn't look upset.

"I didn't want to. I just couldn't see any way to do everything." She shrugged, unprepared for his next suggestion.

"You and the boys can stay here with me until you find a place."

Her breath sucked in, and the want to take him up on his offer hit her like a bucket of water. "I can't."

She hated saying that to him. She felt she'd said it so much. But she couldn't make it happen. "I haven't introduced you to my boys yet. I think they've both seen you. But there isn't enough time to let them get to know you before we would move in."

He didn't respond and she bolstered her argument. "There's a lot going on for them. They both just lost their fathers—not that they were good, or that the boys miss them much—but it's a big change. And the move on top of that, I can't add a new man."

"Do I get to meet them at least?" he seemed frustrated.

"Of course. We can take them out with us." She looked around wondering what a real date with Craig would be like. She couldn't take her boys into a bar. Could she take Craig bowling? The idea required some imagination. "You can come over for dinners. I know they'd love to play with the puppies. I want this to work, Craig."

"Then we'll make it work." He fisted his hands into her shirt and pulled her closer for a kiss. "I just don't know how I'll make it three more weeks."

"We've already gone much longer than that." She smiled up at him.

"Sure, but I never knew you'd come back those times. I was trying to forget you. Now, I'm waiting."

Stretching up on tiptoe, she pressed her lips to his, firmer this time, rolling into him. Need hit her again, like it always did when he touched her. But this time she wasn't afraid of it. She had faith that he wasn't trying to use her. He'd never raise a hand to her. But how would he fare with the boys? They would always be in the way. Kids were like that. She'd chosen to have them. He hadn't.

Brian had never taken to Owen. Sometimes he'd been nice, but her second husband had never loved her first son. It was unfair to compare Craig to Brian. To any of them really. He was a breed of his own. She'd just have to wait and see how things panned out between them. She wasn't rushing into anything this time.

When his tongue pushed softly against her lips, looking to take the kiss a little deeper, she smiled at him but pulled back. "I can't leave Zoe with the boys that long."

He frowned down at her. "Do you worry about her with them? Didn't she have them when you were in Miami? That was longer."

"No, it's not that. This is the second time she's been out since the wedding, and she's in grad school. I don't want her to miss any more of it for me than she already has. I mean, she says it's okay, that she doesn't have to show up for her classes this term, but I don't want her saying that if it's not right." She was rambling, but he didn't seem to care. Still, she changed topics. "I need to get breakfast and I need to find a suitable apartment."

"Do you need company?"

"I would love some. But you're not dressed."

"Gimme a sec." He went down the hallway, puppies scampering at his heels, probably not yet having figured out that they were about to get put into their crate. Then she heard a few whines and the sounds of him changing clothes.

Shay wanted to go watch, but she shouldn't. If things worked out, maybe she'd be able to watch him get dressed in the mornings from curled up under the covers. A girl could dream.

"Do you know any apartments that might hold me and my two boys around here?"

"I can think of a few. I also know good breakfast spots."

Soon after that, she was in the passenger seat of his truck, him insisting she let him drive. He took her to a breakfast specialty restaurant at an area that was apparently up and coming. Shay looked around while she was there, hoping that she could get her business up and running soon. That she wouldn't have to budget so tightly and save so much, that she could bring the boys to a place like this. It wasn't expensive, but it wasn't cheap either.

As they walked out to the truck, Craig pointed beyond the stores. "There are apartments over there. There's another set up behind the movie theaters. Unless you're looking to rent a house again, you'll likely wind up in one of these big complexes on the main streets. You can find smaller rentals off the back roads, but I don't know much about them."

They spent most of the day getting turned away by places that didn't have month to month options, but she took two applications for places that allowed her to either break the lease for a fee, or pay a different rate for the non-contract option.

They found one small house at a decent price, but Shay didn't like the neighborhood, and there was another set of duplexes in an area called "the Bend." She turned down a couple for not having yards or play areas. A quadruplex in the Bend scared her a little because of traffic, but had a good sized communal area, and she saw kids playing on the monkey bars set in the back. But the units were all rented out and she couldn't tour the one that would become available until the next day.

"I won't still be in town then, but I'll keep the place in mind." She said into the phone from where they sat in the parking lot. After she hung up with the manager, she turned to Craig and sighed. "I have to head home or I won't make it today. Surely you have places you need to be, too."

"I have rehearsal in a few hours." He grinned at her. "I want you to come back sooner."

Her heart almost melted. "Owen is in first grade, and he needs to finish the semester. I told him we were moving, but he needs to know where, and I want to have a picture to show him. Time to get him excited about it."

"What about the other one?"

"Aaron?" She wasn't keen on his calling her younger son 'the other one' but she didn't mention it. "He's still good at getting excited about what I tell him will be exciting. Owen is starting to think for himself."

Craig nodded at that as though what she said made sense, as though he had some understanding of little boys. "I'll miss you."

They didn't speak much, but he held her hand as they drove back to his place, the distance shorter than she'd thought it would be. They must have looped around a bit. She didn't even have anything to gather up, so she kissed him outside on the front lawn, giving the neighbors a show, and not tempting herself into staying just a little longer.

Before she knew it, she was on the road home. But her heart was light. She was on the road to adventure. To a bright new future.

CHAPTER 29

Craig had intended to help Shay move. He'd envisioned himself staying over at her house for several days, spending the daytimes packing her home in Bristol into boxes and his nights making love to her.

Instead he was on tour.

He was in his room on the bus talking to Shay on the phone in a low, soft tone. He'd seen JD and Alex both disappear into their rooms—sleeping cubbies really—for nightly chats with their wives. Now here he was, doing the same thing.

"How's the moving going?" He asked her.

"I got the kitchen packed. And I tried to do the living room, but didn't realize that I can't do that. We have another five days here, and not having TV or couches is just too much. I can't do their room for the same reason."

Just the sound of her voice was comforting, even if he couldn't be there with her. She'd actually get into Nashville two days before him. "Can you make it?"

"Of course. This isn't my first move. I've gotten pretty good at this. And Owen is actually helpful now even if Aaron needs as much supervision as if I'd done it myself. So I'll be okay."

"I know you will." He laid back onto the small bed wishing she was with him, wishing he would be there to help her. "I'll be on stage in Denver the night you get into town. Did you get the final pictures of the rental?"

Shay had chosen the townhouse in the Bend after seeing pictures of the inside of the unit. Her son would go to an elementary school just a few blocks away and the units were on a bus stop, so Shay and Aaron could stand out with him in the mornings. She sounded almost as excited as she said Owen was.

Craig was trying to pay attention. Owen was the older one and a bookworm. In his head, Aaron was like JD and Kelsey's daughter Allie when he'd met her at age three. He sounded like a typical toddler to Craig, not that he knew.

He'd watched some children's shows the other day, too, while TJ made fun of both the show and him, in an attempt to get familiar with something the kids might like. He'd picked up a few toys along the way, his heart racing each time he made a purchase. That reaction told him the outcome was important to him. So he didn't tell her, but he talked to her on the phone with toys stashed under his bed.

He left TJ to go out partying by himself most nights. TJ was not amused. He'd even commented that he missed his wingman. The few times Craig had gone out, he'd been a really crappy second. He was not there to meet women, though he'd paid for a few drinks for the friend of whomever TJ was hitting up. Nothing more. He didn't even really flirt with them. He'd somehow forgotten how to do it.

Mostly, Craig talked to Shay each night until she had to go, and he counted down the days until he was home. Each night he went out on stage and played with everything he had, as though if he screwed it up he'd have to stay on tour longer. The days couldn't pass fast enough, but he was still nervous about getting back to Nashville. About having her in town. About it finally being *real*.

Then it was 4a.m. and the bus was turning into the lot at the HeartBeats studio. Craig took a deep breath before stepping down the big bus steps and over to his car. Setting the guitar in the back seat, he cranked the cold engine but didn't wait for it to warm up. Despite the early morning hour, he drove by Shay's new place, knowing they were all still asleep, knowing he couldn't wake her and that it wouldn't look any different from the outside than it had before. But it did.

Shay's old beater car sat in the parking spot in front of the third red door and the very sight of it warmed him in ways that also disturbed him by their depth. He didn't honk or call her. Even if she was awake, she could hardly come to the door. If the boys were up, they'd see Craig and she wanted to really introduce him, something more formal than just "the man that was here that day." Though both boys had at one time or other seen him around a corner or when their dad dropped them off, he still had never been introduced. He had no idea if either child even knew his name.

Then again, he did know. Shay said she'd been talking up all the people they would know in Nashville. Hailey was here—and the boys already loved Hailey. It seemed they'd been mortified not to be at the wedding until Shay had convinced them that it wouldn't be any fun.

She'd also told them about Kelsey and JD, whom she met at the wedding, when she'd hung out with Kelsey and Bridget a little. Kelsey liked her and had kids whose ages lined up with Shay's boys, so that was a plus.

He sat parked in the space, looking at the red door, thinking about how excited Shay had sounded and how he wanted to take even a little credit for it. She never said, "And I'm so excited because you'll be there," but she'd asked him before she came and she'd said if he didn't want her, how could she possibly live near him.

If it was anything like what he felt for her, he understood. Not seeing her, not having her had been okay when she was far away, when she didn't think she could work it out. He'd survived it. But having her here? If she didn't want him? He'd never make it through that. So he put the car in gear and backed out of the spot, heading for home, wondering when he could call her.

After setting his stuff down inside the door and taking the dogs outside—earlier than usual, but they woke up when he came home—he paid the sitter he'd also woken up and she headed out. He wasn't sure if she just didn't want to be in the house with him, or if she really did just want to be home with her own things since she could. He suspected the latter. If it was the first, she was a good liar, and Craig knew liars.

It was probably part of the appeal of Shay. She was never coy. She told him the truth, flat out, even when she knew he wouldn't want to hear it. Even when it hurt them both to admit that she was a prisoner of her two ex-husbands and that they couldn't be together. Even when it was because the blowback on her sons was more than she could stand. She might evade, she might try not to answer him, but she never lied. She told him what she had straight up.

He tried to catch some sleep, but even though for once the puppies laid right down and passed out after doing their pre-dawn business, his mind was racing. He found himself in the living room, picking out chords as the sun came up. Something was coming together in the back of his brain. He could hear the strains of a melody and tried combination after combination until it struck him that he had it right.

He was playing through several parts of it, the words still not formed but still scratching at some silent lobe of his brain, when he realized that it was eight o'clock. For all his excitement, for all he and Shay had decided that they would have lunch together today with the boys, they hadn't pinned down a time or a plan. His day was at the mercy of a six-year-old and a three-year-old. But it was eight, so he grabbed the phone to call her right as it rang.

"Hey, Shay." Even as the words fell off his tongue, he realized that was hardly the way to greet her. "I was just picking up the phone to call you."

I was just picking my heart up off the floor where it's been since I last saw you.

The words jolted him and he reached out to write them on the paper as she spoke something odd to him. Something that after a moment was clearly to the boys. Then she turned back to him. "I talked to the boys and while they love the new apartment and want to stay here, they heard you have puppies."

"Ah, so they have no concerns about meeting me. Just the puppies."

"I hate to say it, but that's probably true. Boys and puppies. You understand." Her tone was lilting, like she was happy just to be on the phone with him.

"Why don't you come by around eleven? We'll take the puppies out for their walk and we can figure out lunch from there."

"That sounds great." She sounded reluctant to hang up and Craig's heart swelled at the thought of it.

Even as he clicked the button and turned back to his guitar, his brain raced. When had anyone ever just loved the sound of his voice?

Okay, that was a stupid question. He had fans. But they liked the tone and timbre of his voice, they liked the sound. Shay seemed to like that it was actually him on the other end of the line.

He'd written for another hour when he had a disturbing thought: his fridge was completely bare. He already didn't know if he had anything her boys would want to play with besides the dogs, and he didn't even have food if they wanted sandwiches. Or chips. Or soda. Did she let her boys drink soda? He needed juice. And soda. Because if she did let them drink it and he didn't have it . . .

His heart rate kicked up, thinking how important it was that he make a good first impression on her kids. He had sized up his foster parents, his case workers, even his tricks, at the drop of a dime. He expected her kids to do the same. Then again, maybe they didn't have the practice that he'd had at it, by even a young age. He hoped not. But he was going to do his damnedest to make sure he got it right. Just in case.

With the guitar abandoned on the couch, rather than set back up into its holder, he grabbed his wallet and keys and dashed out the door.

CHAPTER 30

S hay shuffled the boys into the car, surprised how nervous she was. It was not only the first time the boys were really meeting Craig, it was her first time seeing him on his turf. She'd been to his house before. That wasn't the issue. But she'd moved herself and her kids here because he was here. This was permanent, even if Craig turned out not to be.

She had just started the engine when she realized she'd moved to be with a man. *Again.*

It was how she'd wound up in Bristol in the first place. She'd grown up in a small town in the western corner of Virginia, but Jason had wanted to hit the big city and she'd followed him.

Her breath came fast as she wondered if she'd made another monumental mistake. She'd been thinking about kids with Craig. Her kids and maybe a few more. She'd been thinking about his offer to move in while she house hunted and that she was holding out until it was a permanent offer.

Was she falling into old patterns? This smacked of Old Shay, not New Shay. *Shit.*

"Mommy. Let's go. Want to meet the puppies." Aaron whined.

Owen was probably whining in his head. He wasn't much of an external whiner. He had only two modes, low key and full blown, depressive, angry, everything is wrong. Luckily he didn't go there much.

She pulled out of the spot, realizing she had no options except to go to Craig's. She'd promised her boys a chance to play with puppies. There was no way to explain the old habits that had gotten her into all her messes in the first place. Not to the kids who were the results of those messes.

But she was here now. And there was no going back, even if just because her boys didn't deserve another move, another change of scenery. She was going to have to watch herself carefully. No pushing Craig to suggest she move in with him. No asking for extra favors; he'd already done more than anyone else.

She took the last turn into his neighborhood with a deep breath and a glance around at the other houses on his street. Pushing down the sigh and the desire to have a house like his, she fought against it. The very last thing she should do was move into his neighborhood. That was incredibly poor planning. What if it all fell apart? What if her boys had to deal with their mom seeing her ex every day? She hadn't even had to deal with that shit with Jason or Brian.

She parked on the street and watched as his front door swung open. He didn't come down the walk. Probably not wanting to overwhelm the boys, he stood there with one shoulder pressed against the door frame, arms casually crossed. He looked like a sin waiting to happen.

His white thermal shirt had some black print design on it. It was pushed up at the sleeves, giving peeks of the black ink tattoos that snaked down his biceps and just beyond his elbow. They looked like a continuation of the design from the shirt. His jeans clung to him, and she knew what his ass looked like both in and out of them.

Over the roof of the car she offered him a smile that she hoped looked sincere and not horribly nervous. If her boys didn't like Craig, she didn't know what she would do. But Owen was already out of the car and Aaron was jumping against her hands as she tried to unsnap him from his five-point harness, then walk him around to the side of the car with the sidewalk. Both boys came to a dead halt about halfway up the sidewalk until Craig smiled at them, his arms unfolding.

Shay jumped in. "This is my friend Craig that I told you about. And he has two puppies inside."

"They're really excited to meet you." He offered up and stepped out of the doorway inviting them inside. She stepped through the front door, not remembering any of the previous times she'd done that. Each time before had been too fraught with other problems to take notice of the hardwood floors, the open curtains, and light airy feeling. This time she noticed not just that the old furniture made her feel more at home, but it made the whole place feel more like a home.

Craig disappeared into his room, and she watched as Scarlett and Gunnar came scampering down the hallway toward the sound of voices. They skidded to a stop—poorly—as though they wanted to meet the boys up until the point where it actually happened. Shay thought they were a lot like kids that way.

Owen crouched down and stuck out his hand, making her wonder when he'd had experience with dogs before, because he looked like he knew what he was doing. Aaron glanced at his brother then tried to do the same thing, though his chubby little toddler legs didn't quite have the grace of Owen's older frame. For a moment the world disappeared and Shay found herself immersed in a thought she'd had pretty often lately. *Who was Owen's genetic father?*

Given the circumstances, he couldn't be a decent man that she'd want in her son's life. But as she looked at Owen, she was grateful that he'd passed on at least some good genes. Shaking her thoughts off, and trying to pay attention to the moment, she looked up at Craig and softly asked, "Do they bite?"

His eyebrows popped as though he'd never thought about that question. Then he moved in close to her, whispering, "No, but I do."

She couldn't help the grin that spread across her face even as he turned away from her and plopped down on the floor next to her boys. "They don't bite. But sometimes they chew. It shouldn't hurt, but don't let them do it. They have to stop chewing on things, so they don't do it when they're big dogs."

Owen nodded solemnly as he slowly baited the little dog to sit next to him. He stroked the tiny head, petting all the way down to the tip of the tail and pretty much mesmerized the little dog. But when he picked Gunnar up to settle him in the cradle of his lap, Gunnar popped back up and tried to play.

Craig was sympathetic. "He just got up, so he's going to want to be more active. Do you want a toy for him?"

No sooner had Craig fetched a toy for Owen and Gunnar than Aaron had hopped up wanting one for Scarlett—or "Scarret" as he called the puppy. At least she didn't seem to mind.

After they played like that for a while, with Craig monitoring, he suggested they take the puppies out for a walk around the block. It probably took five times as long as it usually took him to get the dogs ready. Kids were like that, Shay knew, but Craig probably didn't.

He decided that Owen could walk Scarlett, holding the leash by himself. Shay had never seen her son light up so bright. The combination of a dog and being thought of as big enough for a bit of responsibility was the best thing Craig could have done for him. It was even better that Owen hadn't earned the privilege from his mom, that it came from someone else. Shay wondered if Craig knew what he'd done.

He didn't seem to. He just crouched down so he looked up to Owen and explained a few things to him. "Don't let her tug. If she tugs on the leash, you have to tug back. If you let her do it, that means it's okay and she'll keep tugging until she trips you. Plus, she'll be really big one day and what's okay for a puppy is not okay for a big dog."

He kept the instructions simple and workable, then turned to Aaron, "You can help me or your Mom walk Gunnar."

When the little boy's face fell, Shay consoled him. "When you're older, honey."

Then they were out on the block, Owen up ahead with Scarlett, gently getting in her face and telling her 'no' when she tugged, and 'good girl' when she did what she was told.

"He's a natural. Has he had a dog before?" Craig asked her as they walked a few feet behind.

"No. I never had time for anything more than I already had." She thought about that. The move was hectic and things were still at a fast pace, but she was convinced her life had taken a serious turn for the better. She wouldn't have to save so much; they could do more fun things together, get the extra school supplies rather than the bare minimum, spend time with Craig.

Craig unknowingly interrupted her deep thoughts, which was fine, she was tired of them. So much had happened, that she was ready to just *be* for a while. But the kitchen still needed to be put together and though the boys' bedroom was set up, hers was not.

"I had to learn all this from a book." He told her. "I had no idea what to do with them, so some teenagers at the pet store took pity on me and got me a great book to help."

Aaron walked in front of her next to Gunnar, his legs working to keep up with the puppy. He babbled to the little dog the whole way, touching Shay's heart with his joy. They looked like a family out walking their dogs.

Her heart surged. Then her brain shut it down.

Her mother had been manipulative. Her husbands had been manipulative. And Shay had to admit that she had, too. She'd learned to work the system and whenever she could work it in her favor, she'd done it.

As she watched Owen give a gentle tug back on the leash as Scarlett tried to surge ahead, she thought that she and Jason had probably never spoken a single true word to each other. Even when she told him she loved him, she'd meant it, but she had been lying, because she hadn't even known what love was then.

She knew it now with her sons.

She almost stumbled at a crack on the sidewalk as her brain turned over.

With a frown, Craig reached out and took the leash from her. As the change moved Gunnar's path on the sidewalk a bit, Aaron noticed and turned around. He opened a wholly unrelated topic, as he often did.

"How come you don't have a Christmas tree?"

"That's a good question. Should I have one?" Craig asked her son through the haze of Shay's thoughts. They were almost around the whole block.

"Yes. You should definitely get one." Aaron declared, looking back at Craig rather than where he was going.

He tripped, too, his chubby toddler body falling without the ability to stop himself. His butt hit the sidewalk as Owen turned the corner, having gotten ahead of the three of them.

Before Shay could do anything, Craig swooped down and scooped her boy up. When she held her hands out, he absently handed her the small dog's leash, rather than her son, like she'd expected.

In a way she didn't have the strength to do, he flipped Aaron upside down and over, checking him for bruises. "Do you have any cuts?"

Her son giggled—the little one who could have a meltdown when something triggered it, and a bump or a bruise could sure do it. But he giggled in Craig's arms until Craig put him back down to join the puppy tugging on the leash. The little procession continued on its way, with Shay calling out for Owen to wait up. At least he hadn't gotten out of her sight in a strange neighborhood.

Her heart tugged again, and she shoved it down again.

"Does it always take this long to go around the block?" Craig's question startled her.

"Yes. It's like standing still, only faster." She responded wryly.

The laugh that burst from his chest lit up her world as she turned up his walkway to head back into the house.

Craig showed Owen how to set up the baby gates so the puppies would stay in the living room. Then when Owen finished, Craig quietly checked his work without letting the boy know. "Who wants lunch?"

Shay grinned. "It depends on what lunch is. We ate out a lot on the road. I don't know if I can handle another burger."

"I have plenty." He grinned and opened his fridge to reveal a stock to rival a grocery store. "I didn't know if you would want soup or sandwiches or both or . . . I don't know."

As she looked at her options, Shay realized nothing had been in the fridge for more than just a few hours. He'd only gotten home at four or five this morning. He must have gone shopping for her and the boys.

She couldn't fight it any longer. She was in love with him. It was as simple and terrifying as that.

CHAPTER 31

Craig insisted on coming over that evening to help with some of the unpacking. He'd waggled his eyebrows at her when he opened the bag containing her lingerie. After a ridiculous tussle, she'd pulled it out of his hands, and he'd finally kissed her.

The boys were playing back in their room on the premise that if they played nice they didn't have to help with the work of setting up the townhome. So she and Craig were finally somewhat alone.

It was the first kiss of her new life, she thought. In her new room, in the new town that she had chosen, in the apartment that she could afford because she didn't have to sock away every penny that wasn't necessary for food, water, or rent.

Craig was here and she wanted to tell him how she felt, but she had no idea how he'd react. Despite the fact that they'd both had traumatic upbringings and that they understood each other on that level, his bad home had been much different from hers. Her mother had smothered her, told her how to do everything, made Shay's purpose in life very clear. Craig's life had been the opposite. So how would he react to having Shay tell him she loved him? She didn't know. So she didn't say it.

Before he even left, he invited her and the boys to come the next day and help him find and decorate a Christmas tree for his house. That had turned into a shopping trip for a six-foot fake tree. They ventured out to find it among the hordes of people finishing up their holiday shopping.

The boys made ornaments for him like it was going out of style. Owen cut slim strips of colored paper that he stapled into a chain, getting frustrated each time he got his colors out of order. Aaron finger-painted hand prints, then demanded that Shay cut them out and string them. Which meant that her job took five times as long as his and she couldn't hope to keep up.

She called her own Mom and again reminded her that she wasn't going to come home for Christmas this year. She'd thought she was abandoning Zoe with their mom, but then Zoe said she'd used all her travel coming to help Shay and the kids. Zoe was going to have to manipulate her mother carefully there. If she'd been helping Shay, that was okay, but if she were just visiting, well she should have visited her mother, too.

Eventually, Mom called Shay back and told her she and the boys couldn't come for the holiday anyway, that she had been invited out to a special Christmas with her latest paramour and the girls needed to find something else to do. *Typical*, Shay thought.

Though the boys had asked after Grandma, they seemed pretty comforted with Christmas Eve dinner at Kelsey and JD's house. Craig attended and so did TJ, as JD and TJ's parents didn't seem to be home for Thanksgiving or Christmas. Shay found out that was normal for them and she couldn't imagine what kind of parents would choose travel over being with their own kids on the holidays. Then again, she'd chosen not to spend the holidays with her own family, so who was she to judge?

After dinner, Craig drove them to her townhouse, the boys

strapped into car seats he'd bought for them. Shay was pretty sure he'd done his research. He'd gotten it right, even getting a booster for Owen that didn't suggest he was a baby in any way. By the time they pulled up to her temporary home, both boys were out cold. She unstrapped Aaron from his car seat behind hers and started to shake Owen and tell him softly to wake up. She really couldn't carry him anymore and there was no way she could haul them both. But Craig was already there, shooing her hand away, unbuckling Owen and letting him loll forward into waiting arms.

She stood there almost dumbfounded as he slowly tipped the sleeping child onto his broad shoulder. It clearly wasn't the practiced movement that she had, but he tried. He was gentle, patient.

In her head a dozen scenes flipped through her thoughts. Craig asking Owen what he was reading and listening with interest as Owen explained the plot in excruciating detail. He never suggested that Owen was reading pussy books because he liked dragons now. Owen read books with female characters as the lead, and Craig reacted exactly the same.

When Aaron was hurt, Craig was the best at soothing him. He even had a routine—check the left arm, then the right, left leg next, followed by the right. The two would methodically look Aaron over and catalog anything that needed to be done. They would then get Band-Aids or declare him boo-boo-free. But in her head Shay saw again when he'd set Aaron on the couch with a foot he'd probably bruised. Craig had fetched an ace bandage, carefully wrapping the little ankle. Aaron had been so enamored by the elastic bandage that the hurt had completely disappeared by the time it was wrapped.

Craig had parenting books beside his bed. They were always marked in different places because he hadn't put them there for show. They weren't bait for her. He hadn't even told her he was reading them. But when she complemented him, he told her he'd just been trying to learn. He didn't take much credit when he'd been better to her boys in two weeks than either of their fathers had been to them in years.

So she stood there with Aaron heavy over her shoulder, and she looked up at Craig as he closed the door to the truck, trying not to wake Owen. When her son jostled a little at the sound, Craig's free hand went to the boy's back. As she watched, Owen laced his arms around Craig's tattooed neck.

The dam broke.

It felt like she'd been holding it back for so long. But she couldn't hold it back any longer. "I love you."

Craig stopped dead in the cold night air. "What?"

He was going to make her say it again. The first time had been easy. Too easy. It had fallen out by mistake. But a second time? She gulped. "I love you."

She'd said it, out loud, she was sure, but Craig still just stared at her. Then, with a dazed look on his face that she really couldn't interpret, he turned and went up the walk, calling back to her, "It's cold. Let's get them inside."

On numb feet and with a numb brain, she followed him to the door, where he stepped back and let her unlock it. Only then did she realize he'd never asked her for a key. Dread settled in the pit of her stomach, as she pushed into the warm air. Then she realized she'd never asked for a key to his place either.

He followed her quietly down the hall to the boys' room. Making tandem motions to hers, he pulled back the covers and laid Owen onto the bed before pulling off his shoes and tucking him in. Her task was a little more complicated—Aaron needed an overnight diaper still.

Craig made a quick motion to her that he would be out in the living room waiting. Her brain ran a thousand miles per hour. She was only renting, month-to-month even. So she could break the lease and get moved in somewhere else before the boys started school. Not that that was fair to them in any sense, but she could do it. What was Craig thinking out there?

He hadn't said anything. Just stared at her like she'd suddenly said, "I like cows" or something equally inane. What if he didn't feel the same way? Or worse, what if he didn't know? At least if he didn't love her, she could pack up her broken heart in cardboard boxes and move it to the next state with all her other belongings. But if he didn't know? How should she handle that? Just wait around to see if he fell in love with her?

It seemed to take forever to get Aaron wrestled into the diaper without waking him. Shay could swear she heard Craig pacing in the other room. *That couldn't be good.*

Sure enough, after she'd covered her son and snuck backward out of the room, closing the door gently behind her though her heart pounded, she turned to find Craig doing exactly that. He paced away from her and when he hit the dining table, he made an abrupt turn and spotted her. He came to a military precise stop and stared at her again.

Shit. Bad move, Shay, bad move. Her heart thudded slowly to nothing and she quit breathing. For a moment, no one said anything, then she opened her mouth to speak, only to hear his voice.

"Say it again."

Jesus. He was putting her through the wringer. She almost told him so, but she didn't have the energy to tell him off, or even just to tell him to leave. So when she opened her mouth, the words came out again, as though, if she said them enough, he'd say them back. The sound was dejected, even to her own ears. She'd given up. "I love you."

He stepped up to her, face to face, not touching other than where he'd suddenly reached out and grabbed her hands. His were warm, nervous, shaking. So was his voice. "No one has ever said that to me before."

Her eyes blinked, her brain stopped. She was stunned. "No one?"

He shook his head.

Now her brain and her mouth flew. "I know you grew up in foster care, but no one?"

He shook his head again as though that was all he would say, but then his mouth started making words, too. Shay pushed to listen, hard. What was monumental to her was beyond earth-shattering to him. No wonder he hadn't simply responded back there on the sidewalk. Then his words overrode her busy thoughts.

"My case workers told me they would keep me safe." He took a breath in. "Some of the families, the good ones, said they would take care of me. Some said they even liked having me there. But most didn't."

Holy shit.

She didn't know how to respond, so she just said it again. "Well, I love you."

This time when she looked at him, his stunned appearance gave way to a phantom of a smile. Shay pushed up on her toes and pulled against his hands, leaning in to kiss him.

His mouth was hot against hers, burning with need. When he dropped her hands, she felt his fingers against the back of her head, tilting her to line up with him as his mouth opened over hers. Without her consent, her hands fisted into his shirt and her hips pushed up against his.

Heat flooded her, bending her backward like melting metal as he leaned further into her. With her head tipped back, his mouth moved to her neck, nipping his way up to her ear, eliciting a soft sigh from her as tongue and teeth found a spot that she didn't know she had.

His words came like fine gravel under her shoes, "I need you."

She needed him, too. He didn't say *the words*. She hadn't

prepared herself for this outcome, but she knew what to do with him.

Walking backward, she tugged at his shirt, pulling him through the door to her bedroom and gently kicking it shut behind her. Muscling him around, she vaguely remembered to punch the lock button, then she fisted her hands into his shirt again and pushed him back onto her bed.

He fell back, his eyes glued to her as she peeled her shirt, revealing a lace bra. She'd shoved all the plain ones into the back of her drawer and started buying nice ones the day after he'd told her to come to Nashville. He'd changed everything.

She felt powerful and sexy standing over him as his eyes dilated. He watched, transfixed, as she shimmied out of her jeans, leaving only the matching lace underwear.

"Good God, Shay." He breathed it out, and it flowed into her.

She'd had two kids and was maybe a little overweight from the stressful life she'd been living. But this man who could pick up any cowgirl in a bar, was leaning back on his hands on her bed, his eyes nearly rolling back into his head at the sight of her. His hands reached out for her hips, grabbing her, nipping at the tops of her breasts and interfering with her plan to pull his shirt off him.

Reaching around him, she managed to get the hem. A schoolgirl giggle escaped her as he nipped at her ribs and she thwarted a second tickle by using the shirt to wrangle him back. Then she climbed over him on the bed and started working the button on his jeans.

"It's almost Christmas." She whispered. "Be my present."

His hands reached out and stopped hers. "I— Jesus, Shay, stop."

She stilled. He was obviously turned on, so why . . . ?

"I—" He sucked in air, breathing heavily. "I don't have any . . . protection."

It hit her that he'd always supplied the condoms. "Craig, I have some."

"Oh, thank God."

But she didn't move. "I have something else. I went on the pill after I left here last time. It's been a month. I got tested." She waited a beat, when he didn't fill it, she continued. "I don't need condoms anymore. You?"

He reached up for her, the words gushing out as his hands found her skin. "I've been tested. I'm clean. Holy shit, and merry Christmas."

She laughed then, joy and humor hitting her in the same wave, as her hands went back to work peeling his jeans, this time with help from him.

His hands fumbled her bra, his voice rasping, "I love this, but I like it better off." Then he pushed her underwear down, too, his mouth roving over her as she scooted the two of them back onto the bed.

Not waiting any longer, she took him in hand and pushed down onto his waiting erection. She gasped at the feel of him, hard and heavy inside her. His breath rushed out at the contact, reminding her body to move. Then, even as they continued in their rhythm, even as his breath escaped in measured groans, she grabbed his face in her hands and said it again. "I love you."

Craig stayed there, hands on her hips, moving her against him, his eyes on hers as his pace picked up. "Again."

She said it for him again, and again, each time he asked until words were beyond her. She came in a flurry of cries and electricity, her body rocking against his, some deep level of her soul aware that he was coming, too.

Her nails raked his back, clutching him even as she collapsed forward and he tipped them both backward until he was lying flat with Shay sprawled on top of him.

Her face nestled in the crook of his neck. He smelled of sweat and sex and the man she loved. His hand came into her hair, the other cupping her ass as he breathed heavily. "I want to stay."

"I want you to. It's Christmas." Her chest still heaved with the effort of the words.

Slowly, her breathing died down to a more normal rate. His hands stroked her hair, her back, making her feel loved. She hadn't been prepared for this. She wasn't prepared when his hands stilled, holding her in place.

"Shay, I've thought it so many times. I've known for a while now, but I've never said it before, so give me a minute."

Her arms clenched around him as her heart thudded in her chest again. Tears leaked and hit the sheets behind his shoulder before he got it out. He did it one word at a time.

"I."

"Love."

"You."

CHAPTER 32

This time Craig hit the tour bus with both a lighter and a heavier heart. Lighter because Shay put Owen on the school bus, then dropped Aaron at daycare, then shirked her sewing for the morning to come tell him goodbye.

She did it with style, too. Interrupting his packing by stripping to show off her new underwear, which she then didn't wear for long. He'd never had sex before without a condom, and he was grateful or he would have become one of those assholes who didn't want to use them. Or maybe it was just because it was Shay.

Each time she came to him, each time she said yes when he went to her, felt better than the time before. She assured him that they could have reunion sex when he returned home from the tour, then she screamed his name. Repeatedly.

He grinned down at her, propped on one elbow, "I think the neighbors heard you."

"I think they maybe heard *you,* cowboy." She swatted at him and he rolled over even though he didn't want to. Once he'd gotten to Nashville and gotten a real job, he'd never been late for anything. He hadn't even asked to change shifts until it was for a gig for Wilder. He wasn't one to show up late to rehearsals despite the fact that he went out drinking and partying just as often as TJ, who occasionally rolled in a little past start time.

Shay always tempted him. But now she pushed against his arm. "You have to get ready. I hate that you have to go, but you have to go." She pushed up onto her elbows, grinning at him. Naked.

He grinned back until her expression changed and she asked, "What's that noise?"

"Shit!" He yelled and ran naked into the living room where Gunnar had one of his sneakers in his paws. No longer quite so small, the dog had his jaws clamped on the back of the shoe and worked a piece of it off as he made satisfied little sounds at his accomplishment.

Craig would have been furious about the rip, but he could clearly see it wasn't the first. The dog had been at it a while. Searching the room for Scarlett, Craig found her sitting in the corner with a rope toy. He petted her and gave her a treat before putting his fingers in Gunnar's jaw and opening them the way the book had demonstrated it. He pulled out the ruined shoe and got angry at the puppy.

He shook the shoe in the little dog's face. "No. Shoe is mad!" Then he bonked Gunnar's paws with the shoe, one at a time until the puppy was afraid of the shoe. "No shoe!" He spoke in a low angry voice, then picked up the pieces and threw all of it into the trash with a weary sigh.

When he stood and turned away, he caught Shay, respectfully back in her underwear, standing at the bedroom door with her hand over her mouth to hide her giggles.

"Hey. Don't." He scolded her, too. "That hurts to be mad at my dog. And right before I leave, too."

Her arms wound around his neck. "Trust me, I know exactly how it feels. But the shoe being mad at him was just . . ."

229

"Shut up." He brushed her aside, a smile on his face as she giggled one last time. "It's what the book said to do."

He shrugged into his traveling clothes—loose jeans, an old t-shirt, and . . . Dammit. "The dog ate the sneakers I was going to wear." He rummaged around under the bed until he found an older pair that would suit and shoved his feet into them. Then he looked at the clock, trying to calculate whether there was possibly time for one more go round with the nymph in the lace underwear. Sadly, there wasn't. "I have to go. Use your key to lock up?"

She nodded at him and he did all the last minute things he normally did, but this time with Shay watching. He put the puppies into the crate, a harder job each time because they were always just a little bigger than before, and the opening seemed a little smaller. Gunnar walked in on his own, his head hanging. Craig couldn't resist giving each of them a good rub behind the ears. He couldn't leave Gunnar that way.

Then he filled their bowls, set timers on the lights, checked all the knobs on the stove, and so on. At last he put his guitar into his traveling case and slung his old duffel bag over his shoulder and turned to find Shay still waiting in the entry to the hallway, still not dressed. "Jesus, you are going to ruin me for this trip."

She smiled and pressed a kiss to his lips. "Travel safe. Call often. And remember, I love you."

"I love you, too." He turned away, biting his lower lip. It got easier each time he said it. It still wasn't something that just rolled off his tongue, but it didn't take deep breaths between each word like it had that first time. Knowing it and saying it had been two different things. He was settling into it.

He climbed behind the wheel and pulled out of the driveway without looking back. For the first time in his life, he believed someone would be waiting when he got home. Not just the dogs, but a person who loved him. This time he drove to pick up

JD, then TJ, then Alex, and the four of them stuffed their crap under the tarp in the back of the truck and headed to the airport. They were flying in to meet the bus in Sacramento. It had headed out days ago, and they'd ride together back across a northern route. Eight days. It never used to seem so long.

They arrived a handful of hours later and went straight to the arena, where they headed to the suites backstage. Invigorated by his morning romp, Craig had been running music in his head all during the flight. Once dressing rooms were assigned, he pulled JD aside and took over a lounge area, forcing his friend and bandmate to listen to what he'd already picked out. He had a few lines of lyrics as well, including the one that had come to him when talking with Shay: *I was just picking my heart up off the floor where it's been since I last saw you.* It took a moment to get back into that frame of mind for the song.

"That goes in the beginning." JD told him, "where the song is sadder. It gets better at the end. Maybe we can alter the lyrics to be the same-ish."

Craig understood, and they played around with words for a while. When that failed, they picked out harmonies until it was time to head to the stage for sound check. After the show, they hit the waiting bus and Craig fell fast asleep to the familiar rumble of wheels below him.

The next morning, he called Shay. Saturday. It meant the boys were up and in the background. It meant he couldn't say anything dirty to her, but he enjoyed the sound of her voice. "Owen is almost through that huge book you got him for Christmas!"

"Which one?"

"The first one in the dragon series."

For Christmas, he'd printed up color covers of a book series about a boy and a dragon. Then he'd done the same for a book on elf and gnome wars after the fall of man. Then added a few others recommended by a librarian for a high-level reading almost-seven-year-old. Owen had opened the biggest box under the tree and found all the book covers.

"Where are the books?" He'd asked Craig.

"Go open your kindle." When they'd started opening presents he'd pulled his phone out and hit send on the order, automatically loading all the books into the device while Owen was opening other gifts. Watching Owen's face light up as he scrolled through all his new books had been worth it.

"That's impressive." He told Shay over the phone. "That's a big book."

"He loves it. It was brilliant."

Aaron had been given a set of Legos that fit his hands. Only Craig had gone a little over the top with that, too, buying way too many sets. In front of the boys, he'd given Shay a purse he'd seen her admire once in a window. But later he'd given her other gifts, including a key to his house.

"I met with a realtor today." Her voice sounded breathy and excited, but his heart sank. She still wanted a house separate from him.

"What did they say?"

She went on to describe what was available in the area and what kind of loan she would probably qualify for. Then she talked about the new job she'd landed at a local theater, before shutting herself up and asking about his trip.

He told her about the song in general, but not the lyrics she'd inspired. About the weather in Sacramento. He told her about the drive into Eugene, Oregon. Something stupid he'd done, something ridiculous TJ had said. Then they'd hung up.

But the house stayed on his mind when they played the next night in Boise. Why did she want a place separate from him? She'd barely been in town a month. So he understood that she didn't want to put another change on the boys that fast, but in his mind she would move in with him. That meant the boys would move in with him, too.

He'd already contemplated which rooms would belong to which kid. He'd contemplated choosing colors of paint with them. He thought that his small, three-bedroom house might need to upgrade to a four-bedroom house. It would give him and Shay an office to share. He'd convinced himself that she'd stay in the rental until she was ready to be with him. That her own house would be *their* house.

Clearly, Shay was not thinking the same way.

Wilder played to packed houses in Cheyenne, Omaha, and Springfield on consecutive nights. Each day he talked to Shay. She got a preliminary order for some rising new country starlet who opened for Hailey. And another for some guy who sang backup for Hailey. So Hailey was finding her more work. Craig wasn't. Not that anyone would listen to him if he told them where to get their fashion from, but he wasn't helping any. It occurred to him that the more Shay worked, the faster she could afford a house that didn't have him in it.

Sure, they were sleeping over, but she'd limited it to one night a week. Apparently, Christmas had been an exception. Since the semester had started, she wouldn't have him over on school nights. His arguments that Aaron only had "school" on Monday, Wednesday, and Friday had fallen on deaf ears.

She loved him, but he couldn't get her to move any faster. Now, with dreams of 'the house,' she was moving further away. Maybe not in miles, but definitely further from the two of them really being together.

He pulled JD out into the common area of the bus while they rolled from Springfield to Lexington—the last stop. Though he wasn't where he'd once been, the song about picking his heart up off the floor had just become easier to write. JD didn't say anything about his mood, just picked chords and offered harmonies and lyrics. They were a good team, always had been. Craig remembered that if something happened with Shay, the guys would still be here for him. It wasn't really comfort, but it would help.

"Try this." JD broke his thoughts with a few chords.

"You want to take the end up like that?"

JD shrugged at him. "If the ending is supposed to be lighter, better? I mean, if they're together at the end of the song, then yes."

That was the big question, wasn't it? Were they together at the end of the song? Craig felt like he was setting his still-beating heart on the table between them. "I don't know yet."

Just then his phone rang. *Shay.*

He stepped away from the table with a motion to JD, who seemed to understand. "Hey, what's going on?"

She took in a deep breath. "I got a preliminary approval on a loan. So I can start house hunting for real!"

Of course she did.

His heart went through the floor.

CHAPTER 33

C raig yelped and reached out for Owen's hand as the boy touched the sizzling bacon.

"No. That's hot!" Craig nearly yelled it, then grabbed the small hand, realizing he didn't know what to do. Then he did. "Shit. You need ice."

He pulled a cube from Shay's freezer and held it to Owen's finger before he realized Shay was staring at him. "What?"

"Don't swear in front of the kids." She frowned then went back to flipping the pancakes and directing Aaron to set the table.

"Shi—shoot." Craig felt the word coming on then quickly corrected himself. "You're right."

He did not have the vocabulary to be around kids, though he usually did better around JD and Kelsey's brood. He looked down at the six-year-old to see if he'd traumatized the kid. Owen was holding back a giggle. Craig remembered Shay told him the kid was reading Stephen King. And he couldn't swear? Maybe she was worried about the little one.

"Hold that." He curled the ice into Owen's hand and went

back to turning the bacon. "And don't touch it again. Anything on the stove that sizzles is definitely too hot to touch."

Owen gave a single nod of acknowledgment to that fact and went back to watching the bacon cook. Craig couldn't remember ever wanting to watch something like that as a kid. Then again, he didn't read adult books when he was six either. So he paid careful attention to Owen to see how the boy reacted to things. Also, Owen had a birthday coming up soon, and Craig needed gift ideas. He couldn't woo the kid with books again.

Shay put pancakes onto plates and handed them to Aaron to take to the table. When he dropped one of them, she helped him throw out the floor-pancakes and wipe the plate and start over. Craig was impressed. He'd lived in families where that kind of clumsiness would have been punished. And a three-year-old wouldn't have a chance to even try to set the table.

"Did you make extra?" Craig asked her, wondering if she planned ahead for messes.

"Always." She gave a wry smile as she carefully mopped the spot up with a paper towel, before popping back up to flip the pancakes that were cooking.

When the bacon was done and laid out on paper towels, Craig handed it to Owen to put on the table. Then he prayed the kid didn't drop all that good bacon. Luckily, Owen was more coordinated than his little brother and there was plenty to have with breakfast.

Afterward, Shay made the boys take their plates to the sink. Even Owen couldn't quite reach down into the sink yet and Craig was relieved to see they simply set the plates on the counter. He wasn't sure what that really accomplished, but it seemed to be a routine. When the boys left the room to go play, Shay set down her fork in an ominous manner.

Craig waited. What could happen next? It was Sunday, and Saturday was his only night to sleep over with her. The only one she would allow. Some weeks even that didn't happen. Despite things being better here than in Bristol, she now had both kids all the time. Aside from three daycare days for Aaron, Shay had no relief, no time off from being a mom. No extra time to spend with Craig.

When she took a breath, Craig held his.

"The Nashville Ballet Theatre has asked to see my portfolio."

"That's great." He tried to be enthusiastic. While he was happy for her business success, he saw it as another move away from him, too. That made sincere joy for her harder to summon.

"They want to meet with me on Tuesday." She paused. "And Aaron's daycare is full and Owen gets home off the bus at two and they want to the meeting at two-thirty."

He waited, knowing there was more.

"Kelsey recommended three sitters and they're all busy. I don't know how to ask you to do this, but can you watch the boys so I can make the meeting?" She looked worried.

Craig was about to jump up and down. *Finally, something to do that was useful.* He figured he had to show her something. She was running around being supermom all the time and shutting him out. "Of course I can. What time do you need me?"

"If you can get here at about one forty-five? Aaron will be here. I'll be ready and I'll leave." She shrugged. "I have no idea how long the meeting will go or what traffic will be like on my way back."

He nodded, knowing he had rehearsal that afternoon and that he wouldn't make it. He would simply work something out. Maybe they could take a different day. Or he could be late. He didn't like the idea, but if ever there was a reason to be late, this was it. He'd talk to JD first.

Her shoulders lost some of the tension and she breathed out the words "Thank you so much," as she picked up her plate and headed for the sink. "It's a big load off my worries."

Had she thought he wouldn't do it?

"Can I take them to my house? We can play with the puppies." He hadn't yet broached the subject of bringing the puppies over here.

"Sure." But when she turned to look at him, she looked like she was calculating something. "Who takes care of the dogs when you're here on Sunday mornings?"

"Daniel."

"Daniel Hewlitt? Kelsey and JD's Daniel!?" Her voice was rising.

She was upset, though Craig couldn't fathom why. He just nodded since she was looking right at him and he had no clue what was going on.

"So Kelsey and JD know you spend the night here on Saturday nights?" Her face was red.

"Yes." Why was she embarrassed? Was she upset? "That or they think I cheat on you only on Saturdays."

She didn't find that funny.

"I don't understand, Shay." He frowned at her, wondering how this conversation had turned from him saving her to him somehow throwing her under the bus. "They know we're together. It's not some big secret."

"Yeah, but they know *when*." Shay was really upset about them knowing, but Craig was frustrated by the rest of it.

"That's because you limit us to Saturday nights and the random daytimes when Aaron is in daycare!" He tried to keep his voice low, but his frustration was growing.

"The boys have to get ready for school the other mornings." She was loading dishes into the dishwasher with a little too much force. But what did she have to be upset about? Only her own prudish ideas. Craig held his tongue on saying that. She had no trouble telling people her boys had different fathers, but god forbid someone realize a decent man was staying over.

He shocked himself with that thought. She wasn't even looking as he realized it had taken comparing himself to her two crappy ex-husbands to finally think of himself as a decent man. Then again, it had taken her to get him to even want to stay with one woman. His shoulders sagged. He *wanted* this, and it kept hovering just out of reach. He had enough to taste a life he wanted, but not have the whole thing. The last time he'd had a taste of something so much better than where he'd come from had been the time he and Alex had hooked up with JD and they'd started playing together. When they talked about staying together, not just practicing, but really becoming a group, he'd voted "Hell, yes!" twice. Now here was Shay— another massively better life than the one he thought he was content in—and he was going to reach out for it with both hands.

"Why can't I be here when they're getting ready for school?"

She turned to face him, soapy hands braced on the counter behind her. She didn't look quite as ready to jump in as he was. "We'll get there. But I've thrown a lot at the boys recently. Even you are something totally new to them. They're handling it well and I want to continue that. Let's see how things go."

So Craig let her throw him out at eleven and he went home to Scarlett and Gunnar, who had been taken out in the backyard and walked and more that morning. Craig grinned. Daniel was better than the dog sitter; he worked with them, teaching them to sit and stay. He loved giving the puppies treats and since Craig had limited treats to good behavior, Daniel made sure they performed. Craig was also pretty convinced that the boy was so ecstatic to play with puppies that he stayed until they fell asleep on him.

When he let them out, they romped around the living room a bit, but were apparently still worn out from Daniel's visit that morning. So Craig looked around the place, thinking about what he could do to have more things for Owen and Aaron around. He had nothing. Unless they wanted to play guitar. That thought perked him up, but if they did, he didn't have anything he was about to let the little one touch. After lunch and a backyard visit for the puppies, he hit the store.

Shay had a bin to put toys in. Well, actually she had three. He would start with one. He added a few dolls, a few robots, some kids percussion sets—kids loved drums didn't they? It was where he had started.

He then hit the grocery store. He had things in the fridge for the boys already, which was something that boggled his brain each time he opened the door and the light shone on the juice boxes. Who would have ever thought Craig Hibbets would have juice boxes and would look forward to having two little kids come to his house so he could be completely responsible for them? Well, a year ago he would have laughed if you'd told him he'd be head over heels for two puppies and a woman, let alone kids. So he sucked it up and bought fruit strips, reading the labels just as Shay had pointed out to him. It was a brave new world, apparently just one without high fructose corn syrup.

On Tuesday, Shay called him at one-fifteen, her voice pitched high. Anxiety radiated in waves through the line. "Can you come sooner? I'm not even dressed yet. Aaron's being . . . He's not letting me get ready."

Craig wasn't ready either, but he grabbed his keys as he said, "I'll be there in five minutes."

Then he realized the puppies were out and both sitting diligently, watching the keys, hoping they could go to the park. He sighed, hating to break their little hearts. So he told them, "The boys will be here soon, and that will make up for it."

He raced out the door a few minutes later, arriving at Shay's to find her running back and forth between the bathroom and a screaming kid. *Lovely.*

But as quickly as the thought crossed his mind, it left. This was it. This was his opportunity to show her that he was fine. And honestly, he was. He'd been in facilities where one kid or another was always screaming. Some of them had been truly mentally ill and getting no help. He'd been through far worse than an upset toddler.

Putting his hands on Shay's shoulders, he turned her toward the bathroom. "I've got this. Go."

In the living room he sat down next to Aaron, who had his head thrown back and was screaming. The kid had lungs. Craig leaned in, trying not to get hit by arms that were pumping with rage, clutching the very Legos he'd bought the kid for Christmas. "Why are we crying?"

He had to ask a second time before Aaron sniffed and looked at him, holding out several pieces.

"You want them together, or apart?" Craig asked as the pieces fell into his outstretched hands.

Shay headed out the door just a few moments later, stopping almost frantically to kiss first Aaron, then Craig, on the tops of their heads. Deftly she sidestepped away from Aaron rubbing his still tearstained face on her skirt, then she was out the door almost before Craig could yell, "You look great. Knock'em dead."

"Well," he looked at Aaron. "It's just you and me now." But it was one fifty-five before he knew it, the small start of a Lego building the only evidence of time passage. "We have to go out and wait for Owen."

"On the bus?" Aaron asked him, and they barely made it in time once Craig got them all bundled up to stand out in the cold. Owen hopped down off bus steps that looked almost as tall as he was, and the three of them trundled inside. Owen wanted a snack and insisted on eating it at home, despite Craig's insistence that he had great snacks at his house. *Oh well, fruit strips keep,* he thought.

Somehow, it took half an hour to make the five-minute drive to his house. Then the puppies were unleashed and the new toys in the bin forgotten. All his work and preparation unnecessary in the face of cute, furry creatures.

For seven minutes, things went well.

"No, Aaron." Craig pushed the toddler's hand off Scarlett's tail. "You can't pull her tail."

Then, "Owen, no. That's too many treats." He sighed. "I know you're working with them, but they need to start learning to sit just to sit. Not only for a treat. And they need to eat their dinner, too."

Owen nodded, and sighed, then went over to the treats box. Craig watched as the kid unloaded about half a box of tiny milkbones from his pockets. Jeez, the kid had loaded up. He was glad he caught it early. Even so, Owen unknowingly spilled a few small bones. Though Owen missed it, Scarlett and Gunnar didn't, and they scarfed up the treats as each hit the floor.

Craig told himself they would be okay. Milkbones weren't bad for them and Owen didn't mean to do it. He helped the kid close up the box then put it on top of the refrigerator. As soon as he turned back around, he saw Aaron walking across the room.

Something was suspicious about it, but he couldn't put his finger on it. Three minutes later when Aaron petted Gunnar and left a sticky spot on the dog, Craig turned to the kid. "Aaron, what is that?"

"Mrhphh?"

He had no clue what the kid said, but the red ring around his mouth was telling.

"Aaron, what is that?" When the kid pushed his lips together, Craig held his hand out. In half a second, a hard candy slithered out of Aaron's mouth, plopping into his waiting palm.

Uuugghh. That was disgusting.

He was walking to the sink even as he tried to figure out what it was. "Oh. No, no candy, Aaron."

Grabbing a paper towel and wetting it, he went back to wipe first the boy, then the dog. It took three tries to leave Gunnar with a wet streak instead of a red, slimy candy one. As soon as he had it finished, he turned to find Aaron with his hand in the dish of jolly ranchers that had been out since Halloween. "No. Aaron, *no candy.*"

The boy dropped what he was holding back into the dish and Craig looked frantically at Owen. At least he was doing well, working with Scarlett, even though she seemed to be losing enthusiasm without the treats as reward. But even as he sighed in relief at that sight, Craig turned back to Gunnar.

"Aaron, *no.* You can't pull their tails." This time he took the boy's hand and shook it.

When the kid made a growl of disappointment, or maybe anger, Owen looked at his face. "Why is your face green?"

CHAPTER 34

S hay was so mad she could spit nails.

Yesterday's meeting with the Nashville Ballet Theatre had gone so well she'd wound up staying until five, talking designs with the costumer, discussing fabrics she could order wholesale if they were in big enough batches.

The Theatre had a new director who wanted to take them in a more modern direction. They had a designer who came into the meeting—apparently once Shay passed the initial inspection by the director—and showed Shay the ideas for the costuming.

She'd put on her best game face and told them what she knew and what she understood. At one point, she even told the designer, "My guess is that a gossamer won't hold up to the program. I mean, they're going to really dance in these, right? Do they get on the floor at all?"

The designer, a tall thin woman who had the figure and fashion style of an ex-ballerina herself, looked at Shay down her nose.

Right then, Shay felt the job slip through her fingers, just like the gossamer they'd wind up being disappointed in. Maybe they'd call her back in three months, when the costumes showed dirt from the stage floor and had snags from lifts and from the sequins she also wanted.

"Well, what else will move like that, and be sheer so the light shows through?" The woman asked.

Still in the game apparently, but maybe giving away all her trade secrets, Shay went on to describe how she would make the flowing outfits. By four thirty, they'd offered her the job. And it had taken until five to discuss what they wanted, what colors were necessary and what could be changed due to pricing of options. They worked out some deadlines and fitting times, with Shay taking furious notes.

Then she'd gone to Craig's to pick up the boys and offer to take everyone out for pizza. She could afford it now. Ecstatic, she'd used her key and thrown open the door to find Craig looking like he'd survived a tornado.

In the middle of the living room sat a new bin full of toys. Owen was on the couch, curled up with his kindle, while Craig and Aaron played with a swank set of drums. They didn't even hear her until she yelled. Despite the fact that Craig was obviously trying to win her kids over with cool toys, she'd felt tired and elated. She couldn't compete, but she could get them all pizza now. It was only later, as she'd put them to bed, that the boys had told her what happened while she was out.

She hadn't slept at all. It had been a trial all morning, to seem chipper and easygoing in front of the kids when she'd been anything but. Eventually, she dropped Aaron off at daycare and, even though she should have been online ordering bolts of fabric, she was trying not to speed to Craig's house or squeal her tires in the driveway. This time, she knocked. And knocked, and knocked again, until a sleepy-headed Craig came to open the door.

"Hey," he smiled and greeted her, "Why didn't you use your key?"

Then he blinked. Must have gotten a good look at her face.

Not wanting to do this on the front stoop, she walked in, trying to hold her anger back. She didn't want to make judgments, but she was pissed.

"What's wrong?" He was frowning now, much more awake and focusing on her.

She blurted it out. "Did you hit Aaron?"

He jerked back as though she'd slapped him. "No." He shook his head at her, like she was crazy.

Her heart rate started to settle. "Because Aaron said you hit him."

Craig managed to look even more offended. "No. I didn't hit him." Then he paused. "Is he talking about when I smacked his hand?"

"You smacked him!?" Her blood boiled again. That time it was just an accusation more than a question. She couldn't see straight. Clearly, he had done it. He was the one who brought it up. "You can't hit a child, Craig!"

His face changed. This time he no longer looked offended, just confused. "I didn't *hit* him, Shay. There's a big difference."

"Not in my book, there's not. You can't hit him!" Her fists clenched. Her breathing and heart rate jacked up. Her mouth opened, and words spewed out, she was so furious. "You don't touch my kids! Do you hear me?"

He jerked back. "Shay, it wasn't like that."

She felt her eyes narrow, saw that he saw the anger in her, and she yelled. "You have no right! You may not think it's anything, but my little boy only knows that you hit him! You don't know what it's like to have someone bigger than you and stronger than you hurt you."

His mouth fell open. For a moment Craig just stared at her.

Her lungs heaved with anger, and she wondered why fire didn't shoot out with her breath. Then his expression changed. Craig's face mottled and his own hands formed fists at his side.

"What the fuck are you talking about, Shay? Do you hear

246

yourself?" His words weren't loud like hers, but low, deep. Only then did she realize her mistake.

Craig didn't let her speak though, didn't let her try to take that back. *"I don't know?* Are you serious? Do you know how many nights I prayed I would grow taller or stronger so I could fight back?"

She stepped back. She'd stepped in it and it was her own fault.

He didn't advance on her, but he didn't shut up either. "I know Jason hit you, I know he beat you up. But . . ." He paused as though he wasn't going to say it, but then he did. "You think I would hit a child? You can fuck off!"

Her head snapped back then, and stayed back with the spew that fell from his mouth. "I get it. It sucks what Jason did to you. It's awful, and I don't want to make light of it, but you have no fucking clue. You were a grown woman. You could have left at any time. You could have chosen someone else and not gotten involved with that asshole in the first place. I was five, Shay. *Five.* It's one of my earliest fucking memories, having that asshole beat on me. And I was smaller than Owen is now."

He sucked in a breath even as Shay felt the pressure of tears behind her eyes. She'd stepped in it for sure. But now her anger had turned to anger *for* Craig, not *at* him.

"He was the one who was supposed to be taking care of me. And when I started to say something, my case worker told me how happy I should be that I was there. Later, when it happened again with another family, I ran away. I went back to the family that had been good to me. I told them about it. And *they sent me back.* They didn't believe me." He breathed in again, almost pacing a short circle in the room, not looking at her as he talked. It made it a little easier to take, but then he focused on her face again, and it felt like physical touch to her.

"So don't you dare come into my house and accuse me of *hitting* a child. And don't you even for one second drag out that shit about abused people becoming abusers. You'll fall right down that same damn rabbit hole, sweetheart."

The last word was not an endearment but an indictment.

She saw his eyes blink as though he were fighting back something too big for him. His shoulders heaved, his fists clenched and opened, but she could see there was no violence in him. Her own shoulders heaved and sagged and when he turned and stared at her, his eyes glassy and hurt at her betrayal, she felt her own tears tip and fall.

"I'm sorry." But she only mouthed the words. Sound wouldn't come out, even when she tried again.

He'd turned away and was shaking his head like he had something awful in him to get out. Feeling like complete shit, she crossed the room to him. As she reached up to put her hand on his shoulder, he shrugged away, somehow knowing she was there.

It was a punch in the gut. She remembered that. The subtle, small movements, involuntary twitches that pulled you away from someone you thought would strike you. She deserved it. She'd stormed in here, full of anger and righteousness, both guns blazing. So she reached out and took his hand in hers and tugged him toward the couch. When he resisted, she pulled harder, until he sat down beside her. He didn't touch her, not even the brush of a knee against hers. It might not be conscious, but it was deliberate. She knew that, too.

She'd sat on a couch much like this, swollen lip, handprint blooming on her arm, hip growing sore from hitting the corner of some piece of furniture. She'd stayed still while Jason apologized, words in her ears that she swore she wouldn't listen to.

Never had she thought she'd be the one on this side of the couch. What she'd done was nowhere near as bad as what had been done to her, she knew that, but the very dynamic of it frightened her. She *owed* him an apology.

"I'm sorry." This time the words came out clear.

The other side of the couch was a hard place to be, too, apparently. She'd been coddled and manipulated enough to know she didn't want to do it. Craig had probably never been apologized to. Jesus, he didn't even have that, didn't even have someone who told him he was loved and that they were sorry when it happened to him. She reminded herself not to be manipulative, but to be clear.

"I shouldn't have accused you of that. I really am sorry."

He nodded. But that was all. His eyes stayed straight ahead, focused on the front door.

"I was scared. I've worked so hard to protect them from what I experienced. Owen even saw it when he was an infant and I don't know how much of it got through. He doesn't seem to remember it." She sighed, as though her explanation just might make sense to anyone other than her. But Craig nodded, and she kept going. "Owen and Aaron heard the way Brian talked to me. He was almost neglectful of Owen."

She felt the punch of Craig's still silent response. "And you're right, I *could* have left. I didn't see it at the time. But I put myself —and eventually my boys—in those positions. So please understand that I feel so very guilty about that, and I've worked hard every day to make up for being a bad mother to them then."

He nodded again, then he spoke, his words pushed out as though rubbed across sandpaper. "I understand that. But I wouldn't hurt your kids, Shay."

This time, she was the one who nodded. "But I don't spank them or smack them. I talk to them. I put them on time out. I have to be sure you won't do that again."

He shook his head, not as if to say 'no, he wouldn't do it' but as if she were trying his patience. He didn't say anything, and she was out of words, so they sat in silence for long moments that drew out into eternity. She was considering getting up and leaving when he finally said something. The rasp of his voice telling her she'd hurt him deep.

"You know, you left me with them and you told me when to pick up Owen at the bus stop and what to feed them, but you didn't tell me this. How was I supposed to know?" He turned and looked at her, truly asking why she thought he should have been psychic about this topic.

She didn't know, and a shrug was all she could offer.

"You know, you've had six years to get this all down. I've had six weeks."

CHAPTER 35

It took Shay three days to convince Craig to come back to her house, to spend Saturday night with them like he always did. Even if it meant calling Kelsey and Daniel. Even if it meant Kelsey and JD knew when she was having sex and when she wasn't. As if that wasn't embarrassing enough, she had to nearly beg to get him back.

He was still angry. Or hurt. Or maybe both.

With Craig, it was sometimes hard to tell. With this situation, she deserved every bit of anger he was throwing her way. She knew it. It was fully her fault that she hadn't told him what her boundaries were, what the boys were used to. So she went about trying to make it up to him.

As he woke up in bed next to her, gloriously naked, she pushed up on her elbows and stroked his chest. "What do you want for breakfast?"

"More of what I had last night." He grinned at her. Real and deep, it helped push her heart back into place, sweep out some of the lingering fear that she'd screwed up too badly.

She was leaning over to kiss him when a knock came at the door. "Mommy?"

Her eyes looked to the ceiling. "Timing is everything. Get dressed and I'll make you food. It's the best I can offer."

Tugging the covers over that fabulous body of his, she rolled out of bed and called out. "Coming."

She was already dressed. She had two small kids, and you didn't lie in bed naked when someone might knock on your door at any minute during the night. Or worse, just open a door you might have forgotten to lock. Sneaking through the door, she slid it shut behind her and looked down at her youngest. "What do you need, punkin?"

"I'm thirsty." He rubbed his eyes, though she suspected by the noise coming up from the living room that he and Owen had gotten up and turned on the TV a while ago.

She headed down the steps and checked the station as she passed by. Totally kid appropriate. Well, she'd slept in an extra half hour later than usual. That had to be marked as progress, right?

She poured milk in a cup and snapped on a lid and straw almost automatically before handing it to him. Then she checked the fridge. She had plenty of eggs and lots of random stuff. Omelets, then. Opening the vegetable drawer, she found breakfast sausage, because who put vegetables in there anyway?

Well, apparently Craig did. While her fridge had bare patches, his was always stocked to the hilt these days. It hadn't been when it had just been her coming around, but now it had finger foods and three flavors of juice boxes. Even she didn't keep three kinds on hand.

She wondered if he was trying to buy her kids' affections even as she set the eggs on the counter and started pulling out anything she could chop to add in. There was that new bin of toys in his living room. There was a kid's guitar, too. It had arrived after their fight, and when she asked about it, he told her he'd ordered it the week before.

The parenting books on his bedside table still rotated,

though she noticed some of them didn't last long. Maybe she needed to be going through them, giving him more input.

"Morning." His voice behind her as he greeted the boys startled her. She hadn't heard him come down.

Turning, she smiled at him. "Are omelets good? With sausage?"

"Sounds great." He smiled back but his attention was on Aaron. "What show is this?"

It took a moment to turn away from watching him patiently listen to Aaron's description of what was a relatively dumb kid's program. He'd dressed in the change of clothes he'd brought with him, refusing to leave anything here. She got the impression that he didn't like the rental townhouse so much. And he didn't like the idea of her buying a house either. But she truly had no idea what else to do.

She needed the house. She needed to own something, to give her boys something more permanent than they'd ever had. But she needed the man on the couch, too. And she couldn't afford a house big enough for all of them. Not one that would fit a man of his means and talent. His house had three bedrooms, and one was a small music room. She was still debating if she could give her boys separate rooms or give herself a sewing office.

With a sigh, she pulled her gaze away from the man on the couch. She turned her focus to the kitchen, her brain secure in the understanding that her kids really were safe with Craig. She chopped and diced and then took individual orders for omelets.

Though breakfast went well, she could feel the tension had come back into Craig now that he had rolled out of bed. He thanked her for cooking, put his dishes in the sink and kissed her on the forehead. Though he touched each of the kids before he went—a rub on the head for Aaron, a hand on the shoulder for Owen—it was a little absent. He went upstairs to grab his things from her room and then waved goodbye at the front door.

Then he was gone.

It didn't feel right, though she didn't know what 'right' really felt like. There were times she'd had it, and she hadn't paid enough attention to know what was different now. Each time she'd had it had been with Craig, though, and she knew enough to know she needed to get it back.

Nothing she could do right now though. So she went about their usual Sunday routine. They did the grocery shopping for the week, picking out things for packed lunches—five for Owen, three for Aaron. As she made the boys decide together on one flavor of juice boxes, she thought of Craig's stash, but quickly put her jealousy out of her mind. When they got home, they packed lunches in bags to be quickly put into the one cooler style lunchbox each boy had. They planned a few dinners, then cleaned the boys' bedroom with Shay doing most of the work. After that, they picked out clothing for the week and did as much as they could ahead of time. All the things a single mom learned to make life as smooth as possible during the week.

She called Zoe to check in on her little sister. Not that Zoe needed it, but it was something Shay liked to do. She wound up confessing. "Zee, I went into his house, guns blazing, and accused him of hitting my kid."

Zoe didn't know the whole truth about Craig's past, and Shay didn't tell it. She was pretty sure she'd mentioned he grew up in foster care, but she'd told no more of it than that. He didn't run around telling people about it, so neither would she.

There was a pause. Even not knowing the whole truth about Craig's past, Zoe gave him more credit than Shay had. "Do you really think he'd hurt Aaron? Because if you do, then you shouldn't have had him over last night. And never again. But I really don't get that impression of him."

"The only impression you have of him is the one I've told you." Her words were a little harsh, but it pissed her off that her sister was reading the situation better than she had. "Aaron told me Craig hit him."

"Honey."

Oh shit. Shay didn't think she ever liked what Zoe had to say when she started by calling her older sister 'honey.' This proved to be no different.

"Aaron is small and has no vocabulary to explain what happened. Craig is an adult that you've tangled yourself up with for over six months now. You've never complained about him before."

"Yes, I have!" Shay returned. It irked her that Zoe seemed to see things more clearly right from the start.

"No, you only complained when you thought he was being too good to you, or you designed some ulterior motive when he really seemed to have none. This is on you. You have to consider the source, and yours is a toddler. Did you even ask Craig what happened?"

"Eventually." She felt her shoulders slump. Zoe was right. She'd been a complete tool. If she was honest, she still didn't know what happened. What she did know was what he'd volunteered in self-defense and it wasn't the whole story, only that he'd just smacked fingers. Not why. Not how.

After she hung up with Zoe, she felt worse than she had before. She went through the motions of putting the boys to bed, going in later and taking the Kindle out of Owen's hands and insisting he get some sleep.

He really needed his own room. No sewing room, she figured. Maybe she'd get lucky and find a house with a den, or an eat-in kitchen and she could use the dining room for her own. She'd figure it out. She'd been figuring it out, step-by-step, from the moment she'd left Brian and decided she didn't need a man to make her whole. From the second she'd decided that her kids were better off with just her than with a father who wasn't a good one.

She sent them off to school and pre-school on Monday, then pulled out her supplies and started sewing a set of clothing—matching fabric, unique designs—for the band that she'd taken a contract for. Up to her neck in orders, which was a good thing, she didn't have time to head over to Craig's and try to make things right. As it was, she was simply grateful that the Ballet wanted a fabric she had to order and she couldn't even start those pieces yet.

Instead, she texted him.

—Can the boys and I come over tomorrow afternoon? Would love to see you. Play with the puppies. Let me know.

It took a while for him to respond. —ok. After 3. I have rehearsal.

She looked forward to it, proud of herself for making everything work out. She could see Craig, see him with the boys, and not lose sewing time, because she couldn't sew in the hours after school anyway. But when they arrived, he paid more attention to the kids than to her.

It wasn't clear if he was trying to show her how good he was with them or if he was ignoring her. The more she tried to strike up a conversation with him, the more he answered in monosyllables. Besides, she had her hands full with Aaron.

"No. You can't pull the dog's tail. It's not nice." She told him. Three minutes later, she was pushing his hand away again. "*No*. You can't pull her ears either. You can't pull anything on the dog."

So he tried to push her into a position he wanted. Like Owen was doing. But Owen was training Scarlett. He'd given her a command, he was gentle. Aaron was doing no such thing. No commands, no nothing, just pushing the dog around. "Aaron, you can't play with the puppies anymore."

It took about three minutes for Craig to see that telling Aaron not to play with a creature that wanted to play with him was too much. He scooped up both the puppies and put them in their crate. Then Owen got mad.

"I didn't do anything wrong! Why can't I play with them!?"

"I'm sorry." Craig knelt down in front of him, having a whole conversation with her oldest. "I can't put one of them in the crate, but not the other. They go together."

Owen headed into meltdown mode then, and she had a hard time being too upset at him. He'd been gypped. So she sighed heavily and packed her kids up. "I'm sorry we're having to leave so soon."

He shrugged. It was no big deal. He didn't really seem to care. Fissures and cracks formed in her heart as he spoke. "I have to pack anyway. Wilder is out of town the next few days."

"On tour?" She was shocked. She hadn't heard about this. She thought the next leg of the tour was in two weeks.

"No, just a round of radio station interviews and such."

"Will you be back Saturday?" She was wondering if he'd stay over when he nodded. "So maybe we could all do something then?"

"Sure." Back to monosyllables.

She made it through the rest of the week. While he called her once from the road, the conversation was short. It wasn't like the easy, flowing hours they'd been on line when he was touring. Shay was getting frustrated. Why couldn't he forgive her?

So she put her best effort in on Saturday. They arrived with cupcakes; she knew he liked strawberry with white icing. They walked the puppies around the block. This time Shay held Aaron's hand. She didn't know why he'd gotten so touchy with the dogs lately, but he'd gotten a bit pushy with everything.

Just the day before, she'd found him on the floor after Owen shoved him. The whole story had turned out that Owen was reading and Aaron had come up and hit him with his plastic bat.

"He almost broke my kindle, Mom! It's not okay."

When she'd offered to buy him a new one if Aaron broke it, Owen had yelled again. "I like *this one.* You can't just buy another one and think it's okay. This one has all my books."

She told him all his books would transfer, but he still held firm. *This one.* It was *his.* Aaron didn't have a right to hit him, and he would push back if he felt he should.

Strong words for a six-year-old. Big concerns for his mother. Sadly, he had a point. Not a complete one, but partly a good one. So she held Aaron's hand tight, even when he squirmed to be let go. Craig volunteered to carry him for a minute. But when Aaron tried to wiggle out, Craig stopped him, earning him a fist on the shoulder.

She watched as Craig grabbed her son's fist. "*No.* You can't hit people."

Aaron got angry and Shay took him back, fighting with him the rest of the way around the block. At least Owen was having a good time.

The cold was too much and they played in the living room with some of the new toys Craig had bought them. He'd put the puppies in their crate again, much to Owen's dismay. But instead of letting her son curl up in a fictional world, he pulled out the new kid's guitar and started teaching him how to play.

Aaron, angry at not being included, hit the guitar as Owen held it.

Shay had to pull him away. She tried to distract him, and eventually got him settled down with the drums. She shrugged at Owen and Craig as Aaron's non-rhythmic noise interfered with the lesson. At least he wasn't touching anything else.

She'd gotten up to get a drink, finally glad that everyone had settled back down, when she heard the noise. Turning the corner to see into the living room, she caught only a bit of the action.

But it was enough to see that Craig had tackled Aaron and angrily had him on the ground.

CHAPTER 36

Craig was in the backyard with the puppies when he heard the front lock twist. Heading up the steps to the small back porch, he looked through the sliding glass doors to see Kelsey and Daniel come in.

She waved at him as he opened the door, stepping inside, then she frowned. "Are we not supposed to be here?"

Shit. He was supposed to be at Shay's. "No, I forgot to call you and cancel. I'm so sorry."

He hated disappointing Kelsey. She'd done so much for all of them. Just one of those naturally open, giving people, she never hesitated to help him or just be there. But she seemed more concerned for him. It was Daniel who looked disappointed.

Craig turned to the kid. "Why don't you go out and play with them? Do what you usually do. No worries. I'll still pay you." He grinned, thinking that was a good solution.

Though Daniel moved toward the door, he didn't seem much happier. Craig frowned a minute, then realized the problem. "Daniel? You still have a job on Sundays. You're welcome over here any time."

SAVANNAH KADE

That perked him up, making Craig happier. Though to say he was happy was too far out of reality for him. As Daniel stepped outside to much barking, Kelsey stepped forward. "Are you okay?"

"I am." He breathed it out.

"What about Shay?"

"She's okay, too, I'm sure." The words were hard. Kelsey picked up on all that he didn't say.

"Oh." Her face fell. She looked sad for him. "I'm so sorry. I was afraid something was up when I saw your car in the driveway. Then you didn't answer when we knocked and I got worried you weren't even up."

"I'm up." Just like before, it wasn't the answer to her real question. But she understood. He motioned to his old, holey sweats, no longer appropriate now that he wasn't alone. "If Daniel has the puppies under control, I'm going to go change. Make yourself at home."

He came back out in jeans and a thermal shirt with some design on it that had appealed to him in the store. His clothing was soft, his bare feet warm in the heat of the house, and Kelsey was taking care of him, making hot cocoa for Daniel and mixing it with coffee for him. She then mixed the tail end of it into her own cocoa.

"Coffee, huh?" He took the mug while nodding to her belly, glad for something other than Shay to think about.

"I'm allowed one cup a day. And I treasure it with everything I have." She grinned. "JD's been really good about getting the kids out from underfoot and getting me some alone and quiet time each day. He's been taking really great care of me."

She seemed both content in her soul and the kind of happy that came with something like a gift. "Well, you take really great care of him, too. He knows that."

Her smile was both grateful and sad. She'd been rooting for

260

him and Shay. He knew it. But this last hurdle was too big to get over. "I'm so sorry, Craig. You deserve so much more."

When she and Daniel left, he pondered that. He didn't know if he deserved more, but he'd lost belief in a just world a long time ago. So whether or not he deserved it, he thought he might be able to find it. He just had to get over Shay first. He couldn't find something that would last while he was still pining away for something that wouldn't.

He and Shay had taken hit after hit, and he was tired. Especially when the hits were all at her hands. All based on circumstance. The circumstance was that she had young kids. That wasn't going to change. He couldn't change it and he clearly couldn't fix it. He'd put his best foot forward and had gotten right back to square one.

Now, of course, she lived in his town. In his area of town. He was going to run into her sooner or later. If nothing else, she'd turn up at anything Hailey invited them to. He would probably avoid those get-togethers. He didn't want to see her; he just wanted to find a way to put his heart back together.

Restless, he tried hooking the dogs up to their leashes. But they didn't even get up. As usual, Daniel had worn them out. That was a good thing, but not what he wanted. He unclipped them, earning a bark from Gunnar that startled him.

"Hey! That was a real bark!" The puppy's voice had dropped. After twenty minutes of trying to see if Scarlett could offer up a real watch-dog bark, or if Gunnar could do it again, he gave up.

Picking his guitar out of the cradle, Craig sat down on the couch and started mapping out tunes. But even that didn't help.

He spent the rest of the week in a daze. He made it to rehearsal and did his part. When TJ invited him out for drinks, he tried it, but wound up catching a cab home early. His heart wasn't in it and his head wasn't in any game at all.

Shay didn't call or text. He wasn't surprised. She'd seen him tackle her errant child and she'd picked up both boys and left, appalled. She didn't want an explanation. Didn't care about his side of things.

He went to the gym a lot. Ate only a little, and spent a lot of time with his guitar and with his dogs. When the knock came at his door on Friday, he just answered it, never suspecting it was Shay.

"Oh." He stood stunned in the doorway. He was shocked by her very presence as much as by her red eyes.

She pushed past him and into the living room, waiting patiently while he closed the door behind her. When he turned to look at her, wondering what she wanted, she only said, "I'm late."

"Then you should go." He headed back to the door to open it, then stopped dead at her next words.

"No. *Late* as in: I might be pregnant."

Frozen, he faced the front door where he'd been aiming.

No. The word rang through his head on endless loop as his brain tried to process the meanings. He tried to find a way out.

Turning, he asked her, "Are you late often?"

"I've only been late two or three times ever." Her face stayed set in a rigid neutral expression. She was waiting on him.

That math—she had two kids, after all—didn't add up in his favor. He thought about talking around it, but he'd had enough talking around things with her. "You have to get rid of it."

She jerked back as if he'd slapped her. "No. I can't do that."

"Trust me. You don't want this kid." He turned away, the bones behind his face felt like they were cracking and breaking. His lungs collapsed inward from the pressure of the conversation, the insult of her presence when she didn't even want him back.

He'd thought he only had to get over her, but no. He was going to have to rip out his own heart, unbury secrets long dead, and hand them to her. She didn't even love him anymore. How could he count on her to keep his past to herself?

He couldn't. But she couldn't have that child. She was already talking and he hadn't been listening.

"—don't expect anything from you. I'll raise it myself."

He laughed at her, a harsh bitter sound that rang hollow in the air. "You can't do that and you know it. You can barely afford a house for the three of you. You can't afford another kid. What will it do to your boys?"

She just breathed in. "You won't help?"

"No. Because you shouldn't have it." He barked at her, not bothering to explain more when she wasn't even listening.

"Well, just because you don't want this child doesn't mean I don't. I can't believe you, of all people would throw a child away." She was marching toward the door, her hand on the knob when he spoke again.

"I'll cover any costs with taking care of the problem now. But you can't have it." He took a deep breath. He'd hoped she would just agree with him, or maybe do it because she was mad at him, or couldn't afford it. But no, she was Shay, stubborn and butt-headed all the time about the way she wanted things done. He was going to have to rip his carefully covered past to shreds to make her stop. "You can't have a child with my genetics."

She stopped, not opening the door, and turned. "What do you mean?"

He tried again to not have to explain in any detail. "You don't want a child with my genes. This is the best course of action."

She didn't take it. "Why?"

So he began the painful process of unraveling things he'd kept locked up tight for so long. He turned away, unable to look at her while he talked. "You know, I was a cute kid. Probably not any worse-behaved than any other, and I was available for adoption from day one. Not one of those kids that came on the market after they were already damaged. No one took me because I was ruined from the very start."

She didn't speak. Didn't say "okay, I guess you're right and I shouldn't do this."

He had to keep talking until he convinced her. "I saw my file when I was ten. I wasn't supposed to; I don't even know if I'd know my history today if I hadn't snuck a look one time. My biological father is unknown, the only thing we do know about him is that he raped a fifteen-year-old girl. I'm that child."

CHAPTER 37

C raig watched as Shay stared at him for a minute.
   "Jesus, Craig." She whispered.

He turned and stared at her. "That's what's in me. I'm a rapist's kid. No one would adopt me when I was even an infant because of it. You don't want that in your child."

She didn't speak for a while and he stood there breathing heavily, watching everything he'd thought he was building collapsing around him in slow motion. He didn't think of it much. Didn't think of what he was in the center of every cell. Ignored it, hoping it would go away. He'd gotten some grand plan to raise Shay's kids. But brick by brick, it was all falling away.

Her words were a whisper. "So it's in your file, but do you know that it was true?"

He just stared at her. "How would it not be true? Wouldn't my case-worker have done something about it if it wasn't?"

"She was fifteen?" Shay asked as she plopped down on the couch. She crumpled there as though her legs couldn't withstand the topic. He understood.

He nodded.

"In those days—well, even now—it's not okay for a fifteen-year-old girl to wind up pregnant. Do you think maybe she said that to justify being fifteen and knocked up?" She asked, her hands worrying together in her lap. "Maybe you were her boyfriend's child and she couldn't tell her parents."

"Hate to dash your hopes, sweetheart, but that's not what I'm made of." He could see she was grasping at straws, trying to keep from believing she carried a child with that history. "There's a police report on it. She was kidnapped and beaten bloody. She's lucky she survived."

Shay cringed as he spoke, but he kept going, driving nails into any hopes that she'd see reason. "They did a kit. His DNA is on file in case anyone ever catches him."

She cringed again, but he didn't have room to let up.

"No one ever caught him, but years later, when I was aged out of the system and my file became my own, I looked into it. They did match his DNA. Guess what they matched it to?" He was leaning in, angry that she'd made him open this old, scarred wound. Angry that she would never just believe him and let it go. So he pushed some of that mad off onto her.

She shook her head. No words.

Good. Maybe it was soaking in.

"He matched to over twenty other aggravated rapes. Four times he killed his victim in the process."

Her face turned white.

"That's just what they found. So it's probably a hell of a lot worse. That's in me. That's *half* of what I'm made up of. Do you want that in your kid? *Do you?*" He pushed, no longer caring that she was near to tears.

She shook her head at him, tears rolling down her cheeks. He wished she'd just get up and leave. Leave him. Leave him alone. She didn't want him, and coming back around and throwing this shit at him was just mean. So he threw it back at her.

"I trusted you. You said you were on birth control. You told me you had it covered. So don't expect me to take this. You take care of it! There shouldn't be any more of that awful man out in the world than there already is! Get rid of it."

"I can't." She whispered.

"You have to! Do you know what it's like to be me? To know that I have that in every last part of me? You can't do that to a kid." He was almost begging her. He almost hated her.

"I won't tell." Another whisper. Less conviction though.

"Great, so the kid's dad has the worst history in the world and the mom is a liar? They won't just hate themselves, they'll hate you, too, when they find out."

She glared at him. He glared back.

"You fucked it up. You fix it, Shay."

For a few minutes, she sat silently on the couch, tears dripping down her cheeks. He wanted to hold her, tell her it would be okay. That this was the best option given the horrible circumstances. He did not want to carry that man's DNA. He couldn't change the fact that he did, but he could change this before it happened.

But she didn't want him to hold her. Once again, they'd wound up on opposite sides of things. He paced the room while she sat there. His brain whirling. Didn't they always wind up on opposite sides of things?

When he wanted to date, she said she couldn't. When he wanted her to move in, she wanted her own house without him. When he wanted to help with her kids, she didn't like the way he did it. Her voice finally came to him, breaking the melancholy of his thoughts.

"You may have that DNA in you, but you aren't like that." The words were soft, floating along behind him.

"I have it. And the truth is, you don't know what I have in me." He put his hands on his hips, hearing the puppies whining from where they'd hid under the table when he and Shay started to fight. They were big enough now that they couldn't just run under the rungs between the legs of the chairs. Like any other parent, his gaze strayed to them, checking on them. He always felt better seeing they were okay. "But Shay, no one wanted a baby with that. Why would you want it now?"

"You're still half your mother." She said. As though that made up for it.

"I don't know anything about her. Even if she was some unlucky angel, I'm still half monster." He shrugged.

"You aren't!" She stood up as she protested, coming over to hug him. As if that would make him feel better.

He shrugged her arms off of him. "You don't believe it."

"Yes, I do." She stood there, hands at her sides, seeming unsure what to do with them in the face of the argument.

"No, you don't!" He blew up then. "You think I'm a monster who hits your kids! You packed them up so fast that I couldn't blink. You didn't speak to me and you didn't come back here until you needed something from me."

He took a deep breath. "Well, I need something from *you*. I need you not to have this kid. I need you to not link us together for the next eighteen years, because I can't handle it."

"Craig." She reached out to touch his shoulder, but he turned and walked away. "Craig." This time she said it with more force, and waited for him to turn around before she said more. "I talked to Owen."

"So? I'm happy for you."

"He told me that you only smacked Aaron's hands. And he told me what Aaron was doing to deserve it." She put her palms out as if to say she was sorry. But Craig didn't care.

"Oh, so it's okay if you hear it from a six-year-old, but not from me? That warms my heart." He pushed his lips together to keep more painful and hurtful things from spilling forth.

"He told me Aaron was stealing candy."

"He was."

268

"So why didn't you put it away?" She tipped her head forward, like she really wanted to know.

"Now? You want to talk about this *now*? You've already tried and convicted me based on the words of a three-year-old, and now you want to know?" He looked at her face, tear stained and sad. But his own had to convey his disbelief.

"I did do that. And I'm trying to be better about it now."

"Because you might be pregnant. Did you take a test?"

She shook her head. "Not yet. Honestly, I only realized it last night. So I wanted to come here first. I was hoping we could work things out."

He couldn't work things out. Not after the way she'd just dismissed him. Not when the reason she wanted to work things out wasn't him. It was never about him, so he told her. "I did put the candy away. I put it in a drawer, and then he snuck it from there, too."

"You told him 'no'?"

"No, Shay." Sarcasm dripped from his lips. "*I gave him candy left and right then I smacked him for taking it.* Don't be stupid."

That was when she flinched. He felt bad about doing it, about calling her stupid, but not bad enough to apologize. "He wouldn't stop."

"Did you put him on time-out?"

"Of course, I did. He wouldn't stay. And Owen didn't deserve to suffer for me sitting on Aaron for his bad behavior. He'd already lost time with the puppies. I had to keep taking things away from Owen when Aaron was bad. That's horrible. I had to put the puppies in the bedroom, just like it happened on Saturday because Aaron wouldn't leave them alone."

That seemed to get her attention. "He's been acting out lately. I told you, this has been a big transition for them."

"I'm sure it has been. But you letting him get away with it isn't helping at all. It's just turning him into more of a brat." Craig lashed out at her. He liked the kid. He really did. But it was hard to love Aaron when he was fighting with everyone and everything and making them suffer for it. Shay wouldn't let Craig do anything to stop it either.

"He's not a brat. He's three." She protested, angry now.

Good. It was easier to not want her when he was angrier at her.

"He's turning into a brat, Shay."

"He is not—"

"Shay." He interrupted her. "He hit me! He balled up his fist and *hit* me when we were out for a walk."

"And I took care of it." She protested again.

"No. You didn't. You took him from me. What did he learn? He learned 'hit Craig and then hit Mom.' I saw him hit you, too. You just moved his hand. No wonder he didn't stop." He was incredulous.

"He'll quit." She seemed so certain.

"When? Why would he?"

"Look, it worked with Owen."

Craig's mouth fell open. "Have you met your children? Owen is a very different kid than Aaron. Just because Aaron is three doesn't mean you can't see his personality. He wants to get into everything, he's curious. He needs a path for that and he needs to be shown when his methods are wrong or dangerous."

"*What!*" She was shouting now, making Scarlett and Gunnar whine slightly from their spot under the table. "You read a few parenting books and suddenly you're an expert? On *my* kids?"

"No, Shay." He backed down a bit. "I'm telling you what I saw. He pulled the puppies' tails and ears and wouldn't quit. They aren't toys to be taken away or put back on a shelf! I had to punish *my* kids because *your* kid couldn't play nicely with them. I should have put *him* away, but there was nowhere to do it, and he won't stay. Do you know what made Aaron behave better?" He was yelling again, but he didn't care. "When I smacked his hand. Not hard, but enough to let him know he had to quit.

Enough so that he knew I wasn't going to sit around like a pansy-ass and let a toddler walk all over me! He's smart, Shay. He knows exactly what he can get away with. And you know what? He had a good time once he shaped up."

"I—"

"Shut up." He leaned in toward her. He'd had enough of her protests, enough of her telling him he wasn't good enough. "I'm not going to make anyone else suffer for Aaron's bad behavior. Not my dogs, and certainly not Owen. Aaron's not like Owen. Telling him 'no' and putting him on time-out are nice ideas, but they don't affect Aaron. If you'd been watching him, you might have seen that." He'd been reading the parenting manuals. He had prepped himself to be the best he could be at it. He did not mention that some of what he thought was good had come from the dog training book. But the part about big breeds and training applied. "The thing is, Shay, he's three now. And you're not stopping him from hitting people. Not you, not me, not Owen! What happens when he gets bigger and he doesn't know not to hit? What then?"

She didn't have an answer.

He wasn't sure his diatribe called for one, but he sure wasn't done. "What about what happened Saturday?"

"I have no idea." Though she'd listened, her face flinching as some of his remarks had no doubt hit home, she was angry again. "All I know is you took my kid to the ground over some imaginary infraction, and he hit his head on the floor."

"Yeah, he did. Good thing, too."

Her mouth fell open.

"Shay, he got a coat hanger from the closet. I told him to put it back. He did. Or he said he did. Then he got it out again. Since I'm not allowed to do anything other than say 'No, Aaron, please don't do that,' he got it out again and played with it. I put it back and closed the damned door. Then I saw him trying to poke it into the fucking outlet! That's what I stopped. I stopped him from electrocuting himself! So I'm glad he hit his head and that's all it was!"

He expected her to absorb that. She didn't.

"Why weren't you watching him!?" She yelled.

"Why weren't *you!*" He hollered back. "You were here, too. Why didn't you take it away from him? Where were *you* when your toddler was trying to stick a coat hanger in an outlet?"

"You should have had outlet covers!" She was furious.

Just like that, he deflated. He was wrong. He should have had outlet covers. He hadn't child-proofed the house. He nodded. "I should have."

He waited a beat, then spoke again. "We can't have anything, Shay. You hide your kids behind your skirts, putting yourself in between any chance of them and me getting to be anything better than acquaintances. And you put them in between anything more growing out of this thing between us. You keep doing it. You keep blocking any path to something better. So don't come here and expect me to be happy about some pregnancy I don't want and didn't agree to. Don't expect me to want another kid for you to hold against me."

"I'm sorry." She whispered, moving toward the door. "It's just that my boys are the most important people in the world to me."

"Trust me. You've made that very clear." He turned and opened the front door. His dogs had suffered enough, listening to them yell. Like always, nothing was solved. "I think you should go."

CHAPTER 38

S hay had marched out to her car and driven madly home, furious with Craig. What had she been thinking? She'd gone over there with a possible pregnancy as an olive branch and she'd been batted back. He didn't even want her to be pregnant, and he wanted nothing to do with her or the kid if she had it.

Once she turned that over in her head, she plopped down on the couch and cried her eyes out. Probably pregnancy hormones. She needed to take a test, but didn't know where to go. She should drive into Nashville proper, it felt like she saw all the same people in these suburbs. Almost like Bristol. Here her next door neighbor worked at the Walgreens down the street. So she couldn't go grab a pregnancy test there. And not at Kroger, either. She'd probably run into Kelsey.

She cried harder.

To top it off, Craig had a point. She'd given her other two kids some pretty bad starts genetically speaking, but she sure hadn't anticipated Craig's background. No wonder he didn't get adopted. Though she might not completely agree with his logic, he wasn't wrong. No one *wanted* a monster's DNA in their kid. It wouldn't change her mind, but it had clearly changed his.

He was also right that she'd fucked it up. She wasn't sure what she might have done wrong. She was pretty damn positive that she'd taken every pill on time, and she'd waited the requisite month before telling him, before making that their sole birth control. But it had been her responsibility, and she was late.

She thought about working, but that was as far as it got. The fabric had arrived for the ballet company, but she couldn't even open the box. Her tears would leave dirty mascara marks on the beautiful gauze. A knock at her door startled her to jumping off the couch and reaching for the Kleenex box on the coffee table. Only it wasn't there.

"One minute!" She hollered out, trying to sound normal and not like she was bawling her eyes out over bad fate while she frantically searched the house for a tissue box hidden by a child. Giving up, she reached into the hall closet and ripped open the spare box, blotting her eyes as she headed toward the door.

With a deep breath, she straightened her shoulders and hoped she could pull off a sane look for long enough to sign for whatever package was there or turn away whatever sales person had shown up. "Hello?"

"Hi." Kelsey stood on the doorstep alone. "Crying jag?"

Pulling the door back to let her new friend in, Shay nodded, feeling the tears start falling again. "That obvious?"

"A little, but the fact that you're hugging a fresh Kleenex box says a lot." She offered a sad grin. "I heard. I'm sorry."

At that point, Shay lost it. Big sobs came, taking her lungs through waves of gasping for air, as though the loss of Craig was also the loss of oxygen. A hand settled first on her back, then moved to become a hug, letting her cry it out.

She didn't notice until later when she'd exhausted herself that Kelsey hadn't even gotten her own coat off. When she finally seemed to deem Shay safe to sit on the couch by herself, she stood and shrugged out of it, revealing a round belly that led the way wherever she went. "I'm going to grab us both some ice water."

That was Kelsey. It wasn't a question, so Shay stayed on her couch, trying to breathe, while she listened to the other woman rattling around in her kitchen, trying to find glasses and scooping ice out of the freezer bin. Then Kelsey was in front of her, holding out the glass, once again gently demanding. "Drink some."

Shay scooted over so Kelsey could sit while she sipped at the cold water, admitting it felt good, and trying not to look at Kelsey's baby bump and wondering if she'd be there herself in a handful of months. Forcing her thoughts somewhere more productive, she turned to the other woman. "I don't know what you heard, and I'm sure you're here to kill me for breaking his heart, but . . ."

"Obviously yours is broken, too. That's the worst part." Kelsey commiserated. "Not everything works out." She waited a beat before adding, "I'm not going to kill you. I'm not sure which of you two to kill, or if it's even appropriate."

Appreciating the sentiment, Shay nodded her thanks. "Did he tell you what happened?"

Who knew what Kelsey had heard? Up until that moment, Shay didn't know if she'd have any friends left here besides Hailey. They were all in Craig's camp. She was consoling herself that there were plenty of other people in town and she'd make new friends as she went, just like the boys. But the boys liked Kelsey's kids. Owen looked up to Daniel, and Daniel was a great role model, taking time to do things at Owen's level with him. She sighed, wondering what she would tell the boys about how she'd screwed it up.

Kelsey grabbed her hand, holding it tight. "I'm not telling you what I heard. You and Craig either already figured it out, and that's why everyone's upset, or you'll have to figure it out in the future. I'm just here for moral support."

With that, Shay blurted everything out. "I think I might be pregnant."

It wasn't like Kelsey wasn't already aware of every freakin' sleepover Shay and Craig had. From the surprise on Kelsey's face, she hadn't heard that part of it before. *Well, shit.*

"Did you take a test?"

Shay shook her head first then said, "Not yet. But I'm late."

"Okay, so not a guarantee." She folded her hands, thinking. "Did you just now realize?"

Another head shake.

"Then why haven't you taken a test?"

"I'm afraid to buy one. I have to drive into town to be sure I don't see anyone I know." It sounded pathetic even to herself.

"Well, if you're anxious to know, I have a few at the house. No one will know you got one."

Shay laughed for the first time probably since she'd walked out on Craig a week ago. "No one will know except JD and all the kids and . . ."

This time it was Kelsey that shook her head. "I had spares from when we were trying. I got sad one day and bought an economy pack of tests. I'll bring you one when no one is looking."

Shay didn't respond.

"Still don't want to know?"

Another mildly amused giggle escaped her. "Are you a therapist?"

Kelsey's laugh was genuine and full. The easy laugh of a woman who had everything all figured out. The bolt of jealousy that hit Shay was like a taking a punch. "I've seen so many therapists in my time that I should have an honorary license. But I promise not to repeat back what you said. That always makes me want to hit people. I'm just asking the questions you may not be facing yet. You have limited time."

Shay nodded at that, thinking that Craig didn't want the kid. And it wasn't that he didn't really want it so much as he thought his line shouldn't continue. He clearly liked her kids. His insight into Aaron's curiosity and the differences between him and Owen were right on target. What would she do if she was pregnant?

"Do you want this child?"

Kelsey's words stunned her. It was a question she hadn't asked herself. Not once. She had a deep-seated belief in not ending a pregnancy herself, but this one was raising a lot of questions, pushing at the boundaries of what she believed. Her words whispered out of her in a fog. "I don't know."

She'd wanted it with Craig. But—

Kelsey's voice cut through her thoughts. "I have to get going. JD will be back with the kids any minute now. I'll bring you a test tomorrow or maybe the next day if you can wait? Then you don't have to find time to drive to town."

Shay nodded as her friend shrugged back into her coat and headed for the door. Before she let herself out, she turned back. "You have a lot of thinking to do. Let me know if I can help in any way."

After a quick "thank you," Kelsey was gone and Shay was left alone with the deep thoughts that were plaguing her.

There was a picture in her head of herself, Craig, and the boys. Happy, together, as a family. Sometimes she inserted a bundle into the image, trying it out, seeing if it fit. She wasn't sure. She did know that the real Craig didn't fit the picture. The real Craig wasn't willing to compromise on the boys. He believed she was raising a brat. He wanted to tell her how to look at, and what to think about the boys she'd been raising almost entirely on her own for six years. As though his six weeks with some random visits gave him any insight.

The worst part was that even though he was trying, it still didn't work.

On that depressing note, she declared the day completely shot and trundled herself off to bed. At least if she got some sleep, she might be able to stay up late and make up for some of the seams she wasn't serging or the hems she wasn't turning.

Her alarm went off in time to meet Owen at the bus. She hoped her red face could be attributed to the wind, but her oldest was pretty insightful and he wasn't having any of her BS. At least he waited until he was into his peanut butter sandwich before asking things she didn't want to answer.

"Did you and Craig have a fight?"

She nodded, thinking honesty was the best answer, especially when he was seeing straight through her already. Craig had made a comment about lying to kids and them hating you when they found out. It was probably pretty accurate. So she wouldn't tell her six-year-old all the gory details, but she wouldn't lie either.

When he asked if they had broken up and that earned another nod, Owen only gave a thoughtful nod of his own in return. Then he asked, "Are we moving again?"

Her heart about hit the floor. *Shit*. They'd moved when she broke-up-with/divorced Brian. They'd moved here because of Craig and that had obviously not escaped Owen even though she'd had no idea that he knew that until now. "No. We are not moving again. Well . . ." *Crap*. They *were* moving again. "Well, we'll move when we get our house. But you'll stay in the same school and we won't go far."

They weren't going anywhere anytime soon with the results she'd found from the realtor so far. She was holding out for the perfect place. She was hoping for extra bedrooms, but it didn't seem to be in her budget. She still needed a place in the house to work. The only one that had it was too run down for her to afford to fix it up.

Owen didn't know any of that. He just nodded and silently ate his sandwich. Then he ran off to read until it was time to get Aaron. She should have done something more with him. She had just Aaron on Tuesdays and Thursdays, and just Owen after school on the other days. It was supposed to be their time, but she didn't have it in her.

She still didn't have it in her on Thursday morning when Kelsey dropped by with a pregnancy test. Just a quick knock at the door and her new friend was on her way to run errands, kids waiting in the car.

Shay's knees had been knocking every day she didn't start. Having the test in hand now was almost too much, so she stashed it in the bathroom cabinet for when the boys were in bed. It would be too much to have them watch while she fell apart or whatever her reaction might be.

The day dragged forever, probably because of that stupid stick taunting her from under the sink. She set Aaron up with activities, sat down and ate lunch with him, then spent as much time as she could getting ahead on sewing.

Just before two, she bundled herself and Aaron up against the cold and went to wait with the other parents at the bus stop. She was freezing by the time the bus arrived, releasing a knot of kids before pulling away.

It turned the corner before she realized all the kids had dispersed and Owen wasn't there.

CHAPTER 39

C raig had just set his guitar down for a moment when he heard JD's phone ring. Turning away, knowing it was Kelsey, he grabbed the soda he'd bought on the way over. His stomach was upset and no wonder. He felt like shit.

JD had been gracious enough to stay after rehearsal and run songs with him. They'd started with JD's latest piece, with Craig adding a bass line to it, then working through harmonies. They'd been hammering out one of Craig's songs just then, but even Craig knew he was once again turning a good song melancholy. Not the right day to work on that one. Probably not the right month for it, if he was honest.

"Hey," JD's voice made him turn to see his best friend hold his phone up. "Have you heard from Shay?"

"No." *Why would I?* But he didn't say it.

"You should check your messages." JD looked worried and Craig frowned at him. "Shay's been frantic. Apparently Owen wasn't on the bus today."

"What?" His heart rate kicked up. *Why wouldn't Owen be on the bus?* "He's missing?"

JD nodded. "Check your phone."

Already, Craig was digging through his bag, pulling out a phone lit up with messages from Shay. Owen was gone. Had he seen the boy? Had Owen contacted him?

He dialed before thinking.

"Craig?" She was frantic, but the sound of her voice was still a punch to his gut. One that apparently none of them had time for.

"Did you find him?" He asked, maybe a little harshly in his worry.

"No." The word was drawn out, desperate. "I called the elementary, but they haven't gotten back to me. They don't even know if he got on the bus after school. They called the bus driver, but he isn't answering."

"So the bus came, but Owen didn't get off?"

"Right. All the other kids did, but they were talking and I grabbed two kids and neither remembered Owen."

He did have a tendency to read wherever he went. The introvert status wasn't helping anyone today. "I'm at rehearsal—"

"Oh. I'm so sorry to interrupt."

"Shay." He stopped her from being polite in a situation that didn't call for it at all. "Your son is missing. I'm just sorry that I didn't check sooner. I'm packing up and heading home to see if he's there and then I'll call you back."

"Kelsey drove by but didn't see him."

Craig didn't answer. He didn't want to give her false hope, but Owen knew his house. He wouldn't be surprised if the boy was in back playing with the dogs. "I'll call you with an update when I get there and then I'll join the search. Okay?"

"Yes, thank you." She hung up on him, but he didn't think much about it.

When he turned, JD was standing there with Craig's bag, packed and ready, in his outstretched hand. "Get going. We'll all keep each other posted."

It was grim, but Craig held out hope. Even so, he didn't think he'd ever driven so fast. Only as he pulled into his driveway did he realize how confident he'd been that Owen would be sitting on the front step. He'd been wrong.

His heart, already beating frantically, slowed to a stop and sank. *Shit. Where was Owen?* A second thought tagged closely on the heels of the first one. What if someone had taken him? Craig had been so certain that Owen would be here, that he hadn't even stopped to give something more sinister a foothold in his brain. He did now.

Not wanting to call Shay with bad news, he sat in the car. Looking around the side of the house, still trying to be hopeful, he texted her.

—Not here. I'm putting on a better jacket, checking the neighborhood. Let me know where else I should look.

As soon as he hit 'send' he realized that was bad. Shay shouldn't be organizing this. Someone else should. Kelsey, probably. Or maybe him. He didn't have kids of his own to look after, to worry about.

But he did have dogs. He wondered if he should take them around the neighborhood? Not that they were trained to find Owen, but they would go toward him if they could smell him. They both loved the boy. A greater likelihood was that Owen— if he were hiding nearby—would come out to say hello to the dogs even if he wouldn't to Craig.

Sprinting from the car, Craig dashed to the front step, jamming his key into the lock. It gave way and he slammed the door behind him, making it halfway down the hall before his brain registered the small person sitting at his table, tucked in the back out of the way.

"Owen!" Craig almost fell over. Then he almost fell over the other chairs as he made his way around to where the boy sat and hugged him until he squirmed.

This wasn't even his kid. So why was he so very relieved? But he was.

"Thank God you're okay." Craig was pulling out his phone, pulling up his call list.

"Don't call my mom!" Owen's hands came out, and he looked way too hot and way too upset sitting there still bundled in his winter coat.

Pausing, Craig waited to hear why he couldn't call Shay. "I need to call her. She's worried."

"But she'll come right over here. I don't want her to." Owen's face fell.

"Okay. Take off your jacket." Craig held his hand out, unwilling to make Shay wait long, but he needed to get to the bottom of this. When Owen held out the coat, Craig went and hung it in the front closet, the one he now scrounged for fallen coat hangers despite the fact that there were no more three-year-olds coming to his house. Then he went back and pulled out a chair.

"I want to tell your mom that you're okay."

Owen shook his head and Craig tried again. "What if your mom was missing and you didn't know where she was? What if you asked me and I said I'd call you when I found her and then I didn't? You'd be pretty mad at me for letting you worry about her when I'd already found her."

His shoulders falling in defeat, Owen nodded.

"I'll tell her not to come. I'll take you home when you're ready."

That earned him a nod and Craig texted Shay. —He's here. Don't come. I'll bring him home. He's fine. Unharmed.

Though he expected it, he was opening his mouth to say something to Owen when the phone rang. *Shay.*

With a finger up to the boy, he answered. Owen tensed. "Hi Shay. He's here."

"I'll be there in three minutes. I'm getting in the car." He could hear the sound of the car door, and the dinging as she put in the key.

"Don't. I've got him." His eyes were on Owen. Clearly, Owen had something to say, and not in front of Shay.

"You can't just keep him, Craig." She protested. It was shocking how quickly his back stiffened.

"I'm not keeping him." He turned away from Owen as though it would keep the boy from hearing it. "He asked me to take him home later. This isn't on me, Shay. Just let me bring him home, he's fine. Stop worrying."

Her silence was the only thing that answered. He shouldn't have told her not to worry.

An audible sigh came through the line followed by a sullen voice. "Fine."

Then she hung up on him.

He turned back to Owen who spoke before he could.

"She's going to come get me, isn't she?"

Craig's heart wanted to break for the boy. Something was up. "No, she's not. I'll take you home later."

"Thank you." It was quiet, relieved, simple. Of course he followed it up with, "I'm sorry I stole the key from my mom, but the weather said it would be cold today. Mom says not to sit outside in the cold."

Craig almost laughed at that. Then quickly he thought about JD and Kelsey. He tapped out a quick text —Got him. All's well. — then set the phone down and turned to Owen. "Do you want a snack?"

With a quick nod of 'yes,' the kid jumped up and followed Craig into the kitchen where they looked through his fridge. In near silence, they worked together to make half ham sandwiches then plated them with Cheetos and a juice box. It wasn't what Craig would have eaten, but he wasn't about to pop a celebratory beer in front of the six-year-old.

When they were settled at the table again, Craig started

talking. He didn't ask Owen why he'd run away. The kid probably didn't even know that he had. Craig had hated it whenever he was late or even when he had run away that he was first accused of doing something bad. So he didn't use that phrase. "You needed to tell me something?"

Owen nodded. It took a moment of silence before he realized he should be filling it. "Can I still come see the puppies?"

"Of course you can." Maybe later would be a better time to talk about the appropriate way to ask. *Was that it? No.* He was shocked by the next question.

"Will you teach me to play guitar like you?"

His heart stuttered again. He'd been wholly unprepared for that. For the feeling that socked him in the chest that this kid wanted to be like him. He'd been asked to teach it before. Kids in L.A. on the street. Other musicians. But it had been strictly for skills, or to fill dull time. Owen wanted to be like him.

Then he hit Craig with another one. "What's your dad like?"

Well, shit. First, Craig shrugged. He opened his mouth, wanting to say "I don't know," but he couldn't make it come out. He *did* know, and he didn't want to lie. Besides, he felt a strange kinship to this little boy who seemed concerned about what he was made of long before kids should have to worry about that. So he took a deep breath. He couldn't make Shay any angrier at him than she already was; he couldn't lose what he'd already lost.

"I didn't ever meet him, but he was a pretty bad person." The words hurt more than he'd thought they would. They'd never quite achieved the status of 'simple fact.'

"Are you a bad person?" Owen put down the sandwich and was looking at him through clear eyes. He *needed* this answer and he obviously didn't trust Shay to give it.

"No. I'm the person I choose to be. So are you." He said it again, feeling it inside him. He wouldn't lie to the kid. He was saying it for Owen, but still it felt almost like he was telling his ten-year-old self the same thing. Telling his nineteen-year-old self—the one who'd found the police records letting him know his father wasn't a monster just in theory but in glaring, serial-offender fact. "We are who we choose to be."

"What about when I'm bad?"

"Everyone's bad sometimes. It doesn't make you bad. You're nothing like your Dad." He took another bite of his sandwich in an effort to keep himself together.

"He's not my dad." Owen said it matter-of-fact-ly. "Mom tested me and Jason isn't my dad. That's why I don't have to see him again. I don't think she knows who my dad is."

Craig just nodded and chewed, not knowing how to field that one.

Owen did it for him. "I know how babies are made."

Craig nearly choked, but tried to keep his expression neutral.

"Does that make my mom bad? That she doesn't know who my dad is?" Again, the clear eyes, the focus on Craig as though he had all the answers.

"No. She's not bad." *Jesus, the kid was killing him.* "We all get confused sometimes, especially if we love someone. Sometimes we do really stupid things for the people we think we love."

It was the best he could do. But he'd fucked it up again, because the six-year-old was playing hardball and lobbed it back at him. "Are you doing something stupid right now because you love my mom?"

He really should quit even trying to eat, or else he should pray that Owen was proficient in the Heimlich Maneuver. He didn't think the latter was an option, so he set down his sandwich. "No, I'm not. Your mom . . . She decided that we don't fit together. Honestly, so did I."

"Was it me?" The words were a bare whisper, so scared they made Craig ache.

"No, honey, it wasn't you." He put his hand on Owen's hand, holding it until the little boy looked up.

"Was it Aaron? Because he's being a dickhead."

Unable to help it, Craig tipped his head back and belly-laughed. Tears leaked from his eyes and he felt bad, because Owen was asking the question honestly, but God—he tried to get himself together. "No. It's not Aaron either. And all three-year-olds are buttheads sometimes. You might want to choose a better word than you did the first time."

"Fine. But Aaron's a butthead *all* the time." He crossed his arms, almost pouting his face into a mask.

"Yeah, that's part of being three. You probably weren't so great at three either. Me either." Craig tried to get the kid to look up at him. "The only difference was you didn't have a big brother to hit you back, or to point out what a butthead you were being. You also didn't have a cool big brother who could play guitar or walk a puppy when you were too little. He's really jealous of you. You can read, and train the dogs, and do all kinds of things he just can't do yet."

Owen nodded, the explanation making some sense.

"He gets frustrated when he tries to be like you and he can't. He hits because he's three."

"He hits because mom won't stop him."

Now what? Because he totally agreed with the six-year-old. "Your mom said you turned out fine with the way she did things and she's waiting for Aaron to grow out of it."

Craig thought he'd done pretty well. Statements of fact only. No bashing Shay as a parent, no saying what he really thought.

"But I didn't have an older brother getting hit all the time and almost getting his things broken! I have to share a room with him!" Another pout. Another point he was legitimately angry about.

"Did you tell your mom about this?"

He nodded but didn't elaborate. Silence reigned for a few

moments, broken only by the sounds of a six-year-old munching Cheetos. Craig was pretty certain Shay didn't give them Cheetos on a regular basis. But her kid was found, he was safe, and he'd be home to her soon. Craig enjoyed watching Owen enjoy the Cheetos.

He put the last one down and politely wiped his small fingers on a napkin. Then Owen threw his last hardball. "Can you be my dad?"

CHAPTER 40

S hay slept in the hallway outside the boys' room that night.
Or she tried to. Several times she told herself it was the
hard floor that kept her awake, but that wasn't it. It was her
brain. Owen had made a mad mess of it, that was for sure.

She couldn't recall a single time when she'd ever been so
terrified. Even when Brian had drugged Aaron and he wouldn't
wake up. She'd been scared moving here, putting all her eggs in
the "Nashville and Craig" basket. But even when Jason had held
baby Owen aloft as a threat should Shay not do as he wanted, it
had only lasted a few minutes.

This had gone on for over an hour. Though it was nothing
compared to what some parents went through, it was nerve
wracking. Exhausting. Terrifying.

By the time the school had gotten hold of the bus driver and
found out that yes, Owen was on the afternoon bus, she'd just
heard from Craig. Then Craig wouldn't bring him home. Said it
was Owen who didn't want her to come get him.

Apparently, as terrified as she had been she was "not to
worry" because Craig and Owen had it "under control." She was
still shaking with anger each time she thought about it. She was

their mother, and Craig's lack of respect for that had already torn them apart. She hadn't thought it could do more damage until this afternoon.

Craig had pulled up in his truck, Owen in the backseat, buckled into the booster seat. She'd stood in the front door watching—her heart wrenching—as Craig helped Owen down, then Owen reached up and gave Craig a big hug before running inside.

Shay hadn't known what to say.

Craig seemed to have known not to say anything. He only offered a small nod before climbing back into his truck and backing out of her driveway, out of her life once again.

She couldn't count the number of times they'd left each other. Each one hurt worse than the one before. Somehow this time still managed to continue that trend. She turned and peeked into the bedroom door, looking at her sleeping boys from her spot on the floor. A blanket and a few cushions kept her company.

A cat would be good company. The boys could clearly use a pet; Owen had run away to see the puppies. She didn't let her mind even consider that he'd gone to see the man.

What was she thinking? She couldn't get a cat! She was a seamstress who worked from her own home. She'd seen what cats did to couches. She cringed just thinking about what one could do to a whole bolt of twenty-dollar-a-yard fabric.

No cat.

Just a mom, sitting in the hallway. She could practically hear Owen yelling at her that she'd ruined things with Craig. He'd called Aaron a butthead, then said Aaron was only three, so it was okay, but he had to stop.

Sitting on the couch with Owen after Aaron had been put to bed, she'd stroked his head and tried to explain that sometimes things just didn't work out with adults. Owen pointed out that things didn't work out with his dad because his dad was an asshole. Though she'd let calling his brother a 'butthead' ride because Aaron wasn't around to hear it and Owen was clearly getting some things off his chest, she put her foot down about her six-year-old wielding 'asshole' like a brandish. Unfortunately, he'd done it well—good inflection and tone, and he'd applied it to the right person. His father *was* an asshole. There wasn't another word that really got the whole of Jason the same way. Calling him a jerk sounded like he didn't take out the trash or help with the household chores. Owen didn't even know the half of it.

Owen used slightly calmer language about Brian, telling her that things didn't work out with him because he was bad, too. But Craig was good. Her son didn't accept that things 'didn't work out' when both people were good.

Maybe that was why he was convinced the breakup was her fault. Though he had his head in her lap, it clearly wasn't what he wanted.

Before bed, he'd been full-blown angry again. Maybe that was why she was sitting out here in the hallway. Maybe she was afraid he'd go out the window. And he might not go to Craig if he knew her ex was going to return him home. She had to keep an eye on him.

She was, but his last words before bed were sticking with her. "Mrs. Vreeland says 'you get what you get and you don't get upset' or you choose 'you can be the change you wish to see.'"

Shay had told him thank you, then kept it to herself that first grade philosophy lessons were not going to turn her life around. But Owen hadn't been done with that.

"You're sad. You're upset, Mom. So you have to change." He'd looked at her wide-eyed, pleading with her to be some better person that she didn't know how to be. He'd repeated it as he climbed under his Spiderman comforter, "If you want things to change, you have to change, Mom."

The dichotomy had made her smile at him and thank him

again. But now as she sat in the hallway she wondered if her usually silent six-year-old had a point.

Then she reminded herself that maybe he was mad because she had changed. She'd allowed Craig in. It had been an experiment—one that failed, surely—but an experiment. And it wasn't all bad. She and her boys had seen that not all men were bad people. But they were a unit. The three of them.

Somewhere in the middle of the night she remembered to take the pregnancy test. If she hadn't had a heart attack from Owen going missing, then she wasn't going to have one from this.

Still, the three-minute wait was the longest stretch of time since . . . Well, since that afternoon, but it didn't make the time go by any faster. Shay waited four minutes. She told herself it was because she wanted the test to be sure. But the real reason was because she was a wimp.

It was one-thirty in the morning when she read the stick. *Negative.*

Her lungs whooshed out, her shoulders sagged, her whole body slumped until she was sitting on the closed toilet lid. She hadn't been ready. Clearly, she could barely handle the two that she had. Chalking it up to stress—which she'd had a heaping ton of lately—she took the stick and the wrapper out to the kitchen trash, because it was the deepest. She buried it.

Owen seemed to know a lot more than he was letting on. She didn't need him burdened with this, too. When she got back into the hallway, Shay nestled into the blankets and finally found some sleep.

Until Owen shook her awake in the morning. "What are you doing out here, Mom?"

She hugged him, still a little tight. "I missed you yesterday. I was so scared when you were gone."

"You didn't have to."

"It's what moms do." She countered as she climbed out of her little nest.

"It's what good moms do." Owen told her as Aaron came out of the room behind him, rubbing his eyes. Shay's heart warmed at his words. He didn't hate her after all. Then Owen continued. "There are bad moms, too, you know. Just like there are good and bad dads."

That was all he had to say about it. He was obviously lobbying hard for her and Craig to get back together. Shay only nodded in return and began fixing cereal.

She'd gotten Craig's key back from Owen, debated returning it to Craig, then thought better of it. She went about packing lunches and fixing oatmeal that she seeded with chocolate chips. Then Owen was on the bus and she was driving Aaron to daycare. Just that was scary to her.

She wanted to take the day off, hold them both close, but she couldn't. It wouldn't be right. So she was at home alone, sewing, when Kelsey came by. This time the other woman peeled her coat to stay a little while.

"Hey, just wanted to check in. I won't overstay, I know you have work." She smiled and refused a drink when Shay offered.

"Thank you for stopping by. It's a hard day."

Kelsey nodded. "I figured. But you sent them both off? Didn't cry?"

"Nope. I wanted to." Shay grinned. "But I didn't." It felt good to know that Kelsey was still her friend even if she wasn't still with Craig. It was unexpected and wonderful.

"And?" Kelsey prompted, her hands clasped.

"Oh! Not pregnant." Shay laughed this time. "So once I had Owen home and the test was negative, I started later in the night. Must have just been stress."

"They say that can happen."

"Yeah, well, it's a crap method if you ask me. There you are, all stressed out, so your body adds another one."

They chatted a bit before Kelsey offered a hug Shay hadn't realized was sorely needed. Her baby bump—now practically a mountain—hit Shay as they embraced.

Shay laughed, "I'm so glad that's just you and not me on that bandwagon."

"That's the way it should be." Kelsey grinned before heading out the door and back to her hectic life.

Somehow Shay made it through the rest of the day. She'd texted Craig that morning with the non-news. He'd only said "Thanks" several hours later.

Owen climbed off the bus right at two p.m.—which was wonderful. Then he pushed right past her, marching into the townhouse—which was not. He resisted mom-time, then stayed quiet even through picking up Aaron, despite her entreaties to get him to talk. He resisted all questioning until dinner time when he asked if he could get off the bus at Craig's house the next day.

"No, honey, you can't." She frowned.

"Then when can I go?" His stubbornness was gaining traction. She'd not seen him like this before, but told herself both boys were acting out about the move. It would pass. But Owen didn't let it.

When he was climbing into bed, he brought it up again. "Craig said I could go to his house whenever I wanted. Well, I want to go tomorrow."

"You can't just go there. He's a grown man, he has a job. Lots of times he's not home." She stroked his head, but her oldest rolled away.

"He'll be home tomorrow after school."

"Did he tell you that?" She asked softly, this time keeping her hands to herself, no matter how much it made her heart hurt.

"He will be."

Not quite a real answer. But when she headed downstairs, she picked up her phone to call Craig.

Then she set it back down. She didn't have the right to just call him up and ask what was going on. Then again, he didn't have the right to just tell her kid to stop by after school. She picked up her cell again, then set it down again. The third time she pushed the buttons too fast to let her brain talk her out of it. He answered on the fourth ring. Just when she thought he wouldn't.

"Hello, Shay."

His voice shouldn't still have the power to do that to her, but it always did. Even that first evening on the beach, she'd heard him before she saw him and the very sound of him had melted her. "Hi."

"What can I help you with?" He was so matter-of-fact, she practically froze in the puddle she'd melted into. She'd crack any moment.

So she bucked up and asked. "Owen just told me that you said he could come over any time."

"He's up pretty late, isn't he?"

"Yes, it's past his bedtime, but he was talking a lot finally, so I let him stay up."

"He had a lot to say the other day." Craig commented.

"Are you going to tell me what he told you? What you said to him?" She demanded. It irked her that he was calling her on letting her son stay up.

"No. Not all of it."

"He's my son, I have a right—"

He interrupted, but wasn't mad. "Shay, he showed up inside my house, having used a key I gave you. I don't think my breaking a confidence he asked me to keep—when no one is hurt or in danger at all—is wise. He's my friend, I'm not going to betray that."

"He's not your friend, Craig. He's six." She protested, wondering if he would interrupt her again. He didn't. This time he waited a full beat.

"Shay, he's my friend. It's all I have left of it. He wanted me to teach him to play guitar, and I want to do it. Of course I told him he had to ask you for permission."

"He didn't." She sighed, getting ready to apologize, but she didn't get the opportunity.

"Of course not, Shay. He's a six-year-old. Weren't you just telling me that? You don't trust me with anything where they're concerned. Nothing. And that's the main problem."

He was getting angry now. For some reason that made her wicked heart just a little glad. Contrarily, it irked her that he said that as though they could work it out.

"Craig." This time she felt so very tired. "I'm their only line of defense. I protect them from abusive fathers. I keep them safe from the world. I'm all they have."

"I know. But it's that way because you choose it. You did such a good job, they now have a good stable home, no bad fathers, and a better life ahead of them." He paused, his voice quiet, soft, resigned. "Congratulations. You only have fifteen years to go. Good luck."

Then the phone clicked and she hung up, none the wiser.

CHAPTER 41

Craig fumbled in his wallet to pay the cabbie. It was damned expensive getting from downtown to out in the burbs. There was a card reader right there in the back seat. So why was he digging for cash?

Well, probably for the same reason he'd taken a cab. Three beers in two hours was too many. He made TJ promise not to drive home. Yup, his brain was good, but not all there. Patting his pocket, he felt for keys, then had to pull them out. Even as he looked at them, he remembered, he hadn't driven, so his only key was a house key. The ring belonged to TJ. His friend would get home safe—if he still remembered his address after all the fine beer he'd consumed.

It was also possible that TJ would have to remember his address in the morning, when he woke up in some strange woman's house. Maybe Craig would go fetch him. He didn't have anything better to do.

He calculated what he thought was the right tip, then realized the little screen had done it for him. Good, he was on spot, then climbed out of the car and stood on the sidewalk, breathing in the night air, coming close to fully sober, then headed up his front walk.

Once inside, he walked through the front hall, and turned to push the phone into the charger, checking that the volume was all the way up. He would want to hear the ring if TJ called in the morning.

Only as he turned did he remember that he hadn't left the lights on. He would have blinked a few times to get it straight had he not spotted the cause sitting on his couch.

"Why are you here?" He asked her point blank. He couldn't handle this tonight.

"You don't sound happy to see me." Shay stayed put, her hands folded in her lap, her expression contrite.

"I'm not."

"Oh." She took a deep breath in reaching for her purse.

It had to be the extra beer. He thought he'd breathed out the last of it on the sidewalk in the cold of night, but his mouth ran off without his brain. "Why would I be? You've managed to leave me so many times. In fact, you're so good at it that you can leave me when we aren't even together."

Her eyebrows climbed. "Were you out drinking?"

"Yes. But I'm not drunk. Just a shade past rock sober. Where are the boys?" He looked around the room as though expecting them to come out of the hallway, or for her to say she stashed them in his music room.

"They're staying over at Kelsey and JD's."

"A night off for Super-Mom? Wow." He walked past her and into the kitchen where he poured himself an ice water without offering her any.

"Maybe this isn't the right time for this." She was standing now, her purse having made it into position over her shoulder.

"Oh please!" He gestured wildly, "Don't go. Just get it out tonight so I don't have to wait for it tomorrow. I'm really anxious to hear how you came over just so you can leave again."

Yeah, he was definitely a shade past sober, and she was eying him like she knew it. As he watched, she thought about something, but he had no idea how long it took, his timing was off.

Eventually, she set the purse on the coffee table, but stayed on her feet. Following suit—and maybe so he didn't throw it against the wall and prove to her that he was a horrible, violent, child abuser—he set the water glass down and waited while she gathered whatever courage she needed.

"I don't want to leave." She pushed out the words. When he didn't respond, she went further. "I want to stay with you."

"You can't just waltz back in—"

"I'm not. I want to fix this. Craig, you were right. I was right, too, but now I'm not." She stumbled.

"You aren't making any sense, and I'm in no shape to unscramble it." He put his hands on the counter dividing the kitchen from the dining area. Keeping it between them helped him feel steady, as though anything could protect him from hurricane Shay. Any moment he'd be ripped to shreds.

"I was right. I was my boys' only line of defense. Against horrible men. And you were right, too. I picked those men. I put my boys there. I didn't mean to, and I'm still trying to forgive myself for being a terrible idiot on those counts. But I got better. I saved myself and my boys. And I learned to fall in love with someone good."

What the hell was she saying? He could feel the first sharp pains as his skin flayed.

Shay kept at it. "And even though I changed, the way I acted didn't. You're right. I'm not the first line of defense for my boys anymore." She paused, looked to the side. "Or I am, but I'm not the only one. You were right there beside me, and I didn't know what to do with you. I treated you like I treated Jason and Brian. I didn't trust you with the boys when I could, and I still didn't when I should have. You have every right to hate me, Craig. I was awful."

He nodded, but he couldn't ever seem to get himself to hate her, whether he had the right to or not. Those words didn't come out.

"I don't know if you can give me another chance. And I don't know if I concede on smacking Aaron's hands. But I want to try. I want to trust you. I want you there with me. I love you. I really do."

Words came then. "You can't just *want* to trust me Shay. You have to actually *do* it."

"I know." She'd taken a step toward him, then stopped. "I do actually trust you. When you wouldn't tell me what Owen said to you when he ran away, I realized it didn't matter. That you wouldn't hold anything important from me, or that if you had to, you'd handle it. I've never had that thought before. Even with Zoe. She's an alarm system; she'll let me know if something goes wrong, but you can handle things."

She looked frightened, but the corner of her mouth turned up in a small smile.

"He didn't run away." Craig had no idea why that was the thing he'd latched onto, but it was all the words he could form when his heart was starting to pound. He shouldn't have had the third beer. Hell, he shouldn't have had the first. "He ran here. There's a big difference. I know. Don't call it that to him."

"Okay. You're right." She nodded. "I don't know how you're so good with them, but you are."

"I'm not. I try to read up on it, but all the advice contradicts other advice." He shrugged, wondering when the conversation had turned surreal. Or if he'd had a lot more to drink than he remembered. "Mostly, I remember what it was like. That no one cared what I wanted and no one heard my voice. The band was the first time anyone ever cared what I thought, or thought I made a worthwhile contribution."

"You make an unbelievable contribution to me. To my boys."

"You can't just go shopping for a father for your kids." He told her, some part of him still keeping her at bay.

"I'm not. Honestly, I'll back down on how you get Aaron to behave, because you do. Even when I can't. And I know he's far better off with you than without you." She turned away, her eyes rolling toward the ceiling. "That still sounds like I'm trying to get you back for them. But I want you for *me*." This time she looked right at him, every word a physical hit. "Each day without you is worse than the one before it. You're right about the boys, and you were right about me."

All he could do was stare. "Where's the old Shay? Where's the woman who would rip me a new one for daring to suggest that I know something about her kid?"

She laughed. "I sent her packing. I'm sorry I did that to you. My only excuse is that I've never met anyone like you. No one I've dated has even been in your stratosphere, Craig. I didn't know what to do with you, so I did what I always did, which was retreat and protect my boys."

"Did?" The counter was holding him up now, his breathing was turning fast and shallow to match his heart rate.

"She's gone. I trust you. I love you." She took a deep breath as though gearing up for something. It turned out to be another deep breath. "I want to be *us* again. I want you back."

It all stopped. His heart, his lungs, his brain.

She stared at him, waiting for something he couldn't give her. He shook his head, while his chest caved in. He couldn't do it. He'd spent his whole life getting kicked around. Even Shay kicked him around. "You may want me back, but you're the most important person in the world to me, and I'm not that person to you."

She rushed him then, closing the distance, coming around the counter and coming at him until his back was against the refrigerator and her hands were on his face. "I'm a complete fucking idiot for ever saying that to you."

He sucked in air while she steamrolled him.

"You *are* that person to me. My boys are a responsibility to me. Don't get me wrong, I love them and I will defend them with my life if I have to. But you're the only one I have *chosen*." She was openly crying now, her hands gripping his shirt, but his hands held tight to the edge of the counter, not quite believing her words. "You are the one I want to be there when the boys are grown and gone. You are the only one I want."

He crumbled in the onslaught of her words. He caved, giving in to her as she rose up on tiptoe to press her mouth to his in a kiss that claimed him. His hands found her hair and held her there so he could kiss her back, hold onto the wave of pure bliss that pushed through every cell in his body.

They clung to each other, there in his small kitchen. His heart pounded, his hands grasped at her, keeping her close when she so easily slipped away. When she pulled back to look at him, it was with tears in her eyes, but a smile on her face.

Putting his hands on her shoulders, he pushed her back farther. "No."

She frowned up at him, not understanding.

"No, Shay, I can't. You'll leave me again and I won't survive that. I've come through so much . . ." His chest heaved and he felt like he was going to retch. "I know now where my breaking point is, and you're it. I can't."

"What? Why?" She stood there, stunned for a moment. Then her feet moved, changing tacks with her voice. "Do you need me to show up every day and choose you? I will. I'll tell you that I love you until you believe it. I need you. And I think you need me."

He broke then, tears crashing over eyelids he'd squeezed shut, fists clenching. "I *can't*. When you find out what I am, what I really am, you'll leave again. I won't survive it this time."

He didn't open his eyes when she spoke.

"I know what you are." Her words were soft, but the blows weren't. He knew what she didn't. What she wouldn't be able to live with. "I love you."

"You don't know!" He yelled it loud enough to wake the neighbors. "You *don't*. You don't know what I did."

"Then tell me." He felt her touch his hand, grab it and pull him. He resisted despite the fact that he didn't have the strength. His body ached like he had sand running through his veins. No matter how he pulled away, she held on. "Tell me."

She'd let go if he did. So he opened his eyes and stared at her. Then he told her what he'd hid from everyone for so many years. "I ran away at sixteen."

"I know." Her words were soft.

He'd kill her with this, dash her sweet, happy hopes. "I ran *away*, not *to*. I'd been beaten, worked to the bone, and even molested by some of the people who were supposed to raise me."

She tugged at his hand.

"You know about my father, Shay. I can't give you more children." He blinked through his cloudy vision as she tugged him closer to the couch.

"I'm good, two is plenty. Also, I don't know who my father is." She returned. "I have three options. The con artist is the best one."

He tried again. "I ended up on Santa Monica Boulevard at night. I pawned my guitar, I sold everything I had, and then when I ran out of money, I sold myself. I hooked. I turned tricks for over a year." He was nearly yelling it, hoping she'd see, hoping each word would be the straw that broke her, so he could finally curl up alone and cry. Maybe some later day, he could scrape himself off his floor and go on.

She didn't see.

She tugged him to the couch next to her, hugged him, sniffled a little and only said, "Me, too."

He told her every horrible act committed against him. Every terrible thing he'd done. Each time she hugged him tighter and said the same two words.

Eventually he ran out of things to try to prod her with. His shoulders heaved, and he found himself undone in her arms, the two of them tucked back into a corner of the couch. She held him there, safer than he'd ever been, while he spewed out every awful thing he'd done, every crime he committed. Every confession was met with, "me, too."

At last, when he ran out of confessions, he whispered, "I did it for money."

She didn't reply, but he felt her nod somewhere over his head. Her hands felt gentle in his hair, even though he was collapsing into her as he waited. Her words were the barest sound on the air. She was crying even as she wrapped herself around him. "I know. And I don't know how you'll ever forgive me for what I've done. Because I did it for *free*."

CHAPTER 42

Craig woke to a pounding headache and the sweetest sense of Shay curled into him. Ignoring the puppies for just a moment, he rolled into her. The sensation of her naked skin against his was comforting and amazing all at the same time.

He'd gutted himself the night before. Said everything he could to make her go away. Now, as he propped himself up on one elbow and reached out to touch her hair, he was starting to feel whole in a way he never had before. Somehow it was far easier to forgive her the exact same sins he'd committed than it was to forgive himself. He'd come a long way on his own, he knew he was a good person *now*, but it had been hard to let go of a past he was more than ashamed of.

She was asleep in his bed, in his arms until he'd started to get up. Responsibility was responsibility. And it was more than that when it was a creature. Human or puppy, he was glad all the small ones in his care had it better than either he or Shay had had it.

So he slipped out of bed and pulled on pants. He was exhausted. He'd cried his eyes out, something he hadn't done but the once since he was a kid. No wonder his head pounded.

Then he and Shay had been up most of the night, making love that was carnal and raw. He had nothing left to put out there, nothing left to push her away with. He watched as she rolled over softly, the covers falling away.

He loved her. All her flaws, all her faults, all her history.

Turning away from his introspection, he answered the soft whines that were getting louder as he dressed. Setting Scarlett and Gunnar free, he slid his feet into shoes and pulled on a t-shirt. That was Nashville for you; fifty degrees in the middle of winter. It would turn cold again, but today, he wore short sleeves.

He headed out the back door, hearing birds chirp and seeing a blue sky above him. He almost laughed at his goofy exuberance. There were still two dogs doing their business on his back lawn—not exactly romantic.

He was tired deep in his bones, but the dogs needed some play time. It wouldn't be long before they needed to be able to be out of the crate overnight. He was able to leave them in the backyard unattended now for short periods of time, but he usually didn't do it in the mornings. Since those deeper barks had started coming in, he'd grown concerned about waking the neighbors.

Keeping an ear out, he went into the kitchen and made himself an industrial strength pot of coffee. He was nearly to the bottom of his first cup, sitting in the one chair he'd put out on his porch and contemplating getting a second, when Shay slid the porch door open.

Her own coffee in hand, she glided out to him looking well-loved—mussed and sated. She settled herself in his lap as it was the only place to sit. Taking what must have been her first sip, she scrunched up her face and made a gagging noise. "What is this?"

"Sludge." He grinned and took the cup from her. "Do you want me to make a pot of actual coffee for you?"

"Like I would trust you after you made that." She swatted at his shoulder and got up.

The heat of her left him and even though she was only in the kitchen, he missed her. Scarlett brought him a ball, dropping it at his feet, so he picked it up and threw it for her, only to have it returned by Gunnar.

He did it mechanically, his brain turning another direction. Each time he and Shay had worked something out, it had broken apart again. He felt this time was different, but he'd felt that before.

When she emerged with her own coffee in hand, she seemed to sense the direction of his thoughts. Her soft words floated to him, even if she stayed put. "Talk to me."

"I just realized it's Sunday morning."

"And?" She prompted. She was right, he wasn't good at going straight into something.

So he looked at her, wanting to not dance around things anymore. "So you spent the night on a Saturday night. Do I get to come stay with you on Saturday night next week? Will you bring the boys after school one day this week?"

He still wasn't getting right at what he wanted, but she understood. Only she said, "No."

"Oh." He looked away, the 'everything' he so desperately wanted still just out of his reach. He was telling himself that she really loved him and that had to mean a lot, when she spoke again.

"You didn't like that arrangement, and that was part of me trying to keep you out of the boys' lives. That was a mistake." She sat on his lap again, an arm around his shoulders. "I don't want to spend another day or night away from you again. But what do *you* want?"

He took a deep breath. It was a good question.

It hit him then. For the first time, it was about him.

"I want to be with you as much as possible. I want to sleep

next to you every night." He shook his head. "I'm sure that can't happen, but it's what I want."

"Let's make it happen." She set down her coffee, wrapping both arms around him.

"What about the boys?"

"My boys need a happy mother. They'll adjust. And they need you. Aaron asks after you, and when Owen ran, he ran to you. I'm the one who's been slow on the uptake here."

Leaning his head into her for a moment before he had to throw the slimy tennis ball again, Craig soaked up her words. "Neither of us has a house big enough for all of us. Not for any length of time, and I know you want to own your own house—"

"No, I don't." When he frowned at her, she continued. "It was a dream I had for a long time. Something I clung to and honestly thought would still be a long way off. It took a while to realize that I didn't like any of the houses I looked at because there wasn't any room for you."

"We haven't been speaking." He reminded her.

"A huge mistake on my part. So huge that even then the houses weren't right." She took a breath. So many big breaths in the last twelve hours, so many big things changed and moved. "I want a house with you. I want to pay my part. I want my name on the deed. But I want it next to yours on the same deed."

When he opened his mouth, she shook her head. "It's a big thing. Big. You should think about it."

"Okay." He nodded. "I would love that." He rested his head on her shoulder. "I understand about wanting the house. I'm still working on my steps to being what I'm capable of. I remember the first time I got a full-time job, it was at Starbucks. I even got health insurance. The first time I visited a real doctor's office, I was excited to pay my co-pay. Buying a house was a really big thing."

She laughed, the sound slipping through him and settling in his soul where it belonged. "The first month I paid all my bills by myself I was so excited. And proud. It was the first time I knew that I would be okay. Owen was a toddler and I was still pregnant with Aaron, and finalizing my second divorce. Until then, I had no idea I would be able to make it on my own."

"You're more than capable." He told her.

"I am. And so are you." She was looking out over the back yard as he looked at her. Mussed morning hair, sleepy eyes, soft glow to her skin. He liked knowing that he put it there. Her voice rolled over him. "I still have a long way to go. But you made me realize I should look back."

He frowned, he did not like looking back. Nothing back there was good or worth saving. Some of it nearly not survivable.

She must have seen his expression out of the corner of her eye. She looked at him. "You and I have already climbed further than most people will ever even have the opportunity to. I'm not done yet, Craig, but of all the thousands of steps I've taken, this one is the biggest and the best. I've been afraid and worried every step I've taken before. But not this time."

CHAPTER 43

M y BookShay looked out the passenger window as Craig
turned off the engine of the old truck. The truck did
not fit in with the neighborhood.

"Is this it, Mom!" It wasn't a question. Owen figured out they
had parked in front of it, so it must be theirs.

"Yes, this one is ours." She turned to Craig, a grin spreading
across her face. Sparks flew between the two of them at the
thought.

Obviously, they'd seen the place before; they'd walked
through, argued the selling price and made counter-offers. But
today they arrived as the new owners, keys in hand.

Owen was the first one out of the car, his feet jumping to the
ground and starting across the lawn.

"I've got him!" Craig announced, breaking the lightning arc
between them and taking off after her oldest. Shay climbed out
only a little more calmly than Owen had and went to unbuckle a
squirming Aaron who was getting upset at being the last one in
the car.

As she set him down, still holding his hand, she wondered if
he would remember this day when he was older. Maybe it was

okay if he didn't. Maybe it was fine if this nice neighborhood with the good school district and the house with his own bedroom was all he remembered growing up. Maybe he would never remember a time when he didn't have Craig.

They joined the others on the front porch until they were standing four across—Shay next to Craig, Aaron's hand in hers. Owen seemed to feel the importance of the moment and tucked his hand into Craig's. These last few months had been nothing but confirmation that she'd finally made the right choice. Craig was the right choice for her boys, but more importantly, he was the right choice for her. In fourteen years, it would just be the two of them. The boys would grow up, move out, get married, just as they should. She knew where she belonged.

"You do the honors." He handed her the key. He'd already done this once—turned the key to his own home. He was giving her the chance. The only one probably. They'd talked about this —they made plans to pay the place off in fifteen years. They weren't going to trade up; neither of them ever wanted to move again. They wanted to leave the boys in one home for the remainder of their childhoods. She knew things could change, the world could fall away from under her, but she finally had the power to influence it.

She pushed the key into the bolt and turned, opening the door into a small foyer that opened immediately in to a large living room.

Owen and Aaron bolted, exploring parts unknown. Craig watched them go then turned to her. "I've been waiting for this."

Her heart pounded. She had plans and she hoped he didn't ruin them. But he scooped her into his arms and kissed her, carrying her over the threshold. She flashed back to a gauzy yellow dress and a tux, a hotel suite and the promise of a single night of freedom.

This was a hell of a lot better than that freedom. She kissed

SAVANNAH KADE

him back with everything she had, hoping to hell that he didn't propose to her.

When Owen yelled out, Craig set her down and asked her what time it was.

"Ten-twelve." She looked at her watch. The movers were supposed to show up around ten thirty. It was going to be a mess. Her things, his things, they didn't have some of what they needed and they'd been donating duplicate items where they could.

Though they'd had to move to a different neighborhood—Craig's had been made up of smaller bungalows—they'd managed to stay close. The boys would have the same bus driver even.

She watched as Craig rounded up the boys from the back of the house where the kitchen overlooked a good-sized back yard. He held Aaron's hand and pointed Owen up the steps as he grinned at her. "Come on, Shay."

Following them upstairs, she made it in time to hear Owen ooh and ahhhh over the attic room. "Can we put toys up here?"

"How about we put *you* up here?" Craig asked. "This is your room."

"All by myself!?" He flung himself at Craig who hugged the boy back, lifting him off the ground and whispering, "Tell your mom thank-you, too. She worked really hard to make this happen."

She was almost bowled over by the hug flung at her waist.

The house wasn't exactly what they needed. The attic room didn't have a door—not a problem for a six-year old, but it would be later. The fence in the backyard wouldn't last when the dogs gained another twenty pounds each, as they were expected to do. But they would fix and change things as they needed. With both of them chipping in, they could make it happen. Even if Wilder tanked tomorrow and never had another hit, they had each other.

312

They were showing Aaron his room when she heard the deep squeal of air brakes. "The moving truck is here."

She spent the rest of the morning directing boxes that she'd tried to label as well as possible over the previous week. It felt like she'd just done this, though the move into and then out of the rented townhouse was by no means her fastest turnaround. It felt good to finally put down real roots.

After a late lunch and a visit to walk the puppies, they started the task of opening boxes and putting things away. She and Craig stayed side by side, working first on the kitchen, then the bedroom. She went to wipe the inside of the cabinets only to remember the cleaning crew they'd sent through two days before.

She'd always before cleaned her own places when she went in. Each motion brought flashbacks of other moves. Chipped tile counters, cracked linoleum floors. In the past, she'd wiped roaches out of kitchens and bathrooms, and in one place out from under the old bed she and Zoe were to share. She'd cleaned detritus from previous tenants, swept broken beer bottles from a living room floor once when kids had broken in during the week the place had been vacant. None of those things bothered her here.

They answered the door at three p.m. to find the front stoop full to overflowing. JD and Kelsey stood at the front, kids lined up in a row. Contrary to Shay's belief that having the boys over would send Kelsey into labor, she was still pregnant. She was now volunteering to do sleepovers in the hopes that Shay was right.

It took about fifteen minutes to organize everyone, but once they did, beds and bookshelves were assembled in record time. The TV was hooked up and someone else dealt with getting Craig the cable he'd come to love. Once again, Craig waved her underthings at her, before putting them into the top drawer of a dresser they were now sharing. He stuffed his own underwear

313

in the drawer beside hers and it was shocking how wonderful something as stupid as an underwear drawer felt.

TJ looked hungover and nursed a coffee, grumbling at Craig about not coming out with him anymore, but he worked as hard as any of them. Bridget ran a load of dishes and organized bookshelves, leaving little stickers behind so they could find things. JD and the rest of the band worked in unison, flipping mattresses and lifting and moving heavy things when they realized what they'd initially told the movers wasn't going to work.

Once it was all put up and the boys had some say in where each of their things went, their friends disappeared as quickly as they came.

"We're going to have to host a big dinner here soon." Shay grinned at the thought. She'd never had enough friends to do that nor enough space. They'd have to squish in even here, but she was ready.

That night they ordered pizza and ate it at her dining room table. Bigger than Craig's had been, it was the one that survived the cut. Though dinner was delivery on paper plates, Shay looked around the table, thinking how all her tries before this had not quite made her place a home, but this time she'd done it.

She had one step left.

It took them forever to get the boys to sleep that night. Between the excitement of the day and the strangeness of a new place, Shay filled spare drinks of milk and fumbled with hall lights until things were perfect. Or until the boys were so exhausted that they didn't have anything left. She wasn't really sure.

Weary in her bones from the long day, Shay felt herself starting to nod off, but quickly jumped up. She needed to do this tonight. "I'm heading to bed. You should join me soon if you're going to."

Her eyebrows raised once and stayed there. She hoped her

words were enough incentive to draw him away from the TV. Maybe it was too much. He didn't give her a chance to head into the bedroom first and change into the half sweet/half sexy gown she'd bought for their first night here. Instead he followed her up the stairs, bounding behind her, then tumbling her onto the bed the moment he got the door locked.

"Shhhh!" She whispered harshly on a laugh as he caged her on the bed. "The boys will hear."

"They're out cold. We can make all the noise we want."

He grinned and began slowly peeling her clothes, his smile giving way to need and awe. He made love to her as though she were precious, fragile, necessary. She touched him, knowing he was her rock, and she was his.

Later, she lay in his arms, both of them breathing heavily as her thoughts swirled around and drifted down to settle in her head. Remembering, she kissed his shoulder and waited another few minutes to roll out from under him.

"Where are you going?" He asked from his position, tangled in the sheets they'd just laid waste to.

Standing, she went to the dresser, thinking to get something to pull over her head. Pausing at the thought, she realized it was almost better just naked. Nothing between them. So she reached into the top drawer and palmed the item before turning back to him. "I have a question for you."

"I have a bunch of questions." He looked at her through slightly narrowed eyes as he made room for her beneath the covers.

"Me first." She slid in beside him taking a deep breath and then letting all her worries go. In a smooth motion, she held out her hand, opening it to show the platinum band embedded with a row of small sapphires. "Will you marry me, Craig Hibbets?"

He looked stunned. "I—yes!"

Then he threw his head back and laughed, a deep satisfied laugh. "You got me a ring."

"I did." She grinned at him. "I asked, so you get an engagement ring. Plus, I want all those girls screaming at you while you're on stage to know that you're taken."

He turned away, reaching for the nightstand he'd tucked up by his side of the bed. She'd watched earlier as he threw in lip balm, a few books, and the condoms he still had. She'd not seen the small velvet box he now produced. "You beat me to it."

He opened it to reveal a simple diamond solitaire, winking at her out of its nest. "I was going to ask you. But I'm guessing I can just put this on."

Shay grinned at him even as tears leaked from her eyes. She'd suspected he might do this. First night in the new place and all. They'd signed the papers together; they'd already thrown in their lots with each other. Rings or weddings or not, it was already done. But she'd wanted to make it official, legal. Still she couldn't help the laughter and smiles and happy tears as her heart swelled, and she watched as he slowly slid the ring onto her finger.

"My turn." She held up the band and took his hand, sliding it on.

"You just had to ask first, huh?"

"I did." She looked him in the eyes, serious and sure. "I've been married before. They weren't right. This time, I needed to be the one asking. It couldn't be just a 'yes' or 'no' for me. I needed to choose. And you needed to be chosen."

He kissed her again, mouth to mouth, and naked flesh to naked flesh. Then rolled her over to wrap himself around her. "I love you."

The words came out of him easier and easier. She could hear it.

"I love you, too. You're my everything."

His fingers laced through hers, resting atop the covers. As she looked down she could see the stones in the two rings winking like promises, like stars, in the night.

AFTERWORD

Thank you for reading! Shay and Craig fought so hard for their happily ever after and I hope you enjoyed the journey as much as I did. When I started writing this book, I knew everything that happened up until the moment Shay opens the door and finds her fantasy fling on her front steps. After that, I was along for the ride, too! Usually, I know the whole story before I start writing, but this was an adventure for me. They had so much to sort out and I hope I did them justice.

If you want to catch up with Shay's little sister Zoe, she's featured in her own story—*Shooting Star*, in the *Love Found Us* series.

I'd love if you'd leave a review for Heartstrings!

PREVIEW OF LOVE NOTES (WILDER - BOOK 3)

He ached everywhere. But mostly his head hurt. It felt like he was coming off the mother of all benders, his brain pounding out his punishment. TJ started to reach up to clamp his hands alongside his head, but his arms ached, too.

He tried to squint so the light wouldn't hurt so much and he could tug himself up and into the kitchen to get a little hair-of-the-dog. But squinting made him feel like someone had taken a baseball bat to his face. He didn't go anywhere.

"Ahhhhh." He wasn't much for complaining about what he did to himself, but this morning he just needed to moan a little of it out.

"TJ?" The voice was soft and female, and contrary to what he expected, he recognized it.

What he couldn't figure out was why his brother's wife was in his bedroom.

"Hhhmmmmm?" He tried again to squint, and again was rewarded with a crank up on the headache-o-meter.

"TJ. Oh, thank God." Her fingers touched his, but he really didn't want that. He pulled away. Lately his brother and his beautiful wife had begun to wear on his nerves.

"Kelsey?" It sounded thick and slurred, even to him. But that was just another good reason for Kelsey not to be in here. From behind his eyelids he could tell that she had turned on the light. "Turn off the light and go, I'll call you later."

"TJ. You need to wake up."

"No, I need to go back to sleep." He tried to roll over, and when that didn't work he just lay still, wondering where the hell what's-her-face had gone to.

"Dammit, TJ!"

That voice he recognized, too. The gods were angry at him.

"JD, get the hell out of my bedroom."

The gods always sent JD to him. JD was their favored son, and in exchange he was given the responsibility of telling TJ when he'd screwed up. The voice was still angry; the gods were still pissed. "TJ, open your eyes. You aren't in your bedroom. You're in the hospital."

Son of a bitch.

He cracked his eyes, ready to face the daylight, if only to tell his brother to stuff it. But, when the pain of light hitting nerve endings receded, he saw that he was, in fact, in the hospital. Well, that explained a lot of the pain. "Shit."

"That's all you have to say for yourself?"

"Oh, God, spare me." TJ actually managed to get a hand to his head this time.

JD's expression went grim. "He usually does. You've been charmed, little brother. You've escaped scrapes that I would never dream of trying out. I'm going to have to let the doctors explain this one, but God didn't spare you this time."

That got his eyeballs all the way open. Taking in a quick perusal of the bed, he saw that all four limbs remained intact, and he heaved a great sigh of relief.

"By the way,"

Uh-oh. From that tone, something horrible he'd done was

about to get thrown at him. He just hadn't decided yet if he cared.

"The girl who was with you, Marcia Winters, was fine."

"Good to know." Although whether it was good to know she was fine, or just to finally know her name, he wasn't sure.

His brother grabbed his hand and squeezed it. "We're going to go. The doctors will be by in just a few minutes to talk to you."

He squeezed the hand back.

Kelsey came right up beside the bed, placing her hand on his shoulder. "I love you, TJ."

He didn't want to say it back, but he had to. "I love you, too, Kelsey."

He had to love her. She had handed Wilder everything they needed to break out of the un-signed rut they'd been in six years ago. She'd also given his brother the sun and the moon, the way JD told it. But, damn, if she wasn't the one focal point of how JD was still the gods' favorite. The beautiful wife who greeted his brother at the end of every tour with open arms and a warm bed. A very warm bed, if the three children they'd cranked out since they'd married were any indication. As they left the room hand in hand, TJ realized it was a good thing he didn't want anything like that, because he was certain the gods would deny him.

When the room was blessedly empty, he attempted to roll his head from side to side. Some joint limbering was part of his usual after-indulgence routine. This time it didn't work and the pounding in his head combined with his presence in the hospital seemed like a good sign that he shouldn't be doing it.

He blinked a few times, orienting himself in the private room. The bed jutted out into the middle of the room. Machines and poles lined one side of the bed, and if he followed the wires and tubes he could see that several were connected to him. Something dripped from a clear bag into his arm, and another machine pulsed a green line in time with his heartbeat. He was no doctor, but it looked pretty good.

On the other side of him was a moveable table, pushed to hang partway over the bed, with a pitcher of ice water and a pink plastic cup. He reached out for it, only to realize that he had died and gone to hell. The water was just beyond his reach. He laughed a hollow sound at himself. Normally, Glenlivet was his drink of choice on mornings like these, but now, even the stupid water was out of range.

He grabbed at the wires and was contemplating yanking them and just sitting up when the doctors came in.

"Oh, no. Don't pull on those." The oldest doctor was trailed by two younger ones.

TJ looked at all of them warily. "I don't really need this. I can feel that my heart is beating just fine. So I'll just get a drink and be going."

He reached again for the wires.

The doctor placed his own hand over TJ's, again stopping him. This time the hand seemed far more grandfather than dictator. "Let's talk first."

TJ just nodded or tried to.

"I'm Doctor Sanbourne." He held out the weathered hand, and reluctantly TJ shook it, though the ache of his hangover had made even his arms sluggish. He proceeded to listen through the introduction of the two other doctors, one dark and Indian, the other female and shy-looking. TJ dismissed them mentally and promptly forgot their names.

Dr. Sanbourne pulled up a swivel stool and seated himself, while his lackeys just hung back and watched. "Do you remember the accident?"

TJ blinked. *Accident?*

He shook his head as a little memory filtered back. "I really just remember that there was one. A semi rear-ended me, right?" In his head he could see it, in the rearview mirror, orange and large . . . and getting larger by the second. But that was all that came through.

The doctor nodded. "Luckily, you have good airbags. They saved your life and that of your passenger."

TJ didn't take the prompt. Didn't ask after whatever her name had been.

Dr. Sanbourne continued. "Unfortunately, you were in a convertible and you didn't have your seatbelt on."

TJ raised his eyebrows. *Tell me something I don't know*, but he didn't say it.

"You suffered a crushing blow to the base of your neck. The C-6 vertebrae," he pointed it out on his own spine, "was cracked."

TJ frowned and reached up to his own neck. He was shocked to find it encased in a hard collar. Well, that explained why his head wouldn't turn. His brain cranked through the possibilities. He flexed his fingers in front of his face.

"You've already had a surgery to put pins in to hold the pieces of bone together. The pins will remain for the rest of your life, but the collar will come off shortly, and the bone will heal."

The sound was dull and dry even in his own head, where he left it. *Whoo hoo.*

"However,"

Oh, shit.

"There was damage to the nerves themselves. Nothing appears to be completely severed, but we can't be sure. Your responses prior to surgery were lacking."

He found his voice, "What do you mean, *lacking?*"

"You were missing basic reflexes in your legs. There was no response. We had hoped that after surgery, after we relieved whatever pressure the cracked bone was placing on the spinal cord, you would regain sensation. It doesn't appear that you have."

What?

He felt fine. TJ flexed his toes, looking just beyond the little table, but nothing happened.

He flexed again. *Nothing.*

It had to be the water table blocking his view.

He gave it a good shove, sending it toppling. The two attendant doctors flinched. Sanbourne did nothing of the sort. He simply watched.

TJ felt his ribcage constrict. He couldn't breathe either. He couldn't bend his knees or curl his toes. After a few tries he decided that it was his brain that was broken, even just thinking about moving his leg felt wrong.

Sanbourne nodded. "Your brain works, son. It's your legs that aren't responding."

TJ pulled back, then realized that he must be having a perfectly normal response to finding out that your legs don't work. Sanbourne wasn't a mind reader. He was a doctor.

And TJ was an invalid.

JD's words came back to haunt him, *God didn't spare you this time.*

His breathing increased rate while the room closed in on him. His hands clutched at the sheet clumsily, gathering fistfuls and squeezing without his usual strength. At least driving his fingernails into his palms would have offered some measure of relief, but it looked like that wouldn't happen either.

Sanbourne stood closer, getting his face into TJ's. "Let's do a few tests and see what the damage is. We'll know how to proceed from there."

How to proceed?

But the blunt statement worked. TJ managed to find air and bring it into his lungs. He nodded as well as he could in the collar.

Dr. Sanbourne turned to his assistant who shook her shy head at him.

No, *what?*

But Sanbourne didn't tell TJ.

He did run his pen up the sole of TJ's foot.

At least it looked like he did. TJ saw the sheet pinch from the pressure. Saw the pen disappear behind his foot. But he didn't feel anything. He thought for a moment that the doctor was playing a cruel trick, but then remembered that he hadn't been able to make it move himself. He saw the doctor try again, and realized that he should have at least been able to feel the sheet pull and tug, because he could sure see that it was moving.

Sanbourne tested various spots on both legs. The doctor tried different pressures, from obviously poking him to running the pen along the leg.

Nothing.

"Let's try your hands."

"My hands are fine." TJ was thanking God for small favors.

"C-6 injuries often involve fine motor control of the hands."

TJ flexed all his fingers, grateful that something worked. "Just fine."

"Good." The doctor held out two fingers. "Squeeze."

TJ squeezed.

"Hard as you can."

He added extra force, but didn't feel any difference.

The expression on Sanbourne's face wasn't good.

"Now do this." Sanbourne held up both hands, then touched his first fingers to his thumbs.

TJ did the same, somehow managing a cocky expression at that.

The expression slipped as Sanbourne demonstrated touching each finger in turn, and none of his others worked individually. Either they all went or none did. TJ discovered that he could move his thumbs to touch each fingertip, but couldn't make the fingertips go to the thumb.

"All right." That was all the doctor said.

"What does that mean?" TJ wasn't sure he really wanted the answer.

"There's some loss of fine motor control in the hands." Sanbourne pulled back the sheet revealing the traitorous legs that no longer looked like they belonged to him. They certainly bore a striking resemblance to his own, but they couldn't be his. "Let's do one more test."

He and the other two doctors carefully positioned TJ upright. Since he didn't have a clue what they were doing, he let them. They moved his legs and dangled them off the bed, then asked if he could stay there by himself.

He managed it, although he had to brace his hands out because his body wanted to slide over.

Sanbourne watched, then pulled his rubber mallet out of his pocket. He whacked at both knees, but TJ couldn't watch.

"That's good news." Sanbourne perked up.

"What?" He needed any good news he could get his less-than-functioning hands on.

"Your patellar reflex is intact in both legs."

"Speak English! What does that mean?"

Sanbourne took no offense. "Those nerves are working."

"How do *I* make them work?"

The doctor shook his head. "You can't, you don't. They're reflexes. We have no control over them."

"Then why is it good news?" He wanted to grab the white lapels of the stitched lab coat and shake the doctor. But he couldn't; he'd already figured out that he'd fall over if he moved his hands.

"It means the nerves may heal."

"*May?*"

"May."

Thank you for reading! I love romances with real love and believable characters, and I hope you found all that in these pages. I want to fall in love right along with the characters, and I do, while I'm writing it.

About Savannah

I started writing when I was eight--I hand wrote an 80-page novella that I believed to be (adult) romantic suspense. I'm proud to say, I've gotten a lot better since then. I've grown up to be a nerd at heart! I love neuroscience and people watching, and if you look, you'll find some of that in each Savannah Kade book. Most days you'll find me in my office, looking out my window at a handful of the neighbor's cows, or watching my dogs or my cat roam the backyard.

Follow me, find me, ask me questions! I would love to hear from you.
www.SavannahKade.com
Savannah@SavannahKade.com

www.ingramcontent.com/pod-product-compliance
Lightning Source LLC
Chambersburg PA
CBHW020217260626
47156CB00002B/422